The Tender Shoot

also by Colette:

GIGI, CHANCE ACQUAINTANCES *and*
JULIE DE CARNEILHAN

CHERI *and* THE LAST OF CHERI

MY MOTHER'S HOUSE *and* SIDO

THE VAGABOND

THE RIPENING SEED

CLAUDINE AT SCHOOL

CREATURES GREAT AND SMALL

MITSOU *and* MUSIC-HALL SIDELIGHTS

CLAUDINE IN PARIS

SEVEN BY COLETTE
contains a selection of the above novels
plus THE CAT, *not available in a separate volume*

The Tender Shoot

AND OTHER STORIES

BY

COLETTE

Translated by

ANTONIA WHITE

FARRAR, STRAUS AND GIROUX
New York

Library of Congress catalog card number: 59–9961
Printed in the United States of America

Contents

Bella-Vista

IT is absurd to suppose that periods empty of love are blank pages in a woman's life. The truth is just the reverse. What remains to be said about a passionate love affair? It can be told in three lines. *He* loved me, I loved *Him*. His presence obliterated all other presences. We were happy. Then *He* stopped loving me and I suffered.

Frankly, the rest is eloquence or mere verbiage. When a love affair is over, there comes a lull during which one is once more aware of friends and passers-by, of things constantly happening as they do in a vivid, crowded dream. Once again, one is conscious of normal feelings such as fear, gaiety and boredom; once again time exists and one registers its flight. When I was younger, I did not realise the importance of these "blank pages". The anecdotes with which they furnished me—those impassioned, misguided, simple or inscrutable human beings who plucked me by the sleeve, made me their witness for a moment and then let me go—provided more "romantic" subjects than my private personal drama. I shall not finish my task as a writer without attempting, as I want to do here, to draw them out of the shadows to which the shameless necessity of speaking of love in my own name has consigned them.

A house, even a very small house, does not make itself habitable or adopt us in the week which follows the signing of the agreement. As a wise man of few words who makes sandals at Saint-Tropez once said: "It takes as much work and thought to make sandals for someone aged six as to make them for someone aged forty."

Thirteen years ago when I bought a small vineyard beside the sea in the south of France with its plumy pines, its mimosas and its little house, I regarded them with the prompt businesslike eye of a camper. "I'll unpack my two suitcases; I'll put the bath-tub and the portable shower in a corner, the Breton table and its armchair under the window, the divan bed and its mosquito-net in the dark room. I'll sleep *there* and I'll work *there* and I'll wash *there*. By tomorrow, everything will be ready." For the dining-room, I could choose between the shade of the mulberry and that of the centuries-old spindle-trees.

Having the necessities—that is to say shade, sun, roses, sea, a well and a vine—I had a healthy contempt for such luxuries as electricity, a kitchen stove and a pump. More prudent influences seduced me from leaving the little Provençal house in its primitive perfection. I gave in to them and listened to the convincing builder whom I went to see in his own home.

He was smiling. In his garden an all-the-year-round mimosa and purple wallflowers set off to advantage the various objects for sale: concrete benches, upended balusters arranged like skittles, drain-pipes and perforated bricks, the lot under the guardianship of a very pretty bulldog in turquoise Vallauris ware.

"You know how things are here," said the builder. "If you need your villa by July or August, you'll have to come and bully the workman on his own ground now and then."

I remember that I kept blinking my eyelids which were hurt by the chalky glare of March. The sky was patterned with great white clouds and the mistral was shaking all the doors in their frames. It was cold under the table but a sunbeam, which fell on the estimate covered with red figures and black dots and blue pencil ticks, burned the back of my hand. I caught myself thinking that warm rain is very agreeable in spring in the Île-de-France and that a heated, draught-proof flat in Paris, staked out with lamps under parchment hats, has an unrivalled charm.

The Midi triumphed. I had indeed just been having attack after attack of bronchitis and the words "warm climate . . . rest . . . open air . . ." became the accomplices of the smiling builder. I decided therefore to try to find a haven of rest, some way away from the port to which I have since become so deeply attached, from which I could sally forth from time to time to "bully the workmen". This would give me an excuse to escape from the most exhausting of all pleasures, conversation.

Thanks to a decorative painter who takes his holidays alone and makes himself unrecognisable, in the manner of Greta Garbo, by wearing sun-spectacles and sleeveless tennis shirts, I learnt that a certain inn, crowded with odd people in the summer but peaceful for the rest of the year, would take me under its roof. I call it "Bella-Vista" because there are as many Bella-Vistas and Vista-Bellas in France as there are Montignys. You will not find it on the Mediterranean coast; it has lost its proprietresses and nearly all its charms. It has even lost its old name which I shall not reveal.

Consequently, at the end of March, I packed a good pound of periwinkle-blue paper in a suitcase. I also put in my heavy wool slacks, my four pullovers, some woollen scarves and my tartan-lined mackintosh—all the necessary equipment, in short, for winter sports or an expedition to the Pole. My previous stays in the Midi, during a lecture tour at the end of one winter, called up memories of Cannes blind with hail and Marseilles and Toulon as white and gritty as cuttlefish bones under the January mistral. They also evoked bright blue and pale green landscapes, followed by grim recollections of leeches and injections of camphorated oil.

These discouraging images accompanied me almost to the "hostelry" I call Bella-Vista. Concerning Bella-Vista I shall give only certain inoffensive details and draw posthumous portraits such as those of its two proprietresses of whom one, the younger, is dead. Supposing the other to be alive, Heaven knows on what work, and in what place of seclusion, those agile fingers and piercing eyes are now employed.

Thirteen years ago, the two of them stood in the doorway of Bella-Vista. One expertly seized my smooth-haired griffon by the loose skin of her neck and back, deposited her on the ground and said to her: "Hallo, dear little yellow dog. I'm sure you is thirsty."

The other held out her firm hand, with its big ring, to help me out of the car and greeted me by name: "A quarter of an hour later, Madame Colette, and you'd have missed it."

"Missed what?"

"The *bourride*. They wouldn't have left you a mouthful. I know them. Madame Ruby, when you can take your mind for one moment off that dog."

Her charming accent took one straight back to the Place Blanche. She had acquired the red, uneven sunburn peculiar to high-coloured blondes. Her dyed hair showed greyish at the roots; there was spontaneous laughter in her bright blue eyes and her teeth were still splendid. Her tailored white linen dress glistened from repeated ironing. A striking person, in fact; one of those who make an instant, detailed physical impression. Before I had even spoken to her, I already knew by heart the pleasant shape of her hands baked by the sun and much cooking, her gold signet ring, her small wide-nostrilled nose, her piercing glance which plunged straight into one's own eyes, and the good smell of laundered linen, thyme and garlic which almost drowned her Paris scent.

"Madame Suzanne," retorted her American partner, "you

is lost in Madame Colette's opinion if you is nicer to her than to her little yellow dog."

Having made this statement, Mme Ruby announced lunch by ringing a little copper bell whose angry voice quite unhinged my griffon bitch. Instead of obeying the bell, I remained standing in the courtyard, a square which, like a stage set, lacked one side. Perched on a modest eminence, Bella-Vista prudently turned its back to the sea and offered its façade and its two wings to the kindly winds, contenting itself with a restricted view. From its paved terrace I discovered in turn the forest, some sheltered fields and a dark blue fragment of the Mediterranean wedged between two slopes of hills.

"You hasn't any other luggage?"

"The suitcase, my dressing-case, the hold-all, the rug. That's all, Madame Ruby."

At the sound of her name, she gave me a familiar smile. Then she called a dark-haired servant girl and showed her my luggage.

"Room Ten!"

But though Room Ten, on the first floor, looked out on the sea, it refused me my favourite south-west aspect. So I chose instead a room on the ground floor which opened directly on to the terrace courtyard. It was opposite the garage and not far from the aviary of parakeets.

"Here you is more noisy," objected Mme Ruby. "The garage . . ."

"It's empty, thank Heaven."

"Quite right. Our car sleeps out of doors. It's more convenient than going in, coming out, going in, coming out. So, you likes Number Four better?"

"I do like it better."

"O.K. Here's the bath, here's the light, here's the bell, here's the cupboards—she swept up my dog and threw her deftly on to the flowered counterpane—"and here's yellow dog!"

The bitch laughed with pleasure while Mme Ruby, enchanted with the effect she had produced, pivoted on her rubber soles. I watched her cross the courtyard and thought that, from head to foot, she was exactly as she had been described to me. She was scandalous, but one liked her at first sight. She was mannish without being awkward; her boy's hips and square shoulders were trimly encased in blue frieze and white linen; there was a rose in the lapel of her jacket. Her head was round and could not have been more beautifully modelled under the smooth cap of red hair. It had lost its golden glint and showed white in places and she wore it plastered to her skull with severe, provocative coquetry. There was something definitely attractive about her wide grey eyes, her unassuming nose, her big mouth with its big, seemingly indestructible teeth and her skin which was freckled over the cheekbones. Forty-five perhaps? More likely fifty. The neck in the open cellular shirt was thickening and the loose skin and prominent veins on the back of the strong hands revealed that she might well be even more than fifty.

Undoubtedly I cannot draw Mme Ruby as well as I heard Mme Suzanne describe her later in a moment of irritation.

"You look like an English curate! You're the living image of a Boche got up as a sportsman! You're the living image of a vicious governess! Oh, I know you were an American schoolteacher! But I'd no more have trusted you with my little sister's education than my little brother's!"

On the day of my arrival, I still knew very little about the two friends who ran Bella-Vista. A sense of well-being, unforeseen rather than anticipated, descended on me and kept me standing there with my arms crossed on the window-sill of Room Four. I submitted myself passively to the reverberations of the yellow walls and blue shutters; I forgot my exacting griffon bitch, my own hunger and the meal now in progress.

In that odd state of convalescence which follows a tiring night journey, my eyes wandered slowly round the courtyard. They came to rest on the rose-bush under my window, idly following every sway of its branches. "Roses already! And white arum lilies. The wistaria's beginning to come out. And all those black and yellow pansies."

A long dog, lying stretched out in the courtyard, had wagged its tail as Mme Ruby passed. A white pigeon had come and pecked at the toes of her white shoes . . . From the aviary came a gentle, muffled screeching; the soft, monotonous language of the green parakeets. And I was glad that my unknown room behind me was filled with the smell of the lavender, dry bunches of which were hung on the bedrail and in the cupboard.

The duty of having to examine them poisons one's pleasure in new places. I dreaded the dining-room as if I were a traveller contemplating the panorama of an unknown town and thinking: "What a nuisance that I'll have to visit two museums, the cathedral and the docks." For nothing will give the traveller as much pleasure as that warm rampart or that little cemetery or those old dykes covered with grass and ivy . . . and the stillness.

"Come along, Pati."

The griffon followed me with dignity because I had only said her name once. She was called Pati when it was necessary for us both to be on our best behaviour. When it was time for her walk, she was Pati-Pati-Pati, or as many more Patis as one had breath to add. Thus we had adapted her name to all the essential circumstances of our life. In the same way, when Mme Ruby spoke French, she contented herself with the single auxiliary verb "to be" which stood for all the others: "You is all you want? . . . You is no more luggage?" and so on. As I crossed the courtyard, I had already assigned Mme Ruby to that category of active, rather limited people who easily learn the nouns and adjectives of a foreign language but jib at verbs and their conjugation.

The prostrate dog half hitched himself up for Pati's benefit. She pretended to ignore his existence and, by degrees, he collapsed again: first his shoulders; then his neck which was too thin; lastly his mongrel greyhound's head which was too large. A brisk, rather chilly breeze was blowing wallflower petals over the sand but I was grateful to feel the bite of the sun on my shoulder. Over the wall, an invisible garden wafted the scent which demoralises the bravest, the smell of orange trees in flower.

In the dining-room, which was far from monumental but low-ceilinged and carefully shaded, a dozen small scattered tables with coarse Basque linen cloths reassured my unsociable disposition. There was no butter in shells, no head-waiter in greenish-black tails and none of those meagre vases containing one marguerite, one tired anemone and one spray of mimosa. But there was a big square of ice-cool butter and on the folded napkin lay a rose from the climbing rose tree: a single rose whose lips were a little harsh from the mistral and the salt; a rose I was free to pin to my sweater or to eat as *hors-d'œuvre*. I directed a smile towards the presiding goddesses, but the smile missed its target. Mme Ruby, alone at a table, was hurrying through her meal and only Mme Suzanne's bust was visible. Every time the kitchen hatch opened, her golden hair and her hot face appeared in its frame against a background of shining saucepans and gridirons. Pati and I had the famous *bourride*, velvet-smooth and generously laced with garlic; a large helping of roast pork stuffed with sage and served with apple sauce and potatoes; cheese, stewed pears flavoured with vanilla and a small carafe of the local *vin rosé*. I foresaw that three weeks of such food would repair the ravages of two attacks of bronchitis. When the coffee was poured out—it was quite ordinary coffee but admirably hot—Mme Ruby came over and vainly offered me her cigarette lighter.

"You is not a smoker? O.K."

She showed her tact by going off at once to her duties and not prolonging the conversation. As she moved away, I admired her rhythmic, swaying walk.

My griffon bitch sat opposite me in the depths of a knitted woollen hood I had presented to her. For correct deportment and silence at table, she could have given points to an English child. This restraint was not entirely disinterested. She knew that the perfection of her behaviour would not only win her general approval but more concrete tributes of esteem such as lumps of sugar soaked in coffee and morsels of cake. To this end she gave a tremendous display of engaging head-turnings, expressive glances, false modesty, affected gravity and all the terrier airs and graces. A kind of military salute invented by herself—the front paw raised to the level of the ear—which one might call the C in alt of her gamut of tricks, provoked laughter and delighted exclamations. I have to admit that she occasionally overdid this playing to the gallery.

I have written elsewhere of this tiny bitch, a sporting dog in miniature with a deep chest, cropped ears like little horns and the soundest of health and intelligence. Like certain dogs with round skulls—bulldogs, griffons and Pekinese—she "worked" on her own. She learnt words by the dozen and was always observant and on the alert. She registered sounds and never failed to attribute the right meaning to them. She possessed a "rule of the road" which varied according to whether we were travelling by train or by car. Brought up in Belgium in the company of horses, she passionately followed everything that wore iron shoes for the pleasure of running behind them and she knew how to avoid being kicked.

She was artful; a born liar and pretender. Once in Brittany I saw her give a splendid imitation of a poor, brave, suffering little dog with its cheek all swollen from a wasp-sting. But two could play at that game and I gave her a slap which made her spit out her swelling. It was a ball of dried donkey's dung which she had stowed away in her cheek so as to bring it home and enjoy it at leisure.

Glutted with food and less overcome with fatigue than I was, Pati sat up straight on the other side of the table and took an inventory of the people and things about us. There was a lady and her daughter who appeared to be the same age: the daughter was already decrepit and the mother still looked young. There were two boys on their Easter holidays who asked for more bread at every course, and, finally, there was a solitary resident, sitting not far from us, who seemed to me quite unremarkable though he riveted Pati's attention. Twice, when he was speaking to the dark-haired maid, she puffed out her lips to snarl something offensive and then thought better of it.

I did not scold myself for sitting on there, with the remains of my coffee cooling in my cup, glancing now at the swaying rose-bush, now at the yellow walls and the copies of English prints. I stared at the sunlit courtyard, then at something else, then at nothing at all. When I drift like that, completely slack, it is a sign not that I am bored but that all my forces are silently coalescing and that I am floating like a seed on the wind. It is a sign that, out of wisps and stray threads and scattered straws, I am fashioning for myself just one more fragment of a kind of youth. "Suppose I go and sleep? . . . Suppose I go and look at the sea? . . . Suppose I send a telegram to Paris? . . . Suppose I telephone to the builder?"

The resident who had not the luck to please my dog said something to the dark-haired girl as he got up. She answered: "In a moment, Monsieur Daste." He passed close by my table, gave a vague apologetic bow and said something like

"Huisipisi" to my dog in a jocular way. At this she put up her hackles till she looked like a bottle-brush and tried to bite his hand.

"Pati! Are you crazy? She's not bad-tempered," I said to M. Daste. "Just rather conventional. She doesn't know you."

"Yes, yes, she knows me all right. She knows me all right," muttered M. Daste.

He bent towards the dog and threatened her teasingly with his forefinger. Pati showed that she did not much relish being treated like a fractious child. I held her back while M. Daste moved away, laughing under his breath. Now that I looked at him more attentively, I saw that he was a rather short, nimble man who gave a general impression of greyness; grey suit, grey hair and a greyish tinge in his small-featured face. I had already noticed his tapering forefinger and its polished nail. The dog growled something that was obviously insulting.

"Look here," I told her. "You've got to get used to the idea that you're not in your own village of Auteuil. Here there are dogs, birds, possibly hens, rabbits and even cats. You've got to accept them. Now, let's take a turn."

At that moment Mme Suzanne came and sat down to her well-earned meal.

"Well? How was the lunch?" she called to me from her distant table.

"Perfect, Madame Suzanne. I could do with one meal like that every day—but only one! Now we're going to take a turn round the house to walk it off a little."

"What about a siesta?"

"Everything in its own good time. I'm never sleepy the first day."

Her plump person had the effect of making me talk in proverbs and maxims and all the facile clichés of "popular" wisdom.

"Will the fine weather hold, Madame Suzanne?"

She powdered her face, ran a moistened finger over her eyebrows and made her table napkin crack like a whip as she unfolded it.

"There's a bit of east wind. Here it rains if there isn't a touch of wind."

She made a face as she emptied the hard-boiled egg salad out of the *hors-d'œuvre* dish on to her plate.

"As to the *bourride*, I'll have to do without, as usual. I don't care—I licked out the bowl I made the sauce in."

Her laugh irradiated her face. Looking at her I thought that, before thin females became the fashion, it was the fair-haired Mme Suzannes with their high colour and high breasts who were the beautiful women.

"You take a hand in the kitchen every day, Madame Suzanne?"

"Oh, I like it, you know. In Paris I kept a little restaurant. You never came and ate my chicken with rice on a Saturday night in the Rue Lepic? I'll make one for you. But what a bloody hell of a place—excuse my language—this part of France is for provisions."

"What about the early vegetables?"

"Early vegetables! Don't make me laugh. Everything's later here than it is in Brittany. Some little lettuces you can hardly see . . . a few beans. The artichokes are hardly beginning. No tomatoes before June except the Spanish and Italian ones. In winter, except for their rotten oranges, almonds, raisins, nuts and figs are all we get in the way of fruit. As to new-laid eggs, you've got to fight for them. And when it comes to fish! . . . The weekly boarders in hotels are the luckiest. At least they pay a fixed price and know where they are."

She laughed and rubbed her hands together; those hands which had been tried and proven by every sort and kind of work.

"I love the kitchen stove. I'm not like Madame Ruby. Lucie!" she called towards the hatch. "Bring me the pork and a little of the pears! Madame Ruby," she went on, with ironic respect, "cooking's not *her* affair. Oh dear, no! Nor is managing things and doing the accounts. Oh dear, no!"

She dropped the mockery and emphasised the respect.

"No, her affair is *chic*, manners and so on. Furnishing a room, arranging a table, receiving a guest—she's a born genius at all that. I admit it and I appreciate it. I really do appreciate it. But . . ."

An angry little spark animated Mme Suzanne's blue eyes.

"But I can't stand seeing her wandering all over the kitchen, lifting up the saucepan lids and throwing her weight about. 'Madame Suzanne, do you know you is made coffee like dish-water this morning? Lucie, you is not forgotten to fill the ice trays in the refrigerator?' No, that's really *too* much!"

She imitated to perfection her friend's voice and her peculiar grammar. Flushed with an apparently childish jealousy and irritation, she seemed not to mind in the least revealing or underlining what people call the "strange intimacy" which bound her to her partner. She changed her tone as she saw Lucie approaching. Lucie had a succulent, foolish mouth and a great mass of turbulent black hair which curled at the nape of her neck.

"Madame Colette, I'm making a special *crème caramel* tonight for Monsieur Daste. I'll make a little extra if you'd like it. Monsieur Daste only likes sweet things and red meat."

"And who is Monsieur Daste?"

"A very nice man . . . I believe what I see. It's the best way, don't you think? He's all on his own, for one thing. So he's almost certainly a bachelor. Have you seen him, by the way?"

"Only a glimpse."

"He's a man who plays bridge and poker. And he's awfully well educated, you know."

"Is this an insidious proposal of marriage, Madame Suzanne?"

She got up and slapped me on the shoulder.

"Ah, anyone can see you're artistic. You still talk the way artistic people do. I'm going up to have half an hour's nap. You see *I* get up every morning at half-past five."

"You've hardly eaten anything, Madame Suzanne."

"It'll make me slimmer."

She frowned, yawned and then lifted one of the coarse red net curtains.

"Where's that Ruby run off to now? Will you excuse me, Madame Colette? If I'm not everywhere at once . . ."

She left me planted there and I invited my dog to come for a walk round the hotel. A sharp wind enveloped us as soon as we set foot on the terrace but the sun was still on the little flight of steps leading up to my french window and on the aviary of parakeets. The birds were billing and cooing in couples and playing hide-and-seek in their still empty birch-bark nests. At the foot of the aviary, a white rabbit was sunning himself. He did not run away and gave my griffon such a warlike glance with his red eye that she went some way off and relieved herself to keep herself in countenance.

Beyond the walls of the courtyard, the wind was having everything its own way. Pati flattened her ears and I should have gone back to my room if, quite close, shut in between two hillocks of forest, I had not caught sight of the Mediterranean.

At that time I had only a rudimentary acquaintance with the Mediterranean. Compared to the low tides of Brittany and that damp, pungent air, this bluest and saltest of seas, so decorative and so unchangeable, meant little to me. But merely sniffing it from afar made the griffon's snub nose turn moist and there was nothing for it but to follow Pati to the foot of a little scarp covered with evergreens. There was no beach; only some flat rocks between which seaweed, with spreading branches like a peacock's tail, waved gently just below the surface of the water.

The valorous griffon wetted her paws, tested the water, approved of it, sneezed several times and began to hunt for her Breton crabs. But no waves provide less game than those which wash the southern coast and she had to restrict herself to the pleasure of exploring. She ran from tamarisk to lentisk, from agave to myrtle till she came on a man sitting under some low branches. As she growled insultingly at him, I guessed that it must be M. Daste. He was laughing at her, wagging his forefinger and saying: "Huisipisi"—doing everything, in fact, calculated to offend a very small, arrogant dog who was eager for admiring attention.

When I had called her back, M. Daste made an apologetic gesture for not standing up and silently pointed to a tree-top. I jerked my chin up questioningly.

"Wood-pigeons," he said. "I think they're going to build their nest there. And there's another pair at the end of the kitchen garden at Bella-Vista."

"You're not thinking of shooting them, are you?"

He threw up his hands in protest.

"Shooting? Me? Good Lord! You'll never see *me* carrying a gun. But I watch them. I listen to them."

He shut his eyes amorously like a music-fiend at a concert. I took advantage of this to have a good look at him. He was neither ugly nor deformed; only rather mediocre. He seemed to have been made to attract as little attention as possible. His hair was thick and white was as plentifully and evenly sprinkled among brown as in a roan horse's hide. His features were decidedly small; he had a stingy face which looked all the more stingy when the long eyelids were closed. If I observed M.

Daste more carefully than he deserved, it was because I am always terrified, when chance throws me among unknown people, of discovering some monstrosity in them. I search them to the core with a sharp, distasteful eye as one does a dressing-table drawer in a hotel bedroom. No old dressings? No hair-pins, no broken buttons, no crumbs of tobacco? Then I breathe again and don't give it another thought.

In the pitiless light of two in the afternoon, M. Daste, medium-sized, clean and slightly desiccated, showed no visible signs of lupus or eczema. I could hardly hold it against him that he wore a soft white shirt and a neat tie instead of a pullover. I became affable:

"Pati, say how d'you do to Monsieur Daste."

I lifted the dog by her superfluous skin—nature provides the thoroughbred griffon with enough skin to clothe about a dog and a half—and held her over my arm for M. Daste to appreciate the little squashed muzzle, the blackish-brown mask and the beautiful prominent gold-flecked eyes. Pati did not try to bite M. Daste, but I was surprised to feel her stiffen slightly.

"Pati, give your paw to Monsieur Daste."

She obeyed, but with her eyes elsewhere. She held out a limp, expressionless paw which M. Daste shook in a sophisticated way.

"Are you in this part of the world for some time, Madame?"

As he had a pleasant voice, I gave M. Daste some brief scraps of information.

"We wretched bureaucrats," he rejoined, "have the choice between three weeks' holiday at Easter or three in July. I need warmth. Bella-Vista is sheltered from the cold winds. But I find the very bright light distressing."

"Madame Suzanne is making you a *crème caramel* for tonight. You see what a lot of things I know already!"

M. Daste closed his eyes.

"Madame Suzanne has all the virtues—even though appearances might lead one to suppose just the opposite."

"Really?"

"I can't help laughing," said M. Daste. "Even if Madame Suzanne practises virtue, she hasn't any respect for it."

I thought he was going to run down our hostesses. I waited for the "They're impossible" I had heard *ad nauseam* in Paris to put an end to our conversation. But he merely raised his small hand like a preacher and remarked:

"What are appearances, Madame, what are appearances?"

His chestnut-coloured eyes stared thoughtfully at the empty sea, over which the shadows of the white clouds skimmed in dark green patches. I sat down on the dried seaweed that had been torn from the sea and piled up in heaps by the last gales of the equinox and my dog nestled quietly against my skirt. The sulphurous smell of the seaweed, the broken shells, the feeble waves which rose and fell without advancing or retreating gave me a sudden terrible longing for Brittany. I longed for its tides, for the great rollers off St. Malo which rush in from the ocean, imprisoning constellations of starfish and jellyfish and hermit crabs in the heart of each greenish wave. I longed for the swift incoming tide with its plumes of spray; the tide which revived the thirsty mussels and the little rock-oysters and reopened the cups of the sea-anemones. The Mediterranean is not the sea.

A sharp gesture from M. Daste distracted me from my homesickness.

"What is it?"

"Bird," said M. Daste laconically.

"What bird?"

"I . . . I don't know. I didn't have time to make it out. But it was a big bird."

"And where are your wood-pigeons?"

"My wood-pigeons? Not *mine*, alas," he said regretfully.

He pointed to the little wood behind us.

"They were over there. They'll come back. So shall I. That slate-blue, that delicate fawn of their feathers when they spread them out in flight like a fan. . . . Coo . . . croo-oo-oo . . . Coo . . . croo-oo-oo," he cooed, puffing out his chest and half-closing his eyes.

"You are a poet, Monsieur Daste."

He opened his eyes, surprised.

"A poet . . ." he repeated. "Yes . . . a poet. That's exactly what I am, Madame. I must be, if *you* say so."

A few moments later M. Daste left me, with obvious tact, on the pretext of "some letters to write". He set off in the direction of Bella-Vista with the short, light step of a good walker. Before he went, he did not omit to stick out his forefinger at Pati and to hiss "Huisipisi" at her. But she seemed to expect this teasing and did not utter a sound.

The two of us wandered alone along a beaten track which ran beside the sea at the edge of the forest which was thick with pines, lentisks and cork-oaks. While I was scratching my fingers trying to pick some long-thorned broom and blue salvia and limp-petalled rock-roses for my room, I was suddenly overcome with irresistible sleepiness. The sunshine became a burden and we hurried back up the green scarp.

Three beautiful old mulberry trees, long since tamed and cut into umbrella shapes, did not yet hide the backside of Bella-Vista. Mulberry leaves grow fast but they take a long time to pierce the seamed bark. The trees and the façade looked to me crabbed and harsh; there is a certain time in the afternoon when everything seems repellent to me. All that I longed to do was to shut myself away as soon as possible and the dog felt the same.

Already I no longer liked my room although it was predominantly pink and red. Where could I plug in a lamp to light the table where I meant to work? I rang for the dark-haired Lucie who brought me a bunch of white pinks which smelt slightly of creosote. She did not fix anything but went off to find Mme Ruby in person. The American winked one of her grey eyes, summed up the situation and disappeared. When she returned, she was carrying a lamp with a green china shade, some flex and a collection of tools. She sat sideways on the edge of the table and set to work with the utmost expertness, her cigarette stuck in the corner of her mouth. I watched her large, deft hands; her brisk, efficient movements and the beautiful shape of her head, hardly spoilt by the thickening nape, under the faded red hair.

"Madame Ruby, you must be amazingly good with your hands."

She winked at me through the smoke.

"Have you travelled a lot?"

"All over the place . . . Excuse my cigarette."

She jumped down and tested the switch of the lamp.

"There. Is light for you to work?"

"Perfect! Bravo, the electrician!"

"The electrician's an old jack-of-all trades. Will you sign one of your books for me?"

"Whenever you like. For . . . ?"

"For Miss Ruby Cooney. C . . . double o, n, e, y. Thank you."

I would gladly have stopped her going but I dared not display my curiosity. She rolled up her little tool-kit, swept a few iron filings off the table with her hand and went out, raising two fingers to the level of her ear with the careless ease of a mechanic.

Sleep is good at any time but not waking. A late March twilight, a hotel bedroom that I had forgotten while I slept, two gaping suitcases still unpacked. "Suppose I went away?" . . .

The noise a bent finger makes rapping three times on a thin door is neither pleasant nor reassuring.

"Come in!"

But it was only a telegram: a few secret, affectionate words in the code a tender friendship had invented. Everything was all right. There was nothing to worry about. Pati was tearing up the blue telegram; the suitcases would only take a quarter of an hour to unpack; the water was hot; the bath filled quite quickly.

I took into the dining-room one of those stout notebooks in which we mean to write down what positively must not be put off or forgotten. I meant to start "bullying the workmen" the very next day. Lucie ladled me out a large bowl of fish soup with spaghetti floating in it and inquired whether I had anything against "eggs . . . you know, dropped in the dish and the cheese put on top" and half a guinea-fowl before the *crème caramel*.

By the end of dinner, all I had entered in the new notebook was "Buy a folding rule". But I had done honour to the excellent meal. My dog, stimulated by it, sparkled with gaiety. She smiled at Mme Ruby, alone at her table at the far end of the room, and pretended to ignore the presence of M. Daste. Either the young mother or the old daughter was coughing behind me. The two athletic boys were overcome by the weariness which rewarded their energetic effort. "Just think," Lucie confided to me, "they've walked right round the headland. Twenty miles, they've done!" From where I sat, I could smell the eau de Cologne of which they both reeked. Planning to shorten my stay, I wrote in the big notebook: "Buy a small notebook."

"You is seen the drawing-room, Madame Colette?"

"Not yet, Madame Ruby. But tonight, I have to admit that . . ."

"You'd like Lucie to bring you a hot drink in the drawing-room?"

I gave in, especially as Mme Ruby was already holding my dear little yellow dog under her arm and Pati was surreptitiously licking her ear, hoping I did not notice. The drawing-room looked out on the sea and contained an upright piano, cane furniture and comfortable imitations of English armchairs. Remembering that my room was almost next door, I eyed the piano apprehensively. Mme Ruby winked.

"You likes music?"

Her quick deft hands lifted the lid of the piano, opened its front and disclosed bottles and cocktail-shakers.

"My idea. I did it all by myself. Gutted the piano like a chicken. You like some drink? No?"

She poured herself out a glass of brandy and swallowed it carelessly, as if in a hurry. Lucie brought me one of those *tisanes* which will never convince me that they deserve their reputation for being soothing or digestive.

"Where is Madame Suzanne?" Mme Ruby asked Lucie in a restrained voice.

"Madame Suzanne is finishing the *bœuf-à-la-mode* for to-morrow. She's just straining out the juice."

"O.K. Leave the tray. And give me an ashtray. "You is too much bits of hair on your neck, my girl."

Her big, energetic hand brushed the black bush of hair which frizzed on Lucie's nape. The girl trembled, nearly knocked over my full cup and hurried out of the room.

Far from avoiding my look, Mme Ruby's own took on a victorious malice which drew attention to Lucie's distress so indiscreetly that, for the moment, I ceased to find the boyish woman sympathetic. I am eccentric enough to be repelled when love, whether abnormal or normal, imposes itself on the onlooker's attention or imagination. Mme Ruby was wise enough not to insist further and went over to the two worn-out boys to ask them if they wanted a liqueur. Her manly ease must have terrified them for they beat a hasty retreat after having asked whether they could do "a spot of canoeing" the next day.

"Canoe? . . . I told them: 'We is not a Suicides' Club here!' "

She lifted the net curtain from the black window-pane. But, in the darkness, only the bark of the mulberry trees and their sparse, luminously green new leaves showed in the beam of light from the room.

"By the way, Madame Ruby . . . When you're shopping to-morrow, will you go to Sixte's and get us some more breakfast cups? The same kind, the red and white ones."

Mme Suzanne was behind us, still hot from coping with the dinner and the *bœuf-à-la-mode*, but neat, dressed in white linen, freshly powdered and smelling almost too good. I found her pleasing from head to foot. She felt my cordiality and returned me smile for smile.

"Are you having a good rest, Madame Colette? I'm almost invisible, you know. Tomorrow I shan't have quite so much to do: my beef stew is in the cellar and the noodle paste's in a cool place, wrapped up in a cloth. Madame Ruby, you must bring me back twelve cups and saucers; that clumsy fool of a Lucie has brought off a double again. For an idiot, there's no one to touch that girl! Now, *you* . . . have you been at the brandy? Not more than one glass, I hope."

As she spoke, she searched Mme Ruby's face. But the latter kept her head slightly downcast and her grey eyes half closed to avoid the accusing glance. Suddenly the suspicious one gave up and sat down heavily.

"You're just an old soak . . . Oh, my legs!"

"You is needing rest," suggested Mme Ruby.

"Easy enough to say. My best kitchen maid's coming back

tomorrow," explained Mme Suzanne. "After tomorrow I'm a lady of leisure."

She yawned and stretched.

"At this time of night, I've no thought beyond my bath and my bed. Madame Ruby, will you try and shut the rabbit in? The parakeets are all behind the screen and covered in. Are you taking Slough in with you? Oh! and then tomorrow morning, while I think of it . . ."

"Yes, yes, yes, yes!" broke in Mme Ruby, almost beside herself. "Go to bed."

"Really, who do you think you're talking to?"

Mme Suzanne wished us good night with offended dignity. I let the little dog out in the courtyard for a minute while Mme Ruby whistled in vain for Baptiste the rabbit. The night was murmurous and warmer than the day. Three or four lighted windows, the clouded sky patched here and there with stars, the cry of some nightbird over this unfamiliar place made my throat tighten with anguish. It was an anguish without depth; a longing to weep which I could master as soon as I felt it rise. I was glad of it because it proved that I could still savour the special taste of loneliness.

The next morning, there was a fine drizzle. Under her folded blanket, Pati lay awake and motionless. Her wide-open eyes said "I know it's raining. There's nothing to hurry for." Through my open window I could feel the dampness, which I find friendly, and I could hear the soft chatter of the parakeets. Their aviary was luxuriously mounted on wheels and had been placed under the shelter of the tiled penthouse.

Promptly renouncing the idea of "bullying" the workmen who, forty miles away, were digging my soil, painting my wall and installing my septic tank, I rang for my coffee and slipped on my dressing-gown.

Out in the courtyard, Mme Ruby, wearing a mackintosh, gloves and a little white cap, was loading hampers and empty bottles into her car. She was agile, without an ounce of superfluous flesh. The beautiful, ambiguous rhythm of her movements and the sexless strength which directed them inclined me to excuse her gesture of the night before. Could I have admitted that a man might desire Miss Cooney? Would I have thought it decent for Miss Cooney to fall in love with a man?

The half-bred greyhound took its place beside her. Just as the rough, battered old car was starting up, M. Daste ran up in his dressing-gown and gave Mme Ruby his letters to post. When she had gone, he crossed the courtyard cautiously, wrinkling up his nose under the rain. He lost one of his slippers and shook his bare foot in a comic, old-maidish way. Lucie, who had just come in behind my back, saw me laughing.

"Monsieur Daste doesn't like the rain, does he, Lucie?"

"No, he simply can't stand it. Good morning, Madame. When it's raining, he stays indoors. He plays *belote* with those two ladies and he always wins. Will Madame have her breakfast in bed or at the table?"

"I'd rather have it at the table."

She pushed my books and papers to one side and arranged the coffee-pot and its satellites. She was very gentle and very concentrated as she slowly and carefully performed these duties. Her skin was smooth and amber-coloured, and her eyelashes, like her hair, thick and curling. She seemed to be rather timid. By the side of the big cup she laid a rain-wet rose.

"What a pretty rose! Thank you, Lucie."

"It's not me, it's Madame Ruby."

She blushed fierily, not daring to raise her eyes. I pitied her secretly for being the victim of a disturbance which she must find surprising and vaguely painful.

The flying, almost invisible rain, so much more springlike than yesterday's parched sunshine, beckoned me out-of-doors. My loyal dog was willing to admit that this fine, powdery rain not only did not wet one but made smells more exciting and was propitious to sneezing.

Under the penthouse, M. Daste was taking a chilly little walk. Shivering slightly, he was walking thirty paces to and fro without putting a foot outside the narrow dry strip.

"It's raining!" he shouted at me as if I were deaf.

"But so little . . ."

I stopped close beside him to admire the sheltered parakeets with their tiny, thoughtful foreheads and their wide-set eyes. To my great surprise, they had all fallen silent.

"Are they as frightened of rain as all that?"

"No," said M. Daste. "It's because I'm here. You don't believe me?"

He went closer to the cage. Some of the parakeets flew away and pressed themselves against the bars.

"Whatever have you done to them?"

"Nothing."

He was laughing all over his face and enjoying my astonishment.

"*Nothing?*"

"Absolutely nothing. That's just what's so interesting."

"Then you must go away."

"Not till it stops raining. Look at that one on the lowest perch."

He slid his manicured forefinger between two bars of the aviary and there was a great fluttering of wings inside.

"Which? There are three all alike."

"Alike to you, perhaps. But not to me. I can pick it out at once. It's the most cowardly one."

One of the parakeets—I think it was the one he was pointing

at—gave a scream. Almost involuntarily, I hit M. Daste on the arm and he stepped back, shaking his hand. He was astonished, but decided to laugh.

"You've only got to leave those parakeets in peace," I said angrily. "Stop tormenting them."

His gaze wandered from the birds to me and back again. I could read nothing in that pleasant neutral face, as far removed from ugliness as it was from beauty, but unresentful surprise and a gaiety that I found extremely ill-timed.

"I'm not tormenting them," he protested. "But they know me."

"So does the dog," I thought, seeing Pati's hackles stiffen all along her back. The idea that I might have to spend three weeks in the company of a maniac, possibly an enemy of all animals, profoundly depressed me. At that very moment, M. Daste produced his "huisipisi" for Pati's benefit. She attacked him with all her might and he fled with a comic agility, his hands in his pockets and his shoulders hunched up. I stood perfectly still while she chased him round me. But the chase turned into a game and when M. Daste stopped, out of breath, the dog counted the truce as a victory. She insisted on my congratulating her and looked graciously on her adversary.

During the following days she accepted that irritating "huisipisi" as the signal for a game. But she growled when M. Daste pointed at her or teased her with that tapering, aggressive, minatory forefinger. Comfortably wedged on my forearm with her chest expanded and her eyes bulging, she sniffed the soft dampness with delight.

"She looks like an owl," said M. Daste dreamily.

"Do you frighten owls too?"

To protest his innocence more effectively, M. Daste drew his white, naked hands out of his pockets.

"Good heavens, no, Madame! They interest me . . . certainly

they interest me. But . . . I keep away. I must admit I keep well away from them."

He hunched his shoulders up to his ears and scrutinised the sky where a diffused yellow glow and pale blue patches that promised fine weather were beginning to appear between the clouds. I went off to explore with my dog.

The well-being that rewards me when I exchange my town flat for a hotel does not last very long. Not only do the obligation to work and my usual everyday worries soon take the edge off it but I know all too well the dangers of hotel life. Unless that drifting, irresponsible existence is either completely carefree or organised according to a strict timetable, it always tends to become demoralising. The main reason for this is that people who really mean nothing to us acquire an artificial importance. At Bella-Vista I had no choice except between the seclusion of a convalescent and the sociability of a passenger on a liner. Naturally, I chose the sociability. I was all the more inclined for it after my first visit to the little house I had bought. I returned from it so disillusioned about landed property that I went and confided my disappointment to Mme Suzanne. I made no secret of the fact that I would be only too glad to sell my bit of land again. She listened earnestly and asked me detailed questions.

"How many square yards did you say you had?"

"Square yards? It comes to five acres. Very nearly."

"But come, that's quite a decent size! What's wrong with it, then?"

"Oh, everything! You should see the state it's in!"

"How many rooms?"

"Five, if you count the kitchen."

"Count it. It sounds more impressive. And you've got the sea?"

"It's practically *in* it."

She pushed away her account book and rubbed her polished nails on her palm.

"In your place, I'd . . . But I'm not in your place."

"Do say what you were going to say, Madame Suzanne."

"*I* should see it as a place where people could stop off. An exclusive little snack-bar, a snug little dance-floor under the pines. With your name, why, my dear, it's a gold-mine!"

"Madame Suzanne, it's not gold I'm wanting. What I want is a little house and some peace."

"You're talking like a child. As if one could have any peace without money! I know what I'm talking about. So it's not getting on as fast as you think it should, your cottage?"

"I can't quite make out. The builders play bowls in the alley under the trees. And they've made a charming little camping-ground by the well. Open-air fire, fish soup . . . grilled sausages, bottles of *vin rosé* too: they offered me a glass."

Mme Suzanne was so amused that she flung herself back in her chair and slapped her thighs.

"Madame Ruby! Come and listen to this!"

Her partner came over to us, with a napkin over one hand and the middle finger of the other capped with a thimble. For the first time, I saw her occupied in a thoroughly feminine way and wearing round spectacles with transparent frames. She went on gravely embroidering drawn-threadwork while Mme Suzanne went over "the misfortunes of Madame Colette".

"You look like a boy sewing, Madame Ruby!"

As if offended, Mme Suzanne took the napkin from her friend's hands and held it under my nose.

"It's true that embroidering suits her about as well as sticking a feather in her behind. But look at the work itself! Isn't it exquisite?"

I admired the tiny regular lattices and Mme Suzanne ordered

tea for the three of us. An intermittent mistral was blowing. It would be silent for some moments, then give a great shriek and send columns of white sand whirling across the courtyard, half-burying the anemones and the pansies. Then it would crouch behind the wall, waiting to spring again.

During this first week, I had not enjoyed one entire warm spring day. We had not had one single day of that real spring weather which soothes one's body and blessedly relaxes one's brain. The departure of the two boys, followed by that of the lady in black and her withered daughter, gave the partners plenty of free time. My only idea was to get away yet, against my will, I was growing used to the place. That mysterious attraction of what we do not like is always dangerous. It is fatally easy to go on staying in a place which has no soul, provided that every morning offers us the chance to escape.

I knew the timetable of the buses which passed along the main road, three miles away, and which would have put me down at a station. But my daily post quenched my thirst for Paris. Every afternoon at tea-time, I left my work, which was sticking badly, and joined "those women" in a little room off the drawing-room which they called their boudoir. I would hear the light step of M. Daste on the wooden staircase as he came down eager for tea and one of his favourite delicacies. This consisted of two deliciously light pieces of flaky pastry sandwiched together with cheese or jam and served piping hot. After dinner I made a fourth at poker or *belote* and reproached myself for doing so. There is always something suspect about things which are as easy as all that.

My griffon bitch, at least, was happy. She was enjoying all the pleasures of a concierge's dog. In the evenings, she left her nest in the woollen hood to sit on Mme Ruby's lap. She noted and listed these new patterns of behaviour, keeping her ears open for gossip and her nose alert for smells. She continued to react against M. Daste but as a wary, intelligent dog rather than as his born enemy.

"Madame Suzanne, what does one do in this part of the world to make workmen get on with the job?"

She shrugged her shoulders.

"Offer them a bonus. I know *I* wouldn't offer one."

"Isn't you better give your camping builders a kick in the pants?" suggested Mme Ruby.

She jabbed the air with her needle.

"Tst, tst!" said Mme Suzanne reprovingly. "Pour us out some tea and don't be naughty. Drink it hot, Madame Colette. I heard you coughing again this morning when I was getting up at six."

"Did I make as much noise as all that?"

"No, but we're next door. And your hanging-cupboard is in a recess so that it juts out right at the back of our . . ."

She stopped short and blushed as violently as an awkward child.

"Our apartment," Mme Ruby suggested lamely.

"That's right. Our apartment."

She put down her cup and threw her arm round Mme Ruby's shoulders with an indescribable look—a look from which all constraint had vanished.

"Don't worry, my poor old darling. When you've said a thing, you've said it. Ten years of friendship—that's nothing to be ashamed of. It's a long-term agreement."

The tweed-jacketed embroidress gave her an understanding glance over her spectacles.

"Of course, I wouldn't talk of such things in front of old Daddy Daste . . . He'll be back soon, won't he?"

"He wasn't at lunch today," I observed.

I was promptly ashamed of having noticed his absence. Petty observations, petty kindnesses, petty pieces of spite—indications, all of them, that my awareness was becoming sharper, yet deteriorating too. One begins by noticing the absence of a M. Daste and soon one descends to "The lady at Table Six took three helpings of French beans . . ." Horrors, petty horrors.

"No," said Mme Suzanne. "He went off early to fetch his car from Nice."

"I didn't know M. Daste had a car."

"Good gracious, yes," said Mme Ruby. "He came here by car and by accident. The car in the ditch and Daddy Daste slightly stunned, with a nest beside him."

"Yes, a nest. I expect the shock is made the nest fall off a tree."

"Wasn't it a scream?" said Mme Suzanne. "A nest! Can't you just see it!"

"Do you like Monsieur Daste, Madame Suzanne?"

She half-closed her blue eyes and blew smoke from her painted mouth and her nostrils.

"I like him very much in one way. He's a good client. Tidy, pleasant and all that. But in another way, I can't stand him. Yet I've not a word to say against him."

"A nest . . ." I said again.

"Ah, that strikes you, doesn't it? There were even three young ones lying dead round the nest."

"Young ones? What kind of bird?"

She shrugged her plump shoulders.

"I haven't any idea. He got off with some bruises and he's been here ever since. It's fifteen days now, isn't it, Ruby?"

"Two weeks," answered Mme Ruby managerially. "He paid his second the day before yesterday."

"And what's Monsieur Daste's job in life?"

Neither of the two friends answered immediately and their silence forced me to notice their uncertainty.

"Well," said Mme Suzanne. "He's the head of a department in the Ministry of the Interior."

She leant forward with her elbows on her knees and her eyes fastened on mine as if she expected me to protest.

"Does that seem very unlikely, Madame Suzanne?"

"No! Oh, no! But I did not know that civil servants were usually so good at climbing. You should just see how that man can climb. *Really* climb."

The two friends turned simultaneously towards the window which was darkening to blue as the night came in.

"What do you mean, really climb?"

"Up a tree," said Mme Ruby. "We is not seen him go up, we is seen him come down. Backwards, a tiny step at a time, like this."

With her hands she mimed an acrobatic descent down a mast on a knotted rope.

"A tall tree in the wood, over towards the sea. One evening before you arrived. One of those days when it was so hot, so lovely you is no idea."

"No," I said sarcastically. "I certainly haven't any idea. For over a week I've been disgusted with your weather. I suppose Monsieur Daste was trying to dazzle you with his agility?"

"Just imagine!" cried Mme Suzanne. "He didn't even see us. We were under the tamarisks."

She blushed again. I liked that violent way she had of blushing.

"Madame Suzanne," said Mme Ruby phlegmatically, "you is telling your story all upside down."

"No, I'm not! Madame Colette will understand me all right! We were sitting side by side and I had my arm round Ruby, like that. We felt rather close to each other, both in the same mood and not spied on all the time as we are in this hole."

She cast a furious glance in the direction of the kitchen.

"After all, it's worth something, a good moment like that! There's no need to talk or to kiss each other like schoolgirls. Is what I'm saying so very absurd?"

She gave her companion a look which was a sudden affirmation of loyal love. I answered "No" with a movement of my head.

"Well, there we were," she went on. "Then I heard a noise in a tree, too much noise for it to be a cat. I was frightened. I'm brave, really, you know, but I always start by being frightened. Ruby made a sign to me not to move, so I don't move. Then I hear someone's shoe-soles scraping and then 'poof!' from the ground. And then we see Daddy Daste rubbing his hands, and dusting the knees of his trousers and going off up to Bella-Vista. What do you think of that?"

"Funny," I said mechanically.

"Very funny indeed, I think," she said. But she did not laugh.

She poured herself a second cup of tea and lit another cigarette. Mme Ruby, sitting very upright, went on embroidering with agile fingers. For the first time, I noticed that, away from their usual occupations, the two friends did not seem happy or even peaceful. Without going back on the instant liking I had felt for the American, I was beginning to think that Mme Suzanne was the more interesting and more worth studying of the two. I was struck, not only by her fierce, indiscreet jealousy which flared up on the least provocation but by a kind of protective vigilance, by the way she made herself a buffer between Ruby and all risks, between Ruby and all worries. She gave her all the easy jobs which a subordinate could have done, sending her to the station or to the shops. With perfect physical dignity, Mme Ruby drove the car, unloaded the hampers of eggs and vegetables, cut the roses, cleaned out the parakeets' cage and offered her lighter to the guests. Then she would cross her sinewy legs in their thick woollen stockings and bury herself in an English or American magazine. Mme Suzanne did not read. Occasionally she would pick up a local paper from a table, saying: "Let's have a look at the *Messenger*," and, five minutes later, drop it again. I was beginning to appreciate her modes of relaxing, so typical of an illiterate woman. She had such an active, intelligent way of doing nothing, of looking about her, of letting her cigarette go out. A really idle person never lets a cigarette go out.

Mme Ruby also dealt with the letters and, when necessary, typed in three languages. But Mme Suzanne said that she "inspired" them and Mme Ruby, nodding her beautiful faded chestnut head, agreed. Tea-time cleared Mme Suzanne's head and she would communicate her decisions in my presence. Whether from trustfulness or vanity, she did not mind thus letting me know that her eccentric summer clients did not mind what they paid and demanded privacy even more than comfort. They planned their stays at Bella-Vista a long time ahead.

"Madame Ruby," said Mme Suzanne suddenly, as if in response to a sudden outburst of the mistral, "I hope to goodness you haven't shut the gate on to the road? Otherwise Daddy Daste won't see it and he'll crash into it with his car."

"I asked Paulius to light the little arc-lamp at half-past six."

"Good. Now, Madame Ruby, we'll have to think about answering those two August clients of ours. They want their usual two rooms. But do remember the Princess and her masseur also want rooms in August. Our two Boche hussies, and the Princess, and Fernande and her gigolo—that's a whole set that's not on speaking terms. But they know each other . . . they've known each other for ages . . . and they can't stand one another. So, Madame Ruby, first of all you're to write to the Princess."

She explained at considerable length, knitting her pencilled eyebrows. She addressed Ruby as "Madame" and used the intimate "tu" with a bourgeois, marital ceremoniousness. As she spoke, she kept looking at her friend just as an anxious nurse might scrutinise the complicated little ears, the eyelids and nostrils of an immensely well looked-after child. She would smooth down a silvery lock on her forehead, straighten her tie, flatten her collar or pick a stray white thread off her jacket.

The expression on her face—it was tired and making no attempt just then to hide its tiredness—seemed to me very far from any "perverted" fussing. I use the word "perverted" in its usual modern sense. She saw that I was watching her and gave me a frank, warm smile which softened the blue eyes that often looked so hard.

"It's no news to you," she said, "that our clientèle's rather special. After all, it was Grenigue who gave you our address. At Christmas and Easter, you won't find a soul. But come back in July and you'll have any amount of copy. You realise that, with only ten rooms in all, we have to put up prices a bit; our real season only lasts three months. I'll tell you something that'll make you laugh. Last summer, what do you think arrived? A little old couple, husband and wife, at least a hundred and sixty between them. Two tiny little things with an old manservant crumbling to bits, who asked if they could inspect the rooms, as if we were a palace! I said to them—as nicely as possible—'There's some mistake. You see this is a rather special kind of inn.' They didn't want to go. But I insisted, I tried to find words to make myself understood, old-fashioned words you know. I said 'It's a bit naughty-naughty, so to speak. People come here and sow their wild oats, as it were. You can't stop here.' Do you know what she answered, that little old grandmother? 'And who told you, Madame, that we don't want to sow some wild oats too?' They went away, of course. But she had me there, all right! Madame Ruby, do you know what the time is? Time you gave that embroidery a rest. I can't hear a sound in the dining-room and the courtyard's not lit up. Whatever's the staff thinking about?"

"I'll go and ask Lucie," said Mme Ruby, promptly getting to her feet.

"No," shouted Mme Suzanne. "I must go and see to the dinner. You don't suppose the leg of mutton's anxiously waiting for *you*, do you?"

She was trembling with sudden rage. Her lips were quivering with desire to burst out into a furious tirade. To stop herself, she made a rush to the door. As she did so, there was the sound of a motor-engine and the headlamps of a car swept the courtyard.

"Daddy Daste," announced Mme Suzanne.

"Why isn't that man switched off his headlights to come in? He might at least do that."

Pati, suddenly woken up, flung herself at the french window, from etiquette rather than from hostility. The dry breath of the mistral entered along with M. Daste. He was rubbing his hands and his impersonal face at last bore an individual accent. This was a small newly-made wound, triangular in shape, under his right eye.

"Hello, Monsieur Daste! You is wounded? Pebble? A branch? An attack? Is the car damaged?"

"Good evening, ladies," said M. Daste politely. "No, no, nothing wrong with the car. She's going splendidly. This," he put his hand to his cheek, "isn't worth bothering about."

"All the same, I'm going to give you some peroxide," said Mme Suzanne who had come up to him and was examining the deeply incised little wound at close range. "Don't cover it up, then it'll dry quicker. A nail? A bit of flying flint?"

"No," said M. Daste. "Just a . . . bird."

"What, *another* one?" asid Mme Ruby.

Mme Suzanne turned to her friend with a reproving look.

"What do you mean, another one? There's nothing so very astonishing about it."

"Quite so. Nothing so very astonishing," agreed M. Daste.

"It's full of night-birds round about here."

"Full," said M. Daste.

"The headlights dazzle them and they dash themselves against the windscreen."

"Exactly," concluded M. Daste. "I'm delighted to be back at Bella-Vista again. That Corniche road at night! To think that there are people who actually drive on it for pleasure! I shall do justice to the dinner, Madame Suzanne!"

Nevertheless we noticed at dinner that M. Daste ate nothing but the sweet. I noticed this mainly because Mme Ruby kept up a stream of encouragement from her table.

"Hallo, Monsieur Daste! Is good for you to keep your strength up!"

"But I assure you I don't feel in the least weak," M. Daste kept politely assuring her.

In fact, his abstinence had endowed him with the bright flush of satiety. He was drinking water with a slightly inebriated expression.

Mme Ruby raised her large hand sententiously.

"Leg of mutton *Bretonne* is very good against birds, Monsieur Daste!"

I remember it was that evening that we played our first game of poker. My three partners loved cards. In order to play better, they retired into the depths of themselves leaving their faces unconsciously exposed. Studying them amused me more than the game. In any case I play poker extremely badly and was scolded more than once. I was amused to note that M. Daste only "opened" when forced to and then only with obvious reluctance but good cards gave him spasms of nervous yawns which he managed to suppress by expanding his nostrils. His little wound had been washed and round it a bruised area was already turning purple, showing how violent the impact had been.

Mme Ruby played a tough game, compressing her full lips, and asking for cards and raising the bid by signs. I was astonished to see her handling the cards with agile but brutal fingers, using a thumb which was much thicker than I had realised. As to Mme Suzanne, she seemed set in her tracks like a bloodhound. She showed not the slightest emotion, pulled each card out slowly before declaring with an air of detachment: "Good for me!"

The smoke accumulated in horizontal layers and between two rounds I reproached myself for the inertia which kept me sitting there. "Perhaps I'm still not quite well," I told myself with a kind of hopefulness.

Suddenly the mistral stopped blowing and the silence fell on us so brutally that it awakened the sleeping griffon. She emerged from her knitted hood and asked clearly, with her eyes and her pricked ears, what time it was.

"Huisipisi, huisipisi!" said M. Daste maliciously.

She stared at him, sniffed the air about his person and put her two front paws on the table. From there, by stretching her thick little neck, she could just reach M. Daste's hands.

"How she loves me!" said M. Daste. "Huisipisi . . ."

The dog seemed to be searching for a particular spot and to find it just under the edge of M. Daste's cuff. She smelt it with her knowing black nostrils, then she tasted it with her tongue.

"She's tickling me! Madame Suzanne, you pray too long to the goddess of luck while you're shuffling the cards. On with the game!"

"Monsieur Daste, why do you always say 'Huisipisi' to my dog? Is it a magic password?"

He fluttered his little hands about his face.

"The breeze," he said. "The wind in the fir trees. Wings . . . Huisipisi . . . Things that fly . . . Even things that skim over the ground in a very . . . very *silky* way. Rats."

"Boo!" cried Mme Suzanne. "I've a horror of mice. So, imagine, a *rat*! On with the game yourself, Monsieur Daste. Madame Colette, don't forget the kitty. I believe you're thinking more about your next novel than our little poker game."

In this she was wrong. Alone in this equivocal guest-house, during the pause before the harvest of its summer debauch, I was aware of a complex and familiar mental state. In that state a peculiar pleasure blunts the sharp edge of my longing for my friends, my home and my real life. Yet is there anyone who is not deluded about the setting of their "real" life? Was I not breathing here and now, among these three strangers, what I call the very oxygen of travel? My thoughts could wander as lazily as they pleased; I was free of any burden of love; I was immersed in that holiday emptiness in which morning brings a light-hearted intoxication and evening a compulsion to waste one's time and to suffer. Everything you love strips you of part of yourself: the Madame Suzannes rob you of nothing. Answering the few careless questions they ask takes nothing out of you. "How many pages do you do a day? All those letters you get every day and all those ones you write, don't you have to cudgel your brains over them? You don't happen to know an authoress who lives all the year round at Nice—a tall woman with pince-nez?" The Madame Suzannes don't catechise you; they tell you about themselves. Sometimes, of course, they keep aggressively silent about some great secret which is always rising to their lips and being stifled. But a secret is exacting and deafens us with its clamour.

In many ways, I found Bella-Vista satisfying. It revived old habits from my solitary days: the itch for the arrival of the postman, my curiosity about passers-by who leave no permanent trace. I felt sympathetic towards the discredited pair of friends. At Bella-Vista I ate admirably and worked atrociously. Moreover, I was putting on weight there.

"Four last rounds," announced Mme Suzanne. "Monsieur Daste, you open for the last time. Afterwards, I'll stand you a bottle of champagne. I think that ought to wake Madame Ruby up. There hasn't been a sound from her all the evening."

Her blue eyes shot a glance of fierce reproach at her impassive friend.

"You is usually hear me play poker at the top of my voice?"

Mme Suzanne did not answer and, as soon as the last round was over, went off to get the champagne. While she was going down to the cellar, Mme Ruby stood up, stretched her arms and her firm shoulders till the joints cracked. Then she opened the door between the dining-room and the boudoir, listened in the direction of the kitchen and came back again. She seemed absent-minded, preoccupied by some care which made her full mouth look ugly and dulled the large grey eyes under the eyebrows which were paler than her forehead. That evening, the ambiguity of all her features, always disturbing, seemed almost repellent. She was biting the inside of her cheek but forced herself to stop gnawing it when her friend returned, out of breath, with a bottle of "*brut*" under each arm.

"This is really old," announced Mme Suzanne. "Some remains of the '06. You don't think I pour *that* down the gullets of the summer visitors. It's not iced but the cellar's cool. I don't know if you agree with me that it's nice to have a wine now and then that doesn't make a block of ice in your stomach. Madame Ruby, where are there some pliers? These bottles are wired in the old-fashioned way."

"I'll call Lucie," suggested the American.

Mme Suzanne looked at her almost furiously.

"For God's sake, can't you give Lucie a little peace? For one thing, she's gone to bed. For another, you'll certainly find some sort of pliers in the office."

We drank each other's healths. Mme Ruby magically gulped down a large glass in one swallow, throwing her head back in a way which proved how much drinking was a habit with her. Mme Suzanne mimicked the tags with which drinkers in the Midi raise their glasses: "To your very good!" "Much appreciated! Likewise!" M. Daste closed his eyes like a cat afraid of splashing itself when it laps. Sitting opposite me in the depths of one of the English armchairs he drank the perfect old champagne, whose bubbles gave out a faint scent of roses as they burst, in tiny sips. The bruise which was now clearly visible round the little triangular wound on his cheek made him seem, for some reason, likeable, less definitely human. I like a fox-terrier to have a round spot by its eye and a tortoiseshell cat to show an orange crescent or a black patch on its temple. A large mole or freckle on our cheek, a neat well-placed scar, one eye that is slightly larger than the other: all such things mark us out from the general human anonymity.

Mme Suzanne inclined the neck of the second bottle over our goblets and drew our attention to the mushroom-shaped cork, which had acquired the texture of hard wood with age.

"Two bottles among four of us. Quite an orgy! But we'll see better than that in this house this summer."

"We can see it here and now, if you like," said Mme Ruby promptly, pushing her empty glass towards the bottle.

Mme Suzanne gave her friend a warning look.

"Moderation in all things, Madame Ruby. Would you be an angel and go and find that fool of a Slough? And shut the rabbit up, if you can! Have you covered up the parakeets?"

Through the light buzzing of the wine in my ears, I listened to those ritual phrases, not unlike "counting-out rhymes". I know by experience how their sound, their fatal recurrence can be like longed-for dew or a faint, neutral blessing. I know, too, that they can also fall like a branding-iron on a place already seared.

But that night I was all benevolence. Pati, who was also getting fatter at Bella-Vista, waddled peacefully into the courtyard and I listened gratefully to Mme Ruby's voice outside announcing that it was going to be fine.

As I stood up, my spectacles and my room-key slipped off my knees. As they fell, M. Dante's hand reached out and caught them with such a swift, perfectly-timed movement that I hardly had time to see his gesture. "Ah," I thought. "So he's not quite human, this climber."

We all separated without further words like people who have the sense not to prolong the pleasures of a superficial gaiety and cordiality to the point of imprudence. Still under the spell of my optimism, I complimented M. Daste on the appearance of his little wound. I did not tell him that it brought out the character, at once intelligent and uninteresting, of his face. He seemed enchanted. He bridled and passed one hand coquettishly over his ear to smooth his hair.

Lucie did not have to wake me the next morning. When she came in with the tray and the rose, I was already dressed and standing at my open french window, contemplating the fine weather.

Thirteen years ago, I did not know what spring or summer in the Midi could be. I knew nothing of that irruption, that victorious invasion of a season of serenity, of that enduring pact between warmth, colour and scent. That morning I took to longing for the sea salt on my hands and lips and to thinking of my patch of land where my picnicking workmen were drinking *vin rosé* and eating salami.

"Lucie, what beautiful weather!"

"The proper weather for the season. About time too. It's kept us waiting long enough."

As she arranged my breakfast and the daily rose on the table, the dark-haired maid answered me absently. I looked at her and saw that she was pale. Her pallor and a certain troubled look made her more attractive. She had put a little rouge on her beautiful mouth.

"Hallo, Madame Colette!"

I answered Mme Ruby who, dressed all in blue, with a narrow tight-fitting shirt and a beret pulled over one ear, was loading up her hampers.

My dog rushed at her, gave her her military salute, and danced round her.

"You is not want to come with me?"

"I'd love to."

"While I do my shopping, you gives good advice to your pioneers."

"Excellent idea!"

"You say the mason: 'Dear friend.' You say the man who does the roof: 'My boy.' You say the little painter: 'Where is you get made the smart white blouse what suits you so well?' You turn on the charm! Perhaps that works."

"Ah, you know how to talk to men, Madame Ruby! Hold Pati. Just let me get a pullover and I'll be with you."

I went into the bathroom for a moment. When I returned, Lucie and Mme Ruby, one standing perfectly still in my room and the other stationed in the courtyard, were looking at each other across the intervening space. The maid did not turn away quickly enough to conceal from me that her eyes were full of fear, gentleness and tears.

Mme Ruby drove us, fast and well, through the sparse forest, still russet from the annual fires. Between two tracts of pineland were carefully cultivated allotments now green with young beans and marrows, and fenced-off tracts of wild quince with great pink flowers. The much-prized garlic and onion lifted their spears from the light, powdery earth and the growing vines were stretching out their first tendrils. The blue air was now chill but kindly, now full of new and subtle warmth. The blue air of the Estérels rushed to meet us, and moistened the dog's nose. Along the lane which ran into the main road, I could put out my hand as we drove and touch the leaves of the almond trees and the fruit already set and downy.

"The spring is born tonight," said Mme Ruby softly.

Up till then, we had only exchanged a few commonplaces and these last words, spoken in such a low, troubled voice that they were almost inaudible, came as a surprise. They did not demand an answer and I made none. My strange companion sat impassive at the wheel, her chin high and her little beret over one eye. I threw a glance at her firm profile, so unlike a Frenchwoman's, and noted again the coarse ruddy texture of her skin. The back of her neck, emerging from her pullover, looked as strong as a coal-heaver's. With a terrible blast of her horn, she swept the sprawling, dusty dogs off the road, to Pati's intense delight, and kept up a stream of blasphemy in English against the heedless cart-drivers. "The spring is born tonight." Imprisoned behind the same ambiguous exterior, a brazen, angular female and a collegian in love with a servant girl were both claiming the right to live and to love. Very likely each hated the other.

It seemed a long time before we came to the coast and drove along the edge of the sea where a few bathers were shrieking with cold as they splashed about. We passed through sham villages; pink, silent and empty, idly blossoming with no one to admire. At last Mme Ruby put me down before my future dwelling. She gave a whistle of ironic commiseration and refused to get out of the car. Raising her forefinger to the level of her pale, bushy eyebrow, she said: "I come and fetch you in three-quarters of an hour. You thinks it is enough for your whole house to be finished?"

She indicated the rampart of hollow bricks, the crater of slaked lime and the mound of sifted sand which defended my gates, and left me to my fate.

But when she returned, I no longer wanted to leave the place. Instead of the workmen who were missing one and all, I had found white arum lilies, red roses, a hundred little tulips with pointed cups, purple irises and pittosporums whose scent paralyses the will. Leaning over the edge of the well, I had listened to the musical noise of drops that filtered through the broken bricks falling into the water below, while Pati rested after her first encounter with a hedgehog. The interior of the house bore not the slightest resemblance to anything which had charmed me about it at first. But, in the little pine wood, the bright drops of liquid resin were guttering in the wind, those drops that congeal almost as soon as they are formed, and tarnish before they fall to the ground. I had treated the mimosa, which flowers all the year round, with scant respect. Feeling like a rich person, I flung my bundle of flowers into the car, on top of the hampers of early artichokes, broad beans and French beans with which the back seats were loaded.

"Not a soul?" asked Mme Ruby.

"Not a soul! Such luck! It was delightful."

"We used to say that at Bella-Vista too, in the beginning. 'Such luck! Not a soul!' And now . . ."

She raised that clerical chin of hers and started up the car.

"And now we is a little *blasé*. A little old, both of us."

"It's very beautiful, a friendship that grows old gracefully. Don't you agree?"

"Nobody loves what is old," she said harshly. "Everyone

loves what is beautiful, what is young—dangerous. Everyone loves the spring."

On the way back, she did not speak again except to the dog. In any case, I should have been incapable of listening intelligently. I was conscious only of the noonday sun drugging me with light, well-being and overwhelming drowsiness. I sat with my eyes closed, aware only of the resonance of a voice which though nasal, was never shrill and whose deep pitch was as pleasant as the lowest notes of a clarinet. Miss Ruby drove fast, pointing out objects of vituperation to Pati, such as small donkeys, chickens and other dogs. The griffon responded enthusiastically to all these suggestions, even though they were expressed in English spoken with an American twang.

"O.K.," approved Mme Ruby. "Good for you to learn English. Holiday task. Look to the left, enormous, enormous goose! Wah!"

"Wah!" repeated the little dog, standing up, quite beside herself with excitement, with her front paws against the windscreen.

Of the few days that followed, I remember only the glorious weather. The weather spread an indulgent blue and gold and purple haze over my work and my worries, over the letters which arrived from Paris, over the full-blown idleness of the workmen whom I found singing and playing "she loves me, she loves me not" with daisy petals when I revisited my little house. Fine weather, day and night, induced in me an oriental rebelliousness against the accustomed hours of sleep. I was wide awake at midnight and overwhelmed with the imperative need of a siesta in the afternoon. Laziness, like work, demands to be comfortably organised. Mine sleeps during the day, muses at night, wakes at dawn and closes the shutters against the unsympathetic light of the hours after lunch. On dark nights and under the first quarter of a slender, rosy moon, the nightingales all burst out together, for there is never a first nightingale.

On this subject, M. Daste made various poetic remarks which did not affect me in the least. For I never bothered less about M. Daste than I did during that week of fine weather. I saw hardly anything even of my hostesses. Their importance faded under the dazzling impact of the season. I did however observe a little poker incident between Mme Ruby and M. Daste one evening. It was a very brief incident, mimed rather than spoken, and in the course of it I had a vision of Mme Ruby flushing the colour of copper and clutching the edge of the green table with both hands. At that, M. Daste gathered himself together in a most peculiar way. He seemed to shrink till he became very small and very compact and, as he thrust his lowered brow forward, he gave the impression of drawing back his shoulders behind his head. It was an attitude that assorted ill with his prim face and that hair which was neither old nor young. Mme Suzanne promptly laid her hand on her friend's well-groomed head.

"Now, now, my pet! Now, now . . ." she said without raising her voice.

With one accord, the two adversaries resumed a friendly tone and the game went on. As I was not interested in the cause of their quarrel, I made no inquiries. Perhaps M. Daste had cheated. Or perhaps Mme Ruby. Or possibly both of them. I only thought to myself that, had it come to a fight, I should not have backed M. Daste to win.

It was that night, if I am not mistaken, that I was awakened by a great tumult among the parakeets. As it was silenced almost at once, I did not get up. The next morning, very early, I saw Mme Ruby, trim as usual in white and blue, her rose in her lapel, standing near the aviary. Her back was turned to me and she was attentively studying some object she was holding in her cupped hand. Then she slipped whatever it was into her pocket. I pulled on a dressing-gown and opened my french window.

"Madame Ruby, did you hear the parakeets in the night?"

She smiled at me, nodded from the distance, and came up the little steps to shake hands with me.

"Slept well?"

"Not badly. But did you hear, about two in the morning . . ."

She drew out of her pocket a dead parakeet. It was soft and the eye showed bluish between two borders of grey skin.

"What! They're capable of killing each other?"

"So we must suppose," said Mme Ruby, without looking up. "Poor little bird!"

She blew on the cold feathers which parted about a torn, bloodless wound. The dog wanted to be in on the affair and sniffed the bird with that mixture of bewilderment and erotism which the sight and smell of death so often excites in the living.

"Not so keen, not so keen, little yellow dog. You begins smell, smell and then you eats. And then ever after, you eats."

She went off with the bird in her pocket. Then she changed her mind and came back.

"Please, it's better to say nothing to Madame Suzanne. Nor Monsieur Daste. Madame Suzanne is super . . . superstitious. And Monsieur Daste is . . ."

Her prominent eyes, grey as agates, sought mine.

"He is . . . sensitive. It's better to say nothing."

"I agree."

She gave me that little salute with her forefinger and I did not see her again till luncheon.

In addition to its usual guests, Bella-Vista was receiving a family from Lausanne; three couples of hiking campers. Their rucksacks, their little tents and battery of aluminium cooking utensils, their red faces and bare knees seemed like the emblems of some inoffensive faith.

Lucie went to and fro between the tables, carrying the chervil omelette, the brains fried in batter and the ragoût of beef. Her face was thickly powdered and she was languid and absent-minded.

Their meal over, the campers spread out a map. With managerial discretion, Mme Suzanne signed to us to come and take our coffee in the "boudoir". There was an expression of faint repugnance on her heated face. She gave off her strong perfume which assorted ill with that of the ragoût and she cooled the fire of her complexion with the help of a vast powder-puff which never left the pocket of her white blouse.

"Pooh!" she sighed as she fell into a chair. "My goodness, how they fell on the stew, those Switzers! You'll eat God knows what tonight: I haven't a thing left. Those people give me the creeps. So I'm going to treat myself to a little cigar. Where are they off to already, Madame Ruby?"

With a thrust of her chin, Mme Ruby indicated the direction of the sea.

"Over there. Somewhere that isn't got a name, provided it's at least thirty miles away."

"And they sleep on the hard ground. And they drink nothing but water. And it's for idiots like that that our wonderful age invented the railway and the motor-car and the *aeroplane*! I ask you! As for me sleeping on the ground, the mere idea of ants . . ."

She bit off the end of her little Havana and rolled it carefully between her fingers. Mme Ruby never smoked anything but cigarettes.

"Come, come!" said M. Daste. "Don't speak ill of camping. You must be used to many forms of camping, Madame Ruby? And I'm sure you looked much more chic in plus-fours and a woollen shirt and hobnailed shoes than those three Swiss females. Come along now, admit it."

She threw him an ironic glance and displayed her large teeth.

"All right, I admit it," she said. "What about you, Monsieur Daste? Camping? Nights under the open stars? Dangerous encounters? You is a slyboots, Monsieur Daste! Don't deny it!"

M. Daste was flattered. He lowered his chin till it touched his tie, passed his hand over his ear to smooth the hair on his temple and coquettishly swallowed a mouthful of brandy which went the wrong way. He was convulsed with choking coughs and only regained his breath under the kindly hammering of Mme Suzanne's hand on his shoulder-blades. I must record that, with his face flushed and his streaming eyes bloodshot, M. Daste was unrecognisable.

"Thank you," he said when he could breathe again. "You've saved my life, Madame Suzanne. I can't imagine what could have got stuck in my throat."

"A feather, perhaps," said Mme Ruby.

M. Daste turned his head towards her with an almost imperceptible movement and then became stock still. Mme Suzanne, who was sucking her cigar, became agitated and said shrilly: "A feather? Whatever will she think of next? A *feather*! You're not ill, are you, Ruby? Now *me*," she went on hurriedly, "you'd never believe what *I* swallowed when I was a kid. A watch-spring! But a *huge* watch-spring, a positive metal snake, my dears, as long as *that*! I've swallowed a lot of other things since those days, bigger ones too, if you count insults."

She laughed, not only with her mouth but with her eyes, and gave a great yawn.

"My children, I doubt very much whether you'll see me again before five o'clock. Madame Ruby, will you look after the Swissies? They're taking sandwiches with them tonight so that they can have dinner on a nice cool carpet of pine-needles which'll stick into their behinds."

"Right," said Mme Ruby. "Lucie is made the sandwiches?"

"No, Marguerite. Go and make sure she packs them in greaseproof paper. I've put it all down on their bill."

Suddenly she extinguished the laugh in her blue eyes and scanned her friend's face closely: "I've sent Lucie to her room. She's not feeling well."

Having said that, she left the room, jerking her shoulders as she did so. The back of her neck suggested a proud determination which I was the only one to notice. M. Daste, shrunken and tense, had still not moved. Mme Ruby paid not the slightest attention either to M. Daste or to myself before she, too, went out.

It was from that moment that I realised I was no longer enjoying myself at Bella-Vista. The saffron walls and the blue shutters, the Basque roof, the plastered Norman beams and the Provençal tiles all suddenly seemed to me false and pretentious. A certain troubled atmosphere and the menace and hostility it breeds can only interest me if I am personally involved in it. It was not that I repented of feeling a rather pendulum-like sympathy with my hostesses which inclined now to Suzanne, now to Ruby. But, selfishly, I would have preferred them happy, serene in their old, faithful, reprehensible love that should have been spiced only with childish quarrels. The fact remained that I did not see them happy. And, as to faithfulness, the yielding gentleness of a dark-haired servant girl gave me matter for thought—and disapproval.

When I ran into Lucie, when she brought me my "rose" breakfast about half-past seven, I found myself feeling as severe towards Mme Ruby as if she had been Philemon deceiving Baucis.

I began to suspect "Daddy" Daste, that climber who had been so ill-rewarded for his bird-watching. I began to suspect his mysterious government employment, his scar adorned with black sticking-plaster and even what I called his malicious good temper. A conversation with Mme Ruby might have taught me more about M. Daste and possibly explained the obvious antipathy he inspired in her. But Mme Ruby made no attempt to have any private talk with me.

I remember that, about that very time, the weather changed again. During the twilight of a long April day, the south-east wind began to blow in short gusts, bringing with it a heat which mounted from the soil as from an oven full of burning bread. All four of us were playing bowls. Mme Suzanne kept shaking her white linen sleeves to "air herself" as she sighed: "If it weren't that I want to slim!"

Bowls is a good game, like all games capable of revealing some trait of character in the expert player. Much to my surprise, M. Daste was "shooter". Before launching his wood, he held it hidden almost behind his back. The arm, the small manicured hand and the wood rose together and the heavy nailed ball fell on his adversary's with a resounding crack which sent M. Daste into ecstasy.

"On his skull! Bang on top of his skull!" he cried.

Mme Suzanne, the "shooter" of the other side, rated about the same as I did as "marker" for M. Daste's. Sometimes I "mark" very well, sometimes like a complete duffer. Mme Ruby "marked" to perfection, rolling her wood as softly as a ball of wool to within a hairbreadth of the jack. Disdaining our heavy woods, Pati snapped and spat out again innumerable insects which had been driven inland by the approach of a solid wall of purple clouds which was advancing towards us from the sea.

"My children, I can feel the storm coming. The roots of my hair are hurting me!" wailed Mme Suzanne.

At the first flash which broke into twigs of incandescent pink as it ran down the sky into the flat sea, Mme Suzanne gave a great "Ha!" and covered her eyes.

A warm gust played all round the courtyard, rolling faded flowers, straws and leaves into wreaths and spirals, and the swallows circled in the air in the same direction. Warm heavy drops splayed on my hands. Mme Ruby ran to the garage, taking great strides, pulled on a black oilskin and returned to her friend who had not stirred. White as chalk, her hands over her eyes, the sturdy Suzanne collapsed, weak and tottering, on the shoulder of Mme Ruby, who looked like a dripping lifeboatman.

The strange couple and I ran towards our twin little flights of steps. Having shut Mme Suzanne in her room, Mme Ruby rushed to the rescue of other shipwrecked creatures, such as the bloodthirsty rabbit and the stupid greyhound. She wheeled the aviary into the garage, shouted orders to the two invisible kitchen maids and to Lucie who stood in a doorway, her loosened hair hanging in a cloud round her pale face. She closed all the banging doors and brought in the cushions from the garden chairs.

From my window, I watched the hurly-burly which the American woman directed with a slightly theatrical calm. Nestled against my arm, my excited dog followed all that was going on while she waited for the battle of the elements. She shone in exceptional circumstances; particularly in great storms which she boldly defied where a bulldog would have panted with fear and done his best to die flattened out under an armchair. A minute dog with a great brain, Pati welcomed tempests on land or sea like a joyous stormy petrel.

Behind me, the violet darkness of the sky, magnificently rent by each flash, was stealing into my red and pink room. Some small, hollow-sounding thunder which echoed back from the hills decided to accompany the lightning flashes and a crushing curtain of rain, which dropped suddenly from the sky, made me hastily shut my window.

It was almost time for the real night to close in. But the passing night of the storm had taken the place of dusk and I sat down, sullen and unwilling, to my work. I had begun it without inclination and continued it in a desultory way without being decided enough to abandon it altogether. The dog, becoming virtuously quiet as soon as she saw me busy with papers, gnawed her claws and listened to the thunder and the rain. I think that both she and I longed with all our hearts for Paris, for our friends there, for the reassuring mutter of a city.

The rain, which had fallen from a moderate-sized cloud which the wind had not had time to shred, stopped suddenly. My ear, made alert by the startling silence, caught the sound of voices on the other side of the partition. I could hear a high voice and a lower one, then the sound of tearful recriminations. "Extraordinary!" I thought. "That fat Madame Suzanne getting herself in such a state because of a storm!"

She did not appear at dinner.

"Madame Suzanne isn't feeling well?" I asked Mme Ruby.

"Her nerves. You is no idea how nervous she is."

"The first storm of the season affects the nerves," said M. Daste whose opinion no one had asked. "This one is the first . . . but not the last," he added, pointing to wavering flashes on the horizon.

I began to think impatiently of my approaching departure. Bella-Vista could no longer assuage my increasing restlessness and my sense of foreboding. I took my dog out into the courtyard before her usual time. Like a child with new shoes, she deliberately splashed through the puddles of rain which reflected a few stars. I had to scold her to get her away from a frog which she doubtless wanted to bring home and add to her collections in Paris: collections of mammoth bones, ancient biscuits, punctured balls and sulphur lozenges. M. Daste undermined my authority and egged Pati on with innumerable "Huisipisis". The night had stayed warm and its scents made me languid. What tropics exhale more breaths of orange-blossom, resin, rain-soaked carnations and wild peppermint than a spring night in Provence?

After reading in bed, I switched off my lamp rather late and got up to open the door and window so as to let in as much as possible of the meagre coolness and the over-abundant scent. Standing in the dark room, I remembered that I had not heard M. Daste come in. For the first time, I found something unpleasant in the thought of M. Daste's small, agile feet walking, on a moonless night, not far from my open and accessible window. I know from experience how easily a fixed idea of a terror can take concrete shape and I invariably take pains to crush their first, faint intimations. Various mnemonic tricks and musical rhymes served to lull me into a dream in which printed letters danced before me and I was asleep when the french window which led into my hostesses' room was clicked open.

I sat up in bed and heard, from the other side, a deep chest inhaling and exhaling the air. In the silence which foreboded other storms, I was also aware of the slither of two bare feet on my neighbours' stone steps.

"You makes me die of heat with your nerves," said Mme Ruby in a muffled voice. "The storm's over."

The rectangle of my open window was suddenly lit up. I realised that Mme Suzanne had turned on the ceiling light in her room.

"Idiot! I'm naked," whispered Ruby furiously.

The light was promptly switched off.

"Too late. Daste's right opposite, in the courtyard."

I heard a stifled exclamation and the thump of two heavy feet landing on the wooden floor. Mme Suzanne went over to her friend.

"Where d'you say he is?"

"Over by the garage."

"It's quite a long way off."

"Not for him. In any case, it is telling him nothing he doesn't know."

"Oh, don't . . . oh, don't."

"Don't get upset, darling. There, there . . ."

"My pet . . . oh! my pet."

"Shut up so I can listen. He's opening the door of the garage."

They were silent for a long moment. Then Mme Suzanne whispered vehemently: "Get it well into your head that if they separate us, if they come here to . . ."

Mme Ruby's light whistle ordered her to be quiet. The dog had growled and I gently closed my hand over her muzzle.

"Suppose I shoot?" said the voice of Mme Ruby.

"Are you quite mad?"

This startling interchange was followed by a scuffle of bare feet. I imagined that Mme Suzanne was dragging her friend back into the room.

"Really, Richard, you must be mad. Aren't we in a bad enough mess as it is? Isn't it enough for you to have got Lucie in the family way without wanting to put a bullet through Daste into the bargain? You couldn't control yourself just for once, could you? No, of course not. You men are all the same. Come on, now. No more nonsense. Come indoors and for heaven's sake, stay there."

The french window shut and there was complete silence.

I made no further attempt to sleep. My astonishment was soon over. Had Mme Suzanne's cry of revelation really given me a genuine surprise? What excited my interest and moved me profoundly was the thought of Mme Suzanne's vigilance, the discreet and devoted cynicism she interposed between the disguised, suspected "Madame" Ruby and the malevolent little Daste.

If the idle looker-on in me exclaimed delightedly "What a story!", my honourable side warned me to keep the story to myself. I have done so for a very long time.

Towards three in the morning, the wind changed and a fresh storm attacked Bella-Vista. It was accompanied by continuous thunder and slanting rain. In the moment or two it took to gather up my strewn, sopping papers, my nightdress was soaked and clung to my body. The dog followed all my movements, holding herself ready for any contingency. "Have we got to swim? Have we got to run away?" I set her an example of immovable patience and made her a cave out of a scarf. In the shelter of this she played at shipwrecks and desert islands and even at earthquakes.

Now against a background of total darkness, now against a screen lit up with lightning-flashes and driving rain, I reconstructed the neighbouring couple, the man and the woman. Two normal people, undoubtedly with the police on their track, lay side by side in the next room, awaiting their fate.

Perhaps the woman's head rested on the man's shoulder while they exchanged anxious speculations. In imagination I saw again the back of "Madame" Ruby's neck, that thumb, that roughened cheek, that large, well-shaved upper lip. Then I dwelt again on Mme Suzanne and wished good luck to that heroic woman; so jealous and so protective; so terrified, yet ready to face anything.

Daybreak brought a grey drizzle on the heels of the tornado and sleep overtook me at last. No hand knocked on my door nor laid my breakfast tray with its customary rose on my table. The unwonted silence awakened me and I rang for Lucie. It was Marguerite who came.

"Where is Lucie?"

"I don't know, Madame. But won't I do instead?"

Under the impalpable rain, the courtyard and climbing roses torn from their trellis had the aspect of October. "The train, the first train! I won't stay another twenty-four hours!"

In the wide-open garage, I caught sight of the white linen overall and the dyed gold hair of Mme Suzanne and I went out to join her. She was sitting on an upturned pail and candidly let me see her ravaged face. It was the face of an unhappy middle-aged wife, the eyes small and swollen and the cheeks scoured with recent tears.

"Look," she said. "A nice sight, isn't it?"

At her feet lay the nineteen parakeets, dead. Assassinated would be a better word for the frenzy with which they had been destroyed. They had been torn and almost pulped in a peculiarly revolting way. The dog sniffed at the birds from a distance and planted herself at my heels.

"Monsieur Daste's car isn't in the garage any longer?"

Mme Suzanne's little swollen eyes met my own.

"Nor is *he* in the house," she said. "Gone. After doing that, it's hardly surprising."

With her foot, she pushed away a headless parakeet.

"If you're sure he did it, why don't you complain to the police? In your place, I should certainly lodge a complaint."

"Yes. But you're not in my place."

She put a hand on my shoulder.

"Ah, my dear, lodge a complaint! You don't know what you're talking about. Besides," she added, "he'd paid his bill for the week. He doesn't owe us a farthing."

"Is he a madman?"

"I'd like to believe so. I must go and find Paulius and get him to bury all this. Was there something you wanted?"

"Nothing special. As I told you already, I'm leaving. Tomorrow. Or even today unless that's quite impossible."

"Just as you like," she said indifferently. "Today, if you'd rather. Because tomorrow . . ."

"You're expecting someone to arrive tomorrow?"

She ran her tongue over her dry, unpainted lips.

"Someone to arrive? I wonder. If anyone could tell me what's going to happen tomorrow."

She got up as heavily as an old woman.

"I'll go and tell Madame Ruby to see about your seat in the train. Marguerite will help you with your packing."

"Or Lucie. She knows where I keep all my things."

The unhappy, tear-washed elderly woman reared herself up straight. Flushed and sparkling with anger, she looked suddenly young again.

"Terribly sorry. Lucie's not there. Lucie's through!"

"She's leaving you?"

"Leaving *me*? Considering I've thrown *her* out, the slut! There are . . . interesting conditions that I find very far from interesting! Really, the things one has to put up with in this world!"

She went off down the muddy path, her white skirt held up in both hands. I did not linger to consider the scattered wreckage at my feet, the work of the civilised monster masquerading in human shape, the creature who lusted to kill birds.

Mme Suzanne did everything possible to satisfy my keen and slightly cowardly desire to leave Bella-Vista that very day. She did not forget Pati's ticket and insisted on accompanying me to the train. Dressed in tight-fitting black, she sat beside me on the back seat and, all through the drive, she preserved a stiffness which was equally suitable to a well-to-do business woman or a proud creature going to the scaffold. In front of us was Mme Ruby's erect, T-shaped torso and her handsome head with its rakishly tilted beret.

At the station, I managed to persuade Mme Suzanne to stay in the car. My last sight of her was behind the windows misted with fine rain. It was Mme Ruby who carried my heaviest suitcase, bought me papers and settled me in my carriage with the greatest possible friendliness.

But I received these attentions somewhat ungraciously. I had an unjust feeling which refused to admit that this easy assurance quite caught the manner of a masculine female, adept at making women blush under her searching glances. I was on the verge of reproaching myself for ever having been taken in by this tough fellow whose walk, whose whole appearance was that of an old Irish sergeant who had dressed himself up as a woman for a joke on St. Patrick's day.

Gribiche

I NEVER arrived before quarter past nine. By that time, the temperature and the smell of the basement of the theatre had already acquired their full intensity. I shall not give the exact location of the music-hall in which, some time between 1905 and 1910, I was playing a sketch in a revue. All I need say is that the underground dressing-rooms had neither windows nor ventilators. In our women's quarters, the doors of the rows of identical cells remained innocently open; the men . . . far less numerous in revues than nowadays . . . dressed on the floor above, almost at street level. When I arrived, I found myself among women already acclimatised to the temperature for they had been in their dressing-rooms since eight o'clock. The steps of the iron staircase clanged musically under my feet; the last five steps each gave out their particular note like a xylophone—B, B flat, C, D and then dropping a fifth to G. I shall never forget their inevitable refrain. But when fifty pairs of heels clattered up and down like hail for the big *ensembles* and dance numbers, the notes blended into a kind of shrill thunder which made the plaster walls between each dressing-room tremble. Half-way up the staircase a ventilator marked the level of the street. When it was occasionally opened during the day, it let in the poisonous air of the street and fluttering rags of paper, blown there by the wind, clung to its grating which was coated with dried mud.

As soon as we reached the floor of our cellar, each of us made some ritual complaint about the suffocating atmosphere. My neighbour across the passage, a little green-eyed Basque, always panted for a moment before opening the door of her dressing-room, put her hand on her heart, sighed: "Positively filthy!" and then thought no more about it. As she had short thighs and high insteps, she gummed a kiss-curl on her left cheek and called herself Carmen Brasero.

Mlle Clara d'Estouteville, known as La Toutou, occupied the next dressing-room. Tall, miraculously fair, slim as women only became twenty-five years later, she played the silent part of *Commère* during the first half of the second act. When she arrived, she would push back the pale gold swathes of hair on her temples with a transparent hand and murmur: "Oh! Take me out of here or I'll burst!" Then, without bending down, she would kick off her shoes. Sometimes she would hold out her hand. The gesture was hardly one of cordiality; it was merely that she was amused by the involuntary start of surprise which an ordinary hand like my own would give at the touch of her extraordinarily delicate, almost melting fingers. A moment after her arrival, a chilly smell like toothpaste would inform us all that the frail actress was eating her half-pound of peppermints. Mlle d'Estouteville's voice was so loud and raucous that it prevented her from playing spoken parts so that the music-hall could only use her exceptional beauty; the beauty of a spun-glass angel. La Toutou had her own method of explaining the situation.

"You see, on the stage I can't say my *a*'s. And, however small a part, there's nearly always an *a* in it. And, as I can't say my *a*'s . . ."

"But you do say them!" Carmen pointed out.

La Toutou gave her colleague a blue glance, equally sublime in its stupidity, its indignation and its deceitfulness. The anguish of her indigestion made it even more impressive.

"Look here, dear, you can't have the cheek to pretend you know more about it than Victor de Cottens who tried me out for his revue at the Folies!"

Her stage costume consisted of strings of imitation diamonds which occasionally parted to give glimpses of a rose-tinted knee and an adolescent thigh or the tip of a barely-formed breast. When this vision, which suggested a dawn glittering with frost, was on her way up to the stage she passed my other neighbour, Lise Damoiseau, on her way back from impersonating the Queen of Torments. Lise would be invariably holding up her long black velvet robe with both hands, candidly displaying her bow-legs. On a long neck built like a tower and slightly widening at the base, Lise carried a head modelled in the richest tones and textures of black and white. The teeth between the sad voluptuous lips were flawless; the enormous dark eyes, whose whites were slightly blue, held and reflected back the light. Her black, oiled hair shone like a river under the moon. She was always given sinister parts to play. In revues, she held sway over the Hall of Poisons and the Paradise of Forbidden Pleasures. Satan, Gilles de Rais, the Nightmare of Opium, the Beheaded Woman, Delilah and Messalina all took on the features of Lise. She was seldom given a line to speak and the dress designers cleverly disguised her meagre and undistinguished little body. She was far from being vain about her appearance. One night when I was paying her a perfectly sincere compliment she shrugged her shoulders and turned the fixed glitter of her eyes on me.

"M'm, yes," said Lise. "My face is all right. And my neck. Down to here, but no further."

She looked into the great cracked glass that every actress consulted before going up the staircase and judged herself with harsh lucidity.

"I can only get away with it in long skirts."

After the grand final tableau, Lise Damoiseau went into total eclipse. Shorn of her make-up and huddled into some old black dress, she would carry away her superb head, its long neck muffled in a rabbit-skin tie, as if it were some object for which she had no further use till tomorrow. Standing under the gas lamp on the pavement outside the stage door, her eyes and teeth would give a last smouldering flash before she disappeared down the steps of the métro.

Several other women inhabited the subterranean corridor. There was Liane de Parthenon, a tall big-boned blonde, and Fifi Soada who boasted of her likeness to Polaire, and Zarzita who emphasised her resemblance to the beautiful Otero. Zarzita did her hair like Otero, imitated her accent and pinned up photographs of the famous ballerina on the walls of her dressing-room. When she drew one's attention to these, she invariably added, "The only difference is that *I* can dance!" There was also a dried-up little Englishwoman of unguessable age with a face like an old nurse's and fantastically agile limbs; there was an Algerian, Miss Ourika, who specialised in the *danse du ventre* and who was all hips; there was . . . there was . . . Their names which I hardly knew have long since vanished. All that I heard of them, beyond the dressing-rooms near me, was a zoo-like noise composed of Anglo-Saxon grunting, the yawns and sighs of caged creatures, mechanical blasphemies and a song, always the same song, sung over and over again by a Spanish voice:

Tou m'abais fait serment
Dé m'aimer tendrement . . .

Occasionally, a silence would dominate all the neighbouring noises and give place to the distant hum of the stage; then one of the women would break out of this silence with a scream, a mechanical curse, a yawn or a tag of song: *Tou m'abais fait serment . . .*

Was I, in those days, too susceptible to the convention of work, glittering display, empty-headedness, punctuality and rigid probity which reigns in the music-hall? Did it inspire me to describe it over and over again with a violent and superficial love and with all its accompaniment of commonplace poetry? Very possibly. The fact remains that during six years of my past life I was still capable of finding relaxation among its monsters and its marvels. In that past there still gleams the head of Lise Damoiseau and the bottomless, radiant imbecility of Mlle d'Estouteville. I still remember with delight a certain Bouboule with beautiful breasts who wept offendedly if she had to play even a tiny part in a high dress and the magnificent, long, shallow-grooved back of some Lola or Pepa or Concha . . . Looking back, I can rediscover some particular acrobat swinging high up from bar to bar of a nickelled trapeze or some particular juggler in the centre of an orbit of balls. It was a world in which fantasy and bureaucracy were oddly interwoven. And I can still plunge at will into that dense, limited element which bore up my inexperience and happily limited my vision and my cares for six whole years.

Everything in it was by no means as gay and as innocent as I have described it elsewhere. Today I want to speak of my début in that world, of a time when I had neither learnt nor forgotten anything of a theatrical milieu in which I had not the faintest chance of succeeding, that of the big spectacular revue. What an astonishing milieu it was! One sex practically eclipsed the other, dominating it, not only by numbers but by its own particular smell and magnetic atmosphere. This crowd of women reacted like a barometer to any vagary of the weather. It needed only a change of wind or a wet day to send them all into the depths of depression; a depression which expressed itself in tears and curses, in talk of suicide and in irrational terrors and superstitions. I was not a prey to it myself but, having known very few women and been deeply hurt by one single man, I accepted it uncritically. I was even rather impressed by it although it was only latent hysteria; a kind of schoolgirl neurosis which afflicts women who are arbitrarily and pointlessly segregated from the other sex.

My contribution to the programme was entitled *Miaou-Ouah-Ouah. Sketch.* On the strength of my first Dialogues de Bêtes, the authors of the revue had commissioned me to bark and mew on the stage. The rest of my turn consisted mainly of performing a few dance steps in bronze-coloured tights. On my way to and from the stage I had to pass by the star's dressing-room. The leading lady was a remote personage whose door was only open to her personal friends. She never appeared in the corridors except attended by two dressers whose job was to carry her head-dresses, powder, comb and hand mirror and to hold up her trailing flounces. She plays no part in my story but I liked to follow her and smell the trail of amazingly strong scent she left in her wake. It was a sweet, sombre scent; a scent for a beautiful negress. I was fascinated by it but I was never able to discover its name.

One night, attired in my decorous kimono, I was dressing as usual with my door open. I had finished making up my face and my neck and was heating my curling-tongs on a spirit lamp. The quick, hurried little step of Carmen Brasero (I knew it was Carmen by the clatter of her heels) sounded on the stone floor and stopped opposite my dressing-room. Without turning round, I wished her good evening and received a hasty warning in reply.

"Hide that! The fire inspectors. I saw those chaps upstairs. I know one of them."

"But we've all got spirit lamps in our dressing-rooms!"

"Of course," said Carmen. "But for goodness' sake hide it. That chap I know's a swine. He makes you open your suit-cases."

I put out the flame, shut the lid and looked helplessly round my bare cell.

"Where on earth can I hide it?"

"You're pretty green, aren't you? Do you have to be told every single thing? Listen . . . I can hear them coming."

She turned up her skirt, nipped the little lamp high up between her thighs and walked off with an assured step.

The fire inspectors, two in number, appeared. They ferreted about and went off, touching their bowler hats. Carmen Brasero returned, fished out my lamp from between her thighs and laid it down on my make-up shelf.

"Here's the object!"

"Marvellous," I said. "I'd never have thought of doing that."

She laughed like a child who is thoroughly pleased with itself.

"Cigarettes, my handbag, a box of sweets . . . I hide them all like that and nothing ever drops out. Even a loaf that I stole when I was a kid. The baker's wife didn't half shake me! She kept saying 'Have you thrown it in the gutter?' But I held my loaf tight between my thighs and she had to give it up as a bad job. She wasn't half wild! It's these muscles *here* that I've got terrifically strong."

She was just going off when she changed her mind and said with immense dignity: "Don't make any mistakes! It's nothing to do with the filthy tricks those Eastern dancers get up to with a bottle! *My* muscles are all on the *outside*!"

I protested that I fully appreciated this and the three feathers, shading from fawn to chestnut, which adorned Carmen's enormous blue straw hat, went waving away along the corridor.

The nightly ritual proceeded on its way. "The Miracle of the Roses" trailed its garlands of dusty flowers. A squadron of eighteenth-century French soldiers galloped up the staircase, banging their arms against the walls with a noise like the clatter of tin cans.

I did my own turn after these female warriors and came down again with whiffs of the smoke of every tobacco in the world in my hair. Tired from sheer force of habit and from the contagion of the tiredness all round me, I sat down in front of the make-up shelf fixed to the wall. Someone came in behind me and sat down on the other cane-topped stool. It was one of the French soldiers. She was young and, to judge by the colour of her eyes, dark. Her breeches were half-undone and hanging down; she was breathing heavily through her mouth and not looking in my direction.

"Twenty francs!" she exclaimed suddenly. "Twenty francs fine! I'm beyond twenty francs fine, Monsieur Remondon! They make me laugh."

But she did not laugh. She made an agonised grimace which showed gums almost as white as her teeth between her made-up lips.

"They fined you twenty francs? Why on earth?"

"Because I undid my breeches on the stairs."

"And why did you undo . . ."

The French soldier interrupted me: "Why? Why? You and your whys! Because when you can stick it, you stick it, and when you can't any more, you can't!"

She leant back against the wall and closed her eyes. I was afraid she was going to faint but, at the buzz of an electric bell, she leapt to her feet.

"Hell, that's us!"

She rushed away, holding up her breeches with both hands. I watched her down to the end of the passage.

"Whoever's that crazy creature?" asked Mlle d'Estouteville languidly. She was entirely covered in pearls and wearing a breastplate in the form of a heart made of sapphires.

I shrugged my shoulders to show that I had not the least idea. Lise Damoiseau, who was wiping her superb features with a dark rag thick with vaseline and grease paint, appeared in her doorway.

"It's a girl called Gribiche who's in the chorus. At least that's who I think it is."

"And what was she doing in your dressing-room, Colette-villi?" asked Carmen haughtily.

"She wasn't doing anything. She just came in. She said that Remondon had just let her in for a twenty-franc fine."

Lise Damoiseau gave a judicial whistle.

"Twenty francs! I say! Whatever for?"

"Because she took her breeches down on the staircase when she came off the stage."

"Jolly expensive."

"We don't know for certain if it's true. Mightn't she just have had a drop too much?"

A woman's scream, shrill and protracted, froze the words on her lips. Lise stood stock still, holding her make-up rag, with one hand on her hip like the servant in Manet's *Olympe*.

The loudness and the terrible urgency of that scream made all the women who were not up on the stage look out of their dressing-rooms. Their sudden appearance gave an odd impression of being part of some stage spectacle. As it was near the end of the show, several of them had already exchanged their stork-printed kimonos for white embroidered camisoles threaded with pale blue ribbon. A great scarf of hair fell over the shoulder of one bent head and all the faces were looking the same way. Lise Damoiseau shut her door, tied a cord round her waist to keep her kimono in place and went off to find out what had happened, with the key of her dressing-room slipped over one finger.

A noise of dragging feet announced the procession which appeared at the end of the passage. Two stage hands were carrying a sagging body; a limp, white, made-up lay figure which kept slipping out of their grasp. They walked slowly, scraping their elbows against the walls.

"Who is it? Who is it?"

"She's dead!"

"She's bleeding from the mouth!"

"No, no, that's her rouge!"

"It's Marcelle Cuvelier! Ah, no, it isn't . . ."

Behind the bearers skipped a little woman wearing a head-dress of glittering beads shaped like a crescent moon. She had lost her head a little but not enough to prevent her from enjoying her self-importance as an eye-witness. She kept panting: "I'm in the same dressing-room with her. She fell right down to the bottom of the staircase . . . It came over her just like a stroke . . . Just fancy! Ten steps at least she fell."

"What's the matter with her, Firmin?" Carmen asked one of the men who was carrying her.

"Couldn't say, I'm sure," answered Firmin. "What a smash she went! But I haven't got time to be doing a nurse's job. There's my transparency for the Pierrots not set up yet!"

"Where are you taking her?"

"Putting her in a cab, I s'pose."

When they had gone by, Mlle d'Estouteville laid her hand on her sapphire breastplate and half collapsed on her dressing-stool. Like Gribiche, the sound of the bell brought her to her feet, her eyes on the mirror.

"My rouge has gone and come off," she said in her loud schoolboy's voice.

She rubbed some bright pink on her blanched cheeks and

went up to make her entrance. Lise Damoiseau, who had returned, had some definite information to give us.

"Her salary was two hundred and ten francs. It came over her like a giddy fit. They don't think she's broken anything. Firmin felt her over to see. So did the dresser. More likely something internal."

But Carmen pointed to something on the stone floor of the passage: a little star of fresh blood, then another, then still others at regular intervals. Lise tightened her mouth, with its deeply incised corners.

"Well, well!"

They exchanged a knowing look and made no further comment. The little Crescent Moon ran by us again, teetering on her high heels and talking as she went.

"That's all fixed. They've packed her into a taxi. Monsieur Bonnavent's driving it."

"Where's he driving her to?"

"Her home. I live in her street."

"Why not the hospital?"

"She didn't want to. At home she's got her mother. She came to when she got outside into the air. She said she didn't need a doctor. Has the bell gone for 'Up in the Moon'?"

"It certainly has. La Toutou went up ages ago."

The Crescent Moon swore violently and rushed away, obliterating the little regularly-spaced spots with her glittering heels.

The next day nobody mentioned Gribiche. But at the beginning of the evening show, Crescent Moon appeared breathlessly and confided to Carmen that she had been to see her. Carmen passed the information on to me in a tone of apparent indifference.

"So she's better then?" I insisted.

"If you like to call it better. She's feverish now."

She was speaking to the looking-glass, concentrated on pencilling a vertical line down the centre of her rather flat upper lip to simulate what she called "the groove of chastity".

"Was that all Impéria said?"

"No. She said it's simply unbelievable, the size of their room."

"Whose room?"

"Gribiche and her mother's. Their Lordships the Management have sent forty-nine francs."

"What an odd sum."

In the mirror, Carmen's green eyes met mine harshly.

"It's exactly what's due to Gribiche. Seven days' salary. You heard them say she gets two hundred and ten francs a month."

My neighbour turned severe and suspicious whenever I gave some proof of inexperience which reminded her that I was an outsider and a novice.

"Won't they give her any more than that?"

"There's nothing to make them. Gribiche doesn't belong to the Union."

"Neither do I."

"I should have been awfully surprised if you *did*," observed Carmen with chill formality.

The third evening, when I inquired "How's Gribiche?" Lise Damoiseau raised her long eyebrows as if I had made a social *gaffe*.

"Colettevilli, I notice that when you have an idea in your head, it stays up in the top storey. All other floors vacant and to let."

"Oh!" sneered Carmen. "You'll see her again, your precious Gribiche. She'll come back here, playing the interesting invalid."

"Well, *isn't* she interesting?"

"No more than any other girl who's done the same."

"You're young," said Lise Damoiseau. "Young in the profession I mean, of course."

"A blind baby could see *that*," agreed Carmen.

I said nothing. Their cruelty which seemed based on a convention left me with no retort. So did their perspicacity in sensing the bourgeois past that lay behind my inexperience and in guessing that my apparent youth was that of a woman of thirty-two who does not look her age.

It was on the fourth or fifth night that Impéria came rushing in at the end of the show and started whispering volubly to my room-mates. Wanting to make a show of indifference in my turn, I stayed on my cane stool, polishing my cheap looking-glass, dusting my make-up shelf and trying to make it as maniacally tidy as my writing-table at home.

Then I mended the hem of my skirt and brushed my short hair. Trying to keep my hair well-groomed was a joyless and fruitless task since I could never succeed in banishing the smell of stale tobacco which returned punctually after each shampoo.

Nevertheless, I was observing my neighbours. Whatever was preoccupying them and making them all so passionately eager to speak, brought out all their various characters. Lise stood squarely, her hands on her hips, as if she were in the street market of the Rue Lepic, throwing back her magnificent head with the authority of a housewife who will stand no nonsense. Little Impéria kept shifting from one leg to the other, twisting her stubby feet and suffering with the patience of an intelligent pony. Carmen was like all those lively energetic girls in Paris who cut out or finish or sell dresses; girls who instinctively know how to trade on their looks and who are frankly and avidly out for money. Only La Toutou belonged to no definite type, except that she embodied a literary infatuation of the time; the legendary princess, the fairy, the siren or the perverted angel. Her beauty destined her to be perpetually wringing her hands at the top of a tower or shimmering palely in the depths of a dungeon or swooning on a rock in Liberty draperies dripping with jasper and agate. Suddenly Carmen planted herself in the frame of my open doorway and said all in one breath: "Well, so what are we going to do? That little Wurzit there—Impéria—says things are going pretty badly."

"What's going badly?"

Carmen looked slightly embarrassed.

"Oh! Collettevilli, don't be nasty, dear. Gribiche, of course. Not allowed to get up. Chemist, medicine, dressings and all that . . ."

"Not to mention food," added Lise Damoiseau.

"Quite so. Well . . . you get the idea."

"But where's she been hurt then?"

"It's her . . . back," said Lise.

"Stomach," said Carmen, at the same moment.

Seeing them exchange a conspiratorial look I began to bristle.

"Trying to make a fool of me, aren't you?"

Lise laid her big, sensible hand on my arm.

"Now, now, don't get your claws out. We'll tell you the whole thing. Gribiche has had a miscarriage. A bad one, four and a half months."

All four of us fell silent. Mlle d'Estouteville nervously pressed both her hands to her small flat stomach, probably by way of a spell to avert disaster.

"Couldn't we," I suggested, "get up a collection between us?"

"A collection, that's the idea," said Lise. "That's the word I was looking for and I couldn't get it. I kept saying a 'subscription'. Come on, La Toutou. How much'll you give for Gribiche?"

"Ten francs," declared Mlle d'Estouteville without a second's hesitation. She ran to her dressing-room with a clinking of sham diamonds and imitation sapphires and returned with two five-franc pieces.

"I'll give five francs," said Carmen Brasero.

"I'll give five too," said Lise. "Not more. I've got my people at home. Will you give something, Colettevilli?"

All I could find in my handbag was my key, my powder, some sous and a twenty-franc piece. I was awkward enough to hesitate, though only for a fraction of a second.

"Want some change?" asked Lise with prompt tact.

I assured her that I didn't need any and handed the louis to Carmen who hopped on one foot like a little girl.

"A louis . . . oh, goody, goody! Lise, go and extract some sous out of Madame . . ." (She gave the name of the leading lady.) "She's just come down."

"Not me," said Lise. "You or Impéria if you like. I don't go over big in my dressing-gown."

"Impéria, trot round to Madame X . . . And bring back at least five hundred of the best."

The little actress straightened her spangled crescent in her mirror and went off to Madame X's dressing-room. She did not stay there long.

"Got it?" Lise yelled to her from the distance.

"Got what?"

"The big wad."

The little actress came into my room and opened her closed fist.

"Ten francs!" said Carmen indignantly.

"Well, what she said was . . ." Impéria began.

Lise put out her big hand, chapped with wet white.

"Save your breath, dear. We know just what she said. That business was slack and her rents weren't coming in on time and things were rotten on the Bourse. That's what our celebrated leading actress said."

"No," Impéria corrected. "She said it was against the rules."

"What's against the rules?"

"To get up . . . subscriptions."

Lise whistled with amazement.

"First I've heard of it. Is it true, Toutou?"

Mlle d'Estouteville was languidly undoing her chignon. Every time she pulled out one of the hideous iron hairpins, with their varnish all rubbed off, a twist of gold slid down and unravelled itself on her shoulders.

"I think," she said, "you're too clever by half to worry whether it's against the rules. Just don't mention it."

"You've hit it for once, dear," said Lise approvingly. She ended rashly: "Tonight, it's too late. But tomorrow I'll go round with the hat."

During the night, my imagination was busy with this unknown Gribiche. I had almost forgotten her face when she was conscious but I could remember it very clearly white, with the eyes closed, dangling over a stage-hand's arm. The lids were blue and the tip of each separate lash beaded with a little blob of mascara . . . I had never seen a serious accident since I had been on the halls. People who risk their lives daily are extremely careful. The man who rides a bicycle round and round a rimless disk, pitting himself against centrifugal force, the girl whom a knife-thrower surrounds with blades, the acrobat who swings from trapeze to trapeze high up in mid-air—I had imagined their possible end just as everyone does. I had imagined it with that vague, secret pleasure we all feel in what inspires us with horror. But I had never dreamt that someone like Gribiche, by falling down a staircase, would kill her secret and lie helpless and penniless.

The idea of the collection was enthusiastically received and everyone swore to secrecy. Nothing else was talked about in the dressing-rooms. Our end of the corridor received various dazzling visitors. The "Sacred Scarab", glittering in purple and green ("*You* know," Carmen reminded me. "She's the one who was sick on the stage the night of the dress-rehearsal.") and Julia Godard, the queen of male impersonators who, close to, looked like an old Spanish waiter, came in person to present their ten francs. Their arrival aroused as much curiosity as it would in the street of a little town for they came from a distant corridor which ran parallel to ours and they featured in tableaux we had never seen. Last of all Poupoute ("wonder quick-change child prodigy") deigned to bring us what she called her "mite". She owned to being eight and, dressed as a polo player ("Aristocratic Sports" Tableau 14), she strutted from force of habit, bowed with inveterate grace and overdid the silvery laugh. When she left our peaceful regions, she made a careful exit backwards, waving her little riding-whip. Lise Damoiseau heaved an exasperated sigh.

"Has to be seen to be believed! The nerve of Her Majesty! Fourteen if she's a day, my dear! After all that, she coughed up ten francs."

By dint of one- and two-franc and five-franc pieces and the pretty little gold medals worth ten, the treasurer, Lise Damoiseau, amassed three hundred and eighty-seven francs which she guarded fiercely in a barley-sugar box.

The troupe of "Girls" she left out of the affair. ("How on earth can I explain to them when they only talk English that Gribiche got herself in the family way and had a 'miss' and all the rest of it?") Nevertheless "Les Girls" produced twenty-five francs between them. At the last moment, a charming American who danced and sang (he still dances and he is still charming) slipped Carmen a hundred-franc note as he came off the stage, when we thought the "subscription" was closed.

We received some unexpected helps. I won fifty francs for Gribiche playing bezique against a morose and elderly friend.

Believe me, fifty francs meant something to him too and made their hole in the pension of a retired official in the Colonial Service. One way and another, we collected over five hundred francs.

"It's crazy," said Carmen, the night that we counted out five hundred and eighty-seven francs.

"Does Gribiche know?"

Lise shook her splendid head.

"*I'm* not crazy. Impéria's taken her sixty francs for the most pressing things. It's deducted on the account. Look, I've written it all down."

I leant for some time over the paper, fascinated by the astonishing contrast between the large childish letters, sloping uncertainly now forwards, now backwards, and the fluent, assured, majestic figures, all proudly clear and even.

"I bet you're good at sums, Lise!"

She nodded. Her marble chin touched the base of her full, goddess-like neck.

"Quite. I like adding up figures. It's a pity I don't usually have many to add up. I like figures. Look, a 5's pretty, isn't it? So's a 7. Sometimes, at night, I sees 5's and 2's swimming on the water like swans . . . See what I mean? There's the swan's head . . . and there's its neck when it's swimming. And there, underneath, it's sitting on the water."

She brooded dreamily over the pretty 5's and the 2's shaped in the likeness of Leda's lover.

"Queer, isn't it? But that's not the whole story. We're going to take the five hundred and eighty-seven francs to Gribiche."

"Of course. I suppose Impéria will take care of that."

Lise proudly brushed aside my supposition with a jerk of her elbow.

"We'll do better than that, I hope. We're not going to fling it at her like a bundle of nonsense. You coming with us? We're going tomorrow at four."

"But I don't know Gribiche."

"Nor don't we. But there's a right and a wrong way of doing things. Any particular reason for not wanting to come?"

Under such a direct question, reinforced by a severe look, I gave in, while blaming myself for giving in.

"No reason at all. How many of us are going?"

"Three. Impéria's busy. Meet us outside number 3 —Street."

I have always liked new faces, provided I can see them at a certain distance or through a thick pane of glass. During the loneliest years of my life, I lived on ground floors. Beyond the net curtain and the window-pane passed my dear human beings to whom I would not for the world have been the first to speak or hold out my hand. In those days I dedicated to them my passionate unsociability, my inexperience of human creatures and my fundamental shyness which had no relation to cowardice. I was not annoyed with myself because the thought of the visit to Gribiche kept me awake part of the night. But I was vexed that a certain peremptory tone could still produce an instinctive reflex of obedience, or at least of acquiescence.

The next day I bought a bunch of Parma violets and took the métro with as much bored resentment as if I were going to pay a ceremonial New Year's Day call. On the pavement of —— Street, Carmen and Lise Damoiseau watched me coming but made no welcoming sign from the distance. They were dressed as if for a funeral except for a lace jabot under Lise's chin and a feather curled like a question-mark in Carmen's hat. It was the first time I had seen my comrades by daylight. Four o'clock on a fine May afternoon is ruthless to any defect. I saw with astonishment how young they were and how much their youth had already suffered.

They watched me coming, disappointed themselves perhaps by my everyday appearance. I felt that they were superior to me by a stoicism early and dearly acquired. Remembering what had brought me to this particular street, I felt that solidarity is easier for us than sympathy. And I decided to say "Good afternoon" to them.

"Isn't that the limit?" said Lise, by way of reply.

"What's the limit? Won't you tell me?"

"Why, that your eyes are blue. I thought they were brown. Greyish-brown or blackish-brown. Some sort of brown, anyway."

Carmen thrust out a finger gloved in suède fabric and half pulled back the tissue paper which protected my flowers.

"It's Parmas. Looks a bit like a funeral, perhaps. But the moment Gibriche is better . . . Do we go in? It's on the ground floor."

"Looks out on the yard," said Lise contemptuously.

Gribiche's house, like many in the region of Batignolles, had been new round about 1840. Under its eaves, it still preserved a niche for a statue and in the courtyard there was a squat drinking-fountain with a big brass tap. The whole building was disintegrating from damp and neglect.

"It's not bad," observed Lise, softening. "Carmen, did you see the statue holding the globe?"

But she caught the expression on my face and said no more. From a tiny invisible garden, a green branch poked out. I noted for future reference that the Japanese "Tree of Heaven" is remarkably tenacious of life. Following close behind Lise, we groped about in the darkness under the staircase. In the murk, we could see the faint gleam of a copper door-handle.

"Well, aren't you ever going to ring?" whispered Carmen loudly and impatiently.

"Go on, ring yourself then, if you can find the bell! This

place is like a shoe-cupboard. Here we are, I've found the thing. But it's not electric . . . it's a thing you pull."

A bell tinkled, crystal clear, and the door opened. By the light of a tiny oil-lamp I could make out that a tall, broad woman stood before us.

"Mademoiselle Saure?"

"Yes. In here."

"Can we see her? We've come on behalf of the Eden-Concert Company."

"Just a minute, ladies."

She left us alone in the semi-darkness through which gleamed Lise's inflexible face and enormous eyes. Carmen gave her a facetious dig in the ribs without her deigning to smile. She merely said under her breath: "Smells funny here."

A faint fragrance did indeed bring to my nostrils the memory of various scents which are at their strongest in autumn. I thought of the garden of the peaceful years of my life; of chrysanthemums and immortelles and the little wild geranium they call Herb Robert. The matron reappeared; her corpulence, outlined against a light background, filling the open frame of the second door.

"Be so good as to come in, ladies. The Couzot girl . . . Mademoiselle Impéria, I should say, told us you were coming."

"Ah," repeated Lise. "Impéria told you we were coming. She shouldn't have. . . ."

"Why not?" asked the matron.

"For the surprise. We wanted to make it a surprise."

The word "surprise" on which we went through the door permanently linked up for me with the astonishing room inhabited by Gribiche and her mother. "It's unbelievable, the size of their room . . ." We passed with brutal suddenness from darkness to light. The enormous old room was lit by a single window which opened on the garden of a private house—the garden with the Japanese tree. Thirty years ago Paris possessed —and still possesses—any number of these little houses built to the requirements of unassuming, stay-at-home citizens and tucked away behind the big main buildings which almost stifle them. Three stone steps lead up to them from a yard with anaemic lilacs and geraniums which have all run to leaf and look like vegetables. The one in this particular street was no more imposing than a stage set. Overloaded with blackened stone ornaments and crowned with a plaster pediment, it seemed designed to serve as a backcloth to the Gribiches' heavily-barred window.

The room seemed all the vaster because there was no furniture in the middle of it. A very narrow bed was squeezed against one wall, the wall farthest away from the light. Gribiche was lying on a divan-bed under the dazzling window. I was soon to know that it was dazzling for only two short hours in the day, the time it took the sun to cross the slice of sky between two five-storeyed houses.

The three of us ventured across the central void towards Gribiche's bed. It was obvious that she neither recognised us nor knew who we were, so Carmen acted as spokesman:

"Mademoiselle Gribiche, we've all three come on behalf of your comrades at the Eden-Concert. This is Madame Lise Damoiseau . . ."

"Of the *Hell of Poisons* and Messalina in *Orgy*," supplemented Lise.

"I'm Mademoiselle Brasero of the *Corrida* and the *Gardens of Murcia*. And this is Madame Colettevilli who plays the sketch *Miaou-Ouah-Ouah*. It was Madame Colettevilli who had the idea . . . the idea of the subscription among friends."

Suddenly embarrassed by her own eloquence, she accomplished her mission by laying a manilla envelope, tied up with ribbon, in Gribiche's lap.

"Oh, really . . . I say, really. It's too much. Honestly, you shouldn't . . ." protested Gribiche.

Her voice was high and artificial like that of a child acting a part. I felt no emotion as I looked at this young girl sitting up in bed. I was, in fact, seeing her for the first time since she bore no resemblance either to the white, unconscious lay-figure nor to the French soldier who had incurred a fine of twenty francs. Her fair hair was tied back with a sky-blue ribbon, of that blue which is so unbecoming to most blondes, especially when, like Gribiche, they have thin cheeks, pallid under pink powder, and hollow temples and eyesockets. Her brown eyes ranged from Lise to Carmen, from Carmen to me, and from me to the envelope. I noticed that her breath was so short that I gave the matron a look which asked: "Isn't she going to die?"

I gave her my flowers, putting on the gay expression which the occasion demanded.

"I hope you like violets?"

"Of course. What an idea! Is there anyone who *doesn't* like violets? Thanks so much. How lovely they smell . . ."

She lifted the scentless bunch to her nostrils.

"It smells lovely here too. It reminds me of the smell of the country where I lived as a child. A bit like the everlastings you hang upside-down to dry so as to have flowers in winter . . . What is it that smells so good?"

"All sorts of little odds and ends," came the matron's voice from behind me. "Biche, pull your legs up so as Madame Colettevilli can sit down. Do be seated, ladies. I'll bring you up our two chairs."

Lise accepted her seat with some hesitation, almost as if she had been asked to drink out of a doubtfully clean glass. For a moment that beautiful young woman looked extraordinarily like a prudish chair-attendant. Then her slightly knitted eyebrows resumed their natural place on her forehead like two delicate clouds against a pure sky and she sat down, carefully smoothing down her skirt over her buttocks.

"Well," said Carmen. "Getting better now?"

"Oh, I'll soon be all right," said Gribiche. "There's no reason now why I shouldn't get better, is there? Especially with what you've brought me. Everyone's been ever so kind . . ."

Shyly she picked up the envelope but did not open it.

"Will you put it away for me, Mum?"

She held the envelope out to her mother and my two companions looked decidedly worried as they saw the money pass from Gribiche's hands into the depths of a capacious apron pocket.

"Aren't you going to count it?" asked Lise.

"Oh!" said Gribiche delicately. "You wouldn't like me to do that."

To keep herself in countenance, she kept rolling and unrolling the ribbons of the sky-blue bed-jacket, made of cheap thin wool, which hid her nightdress.

She had blushed and even this faint upsurge of blood was enough to start her coughing.

"Stop that coughing now," her mother urged her sharply. "You know quite well what I said."

"I'm not doing it on purpose," protested Gribiche.

"Why mustn't she cough?" inquired Carmen.

The tall, heavy woman blinked her prominent eyes. Though she was fat, she was neither old nor ugly and still had a ruddy complexion under hair that was turning silver.

"Because of her losses. She's lost a lot, you see. And all that isn't quite settled yet. As soon as she gets coughing, it all starts up again."

"Naturally," said Lise. "Her inside's still weak."

"It's like . . . It's like a girl I know," said Carmen eagerly. "She had an accident last year and things went all wrong."

"Whatever did she take then?" asked Lise.

"Why, what does the least harm. A bowl of concentrated soap and after that you run as fast as you can for a quarter of an hour."

"Really, I can't believe my ears!" exclaimed Madame Gribiche. "My word, you'd think there was no such thing as progress. A bowl of soapy water and a run! Why, that goes back to the days of Charlemagne! Anyone'd think we lived among the savages!"

After this outburst which she delivered loudly and impressively, Mme Saure, to give her her right name, relapsed into portentous silence.

Carmen asked with much interest: "Then she oughtn't to have taken soapy water? According to you, Madame, she'd have done better to have gone to one of those 'old wives'?"

"And have herself butchered?" said Mme Saure with biting contempt. "There's plenty have done that! No doubt they think it funny, being poked about with a curtain ring shoved up a rubber tube! Poor wretches! I don't blame them. I'm just sorry for them. After all, it's nature. A woman, or rather a child, lets a man talk her into it. You can't throw stones at her, can you?"

She flung up her hand pathetically and, in so doing, nearly touched the low ceiling. It was disfigured by concentric brown stains of damp and cracked here and there in zigzags like streaks of lightning. The middle of it sagged slightly over the tiled floor whose tiles had come unstuck.

"When it rains outside, it rains inside," said Gribiche who had seen what I was looking at.

Her mother rebuked her.

"That's not fair, Biche. It only rains in the middle. What d'you expect nowadays for a hundred and forty-five francs a year? It's the floors above that let in the water. The owner doesn't do any repairs. He's been expropriated. Something to do with the house being out of line. But we get over it by not putting any furniture in the middle."

"A hundred and forty-five francs!" exclaimed Lise enviously. "Well, that certainly won't ruin you!"

"Oh, no Sir, no Sir, no Sir!" Gribiche said brightly.

I nearly laughed, for anything which disturbed Lise's serenity—envy, avarice or rage—took away what little feminine softness her statuesque beauty possessed. I tried to catch Carmen's eye and make her smile too but she was absorbed in some thought of her own and fidgeting with the kiss-curl on her left cheek.

"But, look," said Carmen, reverting to the other topic, "if the 'old wife' is no better than the soapy water, what's one to do? There isn't all that much choice."

"No," said Mme Saure professionally. "But there is such a thing as education and knowledge."

"Yes, people keep saying that. And talking about progress and all that . . . But listen, what about Miss Ourika? She went off to Cochin China, you know. Well, we've just heard she's dead."

"Miss Ourika? What's that you're saying?" said the high, breathless voice of Gribiche.

We turned simultaneously towards the bed as if we had forgotten her.

"She's dead? What did she die of, Miss Ourika?" asked Gribiche urgently.

"But she was . . . she tried to . . ."

To stop her from saying any more, Lise risked a gesture which gave everything away. Gribiche put her hands over her eyes and cried: "Oh, Mum! You see, Mum! You see."

The tears burst out between her clenched fingers. In three swift steps Mme Saure was at her daughter's side. I thought she was going to take her in her arms. But she pressed her two hands on her chest, just above her breasts, and pushed her down flat on her back. Gribiche made no resistance and slid gently down below the cheap oriental cushion which supported her. In a broken voice, she kept on saying reproachfully: "You see, Mum, you see. I told you so, Mum . . ."

I could not take my eyes off those maternal hands which could so forcefully push down a small, emaciated body and persuade it to lie prone. Two big hands, red and chapped like a washerwoman's. They disappeared to investigate something under a little blue sateen quilt, under a cretonne sheet which had obviously been changed in our honour. I forced myself to fight down my nervous terror of blood, the terror of seeing it suddenly gush out and spread from its secret channels: blood set free, with its ferruginous smell and its talent for dyeing material bright pink or cheerful red or rusty brown. Lise's head was like a plaster cast; Carmen's rouge showed as two purple patches on her blanched cheeks as they both stared at the bed. I kept repeating to myself: "I'm not going to faint, I'm not going to faint." And I bit my tongue to distract from that pressure at the base of the spine so many women feel at the sight of blood or even when they hear a detailed account of an operation.

The two hands reappeared and Mme Saure heaved a sigh of relief: "Nothing wrong . . . nothing wrong."

She tossed her silvery hair back from her forehead which was gleaming with sudden sweat. Her large majestic features which recalled so many portraits of Louis XVI did not succeed in making her face sympathetic. I did not like the way she handled her daughter. It seemed to me that she did so with an expertness and an apprehension which had nothing to do with a mother's anxiety. A great bovine creature, sagacious and agreeable but not in the least reassuring. Wiping her temples, she went off to a table pushed right up against the wall at the far end of the room. The sun had moved on and the room had grown sombre: the imprisoned garden showed black under its "Tree of Heaven". In the distance Mme Saure was washing her hands and clattering with some glasses. Because of the distance and the darkness, her forehead seemed as if, any moment, it must touch the ceiling.

"Won't you ladies take a little of my cordial? Biche, you've earned a thimbleful too, ducky. I made it myself."

She came back to us and filled four little glasses which did not match. The one she offered me spilled over, so that I realised her hand was shaking. Lise took hers without a word; her mouth half-open and her eyes fixed on the glass. For the first time, I saw a secret terror in those eyes. Carmen said "Thank you" mechanically and then seemed to come out of her trance.

"You know," she said hesitantly. "You know, I don't think she's awfully strong yet, your daughter . . . If I were you . . . What did the doctor say, Gribiche?"

Gribiche smiled at her with vague, still wet eyes and turned her head on the oriental cushion. She pursed up her lips to reach the greenish-gold oil of a kind of Chartreuse which was in the glass.

"Oh well, the doctor . . ."

She broke off and blushed. I saw how badly she blushed, in uneven patches.

"In the case of women," said Mme Saure, "doctors don't always know best."

Carmen waited for the rest of the answer but it did not come. She swallowed half her liqueur in one gulp and gave an exaggeratedly complimentary "Mmm!"

"It's rather sweet, but very good all the same," said Lise.

The warmth returned to my stomach with the peppery taste

of a kind of home-made Chartreuse that resembled a syrupy cough mixture. My colleagues were sufficiently revived to make conversation.

"Apart from that, is there any news at the theatre?" inquired Gribiche.

She had pulled her plait of fair hair over one shoulder as young girls of those days used to do at bedtime.

"Absolutely not a scrap," answered Carmen. "Everything would be as dead as mutton if they weren't rehearsing the new numbers they're putting in for the Grand Prix every day."

"Are you in the new numbers?"

Lise and Carmen shook their heads serenely.

"We're only in the finale. We're not complaining. We've got quite enough to do as it is. I'm getting sick of this show, anyway. I'll be glad when they put on a new one. In the morning, they're rehearsing a sort of Apache sketch."

"Who?"

Carmen shrugged her shoulders with supreme indifference.

"Some straight actors and actresses. A bitch they call . . . Oh, I can't remember. It'll come back to me. There are quite a lot of them but they're mainly comedians. The management wanted to get Otero but she's going into Opera."

"Never!" said Gribiche, excitedly. "Has she got enough voice?"

"She's got something better than voice, she's got *it*," said Lise. "It all goes by intrigue. She's marrying the director of the Opéra, so he can't refuse her anything."

"What's his name, the director of the Opéra?"

"Search me, dear."

I half-closed my eyes to hear it better, this talk which took me back into a world unhampered by truth or even verisimilitude. A dazzling world, a fairy-like bureaucracy where, in the heart of Paris, "artistes" did not know the name of Julia Bartet, where it seemed perfectly natural that the great dancer Otero, dying to sing in *Faust* and *Les Huguenots*, should buy the director of the Opéra . . . I forgot the place and the reason which had drawn me back into it.

"Fierval's back from Russia," said Lise Damoiseau. "They're giving her the lead in the Winter Revue at the Eden-Concert."

"Did she enjoy her tour in Russia?"

"Like anything. Just fancy, the Czar rented a box for the whole season just to look in and see her number every night. And every single night, my dear, he sent her round presents by his own pope."

"His what?" asked Gribiche.

"His pope, dear. It's the same thing as a footman."

But of course! Naturally! Why not? Ah, go on . . . don't stop! How I loved them like that, swallowing the wildest improbabilities like children the moment they drop their outer shell of tough, hardworking wage-earners with a shrewd eye on every sou . . . Let's forget everything except the absurd, the fantastic. Let's even forget this tortured little piece of reality lying flat on her bed beneath a barred window. I hope any moment to hear at the very least that President Loubet is going to elope with Alice de Tender . . . Go on, go on! Don't stop!

"Mum . . . oh, quick, Mum."

The whispered call barely ruffled a silence pregnant with other sensational revelations. But, faint as it was, Mme Saure found it reason enough to rush to the bedside. Gribiche's arm dropped slackly and the little glass which fell from her hand broke on the tiled floor.

"Oh God!" muttered Mme Saure.

Her two hands dived once more under the sheets. She drew them out quickly, looked at them and, seeing us on our feet, hid them in the pockets of her apron. Not one of us questioned her.

"You see, Mum," moaned Gribiche. "I told you it was too strong. Why didn't you listen to me? Now, you see . . ."

Carmen made a brave suggestion:

"Shall I call the concierge?"

The tall woman with the hidden hands took a step towards us and we all fell back.

"Quick, quick, get away from here . . . You mustn't call anyone . . . Don't be afraid, I'll look after her. I've got all that's needed. Don't say anything. You'll make bother for me. Get away, quick. Above all, not a word."

She pushed us back towards the door and I remember that we offered a faint resistance. But Mme Saure drew her hands out of her pockets, perhaps to drive us away. At the sight of them, Carmen started like a frightened horse, while I hustled Lise away, to avoid their contact. I don't know whether it was Lise who opened the door of the room and then the other door. We found ourselves in the mildewed hall under the statue holding the globe, we walked stiffly past the concierge's door and, as soon as we got outside on the pavement, Carmen shot ahead of us, almost at a run.

"Carmen! I say, wait for us!"

But Carmen did not stop till she was out of breath. Then she stood leaning her back against the wall. The green feather in her hat danced to the measure of her heartbeats. Whether from passionate desire for air, or from sheer gratitude, I turned my face up to the sky which twilight was just beginning to fill with pink clouds and twittering swallows. Carmen laid her hand on her breast, at the place where we believe our heart lies.

"Shall we take something to pull ourselves together?" I suggested. "Lise, a glass of brandy? Carmen, a pick-me-up?" We were just turning the corner of a street where the narrow terrace of a little wines and spirits bar displayed three iron tables. Carmen shook her head.

"Not there. There's a policeman."

"What does it matter if there is?"

She did not answer and walked quickly on ahead of us till we came to the Place Clichy whose bustle seemed to reassure her. We sat down under the awning of a large brasserie.

"A coffee," said Carmen.

"A coffee," said Lise. "As for my dinner tonight . . . my stomach feels as if it were full of lead."

We stirred our spoons round and round our cups without saying a word. Inside, in the restaurant, the electric lights went on all at once, making us suddenly aware of the blue dusk of approaching evening flooding the square. Carmen let out a great sigh of relief.

"It's a bit stuffy," said Lise.

"You've got hot walking," said Carmen. "Just feel my hand. I know what I'm like. I'll have to put lots of rouge on tonight. I'll put on some 24."

"Now, I'd look a sight if I put on 24," retorted Lise. "I'd look like a beetroot. What *I* need is Creole 2½ and the same ground as a man."

Carmen leant politely across the table.

"I think Colettevilli's awfully well made up on the stage, very *natural*. When you're not playing character parts, it's very important to look *natural*."

I listened to them as if I were only half-awake and overhearing a conversation which had begun while I was asleep.

That coffee, though sugared till it was as thick as syrup, how bitter it tasted! Beside us, a flower-seller was trying to get rid of her last bunch of lilac: dark purple lilac, cut while it was still in the bud, lying on sprays of yew.

" 'Les Girls'," Carmen was saying, "they've got special stuff they use in England. Colours that make you look pink and white like a baby.

But that's no good in character parts, is it, Colettevilli?"

I nodded, my lips on the rim of my cup and my eyes dazzled by an arrow from the setting sun.

Lise turned over the little watch which she pinned to the lapel of her jacket with a silver olive-branch whose olives pretended to be jade.

"It's half past five," she announced.

"I don't care a damn," said Carmen. "I'm not going to have any dinner, anyway."

Half-past five! What might have happened in half an hour to that girl on her soaking mattress? All we had done for her was to take her a handful of money. Lise held out her packet of cigarettes to me.

"No, thanks, I don't smoke. Tell me, Lise . . . isn't there anything we can do for Gribiche?"

"Absolutely nothing. Keep out of it. It's a filthy business. I've got my people at home who'd be more upset than me to see me mixed up in anything to do with abortion."

"Yes. But it was only falling downstairs at the theatre that brought it on."

She shrugged her shoulders.

"You're an infant. The fall came *after*."

"After what?"

"After what she'd taken. She fell because she was nearly crazy with whatever it was she took. Colic, giddiness and what have you. She told Impéria all about it in their dressing-room. When she came into yours, she was so far gone, she was at her wits' end. She'd stuffed herself with cotton-wool."

"Her old Ma's an abortioness," said Carmen. "Gives you a dose to bring it on. She gave her daughter a lot more than a teaspoonful."

"Anyone can see that Ma Saure's already had some 'bothers' as she calls them."

"How can you tell that?"

"Because she's so frightened. And also because they haven't a bean—no furniture, nothing. I wonder what she can have done to be as hard up as all that."

"Old murderess," muttered Carmen. "Clumsy old beast."

Neither of them showed any surprise. I saw that they were, both of them, thoroughly aware of and inured to such things. They could contemplate impartially certain risks and certain secret dealings of which I knew nothing. There was a type of criminality which they passively and discreetly acknowledged when confronted with the danger of having a child. They talked of the monstrous in a perfectly matter-of-fact way.

"But what about me?" I suggested rashly. "Couldn't *I* try? Leaving both of you right out of it, of course. If Gribiche could be got into a hospital! As to what people might say, I don't care a damn. I'm absolutely on my own."

Lise stared at me with her great eyes.

"'S true? As absolutely on your own as all that? You haven't anyone at all? No one who's close to you? Not even your family?"

"Oh, yes, there's my family," I agreed hastily.

"I thought as much," said Lise.

She stood up as if she considered the subject closed, put on her gloves and snapped her fingers.

"Excuse me if I leave you now, Colettevilli. As I'm not going to have any dinner, I'm going to take my time getting down to the theatre. I'll go by bus; it'll do me good."

"Me, too," said Carmen. "If we're hungry, we can buy a cheese sandwich off the stage doorkeeper."

She hesitated a moment before inviting me to join them.

"You coming too?"

"I'd love to, but I've promised to look in at my place first."

"See you later then. Bye-bye."

They went off arm-in-arm across the square which was now all pink and blue: pink with the lit-up shops and bars, blue with the dusk of the late May afternoon.

My only longing was to get back to my little ground-floor room, to my odd scraps of salvaged furniture, to my books, to the smell of green leaves that sometimes drifted in from the Bois. Most of all I longed for the companion of my good and bad moments, my tabby cat. Once again she welcomed me, sniffing my hands and brooding thoughtfully over the hem of my skirt. Then she sat on the table and opened her golden eyes wide, staring into space at the invisible world which had no secrets for her. Neither of us ate more than a morsel or two and I went off punctually to the theatre.

When I arrived at the Eden-Concert, I found Mlle d'Estouteville in a grubby bath-wrap, with her feet as bare as an angel's and her cape of golden hair over her shoulders, trying to extract every detail of our visit to Gribiche from Lise and Carmen.

"Did it go off well?"

"Oh yes, splendidly."

"Was she pleased?"

"I expect she thought it was better than a slap in the belly with a wet fish."

"And how is she? Is she coming back soon?"

Lise's face was impenetrable. She was occupied in making herself up for her first appearance as the demon Asmodeus.

"Oh, you know, I think it'll be some time yet. I don't think that girl's awfully strong."

"Got a decent sort of place?"

"Yes and no, as you might say. There's lots of space. At least, you can breathe there. I'd get the willies, myself, living in such a huge room."

"Her mother looks after her well?"

"Almost too well!"

"What did she say about the five hundred and eighty-seven francs?"

I took it on myself to answer so as to give Lise a little respite.

"She said we were to thank everyone ever so much . . . everyone who'd taken an interest in her. That she was so awfully touched."

"How did her face look? Quite normal again?"

"She's got a very babyish face, but you can see she's got much thinner. She'd got her hair tied back in a plait like a kid and a little blue bed-jacket. She's very sweet."

The door of Carmen's dressing-room banged, sharply pulled to from inside.

"Who's going to be late?" shouted Lise intelligently. "Colettevilli, of course. And who'll be to blame. That pain in the neck, Toutou d'Estouteville!"

The harsh voice of Mlle d'Estouteville launched into a volley of insults, calmed down and resolved into a laugh. Each of us went on to do what we always did: yawn, sing odd snatches of song, curse the stifling airlessness, cough, eat peppermints and go and fill a tiny water-jug at the tap in the passage.

Towards half-past eleven, I was dressed again and ready to go home. It was the moment when the heat and lack of oxygen got the better of the dead-beat chorus-girls and overworked dressers. As I left my dressing-room, I noticed that the door of Carmen's dressing-room was still shut and I raised my voice to call out my usual good night. The door opened and Carmen signed to me to come in. She was engaged in weeping as one weeps when one is wearing full stage make-up. Armed with a little tube of blotting-paper the size of a pencil, she was pressing it first to her right eyeball, then to her left, between the lids.

"Pay no attention. I've got the . . . I'm unwell."

"Do you feel ill with it?"

"Oh, no. It's just that I'm so awfully relieved. Fancy, I was six days late. I was terrified of doing what Gribiche did . . . So, I'm so relieved."

She put her arm on my shoulder, then clasped it round my neck and, just for the fraction of a second, laid her head on my breast.

I was just turning the corner of the long passage when she called out to me from the distance: "Good night! Don't have bad dreams!"

I had them all the same. I dreamt of anguished anxieties which had not hitherto fallen to my lot. My dream took place under the plant of ill-fame, wormwood. Unfolding its hairy, symbolic leaves one by one, the terrible age-old inducer of abortions grew in my nightmare to monstrous size, like the seed controlled by the fakir's will.

The next evening little Impéria came hobbling hurriedly up to us. I saw her whispering anxiously into Lise's ear. Balanced on one leg, she was clutching the foot that hurt her most with both hands. Lise listened to her, wearing her whitest, most statuesque mask and holding one hand over her mouth. Then she removed her hand and furtively made the sign of the cross.

I am perfectly aware that, in the music-hall world, people make the sign of the cross on the slightest provocation. Nevertheless I knew at once and unerringly why Lise did so at that moment. Weakly, I made a point of avoiding her till the *finale*. It was easy and I think she deliberately made it easier still. Afterwards, fate played into my hands. In honour of the Grand-Prix, the management cut out the sketch *Miaou-Ouah-Ouah* which did not, I admit, deserve any preferential treatment. Months and years went by during which I made a public spectacle of myself in various places but reserved the right to say nothing of my private life.

When I felt that I wanted to write the story of Gribiche, I controlled myself and replaced it by a "blank", a row of dots, an asterisk. Today, when I am allowing myself to describe her end, I naturally suppress her name, that of the music-hall and those of the girls we worked with. By such changes and concealments I can still surround Gribiche's memory with the emblems of silence. Among such emblems are those which, in musical notation, signify the breaking-off of the melody. Three hieroglyphs can indicate that break: a mute swallow on the five black wires of the stave; a tiny hatchet cutting across them, and—for the longest pause of all—a fixed pupil under a huge, arched, panic-stricken eyebrow.

The Rendezvous

A GRASSHOPPER jumped out of the beans and flew past with a metallic whirr, interposing its fine canvas wings, its long dry thighs and its horse's head between the orange-pickers and the sun. It terrified Rose by brushing against her hair.

"Ee," Rose screamed.

"What's the matter? Oh, goodness!" said Odette, drawing back. "What on earth's that creature? Must be a scorpion, at least. Why, it's as big as a swallow. Bernard! I'm asking you what this monster is!"

But Bernard was looking at two frightened blue eyes, at hair that was too curly to be strictly fashionable, at a small hand outstretched to ward off the danger.

He shrugged his shoulders to indicate that he had no idea. The two girls, one dark, the other fair, were recklessly squandering the ripe, juicy fruit whose rind split easily under their nails. They tore them open savagely, sucked the best and easiest ones dry in two mouthfuls and flung away the reddish skin of the Moroccan oranges whose sharp flavour does not cloy.

"I hope Cyril will be jealous," said Odette. "What on earth can he be doing at this hour? Asleep, of course. He's a dormouse. I've married a dormouse!"

Bernard stopped munching the green beans.

"Do you know what a dormouse looks like?"

"No," said Odette, always ready to give battle. "But I know that eating raw beans makes your breath smell horrid."

He spat out his bean so hastily that Odette burst into her malicious, insinuating laugh. That laugh made Rose blush.

"If I called out to Cyril from here, d'you think he'd hear?"

"Not a hope," said Bernard. "The hotel is . . . yes, about five hundred yards away,"

Nevertheless Odette, who was never convinced by anyone's opinion, put her hands up to her mouth like a megaphone and shrieked: "Cyril! Cy-ri-i-il!"

She had a piercingly shrill voice which must have carried far out to sea and Bernard winced with exasperation.

Being tyro travellers, they had let the best hours of the morning go by and the eleven o'clock sun was scorching their shoulders. But the April wind, before it reached the young barley, the orange grove, the well-kept kitchen gardens, the neglected park and Tangiers itself, close by but invisible, had blown across a cool waste of salt water, pale and milky as a Breton sea.

"*I* believe," declared Odette, "Cyril's having a quiet cocktail on the hotel terrace."

"You forget there aren't any cocktails yet at the Mirador. The stuff's on the way."

"So that's what they meant when they warned us that they hadn't finished building it yet," said Odette. "I certainly wouldn't say 'no' to a drink myself. Shall we go and have one at the Petit Socco?"

"Certainly," said Bernard in a gloomy voice.

"Oh, you're the limit as soon as one tries to get you off your orangeades and your malted milks."

She bit into her orange as savagely as if she were biting Bernard himself. Her fierceness was possibly something of a pose. A brunette of the hard type, she exaggerated her cannibal laugh and made great display of crushing nuts and even plumstones between the two rows of teeth of which she was so vain.

A lizard or a tiny snake glided through the fresh grass and Odette lost all her haughtiness.

"Bernard! A viper! Oh, this awful country!"

"Why do you insist that it's a viper? There aren't any vipers here. Ask Ahmed."

"What's the good of asking him anything? He doesn't speak French!"

"I'm not so convinced as you that he doesn't . . ."

An infinite meekness, a gravity tempered by a vague, courteous smile, protected their guide from all suspicion. He was one of the servants of the absent pasha who allowed a few tourists to use his gardens.

"Who is Ahmed, anyway?"

"The eldest son of the bailiff who looks after the property and keeps it up," said Bernard.

"The concierge's kid, in fact," Odette translated.

"I prefer my formula to yours," said Bernard. "It's more . . ."

"More polite, you mean?"

"Also more accurate. Ahmed's not in the least like a concierge,"

Ahmed, who, whether from discretion or disdain, appeared to hear nothing, picked an orange from the tree and offered it on his brown palm to Odette.

"Thank you, blue-eyed boy. Allah have you in his holy keeping!"

She dropped Ahmed a comic curtsy, made some little clucking noises and laid her hand on her heart, then on her forehead. Bernard blushed with shame for her. "After what she's just done, I'd leave them there flat. If it weren't for Rose, they wouldn't set eyes on me again. But there's Rose . . ."

There was indeed Rose, the pink-cheeked widow of the younger Bessier who had been an architect. There was also her brother-in-law Cyril, Odette's husband, whom people still called Bessier Senior. Besides Cyril, there was the deed of partnership, not yet signed, which would substitute Bernard Bonnemains for the younger Bessier. "Bernard had better not count his chickens before they are hatched," Odette was in the habit of saying, whenever she thought it expedient to recall the fact that Bonnemains was exactly thirty, had no rich clients and not much money.

"I've had enough of this," declared Odette. "Let's do something else or I'm going in. Anyway, I'm tired."

"But . . . we haven't done anything tiring," Rose objected.

"Speak for yourself," snapped her sister-in-law.

She stretched, yawned uninhibitedly, then sighed: "Oh, that Cyril! I don't know what's the matter with him here . . ."

"That's her way of flaunting things under our noses," thought Bernard. "If I didn't control myself, I'd remind her there was such a thing as decency."

But he did control himself, wincing like a starving man reminded of food. "Eight days, eight nights since I've had nothing of Rose but little stolen kisses and allusions to our love in cryptic language . . ."

Rose's blue eyes asked him the reason for his sullen silence, and blinked moistly under the sun. Her eyes were a warm generous blue, her cheeks almost too vividly pink, her naturally curly hair frankly and cheerfully golden. Looking at Rose's strong, bright colouring, at the red mouth engaged in sucking the dripping, almost scarlet orange, Bernard was furious that she had not yet given him all this glory of colour. They had only been lovers a very short time and he had had to make love to her on hotel beds, in the dark or under a pallid moon. "One of these days, I'll throw my scruples to the winds—and Rose's too. I'll say to Cryil: 'Look here, old man, Rose and me . . . well, that's the way things are. And I'm going to marry her.'" But he imagined Bessier Senior's faint, distant smile and

Odette's spiteful laugh and ugly thoughts. "And, in any case, I don't call Bessier 'old man'." He threw a bitterly resentful look at the "cannibal". Once again he recognised in Odette an ultra-feminine female, difficult to manage and always ready to pick a quarrel. Once again, his resentment weakened to respect.

A cloud darkened the green of the sea and the leaves: Bernard's desire and his good humour vanished at the same moment.

"Don't you think we might as well stay where we are? I can't help feeling that this pasha's been very amiable and that we're behaving like . . ."

"Like trippers," cut in Odette. "Look at the delightful little 'Bois de Boulogne' we're arranging for him, your pasha. Gold-tipped cigarette ends, cellophane wrappings, bean pods and orange peel. A few greasy newspapers and some métro tickets and the work of civilisation will be complete."

Bernard slid a furtive glance of apology in Ahmed's direction. But Ahmed, facing towards the sea, was a perfect statue of youthful Arab indifference.

"Hi, Ahmed!" shrieked Odette. "We're going! Finish! *Macache!* Walk! Get a move on!"

"Don't muddle him," Rose implored. "What on earth do you expect him to make of all that?"

Odette went up to the youth of sixteen or so, stuck one of her Turkish cigarettes between his lips and held out her lighter. Ahmed took two puffs, thanked her with a gesture and continued to await the Europeans' good pleasure. He smoked nobly, holding the cigarette between two slender fingers and blowing out the smoke through his nostrils in a double jet, like a horse's warm breath.

"He's handsome," said Bernard in an undertone.

"She's quite aware of that," answered Rose in the same low voice.

He was shocked that Rose should have noticed the beauty of their young guide, even if only through the eyes of Odette.

"Well, Ahmed, shall we get going?" said Odette. "Which way?"

With his raised hand, Ahmed indicated the heights of the unknown park. The slopes above them were crowned with pines, gum-cistus with limp petals, and trees imported at the whim of an American who had laid out the park and built his house there half a century earlier. The three French tourists left the orchard and vegetable-garden and climbed up towards blue cascades of wistaria, roses festooned on thuyas, broom over which danced butterflies of a similar yellow, and white transparent clematis grown weak through long neglect. Ahmed walked in front of them with a carefree stride.

"So he understood your question?" Bernard asked Odette.

"Telepathy," said Odette fatuously.

They emerged from the orange grove and took deep breaths, glad to be free of the overpowering scent of its fruit and flowers.

"I shan't go any further this morning," declared Odette. "That blood-orange cocktail has gone to my legs. What'll we see up there, anyway? Only the same as here. Wistaria on trellises, clematis by the yard, and what else? On our right, a bottomless abyss. On our left, unexplored wilderness. It's amost midday. Shall we go back?"

"Quite a good idea," said Bernard blandly.

Ahmed came to a halt and they meekly followed suit. He had stopped in front of a little circle of level ground, an old pond half smothered in young grass and potentilla in flower. Its crumbling stone rim could no longer keep back the invasion of marsh marigolds and poppies. A trickle of water, deserting its dried-up spout in the mouth of a stone lion's head, ran free between the broken flags.

"Oh," cried Rose in delight.

"Rather snappy," declared Odette. "Bernard, what about something like that for a garden terrace at Auteuil?"

Bernard did not answer. He was measuring with his eye the flat space now overrun with wild grasses. He smiled to see that in the middle the slightly crushed grass seemed to indicate that someone had lain there. "One person, or two? Two bodies closely interlocked leave no more trace than one." Without raising his head he darted a covert glance at Rose. It was the look of a lascivious schoolboy which began at her knees and slid upwards to her thighs and thence to her breasts. "*There*, it's firm, almost harsh to the touch, like a very downy peach and, I'm sure, slightly brindled. Real blondes are never all one colour . . . *There*, it's probably bluish white, like milk, and there, oh, there it's as frankly rosy as her name. It was bad enough only being able to see with my eyes and my lips in the dark. But to see nothing at all, touch nothing at all for all these days and nights, no, no, it's unbearable . . . From that appalling hotel to this soft cushiony grass—let me see—it can't be more than five hundred yards."

He stared at Rose with such a harsh explicit look that she blushed almost to tears, her face flooded with the burning colour of the blonde at bay. "If I had her in my arms . . ." he thought. The power they had over each other was so new that they were defenceless against such shocks. Frightened, afraid to move, they were assaulted by identical pangs. And because they were both suffering the same thing, they felt themselves to be one.

"It's not only frightfully amusing," insisted Odette, "it's positively sexy."

Leaving Rose to her troubled feelings, Bernard turned away from her with a cowardice which he told himself was discretion.

"That bitch Odette, she's guessed everything! I'm sure she saw me blush." He mopped his forehead and the back of his strong neck. Rose, who was calming down, smiled as she recognised the blue handkerchief she had given him. "The darling, she's so silly when she loves me!"

Vaguely offended, obscurely jealous of a desire which was not fixed on herself, Odette went and sat down some distance away and put on her "Fiji Island face". The black fringe of her hair was etched sharply against her forehead under the white piqué hat and her hard eyes reviled the resplendent weather. When she sulked, she kept her prominent mouth shut. Usually it was open, showing the importunate whiteness of her teeth.

"She's ugly," Bernard decided on consideration. For he knew what a menace ugly women of that type can be when they decide to attract and infuriate. Bessier Senior, who was ageing, must also know something on that subject!

With a savage heel, the woman he found ugly crushed a scarab-beetle as it laboriously made its way across the clearing and Bernard rushed up to her as if to ward off some danger: "Madame Odette . . ."

"Can't you call me Odette like everyone else? No, of course not!"

"But I should be only too delighted," he said promptly.

"Things are going badly," he thought. "Next week she's capable of insisting on even more intimate terms. But I haven't the least desire to go all out to make things easier." All the same, face to face with the enemy, he accentuated his smile, the smile which had conquered Rose.

"I wanted to make a suggestion, Odette—do you hear, Odette? Hodette?"

She leant back and laughed, showing the interior of her mouth, the moist palate the colour of a ripe fig, and all her even, flawless teeth.

"That's better. I'm not pretending that it's a very inspired suggestion. Still, why shouldn't we have some mint-tea brought up here at tea-time—Ahmed knows how to make it—or some sort of orange drink. And Cadi's horns and gazelle's ears . . ."

"It's the other way round," said Rose with no malice.

"Well, those little cakes made of almonds and pistachio nuts, whatever they're called."

"One word more and I shall be sick," said Odette. "It only needs the vice-principal and the headmaster. And what's the grand climax?"

"I've thought of that," said Bernard in a malicious voice which made him loathe himself. "The grand climax is that we don't have any dinner and go to bed at ten. We go to bed and, thank God, we go to bed without dancers in lock-knit brassières, without the local cinema, without a forced march through that beastly steep town. We even go to bed at half-past nine! It's all my own invention and I'm decidedly proud of it."

They did not answer immediately. Odette yawned. Rose waited for Odette to give her opinion. And Odette was never in a hurry to approve anyone else's suggestion.

"The fact is . . ." she began.

"Oh," put in Rose, "I'm the last person to stop anyone going to bed."

All three of them were thinking of their long evening of the day before, which had begun in a *café-chantant* under the canvas awning of a little courtyard that smelt of acetylene. They had been taken there by a young and voluble guide—who wore a dinner jacket but no hat on his sleek head—to mix with the local gentry as they sat sipping their *anis* and nibbling their nougat. On the platform there had been a Spanish woman in yellow stockings, who looked like a staved-in cask, and two Tunisian *commères*, pale as butter, who sang from time to time.

Next they had stopped at a cleaner place with an arched roof, where they had watched another dancer, a slim, naked, competent little creature with well-set breasts, who stamped on the tiles with a lively business-like step. She displayed everything but her hair, which was tightly tied up in a silk handkerchief, and her eyes, which she kept downcast throughout. When her dance was over, she went and sat cross-legged on a leather cushion. She had no art other than that of moving modestly and keeping her sexual organs ingeniously concealed.

"It was pathetic, that little thing who danced naked," said Rose.

Bernard was grateful to her for having thought, at the same moment, just what he himself was thinking. Odette shrugged her shoulders.

"It's not pathetic. It's inevitable. In Madrid one goes to see the Goyas. Here, you mustn't miss native girls in the nude. But I admit the sight isn't worth the effort of staying up till half-past three."

"But it is," thought Bernard. "Only not with her or Rose. You can't expect women to lay aside their own particular brand of indecency and their instinct for spontaneous comparison. Any pleasure in the world would be spoilt for me if Odette were looking on. I knew everything she was thinking. 'That Zorah . . . her breasts won't last three years. My back's longer than hers. My breasts are more like apples not so much like lemons as hers. I'm made quite differently *there* . . .'"

He was embarrassed to find himself imagining the details of a woman's body over which he had no rights and he blushed as he met Odette's look. "That female guesses everything. I'll never manage to do what I want to do tonight. Rose will never have the courage."

Ahmed seemed to be listening to the distant voice of the invisible Tangiers and pulled up his white sleeve to consult his wrist-watch. He bent over the little circle of lush, trampled grass and picked a blue flower, which he slipped between his ear and his fez. Then he fell back into his immobility, his lids and lashes hiding his great dark eyes.

"Ahmed!"

Bernard had called him almost in an undertone: Ahmed started.

"We're going down again, Ahmed."

Ahmed turned towards Rose and Odette, questioning them with his smile. They both smiled back so promptly and with such obvious pleasure that Bernard was annoyed. Ahmed's slippers and lean, agile ankles led the way: Bernard took note of all the turnings and landmarks. "It's as easy as anything. The first turning that forks upward from the big avenue. Anyway, one can hear the trickling of the water almost at once." But he remained dissatisfied. He was languid under the assault of noon; the growing light and heat sapped his vitality. Nevertheless he would like to have owned that vast domain, which struck him as peculiarly oriental.

"I'll say good-bye to Odette and Bessier. I'll shut myself up with Rose. I'll keep Ahmed and that wild little Arab girl we saw down there."

On their way back down the slope they saw once again the pines and the blue cedars and, lower down, the white arums which Ahmed contemptuously beheaded as he passed.

Lower down still, a little girl, whose skin was almost black, crossed their path, followed by her white hens. Her hair was plaited into a horn, one shoulder was half-bare and her breasts, under the native muslin, were conical.

"Ah, that's the nice little thing we saw over by the kitchens," exclaimed Odette.

The nice little thing shot her an insulting look and disappeared.

"Success! Ahmed, what's she called? Yes, the little thing over there. Don't act the idiot! It doesn't take *me* in for a moment. What's her name?"

Ahmed hesitated and fluttered his lashes.

"Fatima," he said, at last.

"Fatima," echoed Rose. "Isn't that pretty! She had a smile for Ahmed. What a look she gave *us*!"

"She's got a marvellous mouth," said Bernard. "And those thick teeth that I adore."

"That I adore!" mocked Rose. "Merely that! Do you hear that, Odette?"

"I hear all right," said Odette. "But I don't care a damn what he says. My feet are hurting."

They reached the crumbling wall of the park. As he stopped a moment to thank the ever-speechless Ahmed with a handshake, Bernard noticed that a gate was missing and a rusty padlock hung at the end of a useless chain.

The three companions turned into the narrow, almost shadeless path, barbed with prickly-pears. Odette walked ahead, her eyes almost closed between the black fringe of her hair and the white bar of her teeth. Rose twisted her ankle and groaned. Bernard, who was following her, took her by the elbow and mischievously squeezed her arm as he helped her along.

"So you've got the wrong sort of shoes on too? Couldn't either of you come to Africa with any other sort of shoes except those absurd white buckskin things?"

"No, stop, that's the limit," Rose wailed. "As if I hadn't enough to put up with as it is, without your having to . . .

"Oh give over," broke in Odette without turning round. "He's just another of those chaps who say 'For goodness' sake, wear espadrilles!' and then they're furious with you because, with no heels, all your skirts droop at the back."

Bernard made no retort. The noon-day hour, while depressing his two weary companions, was making him turn ferocious. He stared at the sea, which seemed to be going down along with them, sinking back into its depths behind the tufted hills, the empty spring fields, and the silent little gardens where everything was in flower. "This is no time to be trailing round out of doors! And these two women! One teeters along, stumbling over everything, and the other's limping. As to their conversation, one's is as idiotic as the other's. I wonder what the hell I'm doing here!"

Since he knew very well what he was doing there, he forced himself to be less cantankerous and managed to take a little pleasure in the swallows, which were scything the air just above the ground and turning short with a whistle of wings.

The plaster-strewn enclosure, which the Mirador Hotel intended shortly to convert into an Arab garden with formal pools, boasted no more than a yellow patio. Its squat archways threw back blinding reflections of various shades of yellow. A tuft of wild oats made one of these look almost green: some red geraniums turned another to the fleshy pink of watermelons. An Ali-Baba jar of blue cinerarias threw a blue halo on the yellow wall, a kind of azure mirage. The strangled painter revived in the depths of Bernard Bonnemains.

"What light! Why not let myself be tempted by a long, uneventful life here . . . No, further away than this . . . I'd have a little concubine, or two . . . " He pulled himself up out of decency. "Or Rose, of course. But with Rose it wouldn't be possible. And it wouldn't be the same."

A smell of anis whetted his desire for a drink. He turned his head and saw Bessier Senior sitting at one of the little tables, writing.

"So there you are, Cyril!" cried Odette. "I bet you've only just come down!"

But Bonnemains had already noticed that there were three glasses on the table and that on an adjoining one, among squeezed lemons, siphons and tumblers, lay several bluish pages torn from the block Bessier used for making notes. He took in all these details at once glance, with a professional jealousy as swift as a woman's suspicion and far more intelligent.

"You're wrong," answered Bessier laconically. "You three had a good walk?"

For a moment he raised his eyes towards the newcomers, the eyes of a fair man who had once been handsome. Then he went on writing. His hair was still thick, though its gold had faded. He affected a pre-war coquetry. He liked clothes which were almost white, let one silver lock fall over his forehead, and made considerable play with his pale lashes and his short-sighted eyes.

"I find him as embarrassing as a faded beauty," thought Bernard. "I've nothing against him except that he's Rose's brother-in-law."

Accustomed to keeping quiet when Bessier was working, the two women sat down and waited, their hats on their knees. Rose slipped Bernard a faintly imploring smile which revived his sense of the power he had over her. "After all, a real blonde, a hundred per cent blonde, is pretty rare." As Odette so charmingly put it: "Pink cheeks at twenty-five; blotches and broken veins at forty-five." He followed the crimson play of light on Rose's bare neck and under her chin and in her nostrils, and felt an immense desire to paint her. Misunderstanding his look, she lowered her eyes.

"I've finished," said Bessier. "But there's a post out this afternoon . . . Have you three only come back to eat? Bonnemains, you look disappointed. Purple in the face, but disappointed. Wasn't it worth the effort?"

He dabbed his prominent, sensitive eyes with the tips of his fingers and smiled with automatic condescension.

"Oh yes . . . quite," said Bernard uncertainly.

"Oh *yes*!" cried Rose. "It's adorable. And we haven't seen more than a quarter of it! You should have come, Cyril. Such greenery everywhere! And the oranges! I've eaten twenty if I've eaten one! And the flowers! It's crazy!"

Bernard stared at her in surprise. His private Rose bore no resemblance to this pretty, voluble little bourgeoise. Then he remembered that the Rose who belonged to the Bessier brothers was expected to behave childishly, to blush frequently and drop an occasional brick to the accompaniment of tender, indulgent laughs. He clenched his jaws: "Spare us any more, Rose!"

"And the villa?" asked Bessier. "What's the villa like? As hideous as they say?"

"The villa?"

"There's no more a villa than there's a . . ." said Odette.

"Perhaps it was the way up to the villa," interrupted Bernard, "that Ahmed was pointing out near the top of the hill. These women weren't interested in finding out anything. And as Ahmed doesn't speak French . . ."

Bessier raised his eyebrows.

"He doesn't speak French?"

"So *he* says," insinuated Odette. "Personally, I've my own ideas about *that*."

Bessier turned to Bernard and spoke to him as if he were a child of eight.

"My dear little Bonnemains, don't bother yourself about the villa. I've got it all here?"

"You've got it all? All what."

Bessier pushed two or three leaves of his notebook, a creased yellow plan and an old photograph across the iron table.

"There!" he said theatrically. "While you are having a good time, I . . ."

Rose had stood up and her crisp, curly gold hair brushed

Bernard's ear as she bent over the photograph. But Bernard, tense and absorbed, was not giving Rose a thought. The faded old photograph occupied his whole attention.

"The villa," explained Bessier, "here they call it the palace—that's this huge black smudge."

"Mh'm," nodded Bernard. "I see, I see. What else?"

"Well," said Bessier, "I've had some fellows here this morning. One called Dankali. One called Ben Salem, one called—eh—Farrhar with an 'h'—who's got power of attorney. Odette and Rose, let my anis alone, will you? If you want some, make it yourself, as Marius says. Farrhar even told me that he'd once started studying architecture in Paris, so he felt as if he were a sort of colleague of mine. Too honoured! Architecture leads to everything, provided you get out of it. He's extremely elegant. A pearl tie-pin and a blue diamond on his finger."

"Blue?" squealed Rose.

"How big?" asked Odette greedily.

"Big as my fist. Once and for all, have you finished sucking at my anis? I've a horror of people drinking through my straws. It absolutely revolts me. You know that perfectly well!"

"Me too," thought Bernard. The sight of Odette and Rose bending over Cyril's tumbler, each with a straw between her lips, made him pinch his lips wryly and swallow his saliva as he did every time anything showed him Rose in familiar intimacy with the two Bessiers. He loathed it when Bessier lit Rose's cigarette or lent her a handkerchief to wipe her lips or her fingers; when he put a spoon to her mouth with a lump of sugar soaked in coffee.

". . . those three chaps were well worth seeing," Bessier went on. "Dankali is the contractor . . ."

"I know," said Bernard.

Bessier did not conceal his surprise: "But how do you know?"

"All the lorries and timber-yards and fences and houses under construction are plastered with 'Dankali and Sons'," said Bernard. "Haven't you noticed?"

"I haven't, by Jove. But I'll certainly remember it in the future."

He paused awhile, gently tapping his prominent eyeballs.

"It's a big job. They're rasing the villa to its foundations and starting all over again. The Pasha's made up his mind."

"Bravo!" said Bernard. "Isn't that going to mean your staying out here longer?"

"On the contrary. Of course I shall have to come back in September with the plans of the whole thing on paper."

"Ah yes. Quite."

Bessier looked dreamy and appeared to have no more to say.

"He said 'I shall come back.' He didn't say 'We shall come back'," thought Bernard. "So much for you, you thoroughgoing swine."

The two women, used to keeping silence while professional discussions were taking place, sat idle on a bench. "If I were to ask him how he got the job, he might tell me," thought Bernard. "But where would that get me?"

He reproached himself for the little shiver which dried his light sweat and for the terrible professional jealousy which was ruining his day.

"I'll swallow that like all the rest. But *shall* I swallow it?" I've had my back up ever since I came out. The fact is that, except for Rose, I can't bear the sight of these people any more." He looked about him and his eyes came to rest on two hard brown hands, two forearms the colour of oak which, a few steps away, were turning over and pressing down the damp earth at the foot of the daturas under the arcade. On the kitchen doorstep, a small, roly-poly child with a fez on its head tottered, fell on the ground and laughed. Above the whistling of the grey swifts, which were drinking on the wing from the newly-made fountain, rose a quavering song which trailed its long notes and its intervals of augmented seconds in the air and relaxed Bernard Bonnemain's contracted heart. "I'd like to live among them, among the people here. It's true that most of them don't belong here." His eyes returned to Rose. Her cheeks were scarlet and her hair tumbled: he could see that she was worried about him. "That girl's going to pay for the others! I swear that she's going through with it tonight, and how! And if she gets caught, if we both get caught, very well then! I can't see that it matters." He could not stop himself from admiring the attitude of the Fiji Islander. At the mention of the "big job", she had manifested her greed and delight only by a brief flicker in her eye. Now she was combing her fringe and her hair gleamed as blue as a Chinese girl's in the sun. "She keeps all the 'how, why and when?' for when they're alone together. She's an admirable female in her own way." He turned again to Rose, who was disentangling her rough golden curls in imitation and humming as she did so. 'As for her . . . The time it takes her to grasp anything!' But she's entirely made—admirably made too—to be enjoyed." His desire gripped him again. It disturbed him yet, at the same time, it revived his awareness of the African spring, of his own strength, of the agreeable present moment. He leapt to his feet and cried: "Food! Food! Let's eat or I'll not be responsible for my actions!"

Then he rushed, gesticulating, up the steps. Behind him there burst out shrill cries of terror. He realised that they came from the little dimpled child in its miniature fez and he regretted having behaved like a maniac.

A few minutes later, the four of them sat at table eating large, stringy shrimps, stuffed artichokes and baby lamb. Bessier

Senior, a rose in his buttonhole, tried vainly to steer the conversation back to the business of the villa.

"What's your opinion, Bonnemains? Farrhar made no secret of the fact that the Pasha, after spending a summer at Deauville, has developed a passion for Norman buildings with crossbeams and all that. A Norman cottage in Tangiers, no, that's really too much! Bonnemains, my dear chap, I'm talking to you, d'you hear?"

Far less deferential than usual, Bonnemains laughed in his face, displaying his splendid teeth to tempt Rose.

"I hear perfectly, my dear fellow, I hear perfectly. But, in the first place I'm a little drunk with this sun and this country and this heavy white wine that glues one's tongue. And, in the second place, I've a horror of meddling in other people's affairs. Didn't you know that?"

Bessier Senior raised his fair eyelashes and, for no apparent reason, laid his hand on Rose's forearm.

"No, dear boy, I didn't know anything of the kind. Rose, fish me a bit of ice out of the pail. Thank you. I prefer your hand to the Spanish waiter's."

He took his time to drink before adding, with too emphatic graciousness: "My affairs won't always be 'other people's affairs' to you, Bernard. At least, so I dare to hope."

"Yes, yes. Always these old-world courtesies," thought Bernard. "He doesn't give a damn for me, yet I still owe him some thanks. What can I say to him? He's obviously expecting some polite formula of gratitude."

"My dear Cyril, no one's clumsier than I am at showing a gratitude which . . . I should so much like, particularly for your sake, to prove myself before you give me your official confidence . . ."

At the word "official", Bessier once more unveiled his bluish eyes and fixed them for a moment on Bernard. He smiled into space, took the tea-rose out of his buttonhole and inhaled it at length, using the rose and the pale hand as a screen between himself and Bernard. Bernard had to be content with this coquettish gesture which implied: "All in good time", or "That's understood".

Odette, who was smoking discreetly, had allowed herself neither an allusive smile nor a meaning look. "Well trained," thought Bernard. "I'll never get such good results with Rose. Unless by great kicks in the . . ." He laughed and became once more the Bernard Bonnemains whom he himself believed to be the authentic one. This Bernard was a strong, likeable young man, rather an optimistic character, who used anger as a defence against his fundamental shyness and who was inclined to covet his neighbour's goods when they were flourished under his nose.

Some black, bitter coffee kept the two couples sitting on at the table. The hot air rose up from the gravel and a cool salt breeze smelling of cedarwood stirred over their heads. Caught by the sun which had moved round, Bessier folded a newspaper into a hat and put it on. It gave him an intolerable resemblance to a portrait of a middle-aged woman by Renoir. Suddenly, Bernard could stand no more and he stood up, knocking his chair over on the gravel.

"If I die of heart failure," scolded Odette, "I know who'll be responsible."

"Oh, come now . . . come . . ." Rose began plaintively.

"A little touch of colic, dear friend?" simpered Bessier under his wide-brimmed printed hat.

"Oh! Cyril!" said Rose reproachfully.

"I might have replied," thought Bernard, as he reached his room, "that I actually was suffering from violent indigestion. Each one of those three said exactly what one knew they would say. Life is becoming impossible."

He locked his door, pulled down the blinds and flung himself on his bed. The half-open window let in noises, not one of which was African: banging crockery, telephone bells, someone languidly dragging a rake. A ship's siren filled the air, drowning all other sounds, and Bernard, relaxed almost to the point of tears, shut his eyes and opened his clenched fists.

"What's the matter with me? What's the matter with me? The need to make love, obviously. My Rose, my little Rose . . . rose of my life . . ."

He turned over with a leap like a fish. "Those names sound as silly for her as they do for me to say them. She's my Rose, my delicious little blonde slavey, my pretty goldilocks of a washerwoman?" He broke off with a kind of sob of impatience, which he managed to choke down and which had nothing to do with tenderness. "Enough of all this gush! Tonight we're going for a walk, Rose and I."

On the wooden slats of the blinds, he conjured up the old pond in the deserted park, overgrown with delicate wild grasses, the trickle of water diverted from the dried-up lion's mouth and Rose lying on her back. But a kind of ill-will spoilt his pleasure and his hope and he refused to be taken in by himself. "Yes, I know perfectly well that all this story would be much prettier if Rose were poor. But if she were poor, I shouldn't be thinking of marrying her."

Sleep fell on him so suddenly that he had not time to settle himself in a comfortable position. He slept, lying sprawled across the bed, one arm bent and the back of his neck pressing against the feather pillow. When he woke up, which was not till the sun had moved to another window, he was stiff all over. Before raising his perspiring head, he caught sight of the corner of an envelope under the door. "What's the trouble now?"

"*We're going out,*" Rose had written. "*Dear Bernard, we didn't want to disturb your rest . . .*"

"We, we . . . who the hell are 'we'. I'll give her a lesson in family solidarity!" In the glass, he saw his untidy image; his shirt rucked up, his trousers unbelted and his hair on end, and thought he looked ugly.

"*Cyril has an awful migraine and asks us, as a favour, to have dinner at the hotel and go to bed early. As usual, Odette, as a model wife, entirely agrees with Cyril. But I admit that I myself . . .*"

Bernard ran to the window, pulled up the blinds and leaned over the cooling patio. From now until tomorrow it would be bathed in shadow and spray from the fountain. The jet of water, shooting up straight from its basin, quivered in the breeze. Beyond the arcades lay the chalky African soil with its ubiquitous riot of pulpy white arum lilies.

He waited, naked, for his bath to fill. His young, slightly heavy body, without scar or blemish, pleased him. The thought of Rose gave him one of those moments of magical anguish such as he had felt when he was fifteen, moments when desire is so fierce that it almost consumes its object, then forgets it.

Freshly bathed and shaved, dressed in light clothes and smelling good, he went down and stood at the edge of the garden. He was rash enough to let his pleasure show on his face.

"You look like a First Communicant," said the voice of Bessier.

"I can smell you from here," said Odette. "You've put it on with rather a heavy hand. That 'Counter-Attack' of yours . . . I've always said it wasn't a man's toilet water."

"On the other hand, I adore his white woollen socks," said Bessier.

"Personally," went on Odette, "I'd have preferred not *quite* such a blue tie. With a grey suit, a really blue tie looks as silly as a bunch of cornflowers in one's buttonhole."

She was sitting so close to her husband that their shoulders touched. United in their spite, they were summing him up as if he were a horse. It was their unity which struck Bernard as even more offensive than their insolence.

"Have you quite finished?" he said roughly.

"Now then, you! Come off it!" cried Odette.

Bessier restrained her by laying his heavy white hand on her arm. "We've quite finished," he said affectionately to Bernard. "Don't get annoyed because your friends are sensitive to all the outward signs that show you want to be handsome and gay."

"I'm not . . . I don't particularly want to . . ." Bernard clumsily protested.

The blood was singing in his ears and he ran a finger between his neck and his shirt-collar. He was afraid he would not be able to stand Odette's little laugh, but Bessier had the situation well in hand and reproved his wife.

"You've touched him to the quick, otherwise to the tie! Insult my mother but don't dare suggest that I've chosen the wrong tie!"

He was speaking to her with a paternal mildness. Suddenly he grabbed the nape of her neck and kissed her on her peevish mouth, on her moist, shining teeth. "He's indecent, that chap," thought Bernard. But, all the same, it gave him a pang to imagine the chill, the perfect regularity of the teeth Bessier had kissed. He turned away, paced a few steps and returned to the couple.

"For they certainly are a couple," he admitted. Bessier was stroking the shoulder of a silent and softened Odette, stroking it with the hand of an indifferent master. "It's unusual for a husband and wife to be a couple." He felt annoyed, in spite of the soft green twilight and the wind laden with the scent of mint tea.

"Here's our Rose," announced Bessier in a studied voice.

Bonnemains, who had recognised the little short step, carefully avoided turning round, but an exclamation from Odette made him forget his discretion.

"Whatever's the matter with you? What's gone wrong?"

He saw that Rose had thrown her dark blue raincoat over the rather crumpled dress she had kept on ever since the morning and that she was coming towards them with her head bent and wearing a brave little martyred smile.

"Have you lost a relation?" cried Odette.

"Oh, I've such a migraine. It's this afternoon. You dragged me through the bazaars, and I simply can't stand the smell of leather there is everywhere here. Forgive me, Cyril and Bernard, I just hadn't the energy. I've stayed just as I am without changing my frock. I know I look simply frightful."

"You look frightful, but you smell marvellous," observed Odette. "How you can stand scent when you've got a migraine! Doesn't she smell good, Bernard?"

"Delicious," said Bernard easily. "She smells of . . . wait a minute . . . marzipan tart . . . I adore that!"

He even went so far as to pretend to bite Rose's bare arm. Rose looked crosser than ever and went and sat very close to Cyril.

"Either we're the worst actors in the world," thought Bernard, "or else the Bessiers can sense a kind of atmosphere round me and Rose. Which doesn't stop the child being slyer than I supposed. Look at her now, got up in that dark thing over her light dress, a dress that's already been rumpled in full view of everyone. It's true that when it comes to deception, the stupidest of them has a genius for it."

After a thoughtful silence, Odette said in a resigned voice: "Well, we're all going to bed early."

They had a strange dinner, served in the patio under a naked electric bulb, which was soon covered with little moths in a hurry to die. Rose pretended at first that she could not eat;

then devoured her food. Bernard insisted on champagne and pressed his three guests to drink. The two women held back at first, then Odette pushed her empty glass across the tablecloth to Bernard like a pawn on a chessboard and drank glass after glass, only giving herself time to take a deep breath between each refill. She gave great gasps and "Ahs" as if she had been drinking under a tap and the glitter of her teeth between her lips, the sight of her moist palate and tongue in her open mouth dazzled Bernard in spite of himself. "Yet Rose has a lovely, healthy, desirable mouth too. But Odette's great carnivorous mouth suggests something else." After a spasm of uncontrollable laughter, Odette had absurdly to wipe away tears. She clutched Rose's bare arm and Bernard saw the flat fingers, with the nails varnished dark red, print hollows in the flesh. Rose made no sound but seemed terror-stricken and slowly and cautiously removed her arm from the fingers which gripped it, as if disentangling it from a briar. Bernard filled up the glasses and drained his own. "If I stop drinking, if I look at these people too close, I shall chuck everything and clear out."

He went on looking at them, however, and, most of all, he looked at Rose. Her hair was standing out like the spokes of a wheel, her cheeks and ears were crimson and there was a paler ring round her eyes. Her eyes were brilliant and vacant, but her quivering mouth had a majestic and dishonoured expression as if she had just submitted to a long, passionate embrace. At the moment when all four of them stopped drinking and talking, she seemed so overcome that Bernard was afraid she would refuse to follow him.

But suddenly she got up stiffly and announced that she was going up to bed.

"You can't want to more than I do," said Bessier. "But permit me to drink a toast to the lady who's watching us and listening to us."

He grabbed his glass and raised his bluish eyes, clouded by the wine, to the sky. Bonnemains followed his gaze and was astonished to see a pink moon, half-way to being round, appearing in the square of sky above the patio.

"Well, of all things! I'd forgotten the moon. So much the worse. Anyway, what the hell! In its second quarter, and rather misty at that, the moon doesn't give much light. It's not the moon that'll stop us from . . ."

"Well," said Odette gloomily. "I'm going to bed, too. What about you, Bernard?"

"Aha!" said Bonnemains. "I'm not going to commit myself to anything. After all, I'm a bachelor. I haven't renounced the pleasures of Africa."

When he saw all three of them vanish up the staircase, which did not yet boast a lift, he felt at the end of his strength and his patience. His last gesture of sociability cost him an immense effort. With voice and hand, he acknowledged Bessier's "Good night" as the latter went up the stairs behind Rose. "He climbs like an old man. He's got an old man's back." Before the trio disappeared, he thought he saw the hand of the "old man" deliberately touch Rose's buttocks. The second turn of the stairs, on the first landing, allowed him to see that both the women were well ahead of Bessier. "I made a mistake. I've had just one or two glasses too many." He looked questioningly at the half-moon which was rapidly ascending the sky. "Not a cloud. Well, it can't be helped." He waited till the little Spaniards in dirty white jackets had cleared the table and ordered a glass of iced water. "I smell of wine and tobacco. After all, so does Rose. Anyway, thank God she's a woman who's not squeamish about the human body—a real woman."

He watched the light in Rose's room. "Now she's brushing her teeth with lots of scent in the toothglass. She does heaps of little odds and ends of beautifying—unnecessary in my opinion.

Now she's gossiping with Odette through a closed door—or an open door. I've quite a bit of time to wait."

The light in the Bessiers' windows went out. Ten minutes later, Rose's window turned black. Then Bonnemains took cover under the arcades and made his way to a narrow door which opened out of the enclosure on to the waste ground beyond.

Crushing flakes of plaster and scraps of broken crockery under his shoe-soles, caressing the white arums which stood stiff, drinking in the damp night air, he passed through this pallid purgatory.

Half-way along the rough little road which led to the Pasha's park, the sea suddenly appeared in the distance like a misted looking-glass. "How beautiful it is, that horizontal line and the sky gently pressing down on it, and that dim reflection in the shape of a boat. It needs that—and only that—for me to stop being unjust or envious or anything that I don't like being."

Leaning against the broken fence and reassured by the absence of dogs and barriers, he admired the black block of the cedars. Here and there the green showed less dark, softly massed in cloudy shapes which he knew were mimosas loaded with scent and flowers. Below him, the sleeping town gave out only a faint glimmer and, at moments, the silence was like a silence only known in dreams. During one of such moments, Bonnemains became aware of the sound of uneven footsteps and saw a wavering shadow on the broken road. "Amazing," he exclaimed to himself. "I'd stopped thinking about her."

He ran back and once again made contact with an unfettered body, a scent too lavishly applied, some wiry hair and a panting breath.

"Here you are! Nothing broken?"

"No . . ."

"The Bessiers? You didn't make a noise?"

"No . . ."

"You weren't afraid?"

"Oh, yes . . ."

He held her firmly by the elbows, taking a peculiar pleasure in addressing her with a new sense of ownership. She lifted her face up to him and, in the nocturnal light, her lovely cheeks were tinged vivid blue and her painted mouth deep purple. "Am I never to have her all pink and white and red and golden?" He pulled open the silk raincoat to touch her dress, crumpled on purpose ever since the morning, and what the dress covered. Rose stood motionless, so as to lose nothing of the caress.

"Come along, I tell you!"

He passed his arm under her bare one and they crossed the confines of the park through a gap in the fence.

"You see—that path goes straight up and then it divides in two. It's the left one that takes us up to the lawn, to our bed walled in with stone and flowers. Rose, Rose . . . Come along! I'll hold you up."

She hung heavily on his arm, then stopped.

"It's dark."

"So I should hope! You can shut your eyes if you don't want to see the blackness. I'll guide you."

"Are you sure? Bernard, it's so dark."

He gave a low, patronising laugh.

"Shut your eyes, silly! Little funk! I'll tell you when we get there."

Her confidence in him returned and she huddled close against him. But, as they climbed the steep road full of ruts, Bonnemains could not recognise the path which had seemed so easy to find. He withdrew his supporting shoulder and guided Rose by her hand. His free hand fidgeted with the little electric torch in his pocket but he managed to refrain from using it. The forest darkness was impenetrable to the moonlight and after a few moments, Bernard began to be aware of a rising tide of apprehension. He was beset by that nervous terror which afflicts any human being who braves the blackest hour of night in the redoubled darkness of a wooded place. He stumbled, swore and switched on his torch. A round tunnel of light, edged with a rainbow, bored through the blackness.

"No!" shrieked Rose.

"You must really make up your mind, my child! You complain that it's dark and you refuse to see clearly . . ."

He switched it off, having seen that they were on the right road. Moreover, the vault of trees opened out above them, showing a river of sky in which stars twinkled.

"We're nearly there," went on Bernard, more gently, moved to pity by feeling Rose's hand grow damp in his without growing warm. But she said nothing and concentrated on following him: he could hear nothing but her hurried breathing. Twice he shone his torch on the path, just long enough to recognise the white clematis above their heads, then an arch of wistaria with long bunches of flowers.

"Do you smell their scent?" he asked very low.

He ventured a kiss in the dark and found her mouth. Rose's lips took fire again from his. They set off again, going with as much difficulty as if they were hauling a load, helping themselves with occasional spurts of light. At last they found the fork of the avenue, the charming flowery margin of the pool and the lion's mask. The diverted trickle of water sparkled under the white beam of the torch.

"Sit down there while I inspect our lawn."

Rose took off her raincoat and held it out to Bernard.

"There, spread that on the ground, with the lining on top."

"Whatever for?" he asked naïvely.

"But . . . for . . . well, after all."

She put her arm over her eyes to protect herself from the

glare of the torch. He understood and was full of gratitude towards a Rose whom he scarcely knew yet, the Rose who was at once prudish and practical, a good companion in bed, entirely devoted to the material necessities of love.

"I'm putting the lamp on the edge, don't knock it over!" he whispered.

"I've got one in my bag, too," answered Rose. "Look carefully in case there are any creatures."

On its way, the vertical trickle of water, white against the background of greenery, encountered the remains of some mosaic which diverted it beyond the kerb. The grass in the centre was fine and concealed no mysteries. Small frightened wings fluttered from the branches, awakened by the electric beam. Bernard strode over the rim, bent down to feel the grass and reared upright again with a start.

"What is it? Creatures? I'm sure there are creatures! Bernard!"

She went on imploring Bernard in a low voice as he stood there, staring fixedly at his feet.

"Don't be frightened," he said.

At that, Rose raised her hands to her temples and was on the verge of a scream, which Bernard checked by threatening her with his open hand. He bent down again and picked up, in the circle of light, a brown hand and a white sleeve which promptly slid out of his grasp and fell back again.

"He's not dead," he said. "The hand's warm, but . . ."

He held the lamp to his own hand, looked at it close to, then wiped his fingers in the grass. It was only then that he became conscious of Rose's silence. She did not run away but, in the rising shaft of light, he could see that her chin was trembling.

"Above all, don't turn faint," he said gently. "It's only a man who's bleeding."

Instinct made him glance questioningly into the darkness all about him.

"No . . . if there were other men here, the birds wouldn't have been asleep. I don't think there's anyone."

Under the crumpled dress, Rose's knees were trembling.

"Come, darling, give me a hand."

She took a step backwards.

"He's not dead, Rose. We can't leave him like that."

As she remained obstinately silent, he became impatient.

"Give me your electric torch."

She took still another step back and vanished from the zone of light. He heard her clumsily groping in her bag.

"Hurry up."

Rose's hand and the cheap little torch appeared out of Bernard's reach. Squatting down, he lifted a white sleeve and felt carefully all the way up the wounded arm.

"Well, bring it here, can't you?"

"No," said a muffled voice, "I don't want to. I'm afraid."

"Idiot," growled Bonnemains. "At least, put the torch on the coping. And switch it on—if that's not too much to ask you. Don't you realise the man's wounded, Rose?"

With both arms he lifted a light, slender body which he propped up against the coping. The body emitted a moan as it let its head, with eyes closed, fall backwards on the stone kerb.

"But it's Ahmed!" cried Bonnemains.

The injured man unclosed his eyelids and his long lashes and promptly closed them again.

"Ahmed! Poor kid! Rose, it's Ahmed! Do you hear me, Rose?"

"Yes," said the voice. "So what?"

"What d'you mean, so what? He must have—oh, goodness knows—fallen down, hurt himself. What a bit of luck we're here."

"Luck!" repeated the hostile voice.

Bernard's eyes were dazzled so that he could barely make out where Rose was standing in the darkness. He lowered his eyes, saw that his hand and his sleeves were stained with blood, and fell silent. "He's lost a lot of blood. Where is he wounded?"

He arranged the two torches so as to give as much light as possible and carefully tapped Ahmed's body all over with his fingertips. The blood was coming neither from the chest nor from the loins nor from the stomach as hollow as a greyhound's. "His throat? No, he's breathing quietly." At last, on the shoulder, he discovered the source of the blood and, once again, Ahmed groaned and opened his eyes.

"Have you a penknife?" he asked without turning his head.

"A what?"

"A penknife or something of the sort. Doesn't matter what, as long as it cuts. Hurry up, for God's sake, hurry up!"

He listened exasperatedly to the jingle of small objects in the handbag.

"I've got some little scissors."

"Don't throw them to me or they'll get lost in the grass. Bring them here," he ordered.

She obeyed and then drew back into the shadow.

"Can I have my raincoat back?" she asked, after a moment.

Bernard, who was slitting Ahmed's white sleeve, did not raise his head.

"Your raincoat? No, you can't. I'm going to cut it up. I haven't anything else to bandage his shoulder with. The amount he must have bled, this boy."

Rose made no protest, but he heard her breathing in jerks and holding back tears.

"Really, that's too much! My raincoat! To make a bandage for a nigger boy. Couldn't you use his shirt—or yours?"

"Why not your camiknickers?" broke in Bernard.

He felt strangely exalted, almost facetious even, as he worked coolly at baring the wounded shoulder. His ears were alert to every crackle in the undergrowth, every sigh in the boughs. A short blade which lay in the grass caught his eye with its glitter.

"Aha!" said Bernard. "You see that?"

He picked the knife up and, holding it by its point, laid it on the coping.

"Ahmed! Ahmed, can you hear me?"

The black lashes lifted and the eyes appeared, calm and severe, like those of a very young child. But the weight of the lids veiled them again almost at once. Bernard discovered the wound, quite a narrow one, but brutally inflicted. Its brown, swollen lips had still not stopped bleeding. With the palms of both hands, Bernard smoothed the bloodstained area round it so as to isolate the wound. "It's hellishly difficult," he said to himself.

"Ahmed! Who did this to you?"

Ahmed's mouth trembled and said nothing. Then it trembled again and murmured: "Ben Kacem."

"Quarrel?"

"Fatima."

"Fatima? Isn't that the pretty little girl down there?"

"Yes."

"Good. Now I think I see."

"What did he say?" asked Rose from far away.

"Nothing that would interest you. Ahmed, can you rest your weight on your hands for a moment? No? All right, don't move then. I knew very well that you spoke French."

He pulled the slit sleeve towards him. Split into three, it made a bandage long enough for his purpose.

Seized with a sudden lightheartedness, he worked fast, repressing his desire to sing under his breath and whistle. He reckoned that the bandage, passing under the armpit and over the shoulder and tightly wound, would have a reasonable hope of staunching the flow of blood, which was already tending to stop of its own accord. Ahmed made no movement. Bernard could feel him watching his hands.

"The torch!" cried Rose.

The bulb of one of the torches was reddening, preparatory to fading. "Hmm, that's not so funny."

"Stay sitting down," he said to Ahmed. "Try to keep quite still while I put on the bandage. Am I hurting you? Sorry, old chap, it can't be helped. The girl might have helped us, but just you try and make her understand."

His sweat dripped down on his work and, in wiping his forehead, he smeared it with red.

"Talk of antisepsis! By Jove, was it for Fatima you've perfumed yourself so magnificently? You fairly reek of sandalwood. There . . . now you're fine."

He caught Ahmed round the waist, sat him up and brought the torch nearer to the faultless face. The lips, from which the crimson had vanished, the eyes circled with brown and olive, gave the ghost of a smile. Bonnemains, invisible behind the torch, answered with a smile which twisted into a grimace as he suddenly found himself wanting to cry.

"D'you want to drink? Just think, I'd forgotten all about this water."

"No, it's the water that comes from the oleanders. It's bad."

He spoke French without an accent, rolling his r's.

"Cigarette?"

The thumb and forefinger, yellow-stained with nicotine, came forward to accept. Bernard wiped his hands on his stained handkerchief, groped in his pocket without a thought that he was smearing his jacket with blood, and stuck a lighted cigarette between Ahmed's lips. The delight of the first puffs made them both silent. Neither of them moved except to make identical gestures. The smoke showed faintly iridescent, seeming to break off as it touched the edges of the halo of light and reappearing higher up in whorls under the spreading branches of the blue cedar.

A burst of coughing disturbed the repose of the two young men. Bernard turned his head.

"What's the matter?"

"I'm cold," said Rose plaintively.

"You wouldn't be cold if you'd helped us. Here, catch your coat, I didn't use it. Ahmed, my boy, we've got to get down from here somehow. What I've done in the way of a dressing is almost less than nothing. Let's see—what's the time?"

Bonnemains scratched away the blood that was drying on the face of his wrist-watch and exclaimed in astonishment:

"Quarter to three! Impossible."

"It was after one when we left the hotel," came the sulky voice.

He strode over the coping and ran up to Rose.

"Rose, look, here's what we're going to do . . ."

She shrank back.

"Don't touch me, you're covered with blood!"

"I'm quite aware of that! Rose, can you give him your shoulder to get down to the bottom? I'll hold him up on the other side. With stops, it'll take a good half-hour. Or, wait a moment . . . Suppose you take the torch and go by yourself to the hotel or to the caretaker's house and send help? How about that?"

She did not answer at once and he became insistent.

"Tell me! Don't you think it would be better if you went down by yourself?"

"What do I think? I think you're mad," said Rose deliberately. "Whether I go down with you, with a wounded Arab between us, or whether I go by myself to rouse the entire population—it's as broad as it's long. Either way, the Bessiers will know I've been rambling about in the woods with you. Don't you see my point?"

"Yes, but I don't care a damn for the Bessiers."

"But I do. When one can avoid trouble with one's family . . ."

"Well? What solution do *you* propose?"

"Leave this—this wounded man here. Then we'll go down and you must wait till I've got back to my room to call for help. By then, the night will be over. A pretty night, I've had! So've you!"

"Don't pity me," he said shortly. "Mine's been all right."

"Charming!" snapped Rose in a low, savage voice. "If anyone had told me . . ."

"Shut up! Suppose I take Ahmed on my shoulders and that you light the path?"

". . . And that down there, they're already looking for him, and they see the light and come up, how do you expect me to explain?"

"Well? I presume you're of age, aren't you? Are you as ashamed of me as all that?"

He could sense her impatient gesture.

"But no, Bernard, there's no question of that. What's the good of putting people's backs up? You've no idea what the Bessiers have been to me ever since . . ."

"Hell!" Bernard interrupted. "You can go off. I'll manage alone."

"But, Bernard, look!"

"Get out. Go back and have your bottom pinched by Bessier. And drink out of his glass. And all the rest of it."

"What? What on earth? Whatever do you . . ."

"I know what I'm talking about. Be off with you! We're through. Pff! None too soon, either."

He passed his hand over his wet face. With a quick glance, he made sure that Ahmed, who had not moved, had not fainted and was still smoking. His eyes were half-closed and he seemed not even to hear the altercation.

"Bernard!" implored a small voice that had grown soft again. "You can't mean it! Bernard—I assure you . . ."

"What do you assure me? That Bessier has never pinched your behind? That Bessier is just a brother to you?"

"Bernard, if you've come to believe spiteful gossip——"

"No question of gossip!" he broke in violently. "No need for any gossip! Go back and make yourself charming to Bessier! Go back and sit on one of his knees! Go back to everything that suits a selfish little bourgeoise, not very clever but so hard that she's a positive marvel!"

She reacted to each attack with a little gasp of "Oh!" but could find no retort. When he paused for breath, she said at last: "But what are you driving at? Bernard, I'm certain that tomorrow . . ."

He sliced the air between them with his bloodstained hand: "Nothing! Tomorrow, I'll change my hotel. Or I take the boat. Unless I'm needed"—he indicated Ahmed—"as witness."

He drew back as if to let Rose pass.

"You can say exactly what you like to your Bessiers. That I'm the most loathsome of swine. And even that I've got disgusting manners. That I'm sick to death of the lot of you. Anything you like."

They were silent for a moment. Bonnemains' eyes, which were getting used to the darkness, made out Rose's face and her aureole of curly hair. He could see a strip of her light dress between the flaps of her open coat.

"And all for this nigger boy who's too tough to kill!" she flung at him furiously.

Bonnemains shrugged his shoulders.

"Oh, you know, if there hadn't been this little news item, there'd have been something else."

He picked up the one torch alight and thrust it by force into Rose's hand. She clenched her fingers and pushed him away.

"What's the matter? It's blood, it's not dirty. I can't help it, it's blood. Blood that you didn't deign to stop flowing. And now, pleasant journey, Rose!"

As she did not move he put his finger on her shoulder and gave her a push.

"On your way. A bit quicker. Or, I promise you, I'll make you run."

She turned the little bull's-eye of the torch on him. His forehead and one cheek were smeared with blood and his eyes were almost yellow. The beam shone into his open mouth, lighting up both rows of his big teeth. She lowered the torch and went off hurriedly.

Bernard went back and sat down by Ahmed. He watched the tunnel of light going down the hill, slowly pushing back the darkness in the avenue. He laid his hand on Ahmed's unhurt shoulder.

"All right? You don't think you're bleeding?"

"No, Monsieur."

The voice was so much firmer that Bernard was delighted. But it surprised him that Ahmed should call him Monsieur. "Still, after all, what could he call me?"

A bird squawked discordantly. From the height of the cedars there fell, by degrees, a glimmer that was still nocturnal.

"But we can see!" exclaimed Bernard joyfully.

"It'll soon be day," said Ahmed.

"What luck! How are you feeling?"

"All right, thank you, Monsieur."

A slender icy hand slid against Bernard's and stayed there. "He's cold. All that blood he's lost . . ."

"Listen, my dear boy. If I try and take you on my back, that rotten dressing of mine will come unstuck. And if I fall while I'm carrying you, that's another big risk for you. On the other hand . . ."

"I can wait for the day, Monsieur. I know myself. If you'd just give me a cigarette. Aziz comes down every day with his donkey for the watering, he passes this way. He won't be long now."

Reassured, Bonnemains smoked to deaden the hunger and thirst which were beginning to torment him. A cock crowed, other cocks followed its example; the breeze rose, bringing out the accumulated scent of the cedars and the fragrance of the wistarias; gradually the colour of the sky appeared between the trees. Bernard shivered in his shirt which was cold with sweat. From time to time, he touched his companion's wrist, counting the pulse-beats.

"Are you asleep, Ahmed? Don't go to sleep. That Kacem who did this, is he far away?"

He followed the progress of the dawning light on Ahmed's face. The black circles round the eyes, the cheeks shadowed by something other than the first beginnings of a beard, alarmed him.

"Tell me, has he gone? Did you see him run away?"

"Not far," said Ahmed. "I know . . ."

His free hand dropped, without letting go the cigarette, and his eyes closed. Bernard had time to raise the head which had fallen forward: he felt the wounded shoulder. But no warm moisture came through the linen, and the deep breathing of sleep fell rhythmically and reassuringly on Bonnemains' straining ears. He pushed his knee forward to support the sleeping head, took away the fag-end of the cigarette from the fingers which could no longer feel it, and stayed perfectly still. With his head raised, he watched the morning dawn and tasted a contentment, a surprise as fresh as love but less restricted and totally detached from sex. "He sleeps, I watch. He sleeps, I watch . . ."

The colour and abundance of the spilt blood blackened the trampled grass. Ahmed was talking in his sleep in guttural Arabic and Bonnemains laid his hand on his head to drive away the nightmare.

"Rose has got back by now. She'll be in bed. Poor Rose . . ." That was over quickly. She was my woman but this one here is my counterpart. It's queer that I had to come all the way to Tangiers to find my counterpart, the only person who could make me proud of him and proud of myself. With a woman it's so easy to be a little ashamed, either of her or of oneself. My wonderful counterpart! He only had to appear . . ."

Without the faintest sense of disgust, he contemplated his hands, his nails streaked with brown, the lines on his palms etched in red, his forearms marked with dried rivulets of blood.

"They say children and adolescents soon make up what they've lost. This boy must be an only son or the eldest one who'll be well looked after. A young male has his value in this country. He's handsome, he's already loved, he's already got a rival. The fact remains that, but for me . . ."

He swelled out his chest and smiled with pleasure at everything about him.

"Women! I know in advance pretty well what I'll do to them and they'll do to me. I'll find another Rose. A better Rose or a worse one. But one doesn't easily find a child in the shape of a man, hurt enough, unknown enough, precious enough to sacrifice some hours of one's life to him, not to mention the jacket of a suit and a night of love. Obviously it was decreed that I should never know whether Rose's breasts were rosier than her heels or her belly as pearly as her thighs. *Mektoub*, Ahmed would say!"

At the end of the long sloping avenue appeared a pink gleam which showed the place where the sun would rise over the sea: the shattering bray of a donkey and the tinkle of a little bell sounded from the top of the hill.

Before lifting Ahmed, Bonnemains tested the knots of his amateur dressing. Then he wrapped his arms round the sleeping boy, inhaled the sandalwood scent of his black hair and clumsily kissed his cheek which was already virile and rough. He estimated the young man's weight as he might have done that of a child of his own flesh or that of a quarry one kills only once in a lifetime.

"Wake up, dear boy. Here comes Aziz."

The Patriarch

BETWEEN the ages of sixteen and twenty-five, Achille, my half-brother by blood—but wholly and entirely my brother by affection, choice and likeness—was extremely handsome. Little by little, he became less so as a result of leading the hard life of a country doctor in the old days; a life which lacked all comfort and repose. He wore out his boot-soles as much as the shoes of his grey mare; he went out by day and he went out by night, going to bed too tired to want any supper. In the night he would be woken up by the call of a peasant banging his fists on the outer door and pulling the bell. Then he would get up, put on his woollen pants, his clothes and his great plaid-lined overcoat and Charles, the man-of-all-work, would harness the grey mare, another remarkable creature.

I have never known anything so proud and so willing as that grey mare. In the stable, by the light of the lantern, my brother would always find her standing up and ready for the worst. Her short, lively, well-set ears would enquire: "Chateauvieux? Montrenard? The big climb up the hill? Seventeen kilometres to get there and as many on the way back?" She would set off a little stiffly, her head lowered. During the examination, the confinement, the amputation or the dressing, she leant her little forehead against the farmhouse doors so as to hear better what *He* was saying. I could swear that she knew by heart the bits of *Le Roi d'Ys* and the Pastoral Symphony, the scraps of operas and the Schubert songs *He* sang to keep himself company.

Isolated, sacrificed to his profession, this twenty-six-year-old doctor of half a century ago had only one resource. Gradually he had to forge himself a spirit which hoped for nothing except to live and enable his family to live too. Happily, his professional curiosity never left him. Neither did that other curiosity which both of us inherited from our mother. When, in my teens, I used to accompany him on his rounds, the two of us would often stop and get out to pick a bunch of bluebells or to gather mushrooms. Sometimes we would watch a wheeling buzzard or upset the dignity of a little lizard by touching it with a finger: the lizard would draw up its neck like an offended lady and give a lisping hiss, rather like a child who has lost its first front teeth. We would carefully detach butterfly chrysalises from branches and holes in walls and put them in little boxes of fine sand to await the miracle of the metamorphosis.

The profession of country doctor demanded a great deal of a man about half a century ago. Fresh from the Medical School in Paris, my brother's first patient was a well-sinker who had just had one leg blown off by an explosion of dynamite. The brand-new surgeon came out of this difficult ordeal with honour but white-lipped, trembling all over and considerably thinner from the amount he had sweated. He pulled himself together by diving into the canal between the tall clumps of flowering rushes.

Achille taught me to fill and to stick together the two halves of antipyrine capsules, to use the delicate scales with the weights which were mere thin slips of copper. In those days, the country doctor had a licence to sell certain pharmaceutical products outside a four-kilometre radius of the town. Meagre profits, if one considers that a "consultation" cost the consultant three francs plus twenty sous a kilometre. From time to time, the doctor pulled out a tooth, also for three francs. And what little money there was came in slowly and sometimes not at all.

"Why not sue them?" demanded the chemist. "What's the law for?"

Whatever it was for, it was not for his patients. My brother made no reply but turned his greenish-blue eyes away towards the flat horizon. My eyes are the same colour but not so beautiful and not so deeply set.

I was fifteen or sixteen; the age of great devotions, of vocations. I wanted to become a woman doctor. My brother would summon me for a split lip or a deep, bleeding cut and have recourse to my slender girl's fingers. Eagerly, I would set to work to knot the threads of the stitches in the blood which leapt so impetuously out of the vein. In the morning, Achille set off too early for me to be able to accompany him. But in the afternoon I would sit on his left in the trap and hold the mare's reins. Every month he had the duty of inspecting all the babies in the region and he tried to drop in unexpectedly on their wet or dry nurses. Those expeditions used to ruin his appetite. How many babies we found alone in an empty house, tied to their fetid cradles with handkerchiefs and safety-pins, while their heedless guardians worked in the fields. Some of them would see the trap in the distance and come running up, out of breath.

"I was only away for a moment." "I was changing the goat's picket." "I was chasing the cow who'd broken loose."

Hard as his life was, Achille held out for more than twenty-five years, seeking rest for his spirit only in music. In his youth he was surprised when he first came up against the peaceful immorality of country life, the desire which is born and satisfied in the depths of the ripe grass or between the warm flanks of sleeping cattle. Paris and the Latin Quarter had not prepared him for so much amorous knowledge, secrecy and variety. But impudence was not lacking either, at least in the case of the girls who came boldly to his weekly surgery declaring that they had not "seen" since they got their feet wet two months ago, pulling a drowned hen out of a pond.

"That's fine!" my brother would say, after his examination. "I'm going to give you a prescription."

He watched for the look of pleasure and contempt and the joyful reddening of the cheek and wrote out the prescription agreed between doctor and chemist: "*Mica panis*, two pills to be taken after each meal." The remedy might avert or, at least, delay the intervention of "the woman who knew about herbs".

One day, long before his marriage, he had an adventure which was only one of many. With a basket on one arm and an umbrella on the other, a young woman almost as tall as himself (he was nearly six foot two) walked into his consulting-room. He found himself looking at someone like a living statue of the young Republic; a fresh, magnificently built girl with a low brow, statuesque features and a calm, severe expression.

"Doctor," she said, without a smile or a shuffle, "I think I'm three months pregnant."

"Do you feel ill, Madame?"

"Mademoiselle. I'm eighteen. And I feel perfectly all right in every way."

"Well, then, Mademoiselle! You won't be needing me for another six months."

"Pardon, Doctor. I'd like to be sure. I don't want to do anything foolish. Will you please examine me?"

Throwing off the skirt, the shawl and the cotton chemise that came down to her ankles, she displayed a body so majestic, so firm, so smoothly sheathed in its skin that my brother never saw another to compare with it. He saw too that this young girl, so eager to accuse herself, was a virgin. But she vehemently refused to remain one any longer and went off victorious, her head high, her basket on her arm and her woollen shawl knotted once more over her breasts. The most she would admit was that, when she was digging potatoes on her father's land over by the Hardon road, she had waited often and often to see the grey mare and its driver go past and had said "Good-day" with her hand to call him, but in vain.

She returned for "consultation". But, far more often, my brother went and joined her in her field. She would watch him coming from afar, put down her hoe, and, stooping, make her way under the branches of a little plantation of pine-trees. From these almost silent encounters, a very beautiful child was born. And I admit that I should be glad to see, even now, what his face is like. For "Sido" confided to me, in very few words, one of those secrets in which she was so rich.

"You know the child of that beautiful girl over at Hardon?" she said.

"Yes."

"She boasts about him to everyone. She's crazy with pride. She's a most unusual girl. A character. I've seen the child. Just once."

"What's he like?"

She made the gesture of rumpling a child's hair.

"Beautiful, of course. Such curls, such eyes. And such a mouth."

She coughed and pushed away the invisible curly head with both hands.

"The mouth most of all. Ah! I just couldn't. I went away. Otherwise I should have taken him."

However, everything in our neighbourhood was not so simple as this warm idyll, cradled on its bed of pine-needles, and these silent lovers who took no notice of the autumn mists or a little rain, for the grey mare lent them her blanket.

There is another episode of which I have a vivid and less

touching memory. We used to refer to it as "The Monsieur Binard story". It goes without saying that I have changed the name of the robust, grizzled father of a family who came over on his bicycle at dusk, some forty-eight years ago, to ask my brother to go to his daughter's bedside.

"It's urgent," said the man, panting as he spoke. His breath reeked of red wine. "I am Monsieur Binard, of X..."

He made a sham exit, then thrust his head round the half-shut door and declared: "In my opinion, it'll be a boy."

My brother took his instrument case and the servant harnessed the grey mare.

It turned out indeed to be a boy and a remarkably fine and well-made one. But my brother's care and attention was mainly for the far too young mother, a dark girl with eyes like an antelope. She was very brave and kept crying out loudly, almost excitedly, like a child, "Ooh!... Ooh! I say!... Ooh, I never!" Round the bed bustled three slightly older antelopes while, in the ingle-nook, the impassive Monsieur Binard superintended the mulling of some red wine flavoured with cinnamon. In a dark corner of the clean, well-polished room, my brother noticed a wicker cradle with clean starched curtains. Monsieur Binard only left the fire and the copper basin to examine the new-born child as soon as it had been washed.

"It's a very fine child," Achille assured him.

"I've seen finer," said Monsieur Binard in a lordly way.

"Oh! Papa!" cried the three older antelopes.

"I know what I'm talking about," retorted Binard.

He raised a curtain of the cradle which my brother presumed empty but which was now shown to be entirely filled by a large child who had slept calmly through all the noise and bustle. One of the antelopes came over and tenderly drew the curtain down again.

His mission over, my brother drank the warm wine which

he had well and truly earned and which the little newly-confined mother was sipping too. Already she was gay and laughing. Then he bowed to the entire long-eyed troop and went out, puzzled and worried. The earth was steaming with damp but, above the low fog, the bright dancing fire of the first stars announced the coming frost.

"Your daughter seems extremely young," said my brother. "Luckily, she's come through it well."

"She's strong. You needn't be afraid," said Monsieur Binard.

"How old is she?"

"Fifteen in four months' time."

"Fifteen! She was taking a big risk. What girls are! Do you know the . . . the creature who . . ."

Monsieur Binard made no reply other than slapping the hindquarters of the grey mare with the flat of his hand but he lifted his chin with such an obvious, such an intolerable expression of fatuity that my brother hastened his departure.

"If she has any fever, let me know."

"She won't," Monsieur Binard assured him with great dignity.

"So you know more about these things than I do?"

"No. But I know my daughters. I've four of them and you must have seen for yourself that there's not much wrong with them. I know them."

He said no more and ran his hand over his moustache. He waited till the grey mare had adroitly turned in the narrow courtyard, then he went back into his house.

Sido, my mother, did not like this story which she often turned over in her mind. Sometimes she spoke violently about Monsieur Binard, calling him bitterly "the corrupt widower", sometimes she let herself go off into commentaries for which afterwards she would blush.

"Their house is very well kept. The child of the youngest

one has eyelashes as long as *that*. I saw her the other day, she was suckling her baby on the doorstep, it was enchanting. Whatever am I saying? It was abominable, of course, when one knows the facts."

She went off into a dream, impatiently untwisting the entangled steel chain and black cord from which hung her two pairs of spectacles.

"After all," she began again, "the ancient patriarchs . . ."

But she suddenly became aware that I was only fifteen and a half and she went no further.

The Rainy Moon

"OH, I can manage that," the withered young girl told me. "Yes certainly, I can bring you each set of pages as I type them as you'd rather not trust them to the post."

"Can you? That would be kind of you. You needn't trouble to come and collect my manuscript, I'll bring it to you in batches as I go along. I go out for a walk every morning."

"It's so good for the health," said Mademoiselle Barberet.

She gave a superficial smile and pulled one of the two little sausages of gold hair, threaded with white, that she wore tied on the nape with a black ribbon bow, forward again into its proper place, over her right shoulder, just below the ear. This odd way of doing her hair did not prevent Mademoiselle Barberet from being perfectly correct and pleasant to look at from her pale blue eyes to her slender feet, from her delicate, prematurely-aged mouth to her frail hands whose small bones were visible under the transparent skin. Her freshly-ironed linen collar and her plain black dress called for the accessories of a pair of those glazed cotton over-sleeves that were once the badge of writers. But typists, who do not write, do not wear their sleeves out below the elbows.

"You're temporarily without your secretary, Madame?"

"No. The girl who used to type my manuscripts has just got married. But I don't possess a secretary. I shouldn't know what to do with a secretary, you see. I write everything by hand.

And, besides, my flat is small, I should hear the noise of the typewriter."

"Oh! I do understand, I do understand," said Mademoiselle Barberet. "There's a gentleman I work for who only writes on the right-hand half of the pages. For a little while, I took over the typing for Monsieur Henri Duvernois who would never have anything but pale yellow paper."

She gave a knowing smile that lumped together and excused all the manias of scribblers and, producing a file—I noticed she matched the cardboard to the blue of my paper—she neatly put away the sixty or so pages I had brought.

"I used to live in this neighbourhood once. But I can't recognise anything any more. It's all straightened out and built up; even the street's disappeared or changed its name. I'm not wrong, am I, Mademoiselle?"

Mademoiselle Barberet removed her spectacles, out of politeness. Her blue eyes were then unable to see me and her aimless gaze was lost in the void.

"Yes, I believe so," she said, without conviction. "You must be right."

"Have you lived here long?"

"Oh, yes," she said emphatically.

She fluttered her lashes as if she were lying.

"I think that, in the old days, a row of houses opposite hid the rise."

I got up to go over to the window and passed out of the circle of light that the green-shaded lamp threw over the table. But I did not see much of the view outside. The lights of the town made no breaches in the blue dusk of evening that falls early, in February. I pushed up the coarse muslin curtain with my forehead and rested my hand on the window catch. Immediately, I was conscious of the faint, rather pleasant giddiness that accompanies dreams of falling and flying. For I was clutching in my hand the peculiar hasp, the little cast-iron mermaid, whose shape my palm had not forgotten after all these years. I could not prevent myself from turning round in an abrupt, questioning way.

Not having resumed her glasses, Mademoiselle Barberet noticed nothing. My enquiring gaze went from her civil, short-sighted face to the walls of the room, almost entirely covered with gloomy steel engravings framed in black, coloured reproductions of Chaplin—the fair-haired woman in the black velvet collar—and Henner, and even, a handicraft rare nowadays, thatchwork frames which young girls have lost the art of fashioning out of tubes of golden straw. Between an enlarged photograph and a sheaf of bearded rye, a few square inches of wallpaper remained bare; on it I could make out roses whose colour had almost gone, purple convolvulus faded to grey and tendrils of bluish foliage, in short, the ghost of a bunch of flowers, repeated a hundred times all over the walls, that it was impossible for me not to recognise. The twin doors, to right and left of the blind fireplace where a stove was fitted, promptly became intelligible and, beyond their closed panels, I revisualised all I had long ago left.

Behind me, I became unpleasantly conscious that Mademoiselle Barberet must be getting bored, so I resumed our conversation.

"It's pretty, this outlook."

"Above all, it's light, for a first floor. You won't mind if I put your pages in order, Madame, I notice there's a mistake in the sequence of numbers. The three comes after the seven and I can't see the eighteen."

"I'm not in the least surprised, Mademoiselle Barberet. Yes, do sort them out, do . . ."

"Above all, it's light." Light, this mezzanine floor, where, at all times of the year, almost at all times of the day, I used to switch on a little chandelier under the ceiling-rose? On that same ceiling there suddenly appeared a halo of yellow light. Mademoiselle Barberet had just turned on a glass bowl, marbled to look like onyx, that reflected the light up on to the ceiling-rose, the same icing-sugar ceiling-rose under which, in other days, a branch of gilded metal flowered into five opaline blue corollas.

"A lot of mistakes, Mademoiselle Barberet? Especially a lot of crossings-out."

"Oh, I work from manuscripts much more heavily corrected than this. The carbon copy, shall I do it in purple or black?"

"In black. Tell me, Mademoiselle . . ."

"My name's Rosita, Madame. At least, it's nicer than Barberet."

"Mademoiselle Rosita, I'm going to abuse your kindness. I see that I've brought you the whole of my text up-to-date and I haven't a rough copy. If you could type page sixty-two for me. I could take it away with me so as to get my sequence right."

"Why, of course, Madame. I'll do it at once. It'll only take me seven minutes. I'm not boasting, but I type fast. Do please sit down."

All that I wanted to do was just that, to stay a few minutes longer and find in this room the traces, if any, of my having lived here; to make sure I was not mistaken, to marvel at the fact that a wallpaper, preserved by the shade, should not, after all these years, be in tatters. "Above all, it's light." Evidently the sanitary authorities or perhaps just some speculative builder had rased all the bank of houses that, in the old days, hid the slope of one of Paris's hills from my unwitting eyes.

To the right of the fireplace—in which a little wood stove, flanked by its provision of sticks, tarred road-blocks and old packing-case staves, was snoring discreetly—I could see a door and, to the right, a door exactly like it. Through the one on the right, I used to enter my bedroom. The one on the left led into the little hall, which ended in a recess I had turned into a bathroom by installing a slipper-bath and a geyser. Another room, very dark and fairly large, which I never used, served as a boxroom. As to the kitchen. . . . That minute kitchen came back to my memory with extraordinary vividness; in winter, its old-fashioned blue-tiled range was touched by a ray of sun that glided as far as the equally old-world cooking-stove, standing on very tall legs and faintly Louis Quinze in design. When I could not, as they say, stick it any more, I used to go into the kitchen. I always found something to do there; polishing up the jointed gas-pipe, running a wet cloth over the blue porcelain tiles, emptying out the water of faded flowers and rubbing the vase clear again with a handful of coarse, damp salt.

Two good big cupboards, of the jam-cupboard type; a cellar that contained nothing but a bottle-rack, empty of bottles.

"I'll have finished in one moment, Madame."

What I most longed to see again was the bedroom to the right of the fireplace, *my* room, with its solitary square window, and the old-fashioned bed-closet whose doors I had removed. That marvellous bedroom, dark on one side, light on the other! It would have suited a happy, clandestine couple, but it had fallen to my lot when I was alone and very far from happy.

"Thank you so much. I don't need an envelope, I'll fold up the page and put it in my bag."

The front door, slammed to by an impetuous hand, banged. A sound is always less evocative than a smell, yet I recognised that one and gave a start, as Mademoiselle Barberet did too. Then a second door, the door of my bathroom—was shut more gently.

"Mademoiselle Rosita, if I've got through enough work, you'll see me again on Monday morning round about eleven."

Pretending to make a mistake, I went towards the right of the fireplace. But, between the door and myself, I found Mademoiselle Barberet, infinitely attentive.

"Excuse me. It's the one the other side."

Out in the street, I could not help smiling, realising that I had run heedlessly down the stairs without making a single mistake and that my feet, if I may risk the expression, still knew the staircase by heart. From the pavement, I studied my house, unrecognisable under a heavy make-up of mortar. The hall, too, was well-disguised and now, with its dado of pink and green tiles, reminded me of the baleful chilliness of those mass-produced villas on the Riviera. The old dairy on the right of the entrance now sold banjos and accordions. But, on the left, the "Palace of Dainties" remained intact, except for a coat of cream paint. Pink sugared almonds in bowls, red-currant balls in full glass jars, emerald peppermints and beige caramels . . . And the slabs of coffee cream and the sharp-tasting orange crescents . . . And those lentil-shaped sweets, wrapped in silver paper, like worm-pills, and flavoured with aniseed. At the back of the shop I recognised too, under their coat of new paint, the hundred little drawers with protruding navels, the low-carved counter and all the charming woodwork of shops that date from the Second Empire, the old-fashioned scales whose shining copper pans danced under the beam like swings.

I had a sudden desire to buy those squares of liquorice called "Pontefract cakes" whose flavour is so full-bodied that, after them, nothing seems eatable. A mauve lady of sixty came forward to serve me. So this was all that survived of her former self, that handsome blonde proprietress who had once been so fond of sky-blue. She did not recognise me and, in my confusion, I asked her for peppermint creams which I cannot abide.

The following Monday, I would have the opportunity of coming back for the little Pontefract cakes that give such a vile taste to fresh eggs, red wine and every other comestible.

To my cost, I have proved from long experience than the past is a far more violent temptation to me than the craving to know the future. Breaking with the present, retracing my steps, the sudden apparition of a new, unpublished slice of the past is accompanied by a shock utterly unlike anything else and which I cannot lucidly describe. Marcel Proust, gasping with asthma amid the bluish haze of fumigations and the shower of pages dropping from him one by one, pursued a bygone and completed time. It is neither the true concern nor the natural inclination of writers to love the future. They have quite enough to do with being incessantly forced to invent their characters' future which, in any case, they draw up from the well of their own past. Mine, whenever I plunge into it, turns me dizzy. And when it is the turn of the past to emerge unexpectedly, to raise its dripping mermaid's head into the lights of the present and look at me with delusive eyes long hidden in the depths, I clutch at it all the more fiercely. Besides the person I once was, it reveals to me the one I would have liked to be. What is the use of employing occult means and occult individuals in order to know that person better? Fortune-tellers and astrologers, readers of tarot cards and palmists are not interested in my past. Among the figures, the swords, the cups and the coffee-grounds my past is written in three sentences. The seeress briskly sweeps away bygone "ups and downs" and a few vague "successes" that have had no marked results, then hurriedly plants on the whole the plaster rose of a today shorn of mystery and a tomorrow of which I expect nothing.

Among fortune-tellers, there are very few whom our presence momentarily endows with second sight. I have met some who went triumphantly backwards in time, gathering definite, blindingly true, pictures from my past, then leaving me shipwrecked amidst a fascinating welter of dead people, children from the past, dates and places, leapt, with one bound, into my future: "In three years, in six years, your situation will be greatly improved." Three years! Six years! Exasperated, I forgot them and their promises too.

But the temptation persists, along with a definite itch, to which I do not yield, to climb three floors or work a shaky lift, stop on a landing and ring three times. You see, one day, I might hear my own footsteps approaching on the other side of the door and my own voice asking me rudely: "What is it?" I open the door to myself and, naturally, I am wearing what I used to wear in the old days, something in the nature of a dark pleated tartan skirt and a high-collared shirt. The bitch I had in 1900 puts up her hackles and shivers when she sees me double . . . The end is missing. But as good nightmares go, it's a good nightmare.

For the first time in my life, I had just, by going into Mademoiselle Barberet's flat, gone back into my own home. The coincidence obsessed me during the days that followed my visit. I looked into it and I discovered something ironically interesting about it. Who was it who had suggested Mademoiselle Barberet to me? None other than my young typist who was leaving her job to get married. She was marrying a handsome boy who was "taking", as they say, a gymnasium in the district of Grenelle and whom she had been anxious I should meet. While he was explaining to me, thoroughly convinced of my passionate interest, that, nowadays, a gymnasium in a working-class district was a goldmine, I was listening to his slight provincial accent. "I come from B . . . like all my family," he mentioned, in passing. "And like the person who was responsible for certain searing disappointments in my life," I added mentally. Disappointments in love, naturally. They are the least worthy of being brought back to mind but, sometimes, they behave just like a cut in which a fragment of hair is hidden; they heal badly.

This second man from B . . . had vanished, having fulfilled his obligations towards me which consisted of flinging me back, for unknown ends, into a known place. He had struck me as gentle; as slightly heavy, like all young men made tired and drowsy by injudicious physical culture. He was dark, with beautiful southern eyes, as the natives of B . . . often are. And he carried off the passionate young girl, thin to the point of emaciation, who had been typing my manuscripts for three years and crying over them when my story ended sadly.

The following Monday, I brought Mademoiselle Rosita the meagre fruit—twelve pages—of work that was anything but a labour of love. There was no motive whatever for being in a hurry to have two typed copies of a bad first draft, none except the pleasure and the risk of braving the little flat of long ago. "Worth doing just this once more," I told myself, "then I'll put my mind on other things." Nevertheless, my remembering hand searched the length of the door-jamb for the pretty beaded braid, my pretentious bell-pull of the old days, and found an electric push-button.

An unknown person promptly opened the door, answered me only with a nod and showed me into the room with two windows where Mademoiselle Barberet joined me.

"Have you worked well, Madame? The bad weather hasn't had too depressing an effect on you?"

Her small, cold hand had hurriedly withdrawn from mine and was pulling forward the two sausage-curls tied with black ribbon and settling them in their proper place on her right shoulder, nestling in her neck.

She smiled at me with the tempered solicitude of a well-trained nurse or a fashionable dentist's receptionist or one of those women of uncertain age who do vague odd jobs in beauty-parlours.

"It's been a bad week for me, Mademoiselle Rosita. What's more, you'll find my writing difficult to read."

"I don't think so, Madame. A round hand is seldom illegible."

She looked at me amiably; behind the thick glasses, the blue of her eyes seemed diluted.

"Just imagine, when I arrived, I thought I must have come to the wrong floor, the person who opened the door to me . . ."

"Yes. That's my sister," said Mademoiselle Barberet as if, by satisfying my indiscreet curiosity, she hoped to prevent it from going any further.

But when we are in the grip of curiosity, we have no shame.

"Ah! That's your sister. Do you work together?"

Mademoiselle Barberet's transparent skin quivered on her cheekbones.

"No, Madame. For some time now, my sister's health has needed looking after."

This time, I did not dare insist further. For a few moments more I lingered in my drawing-room that was now an office, taking in how much lighter it was. I strained my ear in vain for anything that might echo in the heart of the house or in the depths of myself and I went away, carrying with me a romantic burden of conjectures. The sister who was ill—and why not melancholy mad? Or languishing over an unhappy love-affair? Or struck with some monstrous deformity and kept in the shade? That is what I'm like when I let myself go.

During the following days, I had no leisure to indulge my wild fancies further. At that particular time F.-I. Mouthon had asked me to write a serial-novelette for *Le Journal.* Was this intelligent, curly-haired man making his first mistake? In all honesty, I had protested that I should never be able to write the kind of serial that would have been suitable for the readers of a big daily paper. F.-I. Mouthon, who seemed to know more about it than I did myself, had winked his little elephant's eye, shaken his curly forehead, shrugged his heavy shoulders and—I had sat down to write a serial-novelette for which you will look in vain among my works. Mademoiselle Barberet was the only person who saw the first chapters before I tore them up. For, in the long run, I turned out to be right; I did not know how to write a serial-novelette.

On my return from my second visit to Mademoiselle Barberet, I re-read the forty typed pages.

And I swore to peg away at it, as they say, like the very devil, to deprive myself of the flea-market and the cinema and even of lunch in the Bois. . . . This, however, did not mean Armenonville or even the Cascade, but pleasant impromptu picnics on the grass, all the better if Annie de Pène, a precious friend, came with me. There is no lack of milder days, once we are in February. We would take our bicycles, a fresh loaf stuffed with butter and sardines, two "delicatessen" sausage-rolls we bought at a pork butcher's near La Muette and some apples, the whole secured with string to a water-bottle in a wicker jacket, filled with white wine. As to coffee, we drank that at a place near the station at Auteuil, very black, very tasteless but piping hot and syrupy with sugar.

Few memories have remained as dear to me as the memory of those meals without plates, cutlery or cloth, of those expeditions on two wheels. The cool sky, the rain in drops, the snow in flakes, the sparse, rusty grass, the tameness of the birds. These idylls suited a certain state of mind, far removed from happiness, frightened yet obstinately hopeful. By means of them, I have succeeded in taking the sting out of an unhappiness that wept small, restrained tears, a sorrow without great storms, in short a love-affair that began just badly enough to make it end still worse. Does one imagine those periods, during which anodynes conquer an illness one believed serious at the time, fade easily from one's memory? I have already compared them, elsewhere, to the "blanks" that introduce space and order between the chapters of a book. I should very much like—late in life, it is true—to call them "merciful blanks", those days in which work and sauntering and friendship played the major part, to the detriment of love. Blessed days, sensitive to the light of the external world, in which the relaxed and idle senses made chance discoveries. It was not very long after I had been enjoying this kind of holiday that I made the acquaintance of Mademoiselle Barberet.

It was—and for good reason—three weeks before I went to see her again. Conceiving a loathing for my serial-novelette every time I tried to introduce "action", swift adventure and a touch of the sinister into it, I had harnessed myself to short stories for *La Vie Parisienne*. It was therefore with a new heart and a light step that I climbed the slopes of her part of Paris, which shall be nameless. Not knowing whether Mademoiselle Barberet liked "Pontefract cakes" I bought her several small bunches of snowdrops, that had not yet lost their very faint perfume of orange-flowers, squeezed tight together in one big bunch.

Behind the door, I heard her little heels running forward over the uncarpeted wooden floor. I recognise a step more quickly than a shape, a shape more quickly than a face. It was bright out-of-doors and in the room with the two windows. Between the photographic enlargements, the "studies" of woodland landscapes, and the straw frames with red ribbon bows, the February sun was consuming the last faint outlines of my roses and blue convolvulus on the wallpaper.

"*This* time, Mademoiselle Rosita, I haven't come empty-handed! Here are some little flowers for you and here are two short stories, twenty-nine pages of manuscript."

"It's too much, Madame, it's too much . . ."

"It's the length they have to be. It takes thirteen closely-written pages, a short story for *La Vie Parisienne*."

"I was talking of the flowers, Madame."

"They're not worth mentioning. And you know, on Monday, I've a feeling I'm going to bring you . . ."

Behind her spectacles, Mademoiselle Barberet's eyes fixed themselves on me, forgetting to dissemble the fact that they were red, bruised, filled with bitter water and so sad that I broke off my sentence. She made a gesture with her hand, and murmured:

"I apologise. I have worries . . ."

Few women keep their dignity when they are in tears. The withered young girl in distress wept simply, decently controlling the shaking of her hands and her voice. She wiped her eyes and her glasses and gave me a kind of smile with one side of her mouth.

"It's one of those days . . . it's because of the child, I mean of my sister."

"She's ill, isn't she?"

"In one sense, yes. She has no disease," she said emphatically. "It's since she got married. It's changed her character. She's so rough with me. Of course all marriages can't turn out well, one knows that."

I am not very fond of other people's matrimonial troubles, they bear an inevitable resemblance to my own personal disappointments. So I was anxious to get away at once from the sorrowing Barberet and the unhappily-married sister. But, just as I was leaving her, a little blister in the coarse glass of one of the window-panes caught a ray of sun and projected on to the opposite wall the little halo of rainbow colours I used once to call the "rainy moon". The apparition of that illusory planet shot me back so violently into the past that I remained standing where I was, transfixed and fascinated.

"Look, Mademoiselle Rosita. How pretty that is."

I put my finger on the wall, in the centre of the little planet ringed with seven colours.

"Yes," she said. "We know that reflection well. Just fancy, my sister's frightened of it."

"Frightened? What do you mean, frightened? Why? What does she say about it?"

Mademoiselle smiled at my eagerness.

"Oh! You know . . . silly things, the sort that nervous children imagine. She says it's an omen. She calls it her sad little sun, she says it only shines to warn her something bad is going to happen. Goodness knows what else. As if the refractions of a prism really could influence . . .

Mademoiselle Barberet gave a superior smile.

"You're right," I said weakly. "But those are charming poetic fancies. Your sister is a poet without realising it."

Mademoiselle Barberet's blue eyes were fixed on the place where the rainbow-coloured ghost had been before a passing cloud had just eclipsed it.

"The main thing is she's a very unreasonable young woman."

"She lives in the other . . . in another part of the flat?"

Mademoiselle Barberet's gaze switched to the closed door on the right of the fireplace.

"Another part, you could hardly call it that. They chose . . . Her bedroom and dressing-room are separate from my bedroom."

I nodded "Yes, yes," as my thorough acquaintance with the place gave me the right to do.

"Is your sister like you to look at?"

I made myself gentle and spoke tonelessly as one does to

people asleep so as to make them answer one from the depths of their slumber.

"Like me? Oh dear, no! To begin with, there's a certain difference of age between us, and she's dark. And then, as to character, we couldn't be less alike in every way."

"Ah! She's dark . . . One of these days you must let me meet her. There's no hurry! I'm leaving you my manuscript. If you don't see me on Monday . . . Would you like me to settle up with you for the typing you've already done?"

Mademoiselle Barberet blushed and refused, then blushed and accepted. And, although I stopped in the hall to make some unnecessary suggestion, no sound came from my bedroom and nothing revealed the presence of the dark sister.

"She calls it her sad little sun. She says that it foretells something bad. Whatever can I have bequeathed to that reflection, that looks like a planet in a ring of haze, where the red is never anywhere but next to the purple? In the old days, when the wind was high and the sky cloudy, it would keep vanishing, reappearing, fading away again, and its caprices would distract me for a moment from my state of suspense, of perpetual waiting."

I admit that, as I descended the slope of the hill, I gave myself up to excitement. The play of coincidences shed a false, unhoped-for light on my life. Already I was promising myself that the "Barberet story" would figure in a prominent place in the fantastic gallery we secretly furnish and which we open more readily to strangers than to our near ones; the gallery reserved for premonitions, for the phenomena of mistaken identity, for visions and predictions. In it I had already lodged the story of the woman with the candle, the story of Jeanne D.; the story of the woman who read the tarot pack and of the little boy who rode on horseback.

In any case, the Barberet story, barely even roughly sketched, was already acting for me as a "snipe's bandage". That is what I used to call, and still call, a particular kind of unremarkable and soothing event that I liken to the dressing of wet clay and bits of twig, the marvellous little splint the snipe binds round its foot when a shot has broken it. A visit to the cinema, provided the films are sufficiently mediocre, counts as a snipe's bandage. But, on the contrary, an evening in the company of intelligent friends who know what it is to be hurt and are courageous and disillusioned, undoes the bandage. Symphonic music generally tears it off, leaving me flayed. Poured out by a steady, indifferent voice, pronouncements and predictions are compresses and camomile-tea to me.

"I'm going to tell the Barberet story to Annie de Pène." I mentally began. And then I told nothing at all. Would not Annie's subtle ear and those lively bronze eyes of hers have weighed up and condemned everything in my narrative that revealed no more than the craving to go over old ground again, to deck out what was over and done with in a new coat of paint? "That window, Annie, where a young woman whose man has left her, spends nearly all her time waiting, listening—just as I did long ago."

I said nothing to Annie. It is as well for a toy to be played with in solitude, if something or other about its colour, about its acid varnish, about a chance distortion of its shadow, warns one it may be dangerous. But I went off and translated the "Barberet story" into commonplace language for the benefit of the woman who came by the day to "make and mend" for me, a stout brunette who was relaxing after singing in operetta in Oran by sewing and ironing for other people. In order to listen to me, Marie Mallier stopped crushing gathers under a cruel thumbnail, blew into her thimble and waited, her needle poised.

"And then what happened?"

"That's the end."

"Oh," said Marie Mallier. "It seemed to me more like a beginning."

The words enchanted me. I read into them the most romantic omen and I swore to myself I would not delay another moment in making the acquaintance of the dark, unhappily-married sister who lived in my gloomy bedroom and was frightened of my "rainy moon".

Those tugs on my sleeve, those little presents fate has offered me might have given me the power of escaping from myself, sloughing my skin and emerging in new, variegated colours. I believe they might have succeeded, had I not lacked the society and influence of someone for whom there is hardly any difference between what really happens and what does not, between fact and possiblity, between an event and the narration of it.

Much later on, when I came to know Francis Carco I realised that he would, for example, have interpreted my stay at Bella-Vista and my meeting with the Barberets with an unbridled imagination. He would have plucked out of them the catastrophic truth, the element of something unfinished, something left suspended that spurs imagination and terror to a gallop; in short, their poetry. I saw, years afterwards, how a poet makes use of tragic embellishment and lends a mere news item the fascination of some white, inanimate face behind a pane.

Lacking a companion with a fiery imagination, I clung to a rational view of things, notably of fear and of hallucination. This was a real necessity, as I lived alone. On some nights, I would look very carefully round my little flat; I would open my shutters to let the nocturnal light play on the ceiling while I waited for the light of day. The next morning, my concierge, when she brought me my coffee, would silently flourish the key she had found in the lock, on the outside. Most of the time

I gave no thought to perils that might come from the unknown and I treated ghosts with scant respect.

That was how, the following Monday, I treated a window in the Barberet flat which I had entered at the same moment as a March wind with great sea pinions that flung all the papers on the floor. Mademoiselle Rosita put both hands over her ears, and shrieked "Ah!" as she shut her eyes. I gripped the cast-iron mermaid with a familiar hand and closed the window with one turn of my wrist.

"At the very first go!" exclaimed Mademoiselle Barberet admiringly. "That's extraordinary! I hardly ever manage to . . . Oh, goodness, all these typed copies flying about! Monsieur Vandérem's novel! Monsieur Pierre Veber's short story! This wind! Luckily I'd put your text back in its folder. . . . Here's the top copy, Madame, and the carbon. There are several traces of india rubber. If you'd like me to re-do some of the scratched pages, it'll be a pleasure to me, tonight after dinner."

"Find yourself more exciting pleasures, Mademoiselle Rosita. Go to the cinema. Do you like the cinema?"

The avidity of a small girl showed in her face, accentuating the fine wrinkles round the mouth.

"I adore it, Madame! We have a very good local cinema, five francs for quite good seats, that shows splendid films. But, at this moment, I can't possibly . . ."

She broke off and fixed her gaze on the door to the right of the fireplace.

"Is it still your sister's health? Couldn't her husband take on the job of . . ."

In spite of myself, I imitated her prudish way of leaving her sentences unfinished. She flushed and said hastily:

"Her husband doesn't live here, Madame."

"Ah! he doesn't live . . . And she, what does she do? Is she waiting for him to come back?"

"I . . . Yes, I think so."

"All the time?"

"Day and night."

I stood up abruptly and began to pace the room, from the window to the door, from the door to the far wall, from the far wall to the fireplace; the room where once *I* had waited—day and night.

"That's stupid!" I exclaimed. "That's the last thing to do. Do you hear me, the very last!"

Mademoiselle Barberet mechanically pulled out the spiral of hair that caressed her shoulder and her withered angel's face followed my movement to and fro.

"If *I* knew her, that sister of yours, I'd tell her straight to her face that she's chosen the worst possible tactics. They couldn't be more . . . more idiotic."

"Ah! I'd be only too glad, Madame, if you'd tell her so! Coming from you, it would have far more weight than from me. She makes no bones about making it plain to me that old maids have no right to speak on certain topics. In which she may well be mistaken, moreover . . ." Mademoiselle Barberet lowered her eyes and gave a little resentful toss of her chin.

"A fixed idea isn't always a good idea. She's in there, with her fixed idea. When she can't stand it any more, she goes downstairs. She says she wants to buy some sweets. She says: 'I'm going to telephone.' To other people! As if she thought I was deceived for a moment!"

"You're not on the telephone?"

I raised my eyes to the ceiling. A little hole in the moulded cornice still showed where the telephone wire had passed through it. When *I* was in this place, I had the telephone. I could beg and implore without having to bother to go outside.

"Not yet, Madame. We're going to have it put in, of course."

She blushed, as she did whenever there was a question of money or of lack of money, and seemed to make a desperate resolve.

"Madame, since you think as I do that my sister is wrong to be so obstinate, if you have two minutes . . ."

"I have two minutes."

"I'll go and tell my sister."

She went out through the hall instead of opening the door on the right of the fireplace. She walked gracefully, carried on small, arched feet. Almost at once, she came back, agitated and with red rims to her eyelids.

"Oh! I don't know how to apologise. She's terrible. She says 'Not on your life' and 'What are you sticking your nose in for?' and 'I wish to goodness everyone would shut up.' She says nothing but rude things."

Mademoiselle Barberet blew her distress into her handkerchief, rubbed her nose and became ugly, as if on purpose. I had just time to think: "Really, I'm being unnecessarily tactful with these females" before I turned the handle of the right-hand door which recognised me and obeyed me without a sound. I did not cross the threshold of *my* room whose half-closed shutters filled it with a faintly green dusk. At the far end of the room, on a divan-bed that seemed not to have moved from the place I had chosen for it in the old days, a young woman, curled up like a gun-dog, raised the dim oval of her face in my direction. For a second, I had that experience only dreams dare conjure up; I saw before me, hostile, hurt, stubbornly hoping, the young self I should never be again, whom I never ceased disowning and regretting.

But there is nothing lasting in any touch of the fabulous we experience outside sleep. The young myself stood up, spoke and was no longer anything more than a stranger, the sound of whose voice dissipated all my precious mystery.

"Madame . . . But I told my sister—Really, Rosita, whatever are you thinking of? My room's untidy, I'm not well. You must understand, Madame, why I couldn't ask you to come in."

She had only taken two or three steps towards me. In spite of the gloom, I could make out that she was rather short, but upright and self-assured. As a cloud outside uncovered the sun, the construction of her face was revealed to me, a straight, firm nose, strongly marked brows, a little Roman chin. It is a double attraction when well-modelled features are both youthful and severe.

I made myself thoroughly amiable to this young woman who was throwing me out.

"I understand perfectly, Madame. But do realise that your sister's only crime was to imagine I might be of some use to you. She made a mistake. Mademoiselle Rosita, it'll be all right, won't it, to fetch the typescript as usual, next Monday?"

The two sisters did not notice the ease with which I found the curtained door at the far end of the room, crossed the dark little hall and shut myself out. Downstairs, I was joined by Rosita.

"Madame, Madame, you're not angry?"

"Not in the very least. Why should I be. She's pretty, your sister. By the way, what's her name?"

"Adèle. But she likes to be called Délia. Her married name is Essendier, Madame Essendier. Now she's heartbroken, she'd like to see you."

"Very well then! She shall see me on Monday," I conceded with dignity.

As soon as I was alone, the temptation to be entrapped in this snare of resemblances lost its power; the strident glare of the Rue des Martyrs at midday dissipated the spell of the bedroom and the young woman curled up "day and night". On the steep slope, what quantities of chickens with their necks hanging down, small legs of mutton displayed outside shops, fat sausages, enamelled beer-mugs with landscapes on them, oranges piled up in formation like cannon-balls for ancient artillery, withered apples, unripe bananas, anaemic chicory glutinous wads of dates, daffodils, pink "milanese" panties, camiknickers encrusted with imitation Chantilly, little bags of ingredients for home-made stomach remedies, mercerised lisle stockings. What a number of postiches—they used to call them "chichés"—of ties sold in threes, of shapeless housewives, of blondes in down-at-heel shoes and brunettes in curling-pins, of mother-of-pearl smelts, of butcher-boys with fat, cherubic faces. All this profusion, which had not changed in the least, awakened my appetite and vigorously restored me to reality.

Away with these Barberets! That chit of a girl with no manners was a sniveller, a lazy slut who must have driven her husband's patience beyond all bounds. Caught between a prim, fussy old maid and a jealous young wife, what a charming life for a man!

Thus, wandering along and gazing at the shops, did I indict Madame Délia Essendier, christened Adèle . . . "*Adèle . . . T'es belle . . .*" Standing in front of a sumptuous Universal Provision Store, I hummed the silly, already hoary song, as I admired the oranges between the tumbled rice and the sweating coffee, the red apples and the split green peas. Just as in Nice one longs to buy the entire flower market, here I would have liked to buy a whole stall of eatables, from the forced lettuces to the blue packets of semolina. "*Adèle . . . T'es belle . . .*" I hummed.

"If you ask *me*," said an insolent-eyed local girl, right under my nose, "I'd say *The Merry Widow* was a lot more up-to-date than that old thing."

I did not reply, for this strapping blonde with her hair curled to last a week, planted solidly on her feet and sugared with coarse powder, was, after all, speaking for the whole generation destined to devour my own.

All the same I was not old and, above all, I did not look my real age. But a private life that was clouded and uncertain, a solitude that bore no resemblance to peace had wiped all the life and charm out of my face. I have never had less notice taken of me by men than during those particular years whose date I dissemble here. It was much later on that they treated me again to the good honest offensive warmth of their looks, to that genial concupiscence which will make an admirer, when he ought to be kissing your hand, give you a friendly pinch on the buttock.

The following Monday, on a sultry March morning when the sky was a whitish blue and Paris, dusty and surprised, was spilling her overflow of jonquils and anemones into the streets, I walked limply up the steep slope of Montmartre. Already the wide-open entrances to the blocks of flats were ejecting the air that was colder inside than out, along with the carbonic smell of stoves that had been allowed to go out. I rang the bell of Mademoiselle Rosita's flat; she did not answer it and I joyfully welcomed the idea that she might be out, busy buying a pale escallop of veal or some ready-cooked sauerkraut. . . . To salve my conscience, I rang a second time. Something brushed faintly against the door and the parquet creaked.

"Is that you, Eugène?" asked the voice of Mademoiselle Barberet.

She spoke almost in a whisper and I could hear her breathing at the level of the keyhole.

As if exculpating myself, I cried:

"It's me, Mademoiselle Rosita! I'm bringing some pages of manuscript . . ."

Mademoiselle Barberet gave a little "Ah!" but did not open the door at once. Her voice changed and she said in mincing tones:

"Oh, Madame, what can I have been thinking of. I'll be with you in a moment."

A safety-bolt slid in its catch and the door was half-opened.

"Be very careful, Madame, you might stumble . . . My sister's on the floor."

She could not have spoken more politely and indifferently had she said: "My sister's gone out to the post." I did, in fact, stumble against a body lying prone, with its feet pointing skywards and its hands and face mere white blurs. The sight of it threw me into a state of cowardice which I intensely dislike. Drawing away from the body stretched out on the floor, I asked, to give the impression of being helpful:

"What's the matter with her? Would you like me to call someone?"

Then I noticed that the sensitive Mademoiselle Rosita did not seem to be greatly perturbed.

"It's a fainting fit . . . a kind of dizziness that isn't serious. Let me just get the smelling salts and a wet towel."

She was already running off. I noticed she had forgotten to turn the light on and I had no trouble in finding the switch to the right of the front-door. A ceiling-light in the form of a plate with a crinkled border feebly lit up the hall and I bent down over the prostrate young woman. She was lying in an extremely decent attitude, with her skirt down to her ankles. One of her bent arms, whose hand lay palm upwards, beside her ear, seemed to be commanding attention, and her head was slightly averted on her shoulders. Really, a very pretty young woman, taking refuge in a sulky swoon. I could hear Mademoiselle Rosita in the bedroom, opening and shutting a drawer, slamming the door of a cupboard.

And I found the seconds drag heavily as I stared at the tubular umbrella-stand, at the cane table; in particular, at a door-curtain of Algerian design that roused a regret in my heart for a rather pretty strip of leafy tapestry that used to hang there in the old days. As I looked down at the motionless young woman, I realised, from a narrow gleam between her eyelids, that she was secretly watching me. For some reason, I felt disagreeably surprised, as if by some practical joke. I bent over this creature who was shamming a faint and applied another approved remedy for swoons—a good, hard, stinging slap. She received it with an offended snarl and sat up with a jerk.

"Well! So you're better?" cried Rosita, who was arriving with a wet towel and a litre of salad vinegar.

"As you see, Madame slapped my hands," said Délia coldly. "You'd never have thought of that, would you? Help me to get up, please."

I could not avoid giving her my arm. And, supporting her thus, I entered the bedroom she had practically asked me to leave.

The room reverberated with the noises of the street that came up through the open window. There was just the same contrast I remembered so well between the cheerful noises and the mournful light. I guided the young pretender to the divan-bed.

"Rosita, perhaps you'd have the charity to bring me a glass of water?"

I began to realise that the two sisters adopted a bitter, bantering tone whenever they spoke to each other. Rosita's small steps went off towards the kitchen and I prepared to leave her younger sister's bedside. But, with an unexpected movement, Délia caught hold of my hand, then clasped her arms round my knees and wildly pressed her head against them.

You must remember that, at that period of my life, I was

still childless and that friendship, for me, wore the guise of undemonstrative, off-hand, unemotional comradeliness. You must also take into account that, for many months, I had been starved of the coarse, invigorating bread of physical contact. A kiss, a good warm hug, the fresh touch of a child or anyone young had remained so long out of my reach that they had become distant, almost forgotten joys. So this unknown young woman's outburst, her surge of tears and her sudden embrace stunned me. Rosita's return found me standing just where I was and the imploring arms unloosed their grip.

"I let the tap run for two minutes," explained the elder sister. "Madame, how can I apologise . . . "

I suddenly resented Mademoiselle Barberet's air of businesslike alacrity; her two ringlets bobbed on her right shoulder and she was slightly out of breath.

"Tomorrow morning," I interrupted, "I've got to buy some remnants in the Saint-Pierre market. So I could come and collect the typed copies and you can give me news of . . . this . . . young person. No, stay where you are. I know the way."

What stirred just now in the thicket? No, it isn't a rabbit. Nor a grass snake. Nor a bird, that travels in shorter spurts. Only lizards are so agile, so capable of covering a long distance fast, so reckless . . . It's a lizard. That large butterfly flying in the distance—I always had rather bad eyesight—you say it's a Swallowtail? No, it's a Large Tortoiseshell. Why? Because the one we're looking at glides magnificently as only the Large Tortoiseshell can, and the Swallowtail has a flapping flight. "My husband, such a placid man . . ." a friend of mine used to tell me. She did not see that he sucked his tongue all day long. She thought he was eating chewing-gum, not differentiating between the chewing of gum and the nervous sucking of the tongue. Personally, I thought that this man had cares on his mind or else that the presence of his wife exasperated him.

Ever since I had made the acquaintance of Délia Essendier I had found myself "recapping" in this way lessons I had learnt from my instinct, from animals, children, nature and my disquieting fellow human beings. It seemed to me that I needed more than ever to know of my own accord, without discussing it with anyone, that the lady going by has a left shoe that pinches her, that the person I am talking to is pretending to drink in my words but not even listening to me, that a certain woman who hides from herself the fact that she loves a certain man, cannot stop herself from following him like a magnet whenever he is in the room, but always turning her back to him. A dog with evil intentions sometimes limps out of nervousness.

Children, and people who retain some ingenuous trait of childhood, are almost indecipherable, I realise that. Nevertheless, in a child's face, there is just one revealing, unstable area, a space comprised between the nostril, the eye and the upper lip, where the waves of a secret delinquency break on the surface. It is as swift and devastating as lightning. Whatever the child's age, that little flash of guilt turns the child into a ravaged adult. I have seen a serious lie distort a little girl's nostril and upper lip like a hare-lip . . .

"Tell me, Délia . . ."

. . . but on Délia's features nothing explicit appeared. She took refuge in a smile—for me—or in bad temper directed against her elder sister, or else she entered into a sombre state of waiting, installing herself in it as if at the window of a watch-tower. She would half-sit, half-lie on her divan-bed, that was covered with a green material printed with blue nasturtiums—the last gasps of the vogue for "Liberty" fabrics—clutching a big cushion against her, propping her chin on it, and scarcely ever moving. Perhaps she was aware that her attitude suited her often cantankerous beauty.

"But tell me, Délia, when you got married, didn't you have a presentiment that . . ."

Propped up like that, with her skirt pulled down to her ankles, she seemed to be meditating, rather than waiting. Since profound meditation is not concerned with being expressive, Délia Essendier never turned her eyes to me, even when she was speaking. More often than not, she looked at the half-open window, the reservoir of air, the source of sounds, a greenish aquarium in the shade of the green and blue curtains. Or else she stared fixedly at the little slippers with which her feet were shod. I, too, in the old days, used to buy those little heelless slippers of imitation silk brocade, adorned with a flossy pompon on the instep. In those days they cost thirteen francs seventy-five and their poor material soon tarnished. The young voluntary recluse I saw before me did not bother herself with shoes. She was only half a recluse, going out in the morning to buy a squirrel's provisions, a provender of fresh bread, dry nuts, eggs and apples, and the little meat that sufficed for the appetite of the two sisters.

"Didn't you tell me, Délia . . ."

No. She had told me nothing. Her brief glance accused me of imagining things, of having no memory. What was I doing there, in a place which ought to have been forbidden ground for me, at the side of a woman young enough to give no indication of being a wife and who manifested neither virtues nor nobility of mind nor even as much intelligence as any lively, gentle animal? The answer, I insist, is that this was a period in my life which motherhood and happy love had not yet enriched with their marvellous commonplace.

People might already have taken me to task for my choice of associates—those who tried to got an extremely poor reception—and my friends might have been surprised, for example, to find me pacing up and down the Avenue du Bois in the company of a shabby groom who brought and took away the horses hired out by a riding-school. A former jockey who had been unlucky and come down in the world and who looked like an old glove. But he was a mine of information on everything to do with horses and dogs, diseases, remedies, fiery beverages that would kill or cure, and I liked his meaty conversation even though he did teach me too much about the way animals are "made-up" to get a better price for them. For example, I would gladly have been dispensed from knowing that they pour sealing-wax into a French bulldog's ears if it has slightly limp auricles. . . . The rest of his expert knowledge was fascinating.

With less fundamental richness, Marie Mallier had considerable charm. If any of my circle had decided to be captious about all the things Marie Mallier did in the course of what she broadly described as "touring in Operetta", I would not have stood for it. Reduced to accepting all and sundry, the only transgressions Marie Mallier really enjoyed were the unprofitable delights of sewing and ironing. For the spice of an occupation, generally considered innocent, can be more exciting than many a guilty act performed out of necessity.

"To make a darn so that the corners don't pucker and all the little loops on the wrong side stand out nice and even," Marie Mallier used to say. "It makes my mouth water like cutting a lemon!" Our vices are less a matter of yielding to temptation than of some obsessive love. Throwing oneself passionately into helping some unknown woman, founding hopes on her that would be discouraged by the wise affection of our friends, wildly adopting a child that is not ours, obstinately ruining ourselves for a man whom we probably hate, such are the strange manifestations of a struggle against ourselves that is sometimes called disinterestedness, sometimes perversity. When I was with Délia Essendier, I found myself once again as vulnerable, as prone to giving presents out of vanity as a schoolgirl who sells her books to buy a rosary, a ribbon or a little ring and slips them, with a shy note, into the desk of a beloved classmate.

Nevertheless, I did not love Délia Essendier and the beloved classmate I was seeking, who was she but my former self, that sad form stuck, like a petal between two pages, to the walls of an ill-starred refuge?

"Délia, haven't you got a photograph of your husband here?"

Since the day when her arms had clasped my knees, Délia had made no other mute appeal to me except, when I stood up to go, a gesture to hold me back by the hand, the gesture of an awkward young girl who has not learnt how to grip or offer a palm frankly. All she did was to pull on my fingers and hurriedly let them go, as if out of sulkiness, then turn away towards the window that was nearly always open. Following the suggestion of her gaze, it was I who would go over to the window and stare at the passers-by or rather at their lids for, in those days, all men wore hats. When the entrance down below swallowed up a man with a long stride, dressed in a blue overcoat, in spite of myself I would count the seconds and reckon the time it would take a visitor in a hurry to cross the hall, walk up to our floor and ring the bell. But no one would ring and I would breathe freely again.

"Your husband, does he write to you, Délia?"

This time, the reticent young person whom I continued to ask tactless questions, whether she left them unanswered or not, scanned me with her insulting gaze. But I was long past the stage of taking any notice of her disdain, and I repeated:

"Yes, I'm asking if your husband writes to you sometimes"?

My question produced a great effect on Rosita, who was

walking through the bedroom. She stopped short, as if waiting for her sister's reply.

"No," said Délia at last. "He doesn't write to me and it's just as well he doesn't. We've nothing to say to each other."

At this, Rosita opened her mouth and her eyes in astonishment. Then she continued her light-footed walk and, just before she disappeared, raised both her hands to her ears. This scandalised gesture revived my curiosity which, at times, died down. I must also admit that, going back to the scene of my unhappy, fascinating past, I found it shocking that Délia—Délia and not myself—should be lying on the divan-bed, playing at taking off and putting on her little slippers, while I, tired of an uncomfortable seat, got up to walk to and fro, to push the table closer to the window as if by accident, to measure the space once filled by a dark cupboard.

"Délia, was it you who chose this wallpaper?"

"Certainly not. *I'd* have liked a flowered paper, like the one in the living-room."

"What living-room?"

"The big room."

"Ah! yes. It isn't a living-room, because you don't live in it. I should be more inclined to call it the workroom because your sister works in it."

Now that the days were growing longer, I could make out the colour of Délia's eyes—round her dilated pupils there was a ring of dark grey-green—and the whiteness of her skin, like the complexion of southern women who are uniformly pale from head to foot. She threw me a look of obstinate mistrust.

"My sister can work just as well in a living-room if she chooses."

"The main thing is that she works, isn't it?" I retorted.

With a kick, she flung one of her slippers a long way away.

"*I* work too," she said stiffly. "Only nobody sees what I do. I wear myself out, oh! I wear myself out. In there . . . In there . . ."

She was touching her forehead and pressing her temples. With slight contempt, I looked at her idle woman's hands, her delicate fingers, long, slim and turned up at the tips, and her fleshy palms. I shrugged my shoulders.

"Fine work, a fixed idea! You ought to be ashamed, Délia."

She gave way easily to tempers typical of an ill-bred schoolgirl with no self-control.

"I don't only just think!" she screamed. "I . . . I work in my own way! It's all in my head!"

"Are you planning a novel?"

I had spoken sarcastically but Délia, quite unaware of this, was flattered and calmed down.

"Oh! Well, not exactly so . . . it's a bit like a novel, only better."

"What is it you call better than a novel, my child?"

For I allowed myself to call her that when she seemed to be pitchforked into a kind of brutal, irresponsible childishness. She always flinched at the word and rewarded me with angry, lustrous glance, accompanied by an ill-tempered shrug.

"Ah, I can't tell you that," she said in a self-important voice.

She went back to fishing cherries out of a newspaper cornet. She pinched the stones between her fingers and aimed at the open window. Rosita passed through the room, busy on some errand, and scolded her sister without pausing in her walk.

"Délia, you oughtn't to throw the stones out into the street."

What was I doing there, in that desert? One day, I brought some better cherries. Another day, having brought Rosita a manuscript full of erasures, I said:

"Wait. Could I re-do this page on . . . on a corner of a table, doesn't matter where. There, look, that'll do very well. Yes, yes, I can see well enough there. Yes, I've got my fountain-pen."

Leaning on a rickety one-legged table, I received, from the left, the light of the solitary window and, from the right, the attention of Délia. To my amazement, she set to work with a needle. She was doing the fine beadwork that was all the rage at the moment for bags and trimmings.

"What a charming talent, Délia."

"It isn't a talent, it's a profession," said Délia in a tone of disgust.

But she was not displeased, I think, to devote herself under my eyes to work that was as graceful as a charming pastime. The needles, fine as steel hairs, the tiny multicoloured beads, the canvas net, she manipulated them all with the deftness of a blind person, still half-recumbent on a corner of the divan-bed. From the neighbouring room came the choppy chatter of the typewriter, the jib of its little carriage at every line, and its crystalline bell. What was I doing, in that desert? It was not a desert. I forsook my own three small, snug rooms, my books, the scent I sprayed about, my lamp. But one cannot live on a lamp, on a perfume, on pages one has read and re-read. I had moreover friends and good companions; I had Annie de Pène, who was better than the best of them. But, just as delicate fare does not stop you from craving for saveloys, so tried and exquisite friendship does not take away your taste for something new and dubious.

With Rosita, with Délia, I was insured against the risk of making confidences. My hidden past climbed the familiar stairs with me, sat secretly beside Délia, rearranged furniture on its old plan, revived the colours of the "rainy moon" and sharpened a weapon once used against myself.

"Is it a profession you chose yourself, Délia?"

"Not exactly. In January, this year, I took it up again because it means I can work at home."

She opened the beak of her fine scissors.

"It's good for me to handle pointed things."

There was a gravity about her, like the gravity of a young madwoman, that oddly suited Délia. I thought it unwise to encourage her further than by a questioning glance.

"Pointed things," she reiterated. "Scissors, needles, pins . . . It's good."

"Would you like me to introduce you to a sword-swallower, a knife-thrower and a porcupine?"

She deigned to laugh and that chromatic laugh made me sorry she was not happy more often. A powerful feminine voice in the street called out the greengrocer's cry.

"Oh, it's the cherry cart," murmured Délia.

Without taking time to put on my felt hat, I went down bareheaded and brought a kilo of white-heart cherries. Running to avoid a motor-car, I bumped into a man who had stopped outside *my* door.

"Another moment, Madame, and your cherries . . ."

I smiled at this passer-by, who was a typical Parisian, with a lively face, a few white threads in his black hair and fine, tired eyes that suggested an engraver or printer. He was lighting a cigarette, without taking his eyes off the first-floor window. The lighted match burnt his fingers; he let it drop and turned away.

A cry of pleasure—the first I had ever heard from Délia's lips—greeted my entrance, and the young woman pressed the back of my hand against her cheek. Feeling oddly rewarded, I watched her eating the cherries and putting the stalks and stones into the lid of a box of pins. Her expression of greed and selfishness did not deprive her of the charm that makes us feel tender towards violent children, withdrawn into their own passions and refusing to condescend to be pleasant.

"Just imagine, Délia, down there on the pavement . . ."

She stopped eating, with a big cherry bulging inside her cheek.

"What, down there on the pavement?"

"There's a man looking up at your windows. A very charming man, too."

She swallowed her cherry and hastily spat out the stone.

"What's he like?"

"Dark, a face . . . well, pleasant . . . white hairs in his black hair. He's got red-brown stains on his finger-tips, they're the fingers of a man who smokes too much."

As she tucked her slipperless feet under her again with a sudden movement, Délia scattered all her fragile needlework tools on the floor.

"What day is it today? Friday, isn't it? Yes, Friday."

"Is he your Friday lover? Have you got one for all the days of the week?"

She stared full in my face with the insulting glare adolescents reserve for anyone who treats them as "big babies".

"You know everything, don't you?"

She rose to pick up her embroidery equipment. As she flourished a delicate little antique purse she was copying against the light, I noticed her hands were trembling. She turned towards me with a forced playfulness.

"He's nice, isn't he, my Friday lover? D'you think he's attractive?"

"I think he's attractive, but I don't think he looks well. You ought to look after him."

"Oh! I look after him all right, you needn't worry about *him*."

She began to laugh crazily, so much so that she brought on a fit of coughing. When she had stopped laughing and coughing, she leant against a piece of furniture as if overcome with giddiness, staggered and sat down.

"It's exhaustion," she muttered.

Her black hair, which had come down, fell no lower than her shoulders. Combed up on her temples and revealing her ears, it looked like an untidy little girl's and accentuated the regularity of her profile and its childish, inexorable cast.

"It's exhaustion." But what exhaustion? Due to an unhealthy life? No unhealthier than my own, as healthy as that of all women and girls who live in Paris. A few days earlier Délia had touched her forehead and clutched her temples: "It's there I wear myself out . . . And there . . . " Yes, the fixed idea; the absent man, the faithless Essendier. No matter how much I studied that perfect beauty—if you scanned it carefully, there was not a flaw in Délia's face—I searched it in vain for any expression of suffering, in other words, of love.

She remained seated, a little out of breath, with her slender pointed scissors dangling over her black dress from a metal chain. My scrutiny did not embarrass her, but, after a few moments, she stood up like someone getting on her way again and reproaching herself for having lingered too long. The change in the light and in the street-noises told me the afternoon was over and I got myself ready to leave. Behind me, irreproachably slim, with her muted fairness, stood Mademoiselle Rosita. For some time, I had lost the habit of looking at her; she struck me as having aged. It struck me too that, through the wide-open door, she had probably heard us joking about the Friday lover. At the same instant, I realised that, in frequenting the Barberet sisters for no reason, I left the elder sister out in the cold. My intercourse with her was limited to our brief professional conversations and to polite nothings, observations about the weather, the high cost of living and the cinema. For Mademoiselle Rosita would never have allowed herself to ask any question that touched on my personal life, on my obvious freedom of a woman who lived alone. But how many days was it since I had displayed the faintest interest in Rosita? I felt embarrassed by this, and, as Délia was making her way to the bathroom, I meditated being "nice" to Rosita. An exemplary worker, endowed with sterling virtues and even with natural distinction, who types Vandérem's manuscripts and Arthur Bernède's novelettes and my own crossed-out and interlined pages deserved a little consideration.

With her hands clasped palm to palm, her two little ringlets on her right shoulder, she was waiting patiently for me to go. As I went up to her, I saw she was paying not the slightest heed to me. What she was staring at was Délia's back as she left the room. Her eyes, of a middling blue, were hardened; they never left the short, slightly Spanish figure of her sister and the black hair that she was putting up with a careless hand. And, as we take our interior shocks and shudders for divination, I thought as I walked down the hill, whose houses were already rosy at the top: "But it's in the depths of this prim, colourless Rosita that I must find the answer to this little enigma brooding between the divan and the solitary window of a bedroom where a young woman is pretending, out of sheer obstinacy and jealousy, to relive a moment of my own life. The stubborn young woman very likely has few clues to the little enigma. If she knew more about it, she would never tell me. Her mystery, or her appearance of mystery, is a gratuitous gift; she might just as well have had a golden strand in her black hair or a mole on her cheek."

Nevertheless, I continued walking along the pavements where, now that it was June, the concierges sitting out on their chairs, the children's games and the flight of balls obliged one to perform a kind of country-dance, two steps forward, two steps back, swing to the right and turn . . . The smell of stopped-up sinks, in June, dominates the exquisite pink twilights. By contrast I quite loved my western district that echoed like an empty corridor. A surprise awaited me in the form of a telegram: Sido, my mother, was arriving on the morrow and was staying in Paris three days. After this particular one, she only made a single last journey away from her own surroundings.

While she was there, there was no question of the Barberet young ladies. I am not concerned here to describe her stay. But her exacting presence recalled my life to dignity and solicitude. In her company, I had to pretend to be almost as young as she was, to follow her impulsive flights. I was terrified to see her so very small and thin, feverish in her enchanting gaiety and as if hunted. But I was still far from admitting the idea that she might die. Did she not insist, the very day she arrived, on buying pansy-seeds, hearing a comic opera and seeing a collection bequeathed to the Louvre? Did she not arrive bearing three pots of raspberry-and-currant jam and the first roses in bud wrapped up in a damp handkerchief, had she not made me a barometer by sewing weather-predicting wild oats on to a square of cardboard?

She abstained, as always, from questioning me about my most intimate troubles. The sexual side of my life inspired her, I think, with great and motherly repugnance. But I had to keep guard over my words and my face and to beware of her look which read right through the flesh she had created. She liked to hear the news of my men and women friends, and of any newly-formed acquaintances. I omitted however to tell her the Barberet story.

Sitting opposite me at the table, pushing away the plate she had not emptied, she questioned me less about what I was writing than about what I wanted to write. I have never been subjected to any criticism that resembled Sido's for, while believing in my vocation as a writer, she was dubious about my career. "Don't forget that you have only one gift," she used to say. "But what is one gift? One gift has never been enough for anyone."

The air of Paris intoxicated her as if she had been a young girl from the provinces. When she left, I put her on her slow train, anxious about letting her travel alone, yet happy to know that, a few hours later, she would be in the haven of her little home where there were no comforts but also no dangers.

After her departure, everything seemed to me unworthy of pursuit. The wholesome sadness, the pride, the other good qualities she had instilled into me could not be more than ephemeral, I had already lived away from her too long. Yet, when she had gone, I took up my place again in the deep embrasure of my window and once more switched on my green-shaded daylight lamp. But I was impelled by necessity, rather than by love, of doing a good piece of work. And I wrote until it was time to travel by métro up the hill whose slope I liked to descend on foot.

Mademoiselle Rosita opened the door to me. By chance, she exclaimed "Ah!" at the sight of me, which checked a similar exclamation of surprise on my own lips. In less than a fortnight, my withered young girl had become a withered old maid. A little charwoman's bun replaced the bow and the two ringlets; she was wearing a bibbed apron tied round her waist. She mechanically fingered her right shoulder and stammered:

"You've caught me not properly dressed. I've been dreadfully rushed these last days."

I shook her dry, delicate hand which melted away in mine. A rather common scent, mingled with the smell of a frying-pan in which cooking-oil is being heated, revived my old memory of the little flat and of the younger sister.

"Are you keeping well? And your sister too?"

She jerked her shoulders in a way that signified nothing definite. I added, with involuntary pride:

"You understand, I've had my mother with me for a few days. And how's Délia getting on? Still working hard? Can I go and say how d'you do to her?"

Mademoiselle Rosita lowered her head as sheep do when they are mustering up their courage to fight.

"No, you can't. That is to say you can, but I don't see why you should go and say how d'you do to a murderess."

"What did you say?"

"To a murderess. *I* have to stay here. But you, what have *you* got to do with a murderess?"

Even her manner had changed. Mademoiselle Rosita remained polite but she used a tone of profound indifference to utter words that could have been considered monstrous. I could not even see her familiar little white collar; it was replaced by a piece of coarse, sky-blue machine embroidery.

"But, Mademoiselle, I couldn't possibly have guessed. I was bringing you . . ."

"Very good," she said promptly. "Will you come in here?"

I went into the big room, just as in the days when Mademoiselle Rosita used adroitly to bar one from entering Délia's bedroom. I unpacked my manuscript in the intolerable glare of the unshaded windows and gave instructions as if to a stranger. Like a stranger, Rosita listened, and said: "Very good . . . Exactly . . . One black and one purple . . . It'll be finished Wednesday." The frequent, unnecessary interjections—"Madame . . . Yes, Madame . . . Oh! Madame . . ." had vanished from her replies. In her conversation too, she had cut out the ringlets.

As in the days of my first curiosity, I kept my patience at

first, then suddenly lost it. I hardly lowered my voice, as I asked Mademoiselle Barberet point blank:

"Whom has she killed?"

The poor girl, taken by surprise, made a small despairing gesture and leant against the table with both hands.

"Ah! Madame, it's not done yet, but he's going to die."

"Who?"

"Why, her husband, Eugène."

"Her husband? The man she was waiting for day and night? I thought he had left her?"

"Left her, that's easier said than done. They didn't get on but you mustn't think the fault was on his side, very far from it. He's a very nice boy indeed, Eugène is, Madame. And he's never stopped sending my sister something out of what he earns, you know. But she—*she's* taken it into her head to revenge herself."

In the increasing confusion that was overtaking Rosita Barberet, I thought I could detect the disorder of a mind in which the poison of an old love was at work. The commonplace, dangerous rivalry between the pretty sister and the faded sister. A strand of hair, escaped from Rosita's perfunctorily scraped-up bun, became, in my eyes, the symbol of a madwoman's vehemence. The "rainy moon" gleamed in its seven colours on the wall of my former refuge, now given over to enemies in process of accusing each other, fighting each other.

"Mademoiselle Rosita, I do beg you. Aren't you exaggerating a little? This is a very serious accusation, you realise."

I did not speak roughly, for I am frightened of harmless lunatics, of people who deliver long monologues in the street without seeing us, of purple-faced drunks who shake their fists at empty space and walk zigzag. I wanted to take back my manuscript, but the roll of papers had been grabbed by Rosita and served to punctuate her sentences. She spoke violently, without raising her voice:

"I definitely mean, revenge herself, Madame. When she realised he did not love her any more, she said to herself: 'I'll get you.' So she cast a spell on him."

The word was so unexpected that it made me smile and Rosita noticed it.

"Don't laugh, Madame. Anyone would think you really didn't know what you were laughing about."

A metallic object fell, on the other side of the door, and Rosita gave a start.

"Well! right, so it's the scissors now," she said, speaking to herself.

She must have read on my face something like a desire to be elsewhere, and tried to reassure me.

"Don't be afraid. She knows quite well that you're here, but if you don't go into her room, she won't come into this one."

"I'm not afraid," I said sharply. "What has she given him? A drug?"

"She's convoked him. Convoking, do you know what that is?"

"No . . . that's to say I've got some vague idea, but I don't know all the . . . the details."

"Convoking is summoning a person by force. That poor Eugène . . ."

"Wait!" I exclaimed in a low voice. "What's he like, your brother-in-law? He's not a dark young man who's got white hairs among his black ones? He looks rather ill, he's got the complexion of people who have a cardiac lesion? Yes? Then it was him I saw about . . . say two weeks ago."

"Where?"

"Down there, in the street. He was looking up at the window of my . . . the window of Délia's bedroom. He looked as if he were waiting. I even warned Délia she had a lover under her window . . ."

Rosita clasped her hands.

"Oh! Madame! And you didn't tell me! A whole fortnight!"

She let her arms fall and hang limp over her apron. Her light eyes held a reproach, which, to me, seemed quite meaningless. She looked at me without seeing me, her spectacles in her hand, with an intense, unfocused, gaze.

"Mademoiselle Rosita, you don't really mean to say you're accusing Délia of witchcraft and black magic?"

"But indeed I am, Madame! What she is doing is what they call convoking, but it's the same thing."

"Listen, Rosita, we're not living in the Middle Ages now . . . Think calmly for a moment . . ."

"But I am thinking calmly, Madame. I've never done anything else! This thing she's doing, she's not the only one who's doing it. It's quite common. Mark you, I don't say it succeeds every time. Didn't you know anything about it?"

I shook my head and the other faintly shrugged her shoulders, as if to indicate that my education had been seriously lacking. A clock somewhere struck midday and I rose to go. Absorbed in her own thoughts, Rosita followed me to the door out of mechanical politeness. In the dark hall, the plate-shaped ceiling-light chiselled her features into those of a haggard old lady.

"Rosita," I said, "if your sister's surprised I didn't ask to see her . . ."

"She won't be surprised," she said, shaking her head. "She's far too occupied in doing evil."

She looked at me with an irony of which I had not believed her capable.

"And besides, you know, this is not a good moment to see her. She's not at all pretty, these days. If she were, it really wouldn't be fair."

Suddenly, I remembered Délia's extraordinary words: "It's good for me to touch pointed things, scissors, pins." Overcome by the excitement of passing on baleful news, I bent over and repeated them in Rosita's ear. She seized the top of my arm, in a familiar way, and drew me out on to the landing.

"I'll bring you back your typed pages tomorrow evening about half-past six or seven. Make your escape, *she'll* be asking me to get her lunch."

I did not savour the pleasure I had anticipated, after leaving Rosita Barberet. Yet, when I thought over the extravagance, the ambitiousness of this anecdote which aspired to be a sensational news item, I found that it lacked only one thing, guilelessness. A want of innocence spoilt its exciting colour, all its suggestion of old women's gossip and brewings of mysterious herbs and magic potions. For I do not care for the picturesque when it is based on feelings of black hatred. As I returned to my own neighbourhood, I compared the Barberet story with "the story of the Rue Truffaut" and found the latter infinitely pleasanter with its circle of worthy women in the Batignolles district who, touching hands round a dinner table, conversed with the great beyond and received news of their dead children and their departed husbands. They never enquired my name because I had been introduced by the local hairdresser and they slipped me a warning to mistrust a lady called X. It so happened that the advice was excellent. But the principal attraction of the meeting lay in the darkened room, in the table-cloth bordered with a bobble-fringe that matched the one on the curtains, in the spirit of a young sailor, an invisible and mischievous ghost who haunted it on regular days, and shut himself up in the cupboard in order to make all the cups and saucers rattle. "Ah! *that* chap . . ." the stout mistress of the house would sigh indulgently.

"You let him get away with anything, Mamma," her daughter (the medium) would say reproachfully. "All the same, it would be a pity if he broke the blue cup."

At the end of the séance, these ladies passed round cups of pale, tepid tea. What peace, what charm there was in being entertained by these hostesses whose social circle relied entirely on an extra-terrestrial world! How agreeable I found her too, that female bone-setter, Mademoiselle Lévy, who undertook the care of bodies and souls and demanded so little money in exchange! She practised massage and the laying on of hands in the darkest depths of pallid concierges' lodges, in variety artistes' digs in the Rue Biot and dressing-rooms in the music-halls of La Fauvette. She sewed beautiful Hebrew characters into sachets and hung them round your neck: "You can be assured of its efficaciousness, it is prepared by the hands of innocence." And she would display her beautiful hands, softened by creams and unguents, and add: "If things don't go better tomorrow, when I go away, I can light a candle for you to Our Lady of Victories. *I'm* on good terms with everyone."

Certainly, in the practices of innocent, popular magic, I was not such a novice as I had wished to appear in the eyes of Mademoiselle Barberet. But, in frequenting my ten or twenty franc sibyls, all I had done was to amuse myself, to listen to the rich, but limited music of old, ritual words, to abandon my hands into hands so foreign to me, so worn smooth by contact with other human hands, that I benefited from them for a moment as I might have done from immersing myself in a crowd or listening to some voluble, pointless story. In short, they acted on me like a pain-killing drug, warranted harmless to children . . .

Whereas these mutual enemies, the Barberets. . . . A blind alley, haunted by evil designs, was this what had become of the little flat where once I had suffered without bitterness, watched over by my rainy moon?

And so I reckoned up everything in the realm of the inexplicable that I owed to some extent to obtuse go-betweens, to vacant creatures whose emptiness reflects fragments of destinies, to modest liars and vehement visionaries. Not one of these women had done me any harm, not one of them had frightened me. But these two sisters, so utterly unlike . . .

I had had so little for lunch that I was glad to go and dine at a modest restaurant whose proprietress was simply known as "that fat woman who knows how to cook". It was rare for me not to meet under its low ceilings one of those people one calls "friends" and who are sometimes, in fact, affectionate. I seem to remember that, with Count d'Adelsward de Fersen, I crowned my orgy—*bœuf à l'ancienne* and cider—by spending two hours at the cinema. Fersen, fair-haired and coated with brick-red sun-tan, wrote verses and did not like women. But he was so cut out to be attractive to all females that one of them exclaimed at the sight of him: "Ah! What waste of a good thing!" Intolerant and well-read, he had a quick temper and his exaggerated flamboyance hid a fundamental shyness. When we left the restaurant, Gustave Téry was just beginning his late dinner. But the founder of *L'Œuvre* gave me no other greeting than some buffalo-like glares, as was his habit whenever he was swollen with polemic fury and imagined he was being persecuted. Spherical, light on his feet, he entered like a bulky cloud driven by a gale. Either I am mistaken or else, that night, everyone I ran into, the moment I recognised them, showed an extraordinary tendency to move away and disappear. My last meeting was with a prostitute who was eyeing the pedestrians at the corner of the street, about a hundred steps from the house where I lived. I did not fail to say a word to her, as well as to the wandering cat who was keeping her company. A large, warm moon, a yellow June moon, lit up my homeward journey. The woman, standing on her short shadow, was talking to the cat Mimine. She was only interested in meteorology or, at least, so one would have imagined from her rare words. For six months I had seen her in a shapeless coat and a cloche-hat, with a little military plume, that hid the top of her face.

"It's a mild night," she said, by way of greeting. "But you mustn't imagine it's going to last, the mist is all in one long sheet over the stream. When it's in big separate puffs like bonfires, that means fine weather. So you're back again, on foot, as usual?"

I offered her one of the cigarettes Fersen had given me. She remained faithful to the district longer than I did, with her shadow crouched like a dog at her feet, this shepherdess without a flock who talked about bonfires and thought of the Seine as a stream. I hope that she has long been sleeping, alone for ever more, and dreaming of hay-lofts, of dawns crisp with frosted dew, of mists clinging to the running water that bears her along with it.

The little flat I occupied at that time was the envy of my rare visitors. But I soon knew that it would not hold me for long. Not that its three rooms—let's say two-and-a-half rooms—were inconvenient, but they thrust into prominence single objects that, in other surroundings, had been one of a pair. Now I only possessed one of the two beautiful red porcelain vases, fitted up as a lamp. The second Louis Quinze armchair held out its slender arms elsewhere for someone else to rest in. My square book-case waited in vain for another square book-case and is still waiting for it. This series of amputations suffered by my furniture distressed no one but myself, and Rosita Barberet did not fail to exclaim: "Why, it's a real nest!" as she clasped her gloved hands in admiration. A low shaft of sunlight—Honnorat had not yet finished serving his time as a page, and seven on the Charles X clock meant that it was a good seven hours since noon—reached my writing-table, shone through a small carafe of wine, and touched, on its way, a little bunch of those June roses that are sold by the dozen, in Paris, in June.

I was pleased to see that she was once again the prim, neat Rosita, dressed in black with her touch of white lingerie at the neck. Fashion at that time favoured little short capes held in place by tie-ends that were crossed in front and fastened at the back of the waist. Mademoiselle Barberet knew how to wear a Paris hat, which means a very simple hat. But she seemed to have definitely repudiated the two little ringlets over one shoulder. The brim of her hat came down over the sad snail-shaped bun, symbol of all renouncements, on the thin, greying nape and the face it shaded was wasted with care. As I poured out a glass of Lunel for Rosita, I wished I could also offer her lipstick and powder, some form of rejuvenating make-up.

She began by pushing away the burnt-topaz-coloured wine and the biscuits.

"I'm not accustomed to it, Madame, I only drink water with a dash of wine in it or sometimes a little beer."

"Just a mouthful. It's a wine for children."

She drank a mouthful, expostulated, drank another mouthful and yet another, making little affected grimaces because she had not learnt to be simple, except in her heart. Between times, she admired everything her short-sightedness made it impossible for her to see clearly. Soon she had one red cheek and one pale cheek and some little threads of blood in the whites of her eyes, round the brightened blue of the iris. All this would have made a middle-aged woman look younger but Mademoiselle Barberet was only a girl, still young and withered before her time.

"It's a magic potion," she said, with her typical smile that seemed set in inverted commas.

Continuing, as if she were speaking a line in a play, she sighed:

"Ah! if that poor Eugène . . ."

By this, I realised that her time was limited and I wanted to know how long she had.

"Has your sister gone out? She's not waiting for you?"

"I told her I was bringing you your typescript and that I was also going to look in on Monsieur Vandérem and Monsieur Lucien Muhlfeld so as to make only one journey of it. If she's in a hurry for her dinner, there's some vegetable soup left over from yesterday, a boiled artichoke and some stewed rhubarb."

"In any case, the little restaurant on the right as you go down your street . . ."

Mademoiselle Barberet shook her head.

"No. She doesn't go out. She doesn't go out any more." She swallowed a drop of wine left in the bottom of her glass, then folded her arms in a decided way on my work-table, just opposite me. The setting sun clung for a moment to all the features of her half-flushed, half-pale face, to a turquoise brooch that fastened her collar. I wanted to come to her aid and spare her the preamble.

"I have to admit, Rosita, that I didn't quite understand what you were saying to me yesterday."

"I realised that," she said, with a little whinny. "At first I thought you were making fun of me. A person as well-read as you are . . . To put it in two words instead of a hundred, Madame, my sister is in process of making her husband die. On my mother's memory, Madame, she is killing him. Six moons have already gone by, the seventh is coming, that's the fatal moon, this unfortunate man knows that he's doomed, besides he's already had two accidents, from which he's entirely recovered, but all the same it's a handicap that puts him in a state of less resistance and makes the task easier for *her*."

She would have exceeded the hundred words in her first breath, had not her haste and, no doubt, the warmth of the wine slightly choked her. I profited by her fit of coughing to ask:

"Mademoiselle Rosita, just one question. Why should Délia want to make her husband die?"

She threw up her hands in a disclaiming gesture of impotence.

"Ah, as to that . . . you may well hunt for the real reason! All the usual reasons between a man and a woman! And you don't love me any more and I still love you, and you wish I were dead and come back I implore you, and I'd like to see you in hell."

She gave a brutal "Hah!" and grimaced.

"My poor Rosita, if all couples who don't get on resorted to murder . . ."

"But they do resort to it," she protested. "They make no bones about resorting to it!"

"You see very few cases reported in the papers."

"Because it's all done in private, it's a family affair. Nine times out of ten, no one gets arrested. It's talked about a little in the neighbourhood. But just you see if you can find any traces! Fire-arms, poisons, that's all out-of-date stuff. My sister knows that all right. What about the woman who keeps the sweet-shop just below us, whatever's *she* done with her husband? And the milkman at Number 57, rather queer isn't it that he's gone and lost his second wife too?"

Her refined, high-class saleslady's vocabulary had gone to pieces and she had thrust out her chin like a gargoyle. With a flip of her finger, she pushed back her hat which was pinching her forehead. I was as shocked as if she had pulled up her skirt and fastened her suspenders without apologising. She uncovered a high forehead, with sloping temples, which I had never seen so nakedly revealed, from whence I imagined there was to be a burst of confidences and secrets that might or might not be dangerous. Behind Rosita, the window was turning pink with the last faint rose reflection of daylight. Yet I dared not switch on my lamp at once.

"Rosita," I said seriously, "are you in the habit of saying . . . what you've just said to me . . . to just anybody?"

Her eyes looked frankly straight into mine.

"You must be joking, Madame. Should I have come so far if I'd had anyone near me who deserved to be trusted?"

I held out my hand, which she grasped. She knew how to shake hands, curtly and warmly, without prolonging the pressure.

"If you believe that Délia is doing harm to her husband, why don't you try to counteract that harm? Because *you*, at least it seems so to me, wish nothing but good to Eugène Esssendier."

She gazed at me dejectedly.

"But I can't, Madame! Love would have to have passed between Eugène and me. And it hasn't passed between us! It's never passed, never, never!"

She pulled a handkerchief out of her bag and wept, taking care not to wet her little starched neck-piece. I thought I had understood everything. "Now we have it, jealousy of course." Promptly Rosita's accusations and she herself became suspect, and I turned on the switch of my lamp.

"That doesn't mean I must go, Madame?" she asked anxiously.

"Of course not, of course not," I said weakly.

The truth was that I could hardly bear the sight, under the strong rays of my lamp, of her red-eyed face and her hat tipped backwards like a drunken woman's. But Rosita had hardly begun to talk.

"Eugène has never even thought of wanting me," she said

humbly. "If he had wanted me, even just once, I'd be in a position to fight against her, you understand."

"No. I don't understand. I've everything to learn, as you see. Do you really attribute so much importance to the fact of having . . . having belonged to a man?"

"And you? Do you really attribute so little to it?"

I decided to laugh.

"No, no, Rosita, I'm not so frivolous, unfortunately. But, all the same, I don't think it constitutes a bond, that it sets a seal on you."

"Well, you're mistaken, that's all. Possession gives you the power to summon, to convoke, as they say. Have you really never 'called' anyone?"

"Indeed I have," I said laughing. "I must have hit on someone deaf. I didn't get an answer."

"Because you didn't call hard enough, for good or evil. My sister, *she* really does call. If you could see her. She's unrecognisable. Also she's up to some pretty work, I can assure you."

She fell silent, and, for a moment, it was quite obvious she had stopped thinking of me.

"But, Eugène himself, couldn't you warn him?"

"I have warned him. But Eugène, he's a sceptic. He told me he'd had enough of one crack-brained woman and that the second crack-brained woman would do him a great favour if she'd shut up. He's got pockets under his eyes and he's the colour of butter. From time to time he coughs, but not from the chest, he coughs because of palpitations of the heart. He said to me: 'All I can do for you is to lend you *Fantomas*. It's just your cup of tea.' That just shows," added Mademoiselle Barberet, with a bitter smile. "That just shows how the most intelligent men can argue like imbeciles, seeing no difference between fantastic made-up stories and things as real as this . . . as such deadly machinations."

"But what machinations, will you kindly tell me?" I exclaimed.

Mademoiselle Barberet unfolded her spectacles and put them on, wedging them firmly in the brown dints that marked either side of her transparent nose. Her gaze became focused, taking on new assurance and a searching expression.

"You know," she murmured, "that it is never too late to *summon*? You have quite understood that one can *summon* for good and for evil?"

"I know it now that you have told me."

She pushed my lamp a little to one side and leant over closer to me. She was hot and nothing is so unbearable to me as the human smell except when—very rarely indeed—I find it intoxicating. Moreover, the wine to which she was not accustomed kept repeating and her breath smelt of it. I wanted to stand up but she was already talking.

There are things that are written down nowhere, except by clumsy hands in school exercise books, or on thin grey-squared paper, yellowed at the edges, folded and cut into pages and sewn together with red cotton; things that the witch bequeathed to the bone-setter, that the bone-setter sold to the love-obsessed woman, that the obsessed one passed on to another wretched creature. All that the credulity and the sullied memory of a pure girl can gather in the dens that an unfathomable city harbours between a brand-new cinema and an espresso-bar, I heard from Rosita Barberet, who had learnt it from the vaunts of widows who had willed the deaths of the husbands who had deserted them, from the frenzied fantasies of lonely women.

"You say a name, nothing but the name, the name of the particular person, a hundred times, a thousand times. No matter how far away they are, they will hear you in the end. Without eating or drinking, as long as you can possibly keep it up, you say the name, nothing else but the name. Don't you remember one day when Délia nearly fainted? I suspected at once. In our neighbourhood there are heaps of them who repeated the name . . ."

Whisperings, an obtuse faith, even a local custom, were these the forces and the magic philtres that procured love, decided life and death, removed that lofty mountain, an indifferent heart?

". . . One day when you rang the bell, and my sister was lying behind the door . . ."

"Yes, I remember . . . You asked me: 'Is that you, Eugène?'"

"She'd said to me: 'Quick, quick, he's coming. I can feel it, quick, he must tread on me as he comes in, it's essential!' But it was you."

"It was only me."

"She'd been lying there, believe me or not, for over two hours. Soon after that, she took to pointed things again. Knives, scissors, embroidery needles. That's very well-known, but it's dangerous. If you haven't enough strength, the points can turn against you. But do you imagine *that one* would ever lack strength? If I lived the life she does, I should have been dead by now. *I've* got nothing to sustain me."

"Has she, then?"

"Of course she has. She hates. That nourishes her."

That Délia, so young, with her rather arrogant beauty, her soft cheek that she laid against my hand. That was the same Délia who played with twenty little glittering thunderbolts that she intended to be deadly, and she used their sharp points to embroider beaded flowers.

". . . But she's given up embroidering bags now. She's taken to working with needles whose points she's contaminated."

"What did you say?"

"I said, she's contaminated them by dipping them in a mixture."

And Rosita Barberet launched out into the path, strewn with nameless filth, into which the practice of base magic drags its faithful adherents. She pursued that path without blenching, without omitting a word, for fastidiousness is not a feminine virtue. She would not allow me to remain ignorant of one thing to which her young sister stooped in the hope of doing injury, that same sister who loved fresh cherries. . . . So young, with one of those rather short bodies a man's arms clasp so easily, and, beneath that black, curly hair, the pallor that a lover longs to crimson.

Luckily, the narratress branched off and took to talking only about death, and I breathed again. Death is not nauseating. She discoursed on the imminent death of this unfortunate Eugène, which so much resembled the death of the husband of the woman in the sweet-shop! And then there was the chemist, who had died quite black.

"You must surely admit, Madame, that the fact of a chemist being fixed like that by his wife, that really is turning the world upside down!"

I certainly did admit it. I even derived a strange satisfaction from it. What did I care about the chemist and the unlucky husband of the woman who kept the sweet-shop? All I was waiting for now from my detailed informant was one final picture: Délia arriving at the cross-roads where, amidst the vaporous clouds produced by each one's illusion, the female slaves of the cloven-footed one meet for the sabbath.

"Yes, indeed. And where does the devil come in, Rosita?"

"What devil, Madame?"

"Why the devil pure and simple, I presume. Does your sister give him a special name?"

An honest amazement was depicted on Rosita's face and her eyebrows flew up to the top of her high forehead.

"But, Madame, whatever trail are you off on now? The devil, that's just for imbeciles. The devil, just imagine . . ."

She shrugged her shoulders, and, behind her glasses, threw a withering glance at discredited Satan.

"The devil! Admitting he existed, he'd be just the one to mess it all up!"

"Rosita, you remind me at this moment of the young woman who said: 'God, that's all hooey! . . . But no jokes in front of me about the Blessed Virgin!'"

"Everyone's got their own ideas, Madame. Good heavens! It's ten to eight! It was very kind of you to let me come," she sighed in a voice that did not disguise her disappointment.

For I had offered her neither help nor connivance. She pulled down her hat—at last—over her forehead. I remembered, just in time, that I had not paid her for her last lot of work.

"A drop of Lunel before you go, Mademoiselle Rosita?"

Involuntarily, by calling her "Mademoiselle" again, I was putting her at a distance. She swallowed the golden wine in one gulp and I complimented her.

"Oh, I've got a good head," she said.

But, as she had folded up her spectacles again, she searched round for me with a vague eye, and, as she went out, she bumped against the door-post, to which she made a little apologetic bow.

As soon as she had gone, I opened the window to its fullest extent to let in the evening air. Mistaking the feeling of exhaustion her visit had given me for genuine tiredness, I made the error of going to bed early. My dreams showed the effects of it and, through them, I realised I was not yet rid of the two enemy sisters nor of another memory. I kept relapsing into a nightmare in which I was now my real self, now identified with Délia. Half-reclining like her on *our* divan-bed, in the dark part of our room, I "convoked" with a powerful summons, with a thousand repetitions of his name, a man who was not called Eugène. . . .

Dawn found me drenched with those abundant tears we rain in sleep and that go on flowing after we are awake and can no longer track them to their source. The thousand-times repeated name grew dim and lost its nocturnal power. In my own mind, I said farewell to it and thrust its echo back into the little flat where I had taken pleasure in suffering. And I abandoned that flat to those other women, to their stifled, audacious, incantation-ridden lives where witchcraft could be fitted in between the daily task and the Saturday cinema, between the little washtub and the frying steak.

When the short night was ended, I promised myself that never again would I climb the Paris hill with the steep, gay streets. Between one day and the next, I turned Rosita's furtive charm, her graceful way of putting down her slender feet when she walked and the two little ringlets that fluttered on her shoulder, into a memory. With that Délia who did not want to be called Adèle, I had a little more trouble. All the more so, as, after the lapse of a fortnight, I took to running into her by pure chance. Once she was rummaging in a box of small remnants near the entrance of a big shop, and three days later she was buying spaghetti in an Italian grocer's. She looked pale and diminished, like a convalescent who is out too soon, pearly under the eyes, and extremely pretty. A thick, curled fringe covered her forehead to the eyebrows. Something indescribable stirred in the depths of myself and spoke in her favour. But I did not answer.

Another time, I recognised only her walk, seeing her from the back. We were walking along the same pavement and I had to slow down my step so as not to overtake her. For she was advancing by little, short steps, then making a pause, as if out of breath, and going on again. Finally, one Sunday when I was returning with Annie de Pène from the flea-market and, loaded with treasure such as milk-glass lamps and Rubelles plates, we were having a rest and drinking lemonade, I caught sight of Délia Essendier. She was wearing a dress whose black showed purplish in the sunlight, as happens with re-dyed fabrics. She stopped not far from us in front of a fried-potato stall, bought a large bag of chips and ate them with gusto. After that, she stayed standing for a moment, with an air of having nothing to do. The shape of the hat she was wearing recalled a Renaissance "béguine's" and, cupping Délia's little Roman chin was the white crêpe band of a widow.

The Kepi

IF I remember rightly, I have now and then mentioned Paul Masson, known as Lemice-Térieux on account of his delight —and his dangerous efficiency—in creating mysteries. As ex-President of the Law Courts of Pondichéry, he was attached to the cataloguing section of the Bibliothèque Nationale. It was through him and through the Library that I came to know the woman, the story of whose one and only romantic adventure I am about to tell.

This middle-aged man, Paul Masson, and the very young woman I then was, established a fairly solid friendship that lasted some eight years. Without being gay himself, Paul Masson devoted himself to cheering me up. I think, seeing how very lonely and housebound I was, he was sorry for me, though he concealed the fact. I think, too, that he was proud of being so easily able to make me laugh. The two of us often dined together in the little third-floor flat in the Rue Jacob, myself in a dressing-gown hopefully intended to suggest Botticelli draperies, he invariably in dusty, correct black. His little pointed beard, slightly reddish, his faded skin and drooping eyelids, his absence of any special distinguishing marks attracted attention like a deliberate disguise. Familiar as he was with me, he avoided using the intimate "*tu*", and, every time he emerged from his guarded impersonality, he gave every sign of having been extremely well brought up. Never, when we were alone, did he sit down to write at the desk of the man whom I refer to as "Monsieur Willy" and I cannot remember, over a period of several years, his ever asking me one indiscreet question.

Moreover, I was fascinated by his caustic wit. I admired the way he attacked people on the least provocation, but always in extremely restrained language and without a trace of heat. And he brought up to my third storey, not only all the latest Paris gossip but a series of ingenious lies that I enjoyed as fantastic stories. If he ran into Marcel Schwob, my luck was really in! The two men pretended to hate each other and played a game of insulting each other politely under their breath. The *s*'s hissed between Schwob's clenched teeth; Masson gave little coughs and exuded venom like a malicious old lady. Then they would declare a truce and talk at immense length, and I was stimulated and excited by the battle of wits between those two subtle, insincere minds.

The time off that the Bibliothèque Nationale allowed Paul Masson assured me of an almost daily visit from him but the phosphorescent conversation of Marcel Schwob was a rarer treat. Alone with the cat and Masson, I did not have to talk and this prematurely-aged man could relax in silence. He frequently made notes—heaven knows what about—on the pages of a notebook bound in black imitation leather. The fumes from the slow-burning stove lulled us into a torpor; we listened drowsily to the reverberating bang of the street-door. Then I would rouse myself to eat sweets or salted nuts and I would order my guest, who, though he would not admit it to himself, was probably the most devoted of all my friends, to make me laugh. I was twenty-two, with a face like an anaemic cat's, and more than a yard and a half of hair that, when I was at home, I let down in a wavy mass that reached to my feet.

"Paul, tell me some lies."

"Which particular ones?"

"Oh, any old lies. How's your family?"

"Madame, you forget that I'm a bachelor."

"But you told me . . ."

"Ah, yes, I remember. My illegitimate daughter is well. I took her out to lunch on Sunday. In a suburban garden. The rain had plastered big yellow lime leaves on the iron table. She enjoyed herself enormously pulling them off and we ate tepid fried potatoes, with our feet on the soaked gravel . . ."

"No, no, not that, it's too sad. I like the lady of the Library better."

"What lady? We don't employ any."

"The one who's working on a novel about India, according to you."

"She's still labouring over her novelette. Today I've been princely and generous. I've made her a present of baobabs and latonia palms painted from life and thrown in magical incantations, Mahrattas, screaming monkeys, Sikhs, saris and lakhs of rupees."

Rubbing his dry hands against each other, he added:

"She gets a sou a line."

"A sou!" I exclaimed. "Why a sou?"

"Because she works for a chap who gets two sous a line who works for a chap who gets four sous a line, who works for a chap who gets ten sous a line."

"But what you're telling me isn't a lie, then?"

"All my stories can't be lies," sighed Masson.

"What's her name?"

"Her christian name is Marco, as you might have guessed. Women of a certain age, when they belong to the artistic world, have only a few names to choose from, such as Marco, Léo, Ludo, Aldo. It's a legacy from the excellent Madame Sand."

"Of a certain age? So she's old, then?"

Paul Masson glanced at my face with an indefinable expression. Lost in my long hair, that face became childish again.

"Yes," he said.

Then he ceremoniously corrected himself:

"Forgive me, I made a mistake. No, was what I meant to say. No, she's not old."

I said triumphantly:

"There, you see! You see it *is* a lie because you haven't even chosen an age for her!"

"If you insist," said Masson.

"Or else you're using the name Marco to disguise a lady who's your mistress."

"I don't need Madame Marco. I have a mistress who is also, thank heaven, my housekeeper."

He consulted his watch and stood up.

"Do make my excuses to your husband. I must get back or I shall miss the last bus. Concerning the extremely real Madame Marco, I'll introduce you to her whenever you feel inclined."

He recited, very fast:

"She is the wife of V, the painter, a school friend of mine who's made her abominably unhappy; she has fled from the conjugal establishment where her perfections had rendered her an impossible inmate; she is still beautiful, witty and penniless; she lives in a boarding-house in the Rue Demours, where she pays eighty-five francs a month for bed and breakfast; she does writing jobs, anonymous feuilletons, newspaper snippets, addressing envelopes, gives English lessons at three francs an hour and has never had a lover. You see that this particular lie is as disagreeable as the truth."

I handed him the little lighted lamp and accompanied him to the top of the stairs. As he walked down them, the tiny flame shone upwards on his pointed beard, with its slightly turned-up end, and tinged it red.

When I had had enough of getting him to tell me about "Marco", I asked Paul Masson to take me to be introduced to her, instead of bringing her to the Rue Jacob. He had told me in confidence that she was about twice my age and I felt it was proper for a young woman to make the journey to meet a lady who was not so young. Naturally, Paul Masson accompanied me to the Rue Demours.

The boarding-house where Madame Marco V lived has been pulled down. Round about 1897, all that this villa retained of its former garden was a euonymus hedge, a gravel path and a flight of five steps leading up to the door. The moment I entered the hall I felt depressed. Certain smells, not properly speaking cooking smells, but odours escaped from a kitchen, are appalling revelations of poverty. On the first floor, Paul Masson knocked on a door and the voice of Madame Marco invited us to come in. A perfect voice, neither too high nor too low, but gay and well-pitched. What a surprise! Madame Marco looked young, Madame Marco was pretty and wore a silk dress, Madame Marco had pretty eyes, almost black, and wide-open like a deer's. She had a little cleft at the tip of her nose, hair touched with henna and worn in a tight, sponge-like mass on the forehead like Queen Alexandra's and curled short on the nape in the so-called "eccentric" fashion of certain women painters or musicians.

She called me "little Madame", indicated that Masson had talked so much about me and my long hair, apologised, without overdoing it, for having no port and no sweets to offer me. With an unaffected gesture, she indicated the kind of place she lived in, and, following the sweep of her hand, I took in the piece of plush that hid the one-legged table, the shiny upholstery of the only armchair, and the two little threadbare pancake-cushions of Algerian design on the two other chairs. There was also a certain rug on the floor. The mantelpiece served as a bookshelf.

"I've imprisoned the clock in the cupboard." said Marco.

"But I swear it deserved it. Luckily, there's another cupboard I can use for my washing things. Don't you smoke?"

I shook my head, and Marco stepped into the full light to put a match to her cigarette. Then I saw that the silk dress was splitting at every fold. What little linen showed at the neck was very white. Marco and Masson smoked and chatted together; Madame Marco had grasped at once that I preferred listening to talking. I forced myself not to look at the wallpaper, with its old-gold and garnet stripes, or at the bed and its cotton damask bedspread.

"Do look at the little painting, over there," Madame Marco said to me. "It was done by my husband. It's so pretty that I've kept it. It's that little corner of Hyères, *you* remember, Masson."

And I looked enviously at Marco, Masson and the little picture, who had all three been in Hyères. Like most young things, I knew how to withdraw into myself, far away from people talking in the same room, then return to them with a sudden mental effort, then leave them again. Throughout my visit to Marco, thanks to her delicate tact which let me off questions and answers, I was able to come and go without stirring from my chair; I could observe or I could shut my eyes at will. I saw her just as she was and what I saw both delighted and distressed me. Though her well-set features were fine, she had what is called a coarse skin, slightly leathery and masculine, with red patches on the neck and below the ears. But, at the same time, I was ravished by the lively intelligence of her smile, by the shape of her doe's eyes and the unusually proud, yet completely unaffected carriage of her head. She looked less like a pretty woman than like one of those chiselled, clear-cut aristocratic men who adorned the eighteenth century and were not ashamed of being handsome. Masson told me later she was extraordinarily like her grandfather, the Chevalier de Saint-Georges, a brilliant forebear who has no place in my story.

We became great friends, Marco and I. And after she had finished her Indian novel—it was rather like *La Femme qui Tue*, as specified by the man who got paid ten sous a line—Monsieur Willy soothed Marco's sensitive feelings by asking her to do some research on condition she accepted a small fee. He even consented, when I urgently asked him to, to put in an appearance when she and I had a meal together. I had only to watch her to learn the most impeccable table-manners. Monsieur Willy was always professing his love of good breeding; he found something to satisfy it in Marco's charming manners and in her turn of mind which was urbane, but inflexible and slightly caustic. Had she been born twenty years later she would, I think, have made a good journalist. When the summer came, it was Monsieur Willy who proposed taking this extremely pleasant companion, so dignified in her poverty, along with us to a mountain village in Franche-Comté. The luggage she brought with her was heartrendingly light. But, at that time, I myself had very little money at my disposal, and we settled ourselves very happily on the single upper floor of a noisy inn. The wooden balcony and a wicker armchair were all that Marco needed; she never went for walks. She never wearied of the restfulness, of the vivid purple that evening shed on the mountains, of the great bowls of raspberries. She had travelled and she compared the valleys hollowed out by the twilight with other landscapes. Up there I noticed that the only mail Marco received consisted of picture postcards from Masson and "Best wishes for a good holiday", also on a postcard, from a fellow ghost-writer at the Bibliothèque Nationale.

As we sat under the balcony awning on those hot afternoons, Marco mended her underclothes. She sewed badly, but conscientiously, and I flattered my vanity by giving her pieces of advice, such as: "You're using too coarse a thread for fine needles . . . you shouldn't put blue baby-ribbon in chemises, pink is much prettier in lingerie and up against the skin." It was not long before I gave her others, concerning her face-powder, the colour of her lipstick, a hard line she pencilled round the edge of her beautifully-shaped eyelids. "D'you think so? D'you think so?" she would say. My youthful authority was adamant. I took the comb, I made a charming little gap in her tight, sponge-like fringe, I proved expert at softly shadowing her eyes and putting a faint pink glow high up on her cheekbones, near her temples. But I did not know what to do with the unattractive skin of her neck nor with a long shadow that hollowed her cheek. That flattering glow I put on her face transformed it so much that I promptly wiped it off again. Taking to amber powder and being far better fed than in Paris had quite an animating effect. She told me about one of her former journeys when, like a good painter's wife, she had followed her husband from Greek village to Moroccan hamlet, washed his brushes, and fried aubergines and pimentoes in his oil. She promptly left off sewing to have a cigarette, blowing the smoke out through nostrils as soft as some herbivorous animal's. But she only told me the names of places, not of friends, and spoke of discomforts, not of griefs, so I dared not ask her to tell more. The mornings she spent in writing the first chapters of a new novel, at one sou a line, which was being seriously held up by lack of documentation about the early Christians.

"When I've put in lions in the arena and a golden-haired virgin abandoned to the licentious soldiers and a band of Christians escaping in a storm," said Marco, "I shall come to the end of my personal erudition. So I shall wait for the rest till I get back to Paris."

I have said: we became great friends. That is true, if friendship is confined to a rare smoothness of intercourse, preserved by studiously veiled precautions that blunt all sharp points and angles. I could only gain by imitating Marco and her "well-bred" surface manner. Moreover, she aroused not the faintest distrust in me. I felt her to be straight as a die, disgusted by anything that could cause pain, utterly remote from all feminine rivalries. But, though love laughs at difference in age, friendship, especially between two women, is more acutely conscious of it. This is particularly true when friendship is just beginning, and wants, like love, to have everything all at once. The country filled me with a terrible longing for running streams, wet fields, active idleness.

"Marco, don't you think it would be marvellous if we got up early tomorrow and spent the morning under the fir-trees where there are wild cyclamens and purple mushrooms?"

Marco shuddered, and clasped her little hands together.

"Oh, no! Oh, no! Go off on your own and leave me out of it, you young mountain-goat."

I have forgotten to mention that, after the first week, Monsieur Willy had returned to Paris "on business". He wrote me brief notes, spicing his prose, which derived from Mallarmé and Félix Fénéon, with onomatopoeic words in Greek letters German quotations and English terms of endearment.

So I climbed up alone to the firs and the cyclamens. There was something intoxicating to me in the contrast between burning sun and the still-nocturnal cold of the plants growing out of a carpet of moss. More than once, I thought I would not go back for the midday meal. But I did go back, on account of Marco, who was savouring the joy of rest as if she had twenty years' accumulation of weariness to work off. She used to rest with her eyes shut, her face pale beneath her powder, looking utterly exhausted, as if convalescing from an illness. At the end of the afternoon, she would take a little walk along the road that, in passing through the village, hardly left off being a delicious, twisting forest path that rang crisply under one's feet.

You must not imagine that the other "tourists" were much more active than we were. People of my age will remember that a summer in the country, round about 1897, bore no resemblance to the gad-about holidays of today. The most energetic walked as far as a pure, icy, slate-coloured stream, taking with them camp-stools, needlework, a novel, a picnic lunch and useless fishing-rods. On moonlit nights, girls and young men would go off in groups after dinner, which was served at seven, wander along the road, then return, stopping to wish each other good-night. "Are you thinking of bicycling as far as Saut-de-Giers tomorrow?" "Oh, we're not making any definite plans. It all depends on the weather." The men wore low-cut waistcoats like cummerbunds, with two rows of buttons and sham buttonholes, under a black or cream alpaca jacket, and check caps or straw hats. The girls and the young women were plump and well-nourished, dressed in white linen or écru tussore. When they turned up their sleeves, they displayed white arms and, under their big hats, their scarlet sunburn did not reach as high as their foreheads. Venturesome families went in for what was called "bathing" and set off in the afternoons to immerse themselves at a spot where the stream broadened out, barely two and a half miles from the village. At night, round the communal dining-table, the children's wet hair smelt of ponds and wild peppermint.

One day, so that I could read my post which was rich with two letters, an article cut out of *Art et Critique*, and some other odds and ends, Marco tactfully assumed her convalescent pose, shutting her eyes and leaning her head back against the fibre cushion of the wicker chair. She was wearing the écru linen dressing-gown that she put on to save the rest of her wardrobe when we were alone in our bedrooms or out on the wooden balcony. It was when she had on that dressing-gown that she truly showed her age and the period to which she naturally belonged. Certain definite details, pathetically designed to flatter, typed her indelibly, such as a certain deliberate wave in her hair that emphasised the narrowness of her temples, a certain short fringe that would never allow itself to be combed the other way, the carriage of the chin imposed by a high, boned collar, the knees that were never parted and never crossed. Even the shabby dressing-gown itself gave her away. Instead of resigning itself to the simplicity of a working-garment, it was adorned with ruffles of imitation lace at the neck and wrists and a little frill round the hips.

Those tokens of a particular period of feminine fashion and behaviour were just the very ones my own generation was in process of rejecting. The new "angel" hair-style, and Cléo de Mérode's smooth swathes were designed to go with a boater worn like a halo, shirt-blouses in the English style, and straight skirts. Bicycles and bloomers had swept victoriously through every class. I was beginning to be crazy about starched linen collars and rough woollens imported from England. The split between the two fashions, the recent one and the very latest, was too blatantly obvious not to humiliate penniless women who delayed in adopting the one and abandoning the other. Occasionally frustrated in my own bursts of clothes-consciousness, I suffered for Marco, heroic in two worn-out dresses and two light blouses.

Slowly, I folded up my letters again, without my attention straying from the woman who was pretending to be asleep, the pretty woman of 1870 or 1875, who, out of modesty and lack of money, was giving up the attempt to follow us into 1898. In the uncompromising way of young women, I said to myself: "If I were Marco, I'd do my hair like this, I'd dress like that." Then I would make excuses for her: "But she hasn't any money. If I had more money, I'd help her."

Marco heard me folding up my letters, opened her eyes and smiled.

"Nice post?"

"Yes . . . Marco," I said daringly, "Don't you have your letters sent on here?"

"Of course I do. All the correspondence I have is what you see me get."

As I said nothing, she added, all in one burst:

"As you know, I'm separated from my husband. V's friends, thank heaven, have remained *his* friends and not mine. I had a child, twenty years ago, and I lost him when he was hardly more than a baby. And I've never had a lover. So you see, it's quite simple."

"Never had a lover . . ." I repeated.

Marco laughed at my expression of dismay.

"Is that the thing that strikes you most? Don't be so upset! That's the thing I've thought about least. In fact I've long ago given up thinking about it at all."

My gaze wandered from her lovely eyes, rested by the pure air and the green of the chestnut groves, to the little cleft at the tip of her witty nose, to her teeth, a trifle discoloured, but admirably sound and well set.

"But you're very pretty, Marco!"

"Oh!" she said gaily, "I was even a charmer, once upon a time. Otherwise V wouldn't have married me. To be perfectly frank with you, I'm convinced that fate has spared me one great trouble, the tiresome thing that's called a temperament. No, no, all that business of blood rushing into the cheeks, upturned eyeballs, palpitating nostrils, I admit I've never experienced it and never regretted it. You do believe me, don't you?"

"Yes," I said mechanically, looking at Marco's mobile nostrils.

She laid her narrow hand on mine, with an impulsiveness that did not, I knew, come easily to her.

"A great deal of poverty, my child, and before the poverty the job of being an artist's wife in the most down-to-earth way . . . hard manual labour, next door to being a maid-of-all-work. I wonder where I should have found the time to be idle and well-groomed and elegant in secret—in other words, to be someone's romantic mistress."

She sighed, ran her hand over my hair and brushed it back from my temples.

"Why don't you show the top part of your face a little? When I was young, I did my hair like that."

As I had a horror of having my alley-cat's temples exposed naked, I dodged away from the little hand and interrupted Marco, crying:

"No, you don't! No, you don't! *I'm* going to do *your* hair. I've got a marvellous idea!"

Brief confidences, the amusements of two women shut away from the world, hours that were now like those in a sewing-room, now like the idle ones of convalescence—I do not remember that our pleasant holiday produced any genuine intimacy. I was inclined to feel deferent towards Marco, yet, paradoxically, to set hardly any store by her opinions on life and love. When she told me she might have been a mother, I realised that our friendly relationship would never be in the least like my passionate feeling for my real mother, nor would it ever approach the comradeship I should have had with a young woman. But, at that time, I did not know any girl or woman of my own age with whom I could share a reckless gaiety, a mute complicity, a vitality that overflowed in fits of wild laughter, or with whom I could enjoy physical rivalries and rather crude pleasures that Marco's age, her delicate constitution and her whole personality put out of her range and mine.

We talked, and we also read. I had been an insatiable reader in my childhood. Marco had educated herself. At first, I thought I could delve at will into Marco's well-stored mind and memory. But I noticed that she replied with a certain lassitude, and as if mistrustful of her own words.

"Marco, why are you called Marco?"

"Because my name is Léonie," she answered. "Léonie wasn't the right sort of name for V's wife. When I was twenty, V made me pose in a tasselled Greek cap perched over one ear and Turkish slippers with long turned-up points. While he was painting, he used to sing this old sentimental ballad:

Fair Marco, do you love to dance
In brilliant ballrooms, gay with flowers?
Do you love, in night's dark hours,
Ta ra ra, ta ra ra ra . . .

I have forgotten the rest."

I had never heard Marco sing before. Her voice was true and thin, clear as the voice of some old men.

"They were still singing that in my youth," she said. "Painters' studios did a great deal for the propagation of bad music."

She seemed to want to preserve nothing of her past but a superficial irony. I was too young to realise what this calmness of hers implied. I had not yet learnt to recognise the modesty of renunciation.

Towards the end of our summer holiday in Franche-Comté, something astonishing did, however, happen to Marco. Her husband, who was painting in the United States, sent her, through his solicitor, a cheque for fifteen thousand francs. The only comment she made was to say, with a laugh:

"So he's actually got a solicitor now? Wonders will never cease!"

Then she returned the cheque and the solicitor's letter to their envelope and paid no more attention to them. But, at dinner, she gave signs of being a trifle excited, and asked the waitress in a whisper if it was possible to have champagne. We had some. It was sweet and tepid and slightly corked and we only drank half the bottle between us.

Before we shut the communicating door between our rooms, as we did every night, Marco asked me a few questions. She wore an absent-minded expression as she inquired:

"Do you think people will be still wearing those wide-sleeved velvet coats next winter, you know the kind I mean? And where did you get that charming hat you had in the spring—with the brim sloping like a roof? I liked it immensely—on *you*, of course."

She spoke lightly, hardly seeming to listen to my replies and I pretended not to guess how deeply she had hidden her famished craving for decent clothes and fresh underlinen.

The next morning, she had regained control of herself.

"When all's said and done," she said, "I don't see why I should accept this sum from that . . . in other words, from my husband. If it pleases him at the moment to offer me charity, like giving alms to a beggar, that's no reason for me to accept it."

As she spoke, she kept pulling out some threads the laundress had torn in the cheap lace that edged her dressing-gown. Where it fell open, it revealed a chemise that was more than humble. I lost my temper and I scolded Marco as an older woman might have chided a small girl. So much so, that I felt a little ashamed, but she only laughed.

"There, there, don't get cross! Since you want me to, I'll allow myself to be kept by his lordship V. It's certainly my turn."

I put my cheek against Marco's cheek. We stayed watching the harsh, reddish sun reaching the zenith and drinking up all the shadows that divided the mountains. The bend of the river quivered in the distance. Marco sighed:

"Would it be very expensive, a pretty little corset-belt all made of ribbon, with rococo roses on the ends of the suspenders?"

The return to Paris drove Marco back to her novelette. Once again I saw her hat with the three blue thistles, her coat and skirt whose black was faded and pallid, her dark grey gloves and her schoolgirl satchel of cardboard masquerading as leather. Before thinking of her personal elegance, she wanted to move to another place. She took a year's lease of a furnished flat; two rooms and a place where she could wash, plus a sort of cupboard-kitchen, on the ground floor. It was dark there in broad daylight but the red and white cretonne curtains and bedspread were not too hopelessly shabby. Marco nourished herself at midday in a little restaurant near the Library and had tea and bread-and-butter at home at night except when I managed to keep her at my flat for a meal at which stuffed olives and rollmops replaced soup and roast meat. Sometimes Paul Masson brought along an excellent chocolate "Quillet" from Quillet's, the cake-shop in the Rue de Buci.

Completely resigned to her task, Marco had so far acquired nothing except, as October turned out rainy, a kind of rubberised hooded cloak that smelt of asphalt. One day she arrived, her eyes looking anxious and guilty.

"There," she said bravely, "I've come to be scolded. I think I bought this coat in too much of a hurry. I've got the feeling that . . . that it's not quite right."

I was amused by her being as shy as if she were my junior, but I stopped laughing when I had a good look at the coat. An unerring instinct led Marco, so discriminating in other ways, to choose bad material, deplorable cut, fussy braid.

The very next day, I took time off to go out with her and choose a wardrobe for her. Neither she nor I could aspire to the great dress-houses, but I had the pleasure of seeing Marco looking slim and years younger in a dark tailor-made and in a navy serge dress with a white front. With the straight little caracul top-coat, two hats and some underclothes, the bill, if you please, came to fifteen hundred francs: you can see that I was ruthless with the funds sent by the painter V.

I might well have had something to say against Marco's hair style. But, just that very season, there was a changeover to shorter hair and a different way of doing it, so that Marco was able to look as if she were ahead of fashion. In this I sincerely envied her, for, whether I twisted it round my head "à la Ceres" or let it hang to my skirt-hem—"like a well-cord" as Jules Renard said—my long hair blighted my existence.

At this point, the memory of a certain evening obtrudes itself. Monsieur Willy had gone out on business somewhere, leaving Marco, Paul Masson and myself alone together after dinner. When the three of us were on our own, we automatically became clandestinely gay, slightly childish and, as it were, reassured. Masson would sometimes read aloud the serial in a daily paper, a novelette inexhaustibly rich in haughty titled ladies, fancy-dress balls in winter-gardens, chaises dashing along "at a triple gallop" drawn by pure-bred steeds, maidens pale but resolute, exposed to a thousand perils. And we used to laugh wholeheartedly.

"Ah!" Marco would sigh, "I shall never be able to do as well as that. In the novelette world, I shall never be more than a little amateur."

"Little amateur," said Masson one night, "here's just what you want. I've culled it from the Agony Column: 'Man of letters bearing well-known name would be willing to assist young writers both sexes in early stages career.' "

"Both sexes!" said Marco. "Go on, Masson! I've only got one sex and, even then, I think I'm exaggerating by half."

"Very well, I will go on," said Masson. "I will go on to Lieutenant (regular army), garrisoned near Paris, warm-hearted, cultured, wishes to maintain correspondence with intelligent, affectionate woman. Very good, but, apparently, this soldier does not wish to maintain anything but correspondence. Nevertheless, do we write to him? Let us write. The best letter wins a box of Gianduja Kohler—the nutty kind."

"If it's a big box," I said, "I'm quite willing to compete. What about you, Marco?"

With her cleft nose bent over a scribbling-block, Marco was writing already. Masson gave birth to twenty lines in which sly obscenity vied with humour. I stopped after the first page, out of laziness. But how charming Marco's letter was!

"First prize!" I exclaimed.

"Pearls before . . ." muttered Masson. "Do we send it? Poste Restante, Alex 2, Box 59. Give it to me. I'll see that it goes."

"After all, I'm not risking anything," said Marco.

When our diversions were over, she slipped on her mackintosh again and put on her narrow hat in front of the mirror. It was a hat I had chosen, which made her head look very small and her eyes very large under its turned-down brim.

"Look at her!" she exclaimed. "Look at her, the middle-aged lady who debauches warm-hearted and cultured lieutenants!"

With the little oil-lamp in her hand, she preceded Paul Masson.

"I shan't see you at all this week," she told me. "I've got two pieces of homework to do: the chariot race and the Christians in the lions' pit."

"Haven't I already read something of the kind somewhere?" put in Masson.

"I sincerely hope you have," retorted Marco. "If it hadn't been done over and over again, where should I get my documentation?"

The following week, Masson bought a copy of the paper and with his hard, corrugated nail pointed out three lines in the Agony Column: "Alex 2 implores author delicious letter beginning 'What presumption' to give address. Secrecy scrupulously honoured."

"Marco," he said, "you've won not only the box of Gianduja but also a booby prize in the shape of a first-class mug."

Marco shrugged her shoulders.

"It's cruel, what you've made me do. He's sure to think he's been made fun of, poor boy."

Masson screwed up his eyes to their smallest and most inquisitorial.

"Sorry for him already, dear?"

These memories are distant, but precise. They rise out of the fog that inevitably drowns the long days of that particular time, the monotonous amusements of dress rehearsals and suppers at Pousset's, my alternations between animal gaiety and confused unhappiness, the split in my nature between a wild, frightened creature and one with a vast capacity for illusion. But it is a fog that leaves the faces of my friends intact and shining clear.

It was also on a rainy night, in late October or early November, that Marco came to keep me company one night; I remember the anthracite smell of the waterproof cape. She kissed me. Her soft nose was wet, she sighed with pleasure at the sight of the glowing stove. She opened her satchel.

"Here, read this," she said. "Don't you think he's got a charming turn of phrase, this . . . this ruffianly soldier?"

If, after reading it, I had allowed myself a criticism, I should have said: too charming. A letter worked over and recopied; one draft, two drafts thrown into the waste-paper basket. The letter of a shy man, with a touch of the poet, like everyone else.

"Marco, you mean you actually wrote to him?"

The virtuous Marco laughed in my face.

"One can't hide anything from you, charming daughter of Monsieur de La Palisse! Written? Written more than once, even! Crime gives me an appetite. You haven't got a cake? Or an apple?"

While she nibbled delicately, I showed off my ideas on the subject of graphology.

"Look, Marco, how carefully your 'ruffianly soldier' has covered up a word he's begun so as to make it illegible. Sign of gumption, also of touchiness. The writer, as Crépieux-Jamin says, doesn't like people to laugh at him."

Marco agreed, absentmindedly. I noticed she was looking pretty and animated. She studied herself in the glass, clenching her teeth and parting her lips, a grimace few women can resist making in front of a mirror when they have white teeth.

"Whatever's the name of that toothpaste that reddens the gums, Colette?"

"Cherry something or other."

"Thanks, I've got it now. Cherry Dentifrice. Will you do me a favour? Don't tell Paul Masson about my epistolary escapades. He'd never stop teasing me. I shan't keep up my relations with the regular army long enough to make myself ridiculous. Oh, I forgot to tell you. My husband has sent me another fifteen thousand francs."

"Mercy me, be I a-hearing right? as they say where I come from. And you just simply *forgot* that bit of news?"

"Yes, really," said Marco. "I just forgot."

She raised her eyebrows with an air of surprise to remind me delicately that money is always a subject of minor importance.

From that moment, it seemed to me that everything moved very fast for Marco. Perhaps that was due to distance. One of my moves—the first—took me from the Rue Jacob to the top of the Rue de Courcelles, from a dark little cubby-hole to a studio whose great window let in cold, heat and an excess of light. I wanted to show my sophistication, to satisfy my newly-born—and modest—cravings for luxury: I bought white goat-skins, and a folding shower-bath from Chaboche's.

Marco, who felt at home in dim rooms and in the atmosphere of the Left Bank and of libraries, blinked her lovely eyes under the studio skylight, stared at the white divans that suggested polar bears and did not like the new way I did my hair. I wore it piled up above my forehead and twisted into a high chignon; this new "helmet" fashion had swept the hair up from the most modest and retiring napes.

Such a minor domestic upheaval would not have been worth mentioning, did it not make it understandable that, for some time, I only had rapid glimpses of Marco. My pictures of her succeeded each other jerkily like the pictures in those children's books, that, as you turn the pages fast, give the illusion of continuous movement. When she brought me the second letter from the romantic lieutenant, I had crossed the intervening gulf. As Marco walked into my new, light flat, I saw that she was definitely prettier than she had been the year before. The slender foot she thrust out below the hem of her skirt rejoiced in the kind of shoe it deserved. Through the veil stretched taut over the little cleft at the tip of her nose she stared, now at her gloved hand, now at each unknown room, but she seemed to see neither the one nor the other clearly. With bright patience she endured my arranging and rearranging the curtains: she admired the folding shower-bath, which, when erected, vaguely suggested a vertical coffin. She was so patient and so absent-minded that in the end I noticed it and asked her crudely:

"By the way, Marco, how's the ruffianly soldier?"

Her eyes, softened by make-up and short-sightedness, looked into mine.

"As it happens, he's very well. His letters are charming—decidedly so."

"Decidedly so? How many have you had?"

"Three in all. I'm beginning to think it's enough. Don't you agree?"

"No, since they're charming—and they amuse you."

"I don't care for the atmosphere of the *poste restante* . . . It's a horrid hole. Everyone there has a guilty look. Here, if you're interested . . ."

She threw a letter into my lap; it had been there ready all the time, folded up in her gloved hand. I read it rather slowly, I was so preoccupied with its serious tone, devoid of the faintest trace of humour.

"What a remarkable lieutenant you've come across, Marco! I'm sure, that if he weren't restrained by his shyness . . ."

"His shyness?" protested Marco. "He's already got to the point of hoping that we shall exchange less impersonal letters! What cheek! For a shy man . . ."

She broke off to raise her veil that was overheating her coarse-grained skin and flushing up those uneven red patches on her cheeks. But nowadays she knew how to apply her powder cleverly, how to brighten the colour of her mouth. Instead of a discouraged woman of forty-five, I saw before me a smart woman of forty, her chin held high above the boned collar that hid the secrets of the neck. Once again, because of her very beautiful eyes, I forgot the deterioration of all the rest of her face and sighed inwardly: "What a pity . . ."

Our respective moves took us away from our old surroundings and I did not see Marco quite so often. But she was very much in my mind. The polarity of affection between two women friends that gives one authority and the other pleasure in being advised turned me into a peremptory young guide. I decided that Marco ought to wear shorter skirts and more nipped-in waistlines. I sternly rejected braid, which made her look old, colours that dated her and, most of all, certain hats that, when Marco put them on, mysteriously sentenced her beyond hope of appeal. She allowed herself to be persuaded, though she would hesitate for a moment: "You think so? You're quite sure?" and glance at me out of the corner of her beautiful eye.

We liked meeting each other in a little tea-room at the corner of the Rue de l'Échelle and the Rue d'Argenteuil, a warm, poky "British", saturated with the bitter smell of Ceylon tea. We "partook of tea", like other sweet-toothed ladies of those far-off days, and hot buttered toast followed by quantities of cakes. I liked my tea very black, with a thick white layer of cream and plenty of sugar. I believed I was learning English when I asked the waitress: "Edith, please, a little more milk, and butter."

It was at the little "British" that I perceived such a change in Marco that I could not have been more startled if, since our last meeting, she had dyed her hair peroxide or taken to drugs. I feared some danger, I imagined that the wretch of a husband had frightened her into his clutches again. But, if she were frightened, she would not have had that blank flickering gaze that wandered from the table to the walls and was profoundly indifferent to everything it glanced at.

"Marco? Marco?"

"Darling?"

"Marco, what on earth's happened? Have other treasure galleons arrived? Or what?"

She smiled at me as if I were a stranger.

"Galleons? Oh, no."

She emptied her cup in one gulp and said almost in a whisper:

"Oh, how stupid of me, I've burnt myself."

Consciousness and affection slowly returned to her gaze. She saw that mine was astonished and she blushed, clumsily and unevenly as she always did.

"Forgive me," she said, laying her little hand on mine.

She sighed and relaxed.

"Oh!" she said. "What luck there isn't anyone here. I'm a little . . . how can I put it? . . . queasy."

"More tea? Drink it very hot."

"No, no. I think it's that glass of port I had before I came here. No, nothing, thanks."

She leant back in her chair and closed her eyes. She was wearing her newest suit, a little oval brooch of the "family heirloom" type was pinned at the base of the high boned collar of her cream blouse. The next moment she had revived and was completely herself, consulting the mirror in her new handbag and feverishly anticipating my questions.

"Ah, I'm better now! It was that port, I'm sure it was. Yes, my dear, port! And in the company of Lieutenant Alexis Trallard, son of General Trallard."

"Ah!" I exclaimed with relief, "is *that* all? You quite frightened me. So you've actually seen the ruffianly soldier? What's he like? Is he like his letters? Does he stammer? Has he got a lisp? Is he bald? Has he a port-wine mark on his nose?"

These and similar idiotic suggestions were intended to make Marco laugh. But she listened to me with a dreamy, refined expression as she nibbled at a piece of buttered toast that had gone cold.

"My dear," she said at last. "If you'll let me get a word in edgeways, I might inform you that Lieutenant Trallard is neither an invalid nor a monster. Incidentally, I've known this ever since last week, because he enclosed a photograph in one of his letters."

She took my hand.

"Don't be cross. I didn't dare mention it to you. I was afraid."

"Afraid of what?"

"Of you, darling, of being teased a little. And . . . well . . . just simply afraid!"

"But why *afraid*?"

She made an apologetic gesture of ignorance, clutching her arms against her breast.

"Here's the Object," she said, opening her handbag. "Of course, it's a very bad snapshot."

"He's much better-looking than the photo . . . of course?"

"Better looking . . . good heavens, he's totally *different*. Especially his expression."

As I bent over the photograph, she bent over it too, as if to protect it from too harsh a judgement.

"Lieutenant Trallard hasn't got that shadow like a sabre-cut on his cheek. Besides, his nose isn't so long. He's got light brown hair and his moustache is almost golden."

After a silence, Marco added shyly:

"He's tall."

I realised it was my turn to say something.

"But he's very good-looking! But he looks exactly as a lieutenant should! But what an enchanting story, Marco! And his eyes? What are his eyes like?"

"Light brown like his hair," said Marco eagerly.

She pulled herself together.

"I mean that was my general impression. I didn't look very closely."

I hid my astonishment at being confronted with a Marco

whose words, whose embarrassment, whose naïvety surpassed the reactions of the greenest girl to being stood a glass of port by a lieutenant. I could never have believed that this middle-aged married woman, inured to living among Bohemians, was at heart a timorous novice. I restrained myself from letting Marco see, but I think she guessed my thoughts, for she tried to turn her encounter, her "queasiness" and her lieutenant into a joke. I helped her as best I could.

"And when are you going to see Lieutenant Trallard again, Marco?"

"Not for a good while, I think."

"Why?"

"Why, because he must be left to wear his nerves to shreds in suspense! Left to simmer!" declared Marco, raising a learned forefinger. "Simmer! That's my principle!"

We laughed at last; laughed a great deal and rather idiotically. That hour seems to me, in restrospect, like the last halt, the last landing on which my friend Marco stopped to regain her breath. During the days that followed I have a vision of myself writing (I did not sign my work either) on the thin, crackly American paper I liked best of all, and Marco was busy working too, at one sou a line. One afternoon, she came to see me again.

"Good news of the ruffianly soldier, Marco?"

She archly indicated "*Yes*" with her chin and her eyes, because Monsieur Willy was on the other side of the glass-topped door. She submitted a sample of dress material which she would not dream of buying without my approval. She was gay and I thought that, like a sensible woman, she had reduced Lieutenant Alexis Trallard to his proper status. But when we were all alone in my bedroom, that refuge hung with rush matting that smelt of damp reeds, she held out a letter, without saying a word, and, without saying a word, I read it and gave it back to her. For the accents of love inspire only silence and the letter I had read was full of love. Full of serious, vernal love. Why did one question, the very one I should have repressed, escape me? I asked—thinking of the freshness of the words I had just read, of the respect that permeated them—I asked indiscreetly:

"How old is he?"

Marco put her two hands over her face, gave a sudden sob and whispered:

"Oh, heavens! It's appalling!"

Almost at once, she mastered herself, uncovered her face and chided herself in a harsh voice:

"Stop this nonsense. I'm dining with him tonight."

She was about to wipe her wet eyes but I stopped her.

"Let me do it, Marco."

With my two thumbs, I raised her upper eyelids so that the two tears about to fall should be reabsorbed and not smudge the mascara on her lashes by wetting them.

"There! Wait, I haven't finished."

I retouched all her features. Her mouth was trembling a little. She submitted patiently, sighing as if I were dressing a wound. To complete everything, I filled the puff in her handbag with a rosier shade of powder. Neither of us uttered a word meanwhile.

"Whatever happens," I told her, "don't cry. At all costs, don't let yourself give way to tears."

She jibbed at this, and laughed.

"All the same, we haven't got to the scene of the final parting yet!"

I took her over to the best-lighted looking-glass. At the sight of her reflection, the corners of Marco's mouth quivered a little.

"Satisfied with the effect, Marco?"

"Too good to be true."

"Can't ever be too good. You'll tell me what happened? When?"

"As soon as I know myself," said Marco.

Two days later, she returned, in spite of stormy, almost warm weather that rattled the cowls on the chimney-pots and beat back the smoke and fumes of the slow-combustion stove.

"Out of doors in this tempest, Marco?"

"It doesn't worry me a bit, I've got a four-wheeler waiting down there."

"Wouldn't you rather dine here with me?"

"I can't," she said, averting her head.

"Right. But you can send the growler away. It's only half-past six, you've plenty of time."

"No, I haven't time. How does my face look?"

"Quite all right. In fact, very nice."

"Yes, but . . . Quick, be an angel! Do what you did for me the day before yesterday. And then, what's the best thing to receive Alex at home in? Outdoor clothes, don't you think? Anyway, I haven't got an indoor frock that would really do."

"Marco, you know just as well as I do . . ."

"No," she broke in, "I don't know. You might as well tell me I knew India because I've written a novelette that takes place in the Punjab. Look, he's sent a kind of emergency-supply round to my place—a cold chicken in aspic, champagne, some fruit. He says that, like me, he has a horror of restaurants. Ah, now I think of it, I *ought* to have . . ."

She pressed her hand to her forehead, under her fringe.

"I *ought* to have bought that black dress last Saturday—the one I saw in the second-hand shop. Just my size, with a Liberty silk skirt and a lace top. Tell me, could you possibly lend me some very fine stockings? I've left it too late now to . . ."

"Yes, yes, of course."

"Thank you. Don't you think a flower to brighten up my dress? No, *not* a flower on the bodice. Is it true that iris is a scent that's gone out of fashion? I'm sure I had heaps of other things to ask you . . . heaps of things."

Though she was in the shelter of my room, sitting by the roaring stove, Marco gave me the impression of a woman battling with the wind and the rain that lashed the glass panes. I seemed to be watching Marco set off on some kind of journey, embarking like an emigrant. It was as if I could see a flapping cape blowing round her, a plaid scarf streaming in the wind.

Besieged, soon to be invaded. There was no doubt in my mind that an attack was being launched against the most defenceless of creatures. Silent, as if we were committing a crime, we hurried through our beauty operations. Marco attempted to laugh.

"We're trampling the most rigorously established customs underfoot. Normally, it's the oldest witch who washes and decks the youngest for the Sabbath."

"Ssh, Marco, keep still—I've just on finished."

I rolled up the pair of silk stockings in a piece of paper, along with a little bottle of yellow Chartreuse.

"Have you got any cigarettes at home?"

"Yes. Whatever am I saying? No. But *he'll* have some on him, he smokes Egyptian ones."

"I'll put four amusing little napkins in the parcel, it'll make it more like a doll's dinner-party. Would you like the cloth too?"

"No, thanks. I've got an embroidered one I bought ages ago in Brussels."

We were talking in low, rapid whispers, without ever smiling. In the doorway, Marco turned round to give me a long, distracted look out of moist, made-up eyes, a look in which I could read nothing resembling joy. My thoughts followed her in the cab that was carrying her through the dark and the rain, over the puddle-drenched road where the wind blew miniature squalls round the lamp-posts. I wanted to open the window to watch her drive away but the whole tempestuous night burst into the studio and I shut it again on this traveller who was setting off on a dangerous voyage, with no ballast but a pair of silk stockings, some pink make-up, some fruit and a bottle of champagne.

Lieutenant Trallard was still only relatively real to me, although I had seen his photograph. A very French face, a rather long nose, a well-chiselled forehead, hair *en brosse* and the indispensable moustache. But the picture of Marco blotted out his —Marco all anxious apprehension, her beauty enhanced by my tricks, and breathing fast, as a deer pants when it hears the hooves and clamour of the distant hunt. I listened to the wind and rain and I reckoned up her chances of crossing the sea and reaching port in safety. "She was very pretty tonight. Provided her lamp with the pleated shade gives a becoming light. This young man preoccupies her, flatters her, peoples her solitude, in a word, rejuvenates her."

A gust of bad weather beat furiously against the pane. A little black snake that oozed from the bottom of the window began to creep slowly along. From this, I realised that the window did not shut properly and the water was beginning to soak the carpet. I went off to seek floor-cloths and the aid of Maria, the girl from Aveyron who was my servant at that time. On my way, I opened the door to Masson who had just rung three times. While he was divesting himself of a limp mackintosh cape that fell dripping on the tiled floor, like a basketful of eels, I exclaimed:

"Did you run into Marco? She's just this minute gone downstairs. She was so sorry not to see you."

A lie must give off a smell that is apparent to people with sensitive nostrils. Paul Masson sniffed the air in my direction, curtly wagged his short beard and went off to join Monsieur Willy in his white study that, with its brief curtains, beaded mouldings and small window-panes, vaguely resembled a converted cake-shop.

After that, everything progressed fast for Marco. Nevertheless she came back, after that stormy night, but she made me no confidences. It is true that a third person prevented them. That particular day, my impatience to know was restrained by the fear that her confidence might yield something that would have slightly horrified me; there was an indefinable air of furtiveness and guilt about her whole person. At least, that is what I *think* I remember. My memories, after that, are much more definite. How could I have forgotten that Marco underwent a magical transformation, the kind of belated, embarrassing puberty that deceives no one? She reacted violently to the slightest stimulus. A thimbleful of Frontignac set her cheeks and her eyes ablaze. She laughed for no reason, stared blankly into space, was incessantly resorting to her powder-puff and her mirror. Everything was going at a great rate. I could not long put off the "Well, Marco?" she must be waiting for.

One clear, biting winter night, Marco was with me. I was stoking up the stove. She kept her gaze fixed on its mica window and did not speak.

"Are you warm enough in your little flat, Marco? Does the coal grate give enough heat?"

She smiled vaguely, as if at a deaf person, and did not answer. So I said at last:

"Well, Marco? Contented? Happy?"

It was the last, the most important word, I think, that she pushed away with her hand.

"I did not believe," she said, very low, "that such a thing could exist."

"What thing? Happiness?"

She flushed here and there, in dark, fiery patches. I asked her —it was my turn to be naïve:

"Then why don't you look more pleased?"

"Can one rejoice over something terrible, something that's so . . . so like an evil spell?"

I secretly permitted myself the thought that to use such a grim and weighty expression was, as the saying goes, to clap a very large hat on a very small head, and I waited for her next words. But none came. At this point, there was a brief period of silence. I saw nothing wrong in Marco's keeping quiet about her love-affair: it was rather the love-affair itself that I resented. I thought—unjust as I was and unmindful of her past—that she had been very quick to reward a casual acquaintance, even if he were an officer, a general's son and had light brown hair into the bargain.

The period of reserve was followed by the season of unrestricted joy. Happiness, once accepted, is seldom reticent; Marco's, as it took firm root, was not very vocal but expressed itself in the usual boring way. I knew that, like every other woman, she had met a man "absolutely unlike anyone else" and that everything he did was a source of abundant delight to his dazzled mistress. I was not allowed to remain ignorant that Alexis possessed a "lofty soul" in addition to a "cast-iron body". Marco did not, thank heaven, belong to that tribe who boastfully whisper precise details—the sort of female I call a Madame-how-many-times. Nevertheless, by looking confused or by spasms of perturbed reticence, she had a mute way of conveying things I would gladly have been dispensed from knowing.

This virtuous victim of belated love and suddenly-awakened

sensuality did not submit all at once to blissful immolation. But she could not escape the usual snares of her new condition, the most unavoidable of which is eloquence, both of speech and gesture.

The first few weeks made her thin and dry-lipped, with feverish, glittering eyes. "A Rops!" Paul Masson said behind her back. "Madame Dracula," said Monsieur Willy, going one better. "What the devil can our worthy Marco be up to to make her look like that?"

Masson screwed up his little eyes and shrugged one shoulder. "Nothing," he said coldly. "These phenomena belong to neurotic simulation, like imaginary pregnancy. Probably, like many women, our worthy Marco imagines she is the bride of Satan. It's the phase of infernal joys."

I thought it detestable that either of her two friends should call Madame V "our worthy Marco". Nor was I any more favourably impressed by the icily critical comments of these two disillusioned men, especially on anything concerning friendship, esteem or love.

Then Marco's face became irradiated with a great serenity. As she regained her calm, she gradually lost the fevered glitter of a lost soul and put on a little flesh. Her skin seemed smoother, she had lost the breathlessness that betrayed her nervousness and her haste. Her slightly increased weight slowed down her walk and movements; she smoked cigarettes lazily.

"New phase," announced Masson. "Now she looks like the Marco of the old days, when she'd just got married to V. It's the phase of the odalisque."

I now come to a period when, because I was going about more and was also more loaded up with work, I saw Marco only at intervals. I dared not drop in on Marco without warning, for I dreaded I might encounter Lieutenant Trallard, only too literally in undress, in the minute flat that had nothing in the way of an entrance-hall. What with teas put off and appointments broken, fate kept us apart, till at last it brought us together again in my studio, on a lovely June day that blew warm and cool breezes through the open window.

Marco smelt delicious. Marco was wearing a brand-new black dress with white stripes, Marco was all smiles. Her romantic love-affair had already been going on for eight months. She looked so much fatter to me that the proud carriage of her head no longer preserved her chin line and her waist, visibly compressed, no longer moved flexibly inside the petersham belt, as it had done last year.

"Congratulations, Marco! You look marvellously well!"

Her long deer's eyes looked uneasy.

"You think I've got plump? Not too plump, I hope?"

She lowered her lids and smiled mysteriously.

"A little extra flesh does make one's breasts so pretty."

I was not used to that kind of remark from her and I was the one who felt embarrassed, frankly, as embarrassed as if Marco—that very Marco who used to barricade herself in her room at the country inn, crying: "Don't come in, I'll slip on my dressing-gown!"—had deliberately stripped naked in the middle of my studio drawing-room.

The next second, I told myself I was being ungenerous and unfriendly, that I ought to rejoice wholeheartedly in Marco's happiness. To prove my goodwill, I said gaily:

"I bet, one of these days, when I open the door to you, I'll find Lieutenant Trallard in your wake! I'm too magnanimous to refuse him a cup of tea and a slice of bread and cheese, Marco. So why not bring him along next time?"

Marco gave me a sharp look that was like a total stranger's. Quickly as she averted it, I could not miss the virulent, suspicious glance that swept over me, over my smile and my long hair, over everything that youth lavishes on a face and body of twenty-five.

"No," she said.

She recovered herself and looked back at me with her usual doe-like gentleness.

"It's too soon," she said gracefully. "Let's wait till the 'ruffianly soldier' deserves such an honour!"

But I remained appalled at having caught, in one look, a glimpse of a primitive female animal, black with suspicion, hostility and possessive passion. For the first time, we were both aware of the difference in our ages as something sharp, cruel and irremediable. It was the difference in age, revealed in the depths of a beautiful velvety eye, that falsified our relationship and disrupted our old bond. When I saw Marco again after the "day of the look" and I enquired after Lieutenant Trallard, the new-style Marco, plump, white, calm—almost matriarchal—answered me in a tone of false modesty, the tone of a greedy and sated proprietress. I stared at her, stupefied, looking for all the things of which voracious, unhoped-for love had robbed her. I looked in vain for her elegant thinness, for the firmness of her slender waist, for her rather bony, well-defined chin, for the deep hollows in which the velvety, almost black eyes used to shelter. . . . Realising that I was registering the change in her, she renounced the dignity of a well-fed Sultana and became uneasy.

"What can I do about it? I'm putting on weight."

"It's only temporary," I said. "Do you eat a lot?"

She shrugged her thickened shoulders.

"I don't know. Yes. I *am* more greedy, that's a fact, than . . . than before. But I've often seen you eat enormously and *you* don't put on weight!"

To exonerate myself, I made a gesture to signify that I couldn't help this. Marco stood up, planted herself in front of the mirror, clutched her waist tight with both hands and kneaded it.

"Last year, when I did that, I could feel myself positively melting away between my two hands."

"Last year you weren't happy, Marco."

"Oh, so that's it!" she said bitterly.

She was studying her reflection at close quarters as if she had been alone. The addition of some few pounds had turned her into another woman, or rather another type of woman. The flesh was awkwardly distributed on her lightly-built frame. "She's got a behind like a cobbler's," I thought. In my part of the country, they say that the cobbler's behind gets flat from sitting so much but develops a square shape. "And, in addition, breasts like jellyfish, very broad and decidedly flabby." For, even if she is fond of her, a woman always judges another woman harshly.

Marco turned round abruptly.

"What was that?" she asked.

"I didn't say anything, Marco."

"Sorry. I thought you did."

"If you really want to fight against a tendency to put on flesh . . ."

"*Tendency*," Marco echoed, between her teeth. "Tendency is putting it mildly."

". . . why don't you try Swedish gymnastics? People are talking a lot about them."

She interrupted me with a gesture of intolerant refusal.

"Or else cut out breakfast? In the morning don't have anything but unsweetened lemon-juice in a glass of water."

"But I'm hungry in the morning!" cried Marco. "Everything's different, do realise that! I'm hungry, I wake up thinking of fresh butter—and thick cream—and coffee, and ham. I think that, after breakfast, there'll be luncheon to follow and I think of . . . of what will come after luncheon, the thing that kindles this hunger again—and all these cravings I have now that are so terribly fierce."

Dropping her hands that had been harshly pummelling her waist and bosom, she challenged me in the same querulous tone:

"Candidly, could *I* ever have foreseen . . ."

Her voice changed.

"He actually says that I make him so happy."

I could not resist putting my arms round her neck.

"Marco, don't worry about so many things! What you've just said explains everything, justifies everything. Be happy, Marco, make him happy and let everything else go hang!"

We kissed each other. She went away reassured, swaying on those unfamiliar broadened hips. Soon afterwards, Monsieur Willy and I went off to Bayreuth and I did not fail to send Marco a great many picture postcards, covered with Wagnerian emblems entwined with leit-motifs. As soon as I returned, I asked Marco to meet me at our "tea-room". She had not grown any thinner nor did she look any younger. Where others develop curves and rotundity, Marco's fleshiness tended to be square.

"And you haven't been away from Paris at all, Marco? Nothing's changed?"

"Nothing, thank God."

She touched the wood of the little table with the tip of her finger to avert ill luck. I needed nothing but that gesture to tell me that Marco still belonged, body and soul, to Lieutenant Trallard. Another, no less eloquent sign was that Marco only asked me questions of pure politeness about my stay in Bayreuth—moreover I guessed she did not even listen to my answers.

She blushed when I asked her, in my turn:

"What about work, Marco? Any novelettes on the stocks for next season?"

"Oh, nothing much," she said in a bored voice. "A publisher wants a novel for children of eight to fourteen. As if that was up my street! Anyway . . ."

A gentle, cowlike expression passed over her face like a cloud and she closed her eyes.

"Anyway, I feel so lazy . . . oh, *so* lazy!"

When Masson, informed of our return, announced himself with his usual three rings, he hastened to tell me he knew "all" from Marco's own lips. To my surprise, he spoke favourably of Lieutenant Trallard. He did not take the line that he was a tenth-rate gigolo or a drunkard destined to premature baldness or a garrison town Casanova. On the other hand, I thought he was decidedly harsh about Marco and even more cold than harsh.

"But, come now, Paul, what are you blaming Marco for in this affair?"

"Pooh! nothing," said Paul Masson.

"And they're madly happy together, you know!"

"Madly strikes me as no exaggeration."

He gave a quiet little laugh that was echoed by Monsieur Willy. Detestable laughs that made fun of Marco and myself, and were accompanied by blunt opinions and pessimistic forecasts, formulated with complete assurance and indifference, as if the romance that lit up Marco's Indian summer were no more than some stale bit of gossip.

"Physically," Paul Masson said, "Marco *had* reached the phase known as the brewer's dray-horse. When a gazelle turns into a brood mare, it's a bad look-out for her. Lieutenant Trallard was perfectly right. It was Marco who compromised Lieutenant Trallard."

"Compromised? You're crazy, Masson! Honestly, the things you say."

"My dear girl, a child of three would tell you, as I do, that Marco's first, most urgent duty was to remain slender, charming, elusive, a twilight creature beaded with rain-drops, not to be bursting with health and frightening people in the streets by shouting: 'I've done it! I've done it! I've . . .' "

"Masson!"

My blood was boiling; I flogged Masson with my rope of hair. I understood nothing of that curious kind of severity only men display towards an innocence peculiar to women. I listened to the judgements of these two on the "Marco case", judgements that admitted not one extenuating circumstance, as if they were lecturing on higher mathematics.

"She *wasn't* up to it," decreed one of them. "She fondly supposed that being the forty-six-year-old mistress of a young man of twenty-five was a delightful adventure."

"Whereas it's a profession," said the other.

"Or rather, a highly-skilled sport."

"No. Sport is an unpaid job. But she wouldn't even understand that her one and only hope is to break it off."

I had not yet become inured to the mixture of affected cynicism and literary paradox by which, round about 1900, intelligent, bitter, frustrated men maintained their self-esteem.

September lay over Paris, a September of fine, dry days and crimson sunsets. I sulked over being in town and over my husband's decision to cut short my summer holiday. One day, I received an express letter that I stared at in surprise, for I did not know Marco's writing well. The handwriting was regular but the spaces between the letters betrayed emotional agitation. She wanted to talk to me. I was in, waiting for her, at the hour when the red light from the setting sun tinged the yellow-curtained window-pane with a vinous flush. I was pleased to see there was no outward trace of disturbance about her. As if there were no other possible subject of conversation, Marco announced at once:

"Just imagine, Alex is going off on a mission."

"On a mission? Where to?"

"Morocco."

"When?"

"Almost at once. Perhaps in a week's time. Orders from the War Office."

"And there's no way out of it?"

"His father, General Trallard . . . yes, if his father intervened personally, he might be able . . . But he thinks this mission—incidentally, it's quite a dangerous one—is a great honour. So . . ."

She made a little, abortive gesture and fell silent, staring into vacancy. Her heavy body, her full, pale cheeks and stricken eyes made her look like a tragedy queen.

"Does a mission take a long time, Marco?"

"I don't know—I haven't the faintest idea. He talks of three or four months, possibly five."

"Now, now, Marco," I said gaily. "What's three or four months? You'll wait for him, that's all."

She did not seem to hear me. She seemed to be attentively studying a purple ink cleaner's mark on the inside of her glove.

"Marco," I risked, "couldn't you go over there with him and live in the same district?"

The moment I spoke, I regretted it. Marco, with trunks full of dresses, Marco as the European favourite, or else Marco as the native wife going in for silver bangles, couscous and fringed scarves. The pictures my imagination conjured up made me afraid—afraid for Marco.

"Of course," I hastily added, "that wouldn't be practical."

Night was falling and I got up to give us some light but Marco restrained me.

"Wait," she said. "There's something else. I'd rather not talk to you about it here. Will you come to my place tomorrow? I've got some good China tea and some little salted cakes from the Boulevard Malesherbes."

"Of course I'd love to, Marco! But . . ."

"I'm not expecting anyone tomorrow. Do come, you might be able to do me a great service. Don't put on the light, the light in the hall is all I need."

Marco's little "furnished suite" had changed too. An arrangement of curtains on a wooden frame behind the entrance door provided it with a substitute for a hall. The brass bedstead had become a divan-bed and various new pieces of furniture struck me quite favourably, as also did some oriental rugs. A garlanded Venetian glass over the mantelpiece reflected some red and white dahlias. In the scent that pervaded it, I recognised Marco's married, if I can use the expression, to another, full-bodied fragrance.

The second, smaller room served as a bathroom; I caught sight of a zinc bath-tub and a kind of shower arrangement fixed to the ceiling. I made, as I came in, some obvious remark such as:

"How nice you've made it here, Marco!"

The stormy, precociously cold September day did not penetrate into this confined dwelling whose thick walls and closed windows kept the air perfectly still. Marco was already busy getting tea, setting out our two cups and our two plates. "She's not expecting anyone," I thought. She offered me a saucer full of greengages while she warmed the teapot.

"What beautiful little hands you have, Marco!"

She suddenly knocked over a cup, as if the least unexpected

sound upset the conscious control of her movements. We went through that pretence of a meal that covers and puts off the embarrassment of explanations, rifts and silences; nevertheless we reached the moment when Marco had to say what she wanted to say. It was indeed high time; I could see she was almost at the end of her tether. We instinctively find it odd, even comic, when a plump person shows signs of nervous exhaustion and I was surprised that Marco could be at once so buxom and in such a state of collapse. She pulled herself together; I saw her face, once again, look like a noble warrior's. The cigarette she avidly lit after tea completed her recovery. The glint of henna on her short hair suited her.

"Well," she began in a clear voice, "I think it's over."

No doubt she had not planned to open with those words, for she stopped, as if aghast.

"Over? Why, what's over?"

"You know perfectly well what I mean," she said. "If you're at all fond of me, as I think you are, you'll try and help me, but . . . All the same, I'm going to tell you."

Those were almost her last coherent words. In putting down the story that I heard, I am obliged to cut out all that made it, in Marco's version, so confused and so terribly clear.

She told it as many women do, going far back, and irrelevantly, into the past of what had been her single, dazzling love-affair. She kept on repeating herself and correcting dates: "So it must have been Thursday, December 26th. What *am* I saying? It was a Friday, because we'd been to Prunier's to have a fish dinner. He's a practising Catholic and abstains on Fridays."

Then the detailed minuteness of the story went to pieces. Marco lost the thread and kept breaking off to say, "Oh, well, we can skip that!" or "Goodness, I can't remember where I'd got to!" and interlarding every other sentence with "You know." Grief drove her to violent gesticulation: she kept smiting her knees with the palm of her hand and flinging her head back against the chair cushions.

All the time she was running on with the prolixity and banality that give all lovers' laments a family likeness, accompanying certain indecent innuendoes with a pantomime of lowering her long eyelids. I felt completely unmoved. I was conscious only of a longing to get away and even had to keep clenching my jaws to repress nervous yawns. I found Marco all too tiresomely like every other woman in love; she was also taking an unconscionably long time to tell me how all this raving about a handsome young soldier came to end in disaster —a disaster, of course, totally unlike anyone else's; they always are.

"Well, one day . . ." said Marco, at long last.

She put her elbows on the arms of her chair. I imitated her and we both leant forward. Marco broke off her confused jeremiad and I saw a gleam of awareness come into her soft, sad eyes, a look capable of seeing the truth. The tone of her voice changed too, and I will try to summarise the dramatic part of her story.

In the verbosity of the early stage, she had not omitted to mention the "madness of passion", the fiery ardour of the young man who would impetuously rush through the half-open door, pull aside the curtain and, from there, make one bound on to the divan where Marco lay awaiting him. He could not endure wasting time in preliminaries or speeches. Impetuosity has its own particular ritual. Marco gave me to understand that, more often than not, the lieutenant, his gloves and his peaked cap were all flung down haphazard on the divan. Poetry and sweet nothings only came afterwards. At this point in her story, Marco made a prideful pause and turned her gaze towards a bevelled, nickel-plated photograph frame. Her silence and her gaze invited me to various conjectures, and perhaps to a touch of envy.

"Well, so one day . . ." said Marco.

A day of licence, definitely. One of those rainy Paris days when a mysterious damp that dulls the mirrors and a strange craving to fling off clothes incites lovers to shut themselves up and turn day into night, "one of those days," Marco said, "that are the perdition of body and soul. . . ." I had to follow my friend and to imagine her—she forced me to—half-naked on the divan-bed, emerging from one of those ecstasies that were so crude and physical that she called them "evil spells". It was at that moment that her hand, straying over the bed, encountered the peaked forage cap known as a kepi and she yielded to one of those all-too-typical feminine reflexes; she sat up in her crumpled chemise, planted the kepi over one ear, gave it a roguish little tap to settle it, and hummed:

With bugle and fife and drum
The soldiers are coming to town . . .

"Never," Marco told me, "never have I seen anything like Alex's face. It was . . . incomprehensible. I'd say it was hideous, if he weren't so handsome. . . . I can't tell you what my feelings were. . . ."

She broke off and stared at the empty divan-bed.

"What happened then, Marco? What did he say?"

"Why, nothing. I took off the kepi, I got up, I tidied myself, we had some tea. In fact, everything passed off just as usual. But since that day I've two or three times caught Alex looking at me with that face again and with such a very odd expression in his eyes. I can't get rid of the idea that the kepi was fatal to me. Did it bring back some unpleasant memory? I'd like to know what *you* think. Tell me straight out, don't hedge."

Before replying, I took care to compose my face; I was so terrified it might express the same horror, disapproval and disgust as Lieutenant Trallard's. Oh Marco! In one moment I destroyed you, I wept for you—I saw you. I saw you just as Alexis Trallard had seen you. My contemptuous eyes took in the slack breasts and the slipped shoulder-straps of the crumpled chemise. And the leathery, furrowed neck, the red patches on the skin below the ears, the chin left to its own devices and long past hope. . . . And that groove, like a dried-up river, that hollows the lower eyelid after making love, and that vinous, fiery flush that does not cool off quickly enough when it burns on an ageing face. And, crowning all that, the kepi! The kepi—with its stiff lining and its jaunty peak, slanted over one roguishly-winked eye.

With bugle and fife and drum. . . .

"I know very well," went on Marco, "that, between lovers, the slightest thing is enough to disturb a magnetic atmosphere . . . I know very well . . ."

Alas! What did she know?

"And after that, Marco? What was the end?"

"The end? But I've told you all there is to tell. Nothing else happened. The mission to Morocco turned up. The date's been put forward twice. But that isn't the only reason I've been losing sleep. Other signs . . ."

"What signs?"

She did not dare give a definite answer. She put out a hand as if to thrust away my question and averted her head.

"Oh, nothing, just . . . just differences."

She strained her ears in the direction of the door.

"I haven't seen him for three days," she said. "Obviously he has an enormous amount to do getting ready for this mission. All the same . . ."

She gave a sidelong smile.

"All the same, I'm not a child," she said in a detached voice. "In any case, he writes to me. Express letters."

"What are his letters like?"

"Oh, charming, of course, what else would they be? He may be very young but *he's* not quite a child either."

As I had stood up, Marco suddenly became anguished and humble and clutched my hands.

"What do you think I ought to do? What *does* one do in these circumstances?"

"How can I possibly know, Marco? I think there's absolutely nothing to be done but to wait. I think it's essential, for your own dignity."

She burst into an unexpected laugh.

"My dignity! Honestly, you make me laugh! My dignity! Oh, these young women."

I found her laugh and her look equally unbearable.

"But, Marco, you're asking my advice—I'm giving it you straight from the heart."

She went on laughing and shrugging her shoulders. Still laughing, she brusquely opened the door in front of me. I thought that she was going to kiss me, that we should arrange another meeting, but I had hardly got outside before she shut the door behind me without saying anything beyond:

"My dignity! No, really, that's *too* funny!"

If I stick to facts, the story of Marco is ended. Marco had had a lover; Marco no longer had a lover. Marco had brought down the sword of Damocles by putting on the fatal kepi, and at the worst possible moment. At the moment when the man is a melancholy, still-vibrating harp, an explorer returning from a promised land, half-glimpsed but not attained, a lucid penitent swearing "I'll never do it again" on bruised and bended knees.

I stubbornly insisted on seeing Marco again a few days later. I knocked and rang at her door which was not opened. I went on and on, for I was aware of Marco there behind it, solitary, stony and fevered. With my mouth to the keyhole, I said: "It's Colette," and Marco opened the door. I saw at once that she regretted having let me in. With an absent-minded air, she kept stroking the loose skin of her small hands, smoothing it down towards the wrist like the cuff of a glove. I did not let myself be intimidated; I told her that I wanted her to come and dine with me at home that very night and that I wouldn't take no for an answer. And I took advantage of my authority to add:

"I suppose Lieutenant Trallard has left?"

"Yes," said Marco.

"How long will it take him to get over there?"

"He isn't *over there*," said Marco. "He's at Ville d'Avray, staying with his father. It comes to the same thing."

When I had murmured "Ah!" I did not know what else to say.

"After all," Marco went on, "why shouldn't I come and have dinner with you?"

I made exclamations of delight, I thanked her. I behaved as effusively as a grateful fox-terrier, without, I think, quite taking her in. When she was sitting in my room, in the warmth, under my lamp, in the glare of all that reflected whiteness, I could measure not only Marco's decline in looks, but a kind of strange reduction in her. A diminution of weight—she was thinner—a diminution of resonance—she talked in a small, distinct voice. She must have forgotten to feed herself, and taken things to make herself sleep.

Masson came in after dinner. When he found Marco there, he showed as much apprehension as his illegible face could express. He gave her a crab-like, sidelong bow.

"Why, it's Masson," said Marco indifferently. "Hullo, Paul."

They started up an old cronies' conversation, completely devoid of interest. I listened to them and I thought that such a string of bromides ought to be as good as a sleeping-draught for Marco. She left early and Masson and I remained alone together.

"Paul, don't you think she looks ill, poor Marco?"

"Yes," said Masson. "It's the phase of the priest."

"Of the . . . *what*?"

"The priest. When a woman, hitherto extremely feminine, begins to look like a priest, it's the sign that she no longer expects either kindness or ill-treatment from the opposite sex. A certain yellowish pallor, something melancholy about the nose, a pinched smile, falling cheeks: Marco's a perfect example. The priest, I tell you, the priest."

He got up to go, adding:

"Between ourselves, I prefer that in her to the odalisque."

In the weeks that followed, I made a special point of not neglecting Marco. She was losing weight very fast indeed. It is difficult to hold on to someone who is melting away, it would be truer to say consuming herself. She moved house, that is to say she packed her trunk and took it off to another little furnished flat. I saw her often, and never once did she mention Lieutenant Trallard. Then I saw her less often and the coolness was far more on her side than on mine. She seemed to be making a strange endeavour to turn herself into a shrivelled little old lady. Time passed. . . .

"But, Masson, what's happened to Marco? It's ages since . . . Have *you* any news of Marco?"

"Yes," said Masson.

"And you haven't told me anything!"

"You haven't asked me anything."

"Quick, where is she?"

"Almost every day at the Nationale. She's translated an extraordinary series of articles about Ubangi from English into

French. As the manuscript is a little short to make a book, she's making it longer at the publisher's request, and she's documenting herself at the library."

"So she's taken up her old life again," I said thoughtfully. "Exactly as it was before Lieutenant Trallard . . ."

"Oh no," said Masson. "There's a tremendous change in her existence!"

"What change? Really, one positively has to drag things out of you!"

"Nowadays," said Masson, "Marco gets paid two sous a line."

The Tender Shoot

"THERE'S no reason for *you* to stay on in Paris," I said, in May 1940, to my old friend—what shall I call him? Let's say Chaveriat, yes, Albin Chaveriat; in France there are enough Chaveriats, Basque by origin, who have settled in Franche-Comté and all over the place to ensure that none of them will object to the use I make of his name. "As you'll only mope in Paris as long as the war goes on, find somewhere to live in the country for a bit. Why don't you go and join Curnonsky at Mélanie's place in Riec-sur-Belon?"

"I don't like sea-breezes," said Chaveriat. "Also, I don't want to eat too well. I should lose my figure."

"The Midi? Saint-Tropez? Cavalaire?"

Chaveriat bristled his short white moustache.

"Settings for the gay life . . . sinister, now it's dead and gone."

"Do you feel any inclination to be a paying-guest? Go to Normandy, to the Hersents. They won't budge from their estate unless they're dislodged by fire and sword. There's a river, a billiard-room, a badly-kept-up tennis court, a croquet lawn. The entire family is in excellent health and, with their daughters and nieces alone, the place teems with young girls . . ."

"Not another word! You've just said the very thing that would put me off."

"Neither the wind nor good food nor the south of France nor young girls. You're difficult to suit, Albin."

"I've always been difficult, my dear. That is what has made me end up as the pearl of bachelors."

Chaveriat walked across, without his stick, to one of my three windows. When he made a conscious effort, he limped hardly at all. Last year an attack of gout that "ran up to the heart" as they used to say, laid him to rest before his martial figure, still slender at seventy, suffered the humiliation of being definitely crippled. White-haired, with lively black eyes and a clipped moustache, he was presumed to have broken many hearts in his youth. But I can definitely state that, in 1906, he was only a quite ordinary-looking dark man.

Being a good walker, he was as fond of long walks as hairdressers are of fishing. In the country, Albin, who did not shoot, would go off for hours with a gun. He would bring back, by way of game, a little pink peach-tree snapped off by a hailstorm, a stray cat, a handkerchief full of flap mushrooms. Things like that endeared him to me. From time to time, I would search in vain for what was missing from our friendship, a friendship limited by the closely-guarded secrets of Albin Chaveriat's love-life. Before his death, he revealed only one to me and on that very day I suggested he should spend the war—we did not know, in May 1940, what those words implied—in a country house gay with young girls. For I reverted to his refusal which had been uttered with that marked reticence of voice and manner which provokes an inevitable retort from the other person: "My good man, you don't leave this house till you've told me the whole story!"

Albin did not leave the house. It was all the easier for me to make him stay because, for dinner, we had had deliciously fresh fish, mushrooms, taken off the fire before they were reduced to the condition of tasteless rags in which most French people serve them, and a semi-liquid *crème au chocolat* to satisfy those who like eating it with a spoon as well as those who prefer to drink it straight out of the little pot. In 1940, our Paris markets were still so well stocked that we walked through the neighbourhood of Les Halles just to feast our eyes. In talking, we used such expressions as "the phoney war" and "war in disguise" and we were, all of us, rather like animals without a sense of smell.

To break down my guest's inhibitions and loosen his tongue I offered him the last of my good *marc* brandy.

"Is it the Hersents themselves who put you off going to Normandy or their plethora of young girls, Colonel?"

Chaveriat had long ago given up laughing when one called him that. I think he rather liked having the tribute of an imaginary rank paid to his brush of white hair, his moustache and his not unattractive limp.

"Neither one nor the other, my dear. There is nowhere in the world I like better than Normandy and I've always adored young girls, or rather the young girl as a species."

"Well, well, well!"

"Does that astonish you? Why? We've only known each other for twenty-five years and I'm sixty-eight. Do you suppose that for something like forty years I was entirely occupied in living up to your idea of me which, by the way, is certainly very different from my idea of yourself? Yes, my two ruling passions were young girls and shooting. Now, I couldn't even take a shot at a jay and a young girl has, not cured me, but put young girls out of my life for ever . . . You want a story and you shall have it. It isn't a pretty one, far from it. But it can no longer do any harm to anyone and by now I fear its heroine may well have sons of eighteen."

"How did I acquire the taste for young girls? I think it was through a masculine friendship. Between the ages of fifteen and twenty, I had a friend, one of those fellow-adolescents to whom a normal boy is more faithfully devoted than to any mistress. Once turned twenty, a woman, or military service or a profession breaks into one's life and ruins this beautiful mutual affection. Actually, our military service made hardly any difference to Eyrand and me: we went through the mill together. The first betrayal came from him, for that was what I called his marriage. Getting married at twenty-three and a half was, according to my family, an 'imprudence'. I have just told you the name *I* gave our separation. No thanks, one glass of *marc* is enough for me. If I drank more, I should tell my story badly and not as impartially as I should.

"I remember I stubbornly refused to spend my holidays with Eyrand, the first year of his marriage, in a small country house standing in some seventy-odd acres which represented the best part of his wife's dowry and which he farmed himself. It was no good his writing to me over and over again and sending me snapshots of his young wife and his cattle and his farm, my back remained up. I sent him stupid letters in reply, because I thought his wife read them. . . . And also because my friend's expressed nothing but a stolid happiness. Never a doubt or a worry or an anxiety, never anything at all about which I might have consoled him. . . . Actually, I *would* like a drop of *marc*. Just a drop, no higher than the star engraved on the glass.

"In the end Eyrand got tired, as you can well imagine. When I saw that I had lost, and largely through my own fault, a friend I could never replace, I became unsociable with everyone except extremely young females. I was attracted by their sincere bluntness, by an interest that was usually sheer pretence, by beauty in embryo and character still unformed. They were seventeen, eighteen, a little more or a little less, while I was getting on for thirty. In their company, I felt the same age as themselves. In their company . . . It would be truer to say, in their arms. What is there in a young girl that is ripe and ready and eager to be exploited except her sensuality? No, don't let's argue about that, I know you don't agree with me. You won't prevent my having had—and for good reason—an almost terrified preference for that mixture of frenzy and determination, recklessness and prudence you find in a young girl who has, how shall I put it?—gone beyond certain limits. You have to have known a considerable number of young girls to realise that, compared to adult women, the majority of them are the inspired enthusiasts of the sex, ready to take the wildest risks. Also that, in dangerous situations, nothing can equal their complete calm. Public opinion has its set phrase: 'The coward who attacks young girls.' Good Lord! I can assure you that, on the contrary, one needs a very unusual temperament and remarkable self-control to resist them. Only don't get it into your head that my inclination became a monomania or a morbid obsession. In love, I've often been just like any other man, involved for a time in a liaison, attracted towards a sensible marriage, then no less sensibly escaping from it, irresolute . . . I assure you, a man just like other men.

"In 1923, I had already given up shooting but I accepted invitations from sportsmen. One of my friends, a retired chemist—there were parts of the country where, almost overnight, all the big estates had passed into the hands of the said chemists—had just bought such a beautiful property in Doubs that I planned my whole year so as to take a late summer holiday, between the 15th of August and the 15th of October. I did not enjoy it as much as I had hoped, on account of the rather boring collection of people staying there and the continual ostentatious gluttony. Food and drink alike, there was too much of everything, and it went on day after day. Things got to such a point that I had to pretend to be a dreamy recluse suffering from a liver complaint in order to have a right to solitude and sobriety. The owners of the big houses in the neighbourhood used to tap me on the shoulders after meals, belching discreetly:

" 'So you're not quite up to the mark? You ought to see someone.' I abstained from replying that, on the contrary, I would far rather see no one, and I kept myself to myself. Except that I undertook to teach a quite good-looking woman, a cousin of the owner's, how one catalogues a library, and some other pleasant ways of spending a hot afternoon.

"What a country it is my dear, all that region of Doubs! And what an estate! The new owner had not had time to make disastrous 'improvements' or to change that look—burning even more than burnt—that September has up there. The shortened days were still sweltering enough to take the skin off your hands when you lunched out-of-doors and, at night, just before dawn, a marvellous cold came in through the open windows, a cold that turned the leaves of the cherry-trees all red—and the elms and chestnuts prematurely yellow. No season had ever been so yellow, including the grass in the fields which had not had enough rain to give a second hay-crop. But, because the trees were so old and thick, the undergrowth remained and as mushroomy as you could wish. There are lots of 'violets' in Franche-Comté. The violet is a delicate kind of mushroom.

"Sparrowhawks—they were golden, too—would escort me a little way, circling very high above my head to find out my intentions, and, as I was innocent of any evil design, they would abandon me.

"Being a good walker (I'm talking of twenty years ago) I wandered over hill and dale; I discovered a little lock in the park with its sluice-gates rotted away and its pool dried up, the remains of a carved saint in her niche, an ancient 'belvedere', from which it had long been impossible to see anything, full of rabbit dung and prickly broom. I left the park without realising it because the chemist preferred to install bathrooms all over the house rather than rebuild the walls round his property. But a few hundred yards farther on the landscape became tamer and was cut up into small cultivated squares bounded by low, mortarless walls that made warm shelters for vipers. Although the district was fairly thick with small hills, I did not lose my way. I never do get off my track, you know. What's making you smile? Ah, I see what you mean. No thanks, no more brandy. I should love a glass of cold water.

"Perhaps you think I'm overdoing the landscape. But that season of long ago has left me a memory of being severely alone. On certain mornings, the dew was like a white frost, and then you baked for the rest of the day and the evening too, and the grapes—little black grapes in such tight clusters an ant couldn't have made its way into them—ripened ahead of time on the walls of the farm and the gatekeepers' lodges while the blue and mauve scabiouses announced that this blazing summer would soon be termed autumn. I was contented, contented without words and without many thoughts; I was getting tanned and beginning to look pleasingly like a country gentleman. One day . . . Yes, you see, I'm coming to the point.

"One day, I was outside the domain. I had shaken off all the fine-weather enthusiasts. I was on a hillside in the woods, climbing the fairly steep slope of a forest path, grassy but scored with wheel-ruts. I was walking between birches; the wind was already blowing off their little golden leaves, so light that they fluttered a long time before they settled. Towards the top of the hill, I saw that the birches gave way to apple-trees at the edge of a meadow. Behind the apple-trees, a beautiful clump of rather melancholy firs more than half hid an ancient dwelling with a gable of old tiles, set very prettily sideways, as if intentionally, at the top of the slope. A great mantle of Virginia creeper, pink in places, covered its shoulder. An adjoining kitchen garden, a garden overgrown with weeds, a valley whose mist was the typical purple-blue of Franche-Comté. I thought, 'How charming it is—and how neglected', and, as a final touch, I could hear the ripple of water. Running water is a rare blessing in those little mountains. From the other side of the low, crumbling wall, the horned forehead of a goat touched my hand, a pair of spindle-shaped pupils stared me out of countenance. I put out my hand to scratch the pretty black forehead with a white star on it and it did not turn away.

" 'Don't touch her, don't touch her, she'll chase you!' cried a young voice.

"The accent of that part of the world drags out the vowels, as you know. 'Doön't touch her! She'll chaäse you!' Naturally, I stretched out my hand still further and, with one bound, the goat was after me, pretty as a devil, pursued by a female child shouting, 'Stop it, you baäd girl, stop it!' A child . . . no. *I* don't call persons of round about fifteen children. I should lose too much if I did. The young girl grabbed the she-goat by its horns and neatly threw it over on its side. The goat got up and bounded away in little leaps on all four feet.

" 'She's cross,' said the young girl.

"She was recovering her wind and breathing with her mouth half-open. A blonde, even a little more than a blonde, verging on a red-head, with freckles on her cheeks and forehead and fiery eyelashes. But there was nothing of the albino red-head about her. On the contrary, her complexion was extraordinarily vivid under its bevy of freckles and her grey-green eyes, like her cheeks, were powdered with little chestnut freckles. One of the first things I noticed about her was the colour of the little curly tendrils on her forehead and the nape of her neck (she wore her hair pretentiously piled up in a bun), they were almost pink with the midday sun shining through them. For it was noon, and scorching enough on this bare hilltop to peel the skin off your nose.

"I said to her: " 'You've just definitely saved my life, Mademoiselle.'

"She laughed, wriggling her shoulders like a coquettish girl who has no idea of good manners. The inside of her mouth, as she laughed with her chin in the air, was lit up right to the back molars and I thought she was throwing her head back on purpose. You don't often find a flawless set of teeth in country girls. Country girls . . . My young girl had no apron and her clothes were dowdy, rather than rural. A cheap ready-made blue blouse with white spots, a badly cut skirt and a leather belt —that was all as regards the outside. Underneath there was a young creature. The expression 'well-rounded', so long out of fashion, describes a type of beauty which, believe me, is positively intoxicating when that beauty is adolescent. While I was making the little thing laugh at my simple jokes, I kept thinking, as I looked at that tautness and fullness and suppleness, of the drawings Boucher made of Louise O'Morphy, that girl who had not even finished growing before her entire dimpled body proclaimed its pressing need and cried aloud to lovers: 'Deliver me from myself or I shall burst!'

"My little O'Morphy ended by blushing but only when she remembered that she had hung a necklace of 'square-caps' round her neck, as all children do in autumn—you know, those bright pink wild euonymus berries with four lobes. I am stupid, as you have every reason to know. Furiously, she broke the thread and I remarked:

" 'That's a pity, it suited you very well. May I know the name of my protectress?'

" 'Louisette . . . Louise,' she corrected herself with dignity.

"I replied that my name was Albin and she signified with a little twitch of her mouth that she didn't care a rap. She was observing me surreptitiously, putting her hand over her eyes as if to keep the sun out of them. A voice called her and she answered with a shrill 'Yes.'

" 'I live there,' she said before leaving me. 'Over there, in the château.'

"She gave her home its name with a mannered haughtiness. Then she ran off towards her 'château' with long, boyish strides.

"I don't imagine I shall astonish you by telling you that . . . No, not the next day. The day after that, I braved the half-past eleven sun, on the same spot. The day before, I had taken advantage of a motor that went in to do the shopping to go 'into town' and buy a little coral necklace whose beads were exactly the same bright pink as the 'square-cap' berries . . . Excuse me, what were you saying, my dear? That it was a horrid proceeding, and a classic one? Allow me to defend myself. The lover of young girls is neither so simple nor so determined as to imagine the fulfilment of intentions he has not even had time to formulate clearly. But I admit that his method of approach is often of that commonplace kind Faust was taught by a demon whose tactics were far from subtle. Pretty trifles from the squire to the village maiden. So I ambushed myself at the edge of the wood, in that same scorching fine weather that seemed as if it would never end, in that same exacerbating eleven-o'clock sun that was fast ripening the apples and the blackberries and those wall-peaches known, for obvious reasons, as 'hardies'. And there I saw no sign of Louisette, but I could hear the ripple of the running water which marked its path on the other side of the slope by a track of greener herbage, some alders, a few willows. I had walked fast, I was dying to go and drink at it. Suddenly, there was my young girl, a yard away, without the sound of a footstep or the rustle of a branch. She was staring at me with such fixed intensity that I can only convey it by brief ejaculations, such as: 'Well? So you've come? What do you want? I'm waiting. Say something. Do something!' I did not take the risk of using the same language and I greeted her politely as any man would, whether or not he had evil designs.

" 'Good morning, Mademoiselle Louisette.'

She held out her hand like a young girl who does not know how to shake hands, an impersonal little paw.

" 'Good morning, Monsieur.'

" 'I've brought you back the necklace you broke the day before yesterday.'

"And I offered her my little necklace quite naked. Louisette tossed her chin and I observed she had the most delicious neck. An envelope of flesh so perfectly filled, a roundness that revealed not a hint of ligament or bone; never before or since have I seen a neck of such succulent perfection. And, besides, this was no bronzed beach-girl I saw before me. Apart from the glorious colouring of her face and a little sunburnt triangle in the opening of her blouse, the colour of her body began at once at the base of the neck, a colour so light, barely tinged with pink.

"*a lily under crimson skies . . .*

"Oh, you can laugh! Many a time I've felt that poem surging up in me above the purely physical feeling. In similar circumstances, that poem has often saved a young girl—and me—from myself.

"Well, I offered her my necklace, which had a little golden clasp. But Louisette refused it with a shake of the head, adding:

" 'No.'

" 'You don't want it? You think it's ugly?'

" 'No. But I can't take it.'

" 'It's an object of no value,' I said idiotically.

" 'That makes no difference. I can't take it because of Mamma. Whatever would Mamma say if she saw me with a necklace?'

" 'Mightn't you have . . . found it?'

She gave a cynical little smile. She was still keeping her chestnut-flecked eyes fixed on mine. Spots of sunlight danced from her golden lashes to her chin. I have never seen a complexion like hers, such delicate chiselling of the mouth and nostrils. What's that? Was she pretty? It's true I haven't told you whether she was pretty. Actually, I don't think she was very pretty. Untidy, anyway. In her shining hair, I could see the ugly, battered japanned hairpins that kept it in place. I could see that her stockings, beige lisle or cotton, were not very clean. For certain things, I have a remorseless eye.

"She was gazing at me so . . . how can I put it . . . so crudely that for a moment I was afraid there was something wrong with my appearance. But only for a moment. My costume was so simple that it could not make me look absurd: an open-necked shirt and trousers of some smooth material that did not catch on brambles. I was carrying my jacket over my arm—and nineteen less years than now. Long before it became the fashion, I used to walk bareheaded, well thatched as I was with my thick hair, alas! prematurely white. And I was lean, as you've always known me.

"Naturally, I was also gazing at Louisette, but in a more cautious, let us say a more civilised way. But, even so, I saw that she had extended the outer corners of her eyelids by means of two little pencilled lines. Such a preposterous, such an idiotic bit of coquetry made me burst out laughing as one does at children who celebrate Shrove Tuesday by solemnly wearing crêpe-hair beards.

"You can imagine my young girl was not at all pleased. She understood perfectly well and rubbed her two forefingers over the corners of her eyes. I took advantage of this to assert my authority.

" 'That's a nice thing,' I told her. 'At your age? You refuse a trifle because you're afraid of your mother, and you don't hesitate to make up your eyes!'

"She wriggled her shoulders, the way all badly brought-up girls do. But no girl, badly brought-up or not, ever made such shoulders or such a pair of young breasts tightly attached to them heave inside her blouse. I hoped she was going to snivel a little so that I could console her.

" 'Do take this little necklace,' I said. 'Or else I shall throw it away.'

" 'Throw it away, then,' she said at once. 'I certainly shan't pick it up. You'd better give it to someone else.'

" 'Are you so very frightened of your mother?'

"She shook her head again before she spoke, as she had done before.

" 'No. I'm afraid she'd think badly of me.'

" 'And your father, is he a rigid disciplinarian?'

" 'Is he a what?'

" 'Is he strict with you?'

" 'No. He's dead.'

" 'Forgive me. Was he very old?'

" 'Fifty-two.'

"It was within a month or two of my own age and I mechanically stood up straighter.

" 'So you live alone with your mother?'

" 'And there are the Biguets too. They run the farm.'

" 'Is it yours, that water I can hear rippling?'

" 'Yes. It's the spring.'

" 'A spring! And a spring that gives so much water you can hear it from here . . . Why, it's a fortune!'

" 'It's the most beautiful spring in the world,' said Louisette simply.

"Her expression changed and she shot me an angry look.

" 'You're not another of those people who want to buy it from us?'

" 'Who waänt to buy-ee it?' Her accent, stressed on certain words, did not displease me, on the contrary. I reassured her.

" 'No, no, Louisette. I'm on holiday at ——, staying with the new owner. I don't want to take your spring away from you. But I think I could drink it all up, I'm so thirsty.'

"She spread out her hands in a gesture of helpless regret:

" 'Oh dear, I can't take you there to drink. Mamma would think it queer for me to be talking to someone she doesn't know. Unless we went round outside by the back way.'

" 'And which is the back way?'

"She answered me by jerking her eyebrows, winking, and pursing her lips, a sign-language of complicity I had not hoped for and that enchanted me. I saw she was ripe for dissimulation, for forbidden collusion, in other words, for sin. I replied as best I could by making the same sort of faces and we walked back, she in front and I following her, down the sheltered path at the edge of the wood, the whole length of the low, half-collapsed wall the goat had jumped to 'chaäse' me.

" 'Where's my enemy the goat, Mademoiselle Louisette?'

" 'She's out in the fields. We've got three. But that one's the nicest.'

"Louisette answered me without turning her head and I was more than content to have a good chance to study the nape of her neck revealed by her high-pinned bun, the small, ardently pink ears, the flat, well-placed shoulder-blades and the faint swell of the springy hips below the tight leather belt . . . I assure you, a work of art with no hint of angularity or awkwardness, but with nothing noble about it except its precocious perfection. A young creature so frankly inviting one definite thing that an imbecile might have thought her cynical. But I am not an imbecile, my dear. I need to tell you this in so many words because, very late in the day, I'm now introducing you to an unknown Chaveriat who for a long time made a point of remaining unknown. For I have never been vain about my vices, if vices they are.

"Well, I followed this little thing, admiring her. I was trying to find some definite classification for her based on her inborn effrontery, her craving to satisfy my curiosity and to deceive her mother's watchful eye. Already, I mentally called her 'the prettiest little servant-girl in France'. Anyone can make a mistake.

"At the elbow of the crumbling wall, we left the undergrowth. The path was now no more than a track that descended fairly steeply, so that the wall loomed up higher, and hid the 'château' from us. An old wall, as flowery as a herbaceous border. Scabiouses, the last foxgloves, valerians that I've noticed are always very red in Franche-Comté, and begonias slightly choked by ivy.

" 'What a beautiful wall!' I said to Louisette.

"She replied only by a sign and I presumed she preferred her voice not to be heard associated with a stranger's. The enclosing wall bent again at a right-angle, revealing, at the same time, the other side of the hill and the entrance to the grounds of the house. The entrance, however, had been reduced to two pillars crowned with little stone lions, so worn by time that their faces looked more like those of sheep. An avenue of rowan trees, thick with berries and birds, led to the 'château' whose coat of ivy disguised its dilapidation. If you've lived in Franche-Comté . . . yes, you have lived there. Then you know those solid country houses, built to withstand the weight of heavy snow in winter. But this one really was in a bad state. From a distance, it produced an illusion and dominated a valley that, even at midday, was still veiled in blue haze because the spring, now running underground, now enclosed in the bed it hollowed out for itself, filled it with mist.

"Louisette stopped abruptly before she reached the first pillar, so abruptly that I bumped up against her charming back, her red-gold nape, and her whole person, as plump and hard as a wall-peach.

" 'We mustn't go any further,' she said. 'Can you see the spring?'

"I could only half-see it, that is to say, in a stone niche at the end of the rowan avenue, I caught a glimpse of a wild leaping. It was as if the niche, all overhung with plants that love shade and water, was frequented by great silver fish. I could also see that a liquid curtain flowed over the margin and probably ran down into a basin below . . . But I saw no means of quenching my thirst without crossing the barrier of the sheeplike lions. Louisette went in without saying a word and came back carrying a small, brimming watering-can with a long spout.

" 'Drink before I do, Louisette.'

"And I added, without shame:

" 'Then I shall know your thoughts.'

"But she replied with a very curt refusal: 'I'm not thuürsty.' There's no drink to compare with water when it springs, mysteriously cold, straight out of the earth.

" 'Go down again the same way,' Louisette commanded me. 'This is the real entrance, but you might be seen from the house if you went down by the main road.'

"I obeyed without a word. At the spot where the wall overtopped the path by some twelve or fifteen feet, I received a small pebble on my head. Louisette, perched up there, was watching my departure. I waved my hand and blew her a kiss without her smiling or pretending to be embarrassed. The sight of a golden head, motionless and watchful between tufts of scabious and yellow stonecrop, that was all I got from her that day. I remember that, walking back down the hill towards the chemist's domain, I said to myself: 'All the same, she might have thrown me a flower instead of a pebble!' and, in my heart of hearts, I reproached that little girl for her lack of poetry.

"I'm not going to bore you, my dear, with the details of our lovers' meetings that first week. In any case, Louisette and I didn't have any lovers' meetings, properly speaking. I used to climb the little hill round about the really scorching hour, eleven or half-past. The drought was making the leaves fall early. Up at the big house, my host's shooting guests brought bad reports of game grown lean and haggard. But I never listened to them. My own private game was always to be found, now here, now there, fresh, not in the least exhausted by the heat, and plump as ever. The strange thing was that my tentative affair, which was proving pleasant rather than amusing, was making no progress. Louisette, though she laughed easily, showed no fundamental gaiety. Being fifteen and a half and living in extreme and dangerous solitude, probably on the verge of poverty, is not, admittedly, conducive to a very gay life. . . . Her answers to my questions never went beyond the strictly necessary. For example, when I asked her:

" 'Do you live very much alone?'

" 'Oh, yes,' she answered.

" 'Don't you find that rather dreary?'

" 'Oh, no. We have visitors on Sundays. People we know.' She added:

" 'Not every Sunday. That would be a lot.'

"Her little hands, dimpled at the base of each finger, told me more than she did about the heavy household chores imposed on them. Idle, they would have been very pretty and like Louisette herself; rather short, dimpled, with fingers that turned up at the tips. As she walked beside me, she picked a pointed twig and used it as an orange-stick to clean her nails. Another time I said to her:

"'Do you read a great deal?'

"She nodded twice, with the air of an expert.

"'Papa left us a big library.'

"'Are you fond of novels? Would you like me to give you some books?'

"'No thanks.'

"The refusal was always very definite. I could not make her accept either books or a bottle of scent or a suede belt or a trumpery bracelet or a lawn handkerchief . . . Nothing, do you understand? As she said herself: 'Not the leastest thing.' This inflexibility never yielded an inch. 'And what would Mamma say?' She invariably floored me with that one argument, produced in severe, triumphant tones. 'You must have a terrible mother,' I risked saying one day.

"Louisette shot me the same nasty look she had given me when she spoke of selling the spring.

"'No, I haven't. She never does anything wrong, she doesn't. If she knew I talked to you, she'd be very upset. So, as I've got to keep it a secret from her that I do talk to you, I mustn't do *anything* to give it away. I think that's the least I can do for her, take pains to stop her knowing.'

"And in such a tone! The young lady was instructing me in her personal morality and it was I who was being given lessons! To mollify her and flatter her I listened with an air of being much impressed. She was watching me covertly, as if she expected something from me and I did not know what it was she wanted or did not want. We men who fall in love with young girls, we don't take any risks till we're sure of success. The one thing that disconcerts us and holds us back is simplicity, firstly because we don't believe in it, secondly because our success depends on choosing the right moment. Those interviews, with the light beating down on us and Louisette always with one eye or one ear cocked in the direction of her mother, left me nervy and exhausted by so much sunshine. When I returned to —— I found a definite charm in playing bridge on a shady terrace, in reading the illustrated papers with the cool six o'clock wind ruffling their pages. Until the day, when that week had gone by, that I had the idea of telling Louisette 'I've only got ten more days here.' The corners of her mouth quivered, but all she said was: 'Oh!'

" 'Yes, alas. And tomorrow the owner of —— is organising a series of motor expeditions and picnics in the local beauty-spots. I can't always go off on my own, and be unsociable. But if, instead of getting myself roasted up here, I came and took a breath of fresh air on this little mountain in the evening, mightn't I possibly happen to meet you?'

"I assure you I gave a quite marvellous imitation of shyness and I did not even hold her hand. I had the surprise of seeing her begin to fidget, biting one of her nails, and thrusting and re-thrusting the hideous japanned hairpins into her bun from which the little tendrils escaped like a haze of fire. She looked all round her, then said hurriedly: 'I don't know, I don't know . . .' and as she raised her arms, I caught a drift of feminine odour. I pretended to hesitate, then to lose my head and I seized Louisette by that slim waist so many plump little things have. I whispered into her hair, under her ear: 'This evening? . . . Six o'clock?' and I refrained from kissing her on the lips before going off with long, hurried strides. I went down quickly through the undergrowth so as to give her no time to think of calling me back, and, when I had already left her far behind, I realised we had not uttered one word that implied tenderness, desire or friendliness.

"My dear, it isn't only to drink up this glass of water that I'm breaking off. No, thank you, I'm not tired. When one's talking about oneself, one doesn't feel tired till one's finished. But I observe you're looking apprehensive, not to say disapproving. Why? Because my heroine is only aged sixteen minus three months? Because I've fastened my covetous gaze on too young a blossom? Don't be in too much of a hurry to judge me, and, above all, to pity the tender ewe-lamb. At fifteen, or even less, they threw a princess to an heir-apparent, probably an innocuous young man. Queens were married at thirteen. To search even higher than thrones for my justification, do I have to remind you what Juliet meant, at fifteen, by 'hearing the nightingale'? If my memory does not deceive me, didn't you tell me that, at sixteen, you yourself fell madly in love with a bald man of forty who looked twice that age? I think I'm using your very words. Old boughs for tender shoots, as our fathers used to say with genial lechery. I claim indulgence, at least *your* indulgence, considering that, with a few exceptions, I've been mad about tender shoots nearly all my life without withering one of them up or making her produce another shoot. So I will now continue a story you brought on yourself and I shall lower neither my eyes nor my voice.

"Well, I had solicited a meeting at dusk, but, because of my deliberate flight, I was not sure whether Louisette would turn up. I did find her there, however, and in a setting that seemed quite new at that late hour, among long shadows that marked the divisions between the little mountains and made them look higher. You know that country, you know how, as the light goes, valleys take on quite a different colour from the blue of midday. That periwinkle, almost lilac blue, barred with pale yellow and dark green, the humpbacked, complex landscape, hitherto blotted out by the ferocious noonday sun, the smell of wood fires lit for the evening meal, it was all so enchanting that I was not in the least bored as I waited for Louisette. Frankly, I was already consoling myself for not seeing her when she arrived, running, and flung herself, as if in play, into my arms where she was very well received. I admired her at once for having avoided, by an impetuous rush, the usual 'It's you at last!' or 'How sweet of you to come!' Whatever her social level, the female creature does not leave us a wide choice of phrases to greet her arrival. As I say, Louisette flung herself, breathless, into my arms as if she were playing 'Wolf' and had reached 'home'. She laughed, unable to speak, or at least apparently unable to speak. Her ugly metal hairpins dropped out of her pretentious little bun and her hair hung about her head, not very long, but so frizzy that it stood out in a thick, fiery bush. As to her palpitation, I assured myself, with one cupped hand, that it was genuine. Our physical intimacy was established in one moment in an unhoped-for way and on entirely new ground. I say physical, because I can't say plain intimacy. I think an ordinary man, I mean an ordinary lover, would have thought that, in Louisette, he'd met the most shameless of semi-peasant girls. But I was not an ordinary lover.

"I gave Louisette time to calm down before kissing her. When I did, she received my kisses so naturally, so eagerly . . . Don't raise your eyebrows like that, my dear, do I surprise you as much as all that? Yes, with an eagerness that would have been the ruin of a lover who was both careless and in a hurry, as they nearly all are. But I was not a careless lover. So Louisette gave herself up to the pleasure of being kissed, and, in the intervals, she smiled at me and looked at me with wonderfully clear, radiant eyes as if she were delighted to have found the real way to talk to me and not to have to be bored any more with a stranger. The twilight had already fallen and, high in the sky, it was barred by a long cloud, still rosy with the setting sun. And, looking up from my supporting arm, I saw a happy face, exuberant hair, eyes no longer bashfully drooped but wide open, all echoing the colour of the cloud. It was very lovely and, I assure you, I did not miss one iota of it. A cry broke out from the direction of the house and Louisette wrenched away from me everything I was holding fast; her hard little mouth, her slim, rounded torso, her feet I had gripped between mine. She listened, waited for a second cry, her eyes and ears on the alert to decide exactly where the cry came from, then fled full speed, with no good-bye beyond a little wave.

"That night, I made mistake after mistake at bridge. Away from Louisette, it was easier to admit that I was disconcerted. In her presence—as you can well imagine, I met her again the next day and every day after—I let myself be guided not only by my own experience but also by Louisette herself. Without going into a lot of details that would embarrass us both, I admit I have never met anyone like Louisette either in her simplicity or in her baffling mystery. To make myself clear, I believe that the sensuality of any grown-up woman who behaved like Louisette would have revolted me. Louisette was avid in the way children are, she was vicious with grace, with majesty. Physical confidence is always admirable. Louisette's preserved her from certain dangers, it is true, but it must also be said she was lucky to chance on me and not another man. She treated sensual pleasure as a lawful right but nothing gave me reason to think that she had had any previous experience. This strange affair lasted longer than the fine weather and kept me staying on, rather inconveniently, with my friend the ostentatious retired chemist.

"At the end of a fortnight, I told myself quite sincerely: 'You've had enough of this. Any more would be too much.' Perhaps, in my heart, I was . . . how can I put it? I was shocked, I was . . . well . . . a little scandalised that this wild pony caught in the fields didn't show me a little . . . hang it all, a little affection, a little . . .

"What's that, my dear? Begging your pardon, I am *not* a

brute—I proved that at least once every twenty-four hours—and I did not think it was asking too much to hope that Louisette, softened and satisfied, would come to treat her unselfish lover as a friend. So much so that, when my nerves were on edge, for very obvious reasons, it was I who said to Louisette, bending over her little shell-like ear: 'You won't quite forget your old friend when he's far away?' I was sitting on a granite boulder, coated with dry lichen that made it less hard. Louisette, sitting lower down, was leaning her head against my ribs. She turned up a face like a ripe peach—raised her eyes, which at that moment were very bright under their chestnut flecks, and I thought that, for the first time I was going to hear . . . a gentle word, a childish avowal, perhaps just a sigh. She merely said 'Oh, no!' exactly like a child answering an imbecile parent who has asked the imbecile question: 'You don't love Mamma more than Papa, do you?' And I left her that day earlier than usual without her appearing to notice it in the very slightest. We talked so little. She listened to me, certainly. But she was also listening to many other sounds I did not hear and now and then would sign to me, sometimes rather rudely, to be quiet. I was in process of telling her something or other, goodness knows what, to make myself believe we enjoyed talking together, and, seeing the fixed gaze of her beautiful flecked eyes, and her parted lips whose colour I had just warmed to a rich glow, I felt flattered by her attentiveness. She was lying, leaning on her elbow, and we were in one of those tiny clearings that make bare patches among the tall heather. I was sitting, leaning over her, when she suddenly began to flutter her eyelids, overcome by a lassitude that pleased my vanity. One of Louisette's charms was to exclaim suddenly: 'I'm hungry' or 'I'm sleepy', to yawn with hunger or suddenly to fall heavily asleep for a few moments. As I say, she was fluttering her lids and, at every blink, her red eyelashes glinted like fire when suddenly she opened her eyes wide, sat up, grabbed me by the shoulders and pushed me over on the ground, where she held me down by main force. I tried to get up, but she threatened me with her fist, and her child's face became quite terrifying. All this lasted about the space of ten heartbeats. Then Louisette let me go, her cheeks and lips went white and she collapsed, quite limp, on the grass. When her colour returned, she explained:

" 'Your head was showing. There was someone on the path.'

" 'Who?' I asked.

" 'Someone who lives round here.'

"I think she had recognised her mother's footsteps. Without any embarrassment, she fastened up her open blouse. Everything she allowed me to see of herself would have rejoiced what one calls a gay dog. Quite unlike a gay dog and a Don Juan, it made me feel solemn to see how much childhood and newly-achieved womanhood can have in common. So much beauty, with no adornments except cotton underclothes, a little blue ribbon and cheap, coarse stockings. No scent except the slightly russet fragrance of the hair. When she was violently excited I could breathe in the smell of that plant . . . what *is* its name? . . . one of the pea family, with pink flowers . . . that blondes give out when they sweat. Rest-harrow, that's right, thanks. When I was away from Louisette, I used to think what she might have been, which is always a stupid thing to do. I used to imagine her as a nymph, leaning over the spring, naked as she was worthy to be. We never rise to great heights when we try to mingle art and literature with the religious feeling inspired by a beautiful body.

"After a few days Louisette changed the time of our meetings and, for my host's benefit, I had to assume the rôle of poet and night-walker, so as to be able to climb up to the 'château' round about ten at night. 'Why so late?' I asked my little sweetheart.

" 'Because Mamma goes to bed at nine. She gets up before five all the year round. At half-past eight, I've just finished washing up the supper things and putting them away. After that, I can do as I like, as long as I'm very careful.'

" 'You don't sleep near your mother, then?'

"She lowered her red-gold eyebrows.

" 'Fairly near. Look, I'll show you.'

"She led me as far as the lion-guarded entrance, walking along the narrow path as if it were broad daylight.

" 'That square tower, behind the spring. There's only one room on each floor. Mamma has the top one, she's given me the other one because it's nicer. But as soon as it gets cold, Mamma brings her bed down into my room where it's warmer. The cold weather comes early up here.'

"She fell silent. I could hear the spring and its imaginary fishes leaping in their basin.

" 'But, Louisette, darling,' I said, 'it's dangerous for you, going out at night.'

" 'Yes,' she said.

"That considered, almost gloomy 'yes' was so far removed from the cry of a girl in love flinging herself recklessly in the path of danger that I did not express my gratitude. A 'yes' that did not even seem to have any concern with me. She was staring vaguely at the square gable and the silver leaps of the spring at the end of the avenue. The moon was blurred that night, showing pink through its surrounding haze. So near the main gate, we might easily have been seen. But I trusted entirely to my little companion who knew how to make us invisible at the right moment, making me walk in the dark at the foot of the garden wall, pushing me into the thick shadow of a laurel bush that left its fragrance on her hands. We only met stray ramblers she could trust not to betray us; a silent dog, guilty of going off hunting on his own; the white horse belonging to the 'château' who was trailing his chain slackly behind him and taking advantage of the warmth of the night. The clouded moon threw few strong shadows but, from time to time, she emerged from her halo and I could see my long shadow welded to a shorter one, moving ahead of us.

"Don't you get the impression that I'm telling you rather a sad story? Curious, so do I. Yet the story of Louisette starts off as something rather charming, doesn't it? But tonight I'm feeling sentimental. In any case, it's the nature of affairs of this type to get tiresome very soon, to lose their freshness. Otherwise, the only thing that keeps the edge on them for those of us who are addicted to a particular type of woman is when we find ourselves coming to grips with young demons. Oh, they exist all right, there are more of them than you think. Louisette was nothing more than a young girl whose whole body had burst into blossom, a young girl whom I was relieving of her boredom for I was not fatuous enough to think I was relieving her of her innocence. In country girls, there is no such thing as physical innocence. Louisette accepted, she even fixed the character of our relationship. She hardly ever used my Christian name; when she called me 'Albin', she sounded self-conscious. I've always thought she had to restrain herself from calling me 'Monsieur', and I should not have been offended if she had. On the contrary. This reserve redoubled the astonishment—I may also say the desire—that Louisette aroused in me.

"One day, I brought her a little ring, made of diamond chips, a jewel for a child, and, taking her by surprise, I slipped it on her finger. She turned red as . . . as a nectarine, as a dahlia, as the most divinely red thing in the world. But it was with rage, you must understand. She tore the ring off her finger and brutally flung it back at me. 'I've already commanded you (she said *commanded*!) not to give me anything.' When I had sheepishly taken back my humble jewel, she made sure that the little cardboard box, the tissue paper and the blue tinsel ribbon were not still lying about on our chair of rocks and lichen. Odd, wasn't it?

"But otherwise I had no cause but to rejoice in an idyll so exciting and so ideally suited to my natural bent. If Louisette's mutism was merely want of intelligence, I had met other stupid girls and less pleasing ones. All the same, at moments, I could feel something emanating from her that resembled sadness. I felt sorry for anyone whose destiny was as uncertain as Louisette's. And, besides, my holiday, what with consuming heat and consuming passion, was reducing me to something like exhaustion. I was getting impatient at being completely unable to understand a girl who roamed the woods at night, with me, but sprang up as if she had been shot, turned pale and trembled at the knees if she heard the step or the voice of her mother.

"All that, my dear, belongs to the past. But to a past that has remained buried in silence. I am throwing fresh light on it by telling you about it because, looking back on it now, it seems, quite definitely, not to have been such a gay adventure as I thought. At the time, I used to wonder now and then whether Louisette were not exploiting me like a lecherous man who's found a willing girl. This ridiculous notion irritated me to such a point that I had a most unexpected little access of rage. No, not in front of her, but at bridge, in my host's house, one night when I had not arranged to meet Louisette. No one noticed anything, except that I played very badly. I was listening to the noise of the wind which, for the first time since my arrival, was sobbing under the doors and bringing us through the open windows—it was very mild—a poignant smell from the terrace outside—the smell of dampness before rain, of flowers when the season of flowers is over. The song of the wind, the scent of autumn, I knew that they both spoke of my return to Paris and I found myself quite astonishingly upset at the prospect. I thought of my departure, of what the life of two women must be like in winter, in the dilapidated 'château'. I forced myself to imagine the rowan trees without their leaves, green on one side and silvery on the other, without their umbels of red berries; the spring sealed up by the cold, its living water imprisoned between great bars of limpid ice.

"I went to bed early, and the rest, which I badly needed, put everything more or less right. The next morning I allowed myself a long lazy morning in a rocking-chair on the terrace, making idle conversation with the other guests. I found I had got rid of that anxious, indiscreet feeling that made me want to know more about Louisette's private life. Indiscreet is the right word. Didn't she consider it so herself, since, after a whole month of daily meetings, I was still waiting for her to make me any sort of confidence? It gave me a definite pleasure to watch and listen to the people around me, and privately to regard my fellow-quinquagenarians as old men because they were married and getting pot-bellied. The day passed quickly—it was warm, but free of the recent tremendous heat—and in such calm that I hardly thought at all about Louisette. But you know how dangerous the habit of making love is; it is exactly like being addicted to smoking or taking drugs. When the hand of the clock (a Louis XIV clock, I need hardly say) jerked its embossed point towards a tortoise-shell figure X, I could hear it no longer, and I got up from my chair.

" 'What, again, Chaveriat!' exclaimed my host. 'Even tom-cats don't go out when their bellies are full.'

" 'I am not a tom-cat,' I replied. 'I am a martyr to hygiene and vanity. If I didn't take at least an hour's exercise after my meals, I should ruin my waistline and my digestion.'

" 'Look out then, the weather's going to change any moment.'

" 'With a full moon? Nothing could be less likely. After my defeat last night, you can find another victim.'

"All the same, I took a mackintosh and my pocket-torch which Louisette always forbade me to use as soon as I came anywhere near her 'château'. A Gustave Doré moon seemed to be leaping from cloud to cloud, plunging behind cumuli rimmed with fire and emerging naked, dazzling and a little hunchbacked. These games of the moon and the flying clouds made me realise the wind had risen and I promised myself I would only spend a moment with Louisette. It was a wise resolution. Just as I had reached the spot where the garden wall overhung the path and gave it deepest shelter—that was where my sweetheart always waited for me—just as my arms had closed round an adored body, as lovely standing up as lying down, but never freely seen or freely enjoyed, just as the first kiss had assured me, in the darkness, that nothing had ever rivalled that elastic firmness, utterly surrendered to my honour, the wind rose in a fierce gust. I only held my companion all the tighter. From her invisible hair and her mouth that tasted of raspberries, from the smell that came from her already-bared bosom which assured me I was crushing a woman, not a child, against me, I could have guessed all her rose and russet tints. My vague remorse for my day of indifference increased my ardour. Heaven knows where remorse of that kind may lead us! . . . Don't be alarmed, my dear, that last remark is not going to start me off on a digression. I only made it to indicate that, that night, I was on the very verge of behaving like a straightforward normal animal, like a man who knows only one way to possess the woman he desires. And I am not sure that Louisette, who was as frenzied as I was, would have stopped me.

"It was at that moment the rain, fast approaching through the scented darkness and the chirp of insects who thought summer had returned, suddenly burst down on us. A solid sheet of rain, like a ceiling collapsing on our heads, a crushing deluge of rain. I flung my waterproof cape over Louisette and she very deftly draped one half over my shoulders, but what stuff could have stood up to that drenching? The shower poured down in cascades below the bottom of the cape and soaked our feet. Louisette did not hesitate long, she ran, pulling me along with her. The diffused light of the hidden moon showed me we were passing the lions who guarded the non-existent gate, the rowan-trees, the spring lashed by rain that fell dead straight: I felt paving-stones under my feet and bent my head down to Louisette's dripping ear to make myself heard in spite of the thunderous drumming of the raindrops: 'Till tomorrow, darling. Get inside quick!'

"But she did not let go my hand and led me on. I was aware of treading on dry stones, the noise of the rain became less deafening, and I realised, from the denser darkness, that I had crossed a threshold, the threshold of Louisette's 'château'.

"The fitful, stormy light only came in faintly through the open door. Forced inside by the solid curtain of rain, I could breathe the smell of those country-house lobbies where there are old straw hats hanging up and they keep the galoshes and the first windfalls.

" 'I mustn't make any light,' Louisette whispered to me. 'Give me your hand.'

"She pushed me, leaving the door wide open, towards one of those long, severely uncomfortable, cane-bottomed settees you find quite as often in Provence as in Breton country houses. A thin quilted mattress covers the seat without making it any less penitential. I remember you had one, in Brittany, round about 1908. We sat down. Moving my hands cautiously over her, I made sure the rain had not soaked Louisette's thin clothes. And, if she was shivering, it was not with cold. But my spirit of aggression was severely checked by this unfamiliar haven and the total darkness.

" 'As soon as it's raining less, you must go,' whispered Louisette.

"Mentally, I replied that I should not need to be told twice. And I settled Louisette against me, very respectably, with her feet stretched out on the vacant part of the settee and her head on my shoulder. She slipped her arm under mine and we stayed perfectly still. Little by little I made out the size of the room, and some of its features. A staircase with wooden banisters ran down into it just behind us. A bunch of pale flowers gradually grew clearer on a fairly large table that I could touch with my outstretched hand. On my right, an unshuttered window slowly began to show blue. I kept my eyes and ears strained and my jaws clenched. Obviously, what made me uneasy reassured Louisette, for I could feel her warm and relaxed against my arm and as still as a little hare in the hollow of a furrow.

" 'I think it's raining less,' I whispered in her ear.

"Hardly had I spoken than the deluge redoubled and the darkness thickened about us. My dear, I simply cannot tell you how I longed to get away from that place. I had just made up my mind to escape and was already looking forward with positive pleasure to being forced to run, guided by the halo of my torch, to a safe shelter when I realised, from the limpness of her little torso, that Louisette had dozed off. I've told you how promptly she obeyed, as robust temperaments do, the impulses of hunger, sleep and other physical cravings. I was on the point of waking her up, but it was such a new sensation to hold her asleep in my arms that I wanted to wait just a little longer. You can understand what it meant to be, or at least to fancy myself, watching over her protectively for the first time. . . . And I closed *my* eyes too, to give myself a brief illusion that we were sleeping like two lovers. But I opened my eyes at the slightest creak and heaven knows there was nothing that *didn't* creak in that barn of a place!

"A dim light shone down on us and I wanted to wake Louisette to tell her that the moon was out again and I must go. Then I realised that the light was coming neither from the open door nor from the window on the right. Far worse, the light began to move and lit up a landing higher up the staircase. There is a great difference between electric light and any other kind. It was the flame of a lamp, beyond all possibility of doubt, that was coming towards us and the shadows of the banisters began to shift slowly round in the well of the staircase. I whispered urgently into the bush of damp hair that covered my shoulder: 'Louisette! Someone's coming!' The little thing gave a terrible start, and I leapt to my feet to . . . Oh yes, quite frankly, to escape, but she clutched hold of me with the same strength that had knocked me over that day among the brambles. All I succeeded in doing was to produce a tremendous clatter of sofa-legs and chair-legs and all that sprang to my lips was the beginning of a blasphemous oath. The shadows of the banisters swung full circle on to the walls and I saw a woman appear, holding the lamp—quite a small woman, in a mauve dressing-gown tightly girdled round the waist. Her resemblance to Louisette left me no doubt, no hope. Same frizzy hair, but already almost completely white, and faded features that one day would be Louisette's. And the same eyes, but with a wide, magnificent gaze Louisette perhaps would never have, a gaze that was not upturned in anguish but that imperiously insisted on seeing everything, knowing everything. How interminable it seems, a moment like that, and how is it that boredom, yes, sheer boredom, a boredom that tempts one to yawn and chuck the whole thing, manages to intervene between the fractions of dramatic seconds? And that little idiot, clutching tight hold of me and refusing to let me go. With a violent shake, I tore my sleeve out of her fingers and stood up. I remember I said:

" 'Madame, don't be frightened . . .'

"And then, I found myself unable to go on. The little thing, still lying on the settee, was supporting herself on one arm like the *Dying Gladiator*. And, with her other bent elbow, she flung back her hair. She did, poor girl, the only thing she could; she screamed for help:

" 'Mamma!'

"And then she began to cry. The astonishing thing is that I was not in the least touched because, in spite of all my exasperation with everything, myself included, I was spellbound by the principal character who had just made her stage entrance, the mother. She set down her oil lamp, turned to Louisette and asked her:

" 'So that's the man is it, my girl?'

"The little thing raised her face, showing her streaming eyes and a mouth open square, like a crying baby's, and shrieked:

" 'No, Mamma, no, Mamma!'

" 'Not so much noise, my girl,' said the white-haired woman. 'Because it definitely is that man who's been leading you astray all this while. I've seen you, so it's no good lying. I saw you with him in the copse, in among the bushes. As to *him*, I'm not sorry to see his face, no, not at all sorry.'

"She turned to me with a quick movement. The unshaded lamp shone straight in her eyes but she did not blink. I could not prevent myself from noticing the difference between the expression of her face and the words on which she had broken off. I thought I ought to emerge from my silence. You can't imagine how immensely anxious one becomes, at such an unforeseen moment, about what is the proper thing to do or not to do. The decision I made was not the most fortunate one.

" 'Madame,' I said, 'in spite of appearances, which, I admit, are deplorable, I can assure you I have not behaved towards . . . towards Mademoiselle Louisette in a way that could . . .'

"The white-haired lady put her hands on her hips, thrusting her fists into the hollows of her waist. This gossip's attitude was not unbecoming to her, on the contrary.

" 'In a way that could . . .' she repeated.

" 'In a way that could put her into a certain situation . . .'

" 'I know what you're trying to say,' she broke in harshly. 'You think that's an excuse? *I* don't. Do you expect me to say thank you?'

"The little thing stopped sobbing. At the same moment, the rain stopped too and this double truce filled the room with a great silence that seemed to be awaiting my answer. It is extremely unusual for a man who is appearing at a disadvantage in the presence of two women not to be tempted to lose patience and make some stupid retort. That was what happened to me.

" 'Come now, Madame, it's true I'm not a saint, but, in this case, I haven't forced anyone against their will, and your daughter's beauty . . .'

"The feet of the cane settee rasped on the flagstones as it was pushed backwards and I was confronted with Louisette, her face red and inflamed with crying:

" 'I forbid you to talk to my mother in that tone,' she said in a low, harsh voice.

" 'Oh!' I said. 'If I've got the two of you against me, I prefer . . .'

And I made an attempt to retreat, an attempt that was frustrated because the haughty little lady stood between me and the door and made no effort to get out of my way.

" 'You're not here to tell us about your preferences,' she said.

"She had really admirable eyes, and a sunburnt, windburnt face with a shiny glaze on the cheekbones and the bridge of the nose. And she was staring at me as if she were boring into my brain, so much so that it put my back up.

" 'Very well, Madame, if you will be good enough to tell me in what terms I may express my regrets . . .'

" 'Monsieur,' she interrupted me rudely, 'may one know your age?'

"If I had been expecting a question, it was most certainly not not that one. Moreover, I was astonished that this strange mother, finding her daughter in the arms of a man, had not had recourse to any of the classical arguments and vituperations. She had a mouth made for vehemence, a freedom of manner that was half peasant, half middle-class. Her preposterous question shattered me so much that I found myself making a series of idiotic gestures such as running my hand through my hair, pulling my leather belt down over my loins, and drawing myself up to my full height.

" 'I cannot see, Madame, what the precise number of my years has to do with all this. However, I am willing to confess to you that I am forty-nine.'

"For a moment, I thought she was going to laugh. Why not turn the scene into light comedy? The good woman seemed to me to have a sense of humour and she was anything but shy. A kind of laugh did, in fact, run over her features. She seized her daughter by the arm, pulled her close against her, mingling her white hair with the red hair, and whispered passionately:

" 'You hear him, child? You *see* that man there? Child, he's three times as much as your fifteen and a half, and even more! You've let yourself be led astray by a man of fifty, Louise! A young boy such there are plenty of round here, *that* I could understand. But a man of fifty, Louise, of *fifty*! Ah! You may well be ashamed!'

"If I had not controlled myself, I assure you I should have gone for those two cows and knocked them down. Their two heads, close together and so terribly alike, stared me out of countenance. And that blinding, unshaded lamp. The elder let go of the younger's arm, pointing the forefinger of her shrivelled brown hand at me and raised her voice:

" 'If your father were still alive, Louise, he'd be just the age of that man there!'

"Louisette gave a sharp little moan and hid her face in her mother's white mane. Her mother did not repulse her and went on talking:

" 'Yes, now you don't want to see him any more, high time too, Louise! All the same, you've *got* to look at him! Yes, look at him, the man who was born the same year as your own father!'

"Plunging her hand into her daughter's hair, she forced her face round towards me. As if she were brandishing a decapitated head, she held her by her hair so tightly that the little thing's eyes were drawn up slantwise.

" 'That man who would have been fifty years older than his child, suppose you had been pregnant by him, Louise!'

"At that shriek, Louisette freed herself and did indeed begin to look at me. The screaming shrew had not finished with me and she no longer respected the silence of the night.

" 'Do you see what he's got on his temples? White hairs, Louise, white hairs, just like me! And those wrinkles he's got under his eyes! All over him, wherever you look, he's got the stamp of ancience, my girl, yes, ancience.'

"She screamed that peasant word with an air of murderous delight, with a gloating joy that shrivelled me up. Louisette remained looking earnest and stupid as children do when they wake up, the flame of the lamp was reflected yellow in her eyes. She fastened up her open blouse, smoothed down its pleats, buckled her belt again and muttered to her mother:

" 'Do you want me to go for him, Mother? Us two'll "chaäse" him, shall we?'

"The mother had no time to answer before I had shot out of the house. Yes, right out of the house and the Devil himself couldn't have stopped me. You don't understand? You can't understand that I'd rather do anything in the world than fight a woman—or two women. Any set-to between men, even war, is less alarming to us men, less alarming to our nerves, than the fury of a woman. We can never foresee what a woman may do when she loses all control. We never know whether she is going to call us a 'cad' with an air of tremendous dignity or whether she is going to try and tear our nails out or bite our nose off with one snap of her teeth. What's more, she herself hasn't the least idea either. It comes from too deep down in her. Goodness, I ran fast. And I kept my eyes skinned too, so as to dodge stones and ruts. If I've ever laughed about my misadventure, by gad, it certainly wasn't at that moment! The terrace, the spring, the avenue of rowans, the pillars with the lions, I fled past them as if in a nightmare. I outdistanced my two pursuers and I took the narrow path that skirted the outer wall. But the moon had moved across the sky and it now shone full on the path. When I came abreast of the scented laurels, I stopped. I could no longer hear footsteps behind me and I forced myself to recover my breath. To prove to myself I was perfectly calm, I deliberately gazed out over the valley which was once again a clear blue, steaming with warm mists and dotted with delicate birches whose satiny trunks shimmered as if in broad daylight. I mopped my brow and the back of my neck and, as I searched for a cigarette, I noticed that my hands were trembling.

"A shiver of insecurity sharpened my uneasiness; I raised my head, and just above me, just behind the crest of the dilapidated wall I saw the mother and the daughter. Only the top half of their bodies was visible and they were watching me like hawks. It cost me a tremendous effort not to start off again at full speed. I was firm with myself and walked on slowly and nonchalantly, as if absorbed in moonlight meditation. Two heads, close side by side, followed my movement; they must be starting off again in pursuit of me. I was only too right; the two heads reappeared farther on, waiting for me. White hairs and gold hairs fluttered in the air like poplar-seeds.

"Seeing them there, perfectly still, I stopped. It was one of the hardest things I have done in my life. Then I started to walk on again slowly, down the increasing slope of the path. I passed underneath the two women. It was then that a large-sized stone fell from the top of the wall, grazed my shoulder, and rolled ahead of me down the steep path, just in front of my feet. I stepped over it and continued on my way. A little farther on, a second stone just like it took the skin off my ear as it fell before hitting my foot and quite severely bruising my big toe. I was only wearing canvas shoes. I came to a breach that lowered the level of the wall. My tormentresses were standing in the breach and waiting for me. A good honest rage, the rage of an injured man, seized me at last and inspired me to assault the breach and the two hussies. In three bounds, I was up there. No doubt they too suddenly recovered their reason and remembered that they were females, and I was a male, for, after hesitating, they fled and disappeared into the neglected garden behind some pyramid fruit trees and a feathery clump of asparagus.

"I didn't care! I had regained control of myself. I shouted heaven knows what threats in the direction of my fugitives. I grabbed hold of a vine-prop which I brandished like a sword. It was ridiculous, but it did me no end of good. Afterwards, I walked down to the path again and reached the undergrowth, spotted with moonlight like a leopard-skin. Rabbits were already scurrying about and I frightened some birds. But I was much more startled than these timid small folk. However my nerves did not entirely let me down; I dried my bleeding ear and I began to limp because of my crushed foot.

"The next day, I went down with what is called a 'first

class' bout of fever, due, I think, to the warm dampness and to the folly of not having taken a sweater. To emotion as well, I'm not idiotic enough to deny it. No encounter has ever staggered me as much as the one with that moralist, the little lady with the frizzy white hair. For an outraged mother to demand some form of compensation, right, that's logical enough. Even for her to insist on the supreme reparation—marriage—that's all right too. That sort of demand always ends by the lady softening down. But *that* mother, with that fleecy head, those eyes, that way of charging the enemy. She'd have stoned me to death if she could. Yes, yes, she really would have. What risk did she take? A wall that was crumbling of its own accord. The little thing, I think she was just an honest, straightforward, adorable idiot.

"Well, my bout of fever was long and violent, and accompanied by shivering fits that made the bed rattle, by nightmares, even a little delirium—I've always been highly strung. I saw ferocious yellow cats, twin heads on a single neck. My host looked after me admirably, and luckily found in his cupboard various medicaments compounded in his professional days. He made a hole in one of my slippers to make room for my swollen injured toe. And his agreeable female relative sewed a number of medals, all of proven efficacy, into my pyjamas.

"No, I never saw Louisette again. I made no attempt to see her. At one fell swoop, I had lost the taste for the twilights of Franche-Comté and satiny birch-trees and clumps of heather. But, for all too definite reason, there was no question of forgetting her. When I thought about her, I turned hot and cold and disgust came rushing over me, distorting and eclipsing her charms. Infinitely worse, my dear, the most hideous fear of my life unfortunately revived again, insinuating its little icy serpent, its drop of burning wax, between my shirt and my skin, between Louisette and myself, between me and other Louisettes.

Henceforth, it was to deprive your old friend—look, the mere thought of it is making me sweat—of all the Louisettes in this world. What's that you say? A punishment for my sins? Just wait! I have been granted an unexpected kind of compensation. You know the theme, exploited hundreds of times in literature and funny stories: the enemies and the victims of Don Juan substitute the duenna or some overblown chambermaid in his bed for the beautiful quarry. And the next day, the gang of practical jokers assembles round the seducer and informs him, with loud laughter, what they have done. . . . Inform him? Did he really know nothing about it? Wasn't the evidence of his own senses enough? Does that mean that, but for his tormentors, he might have been quite satisfied in the morning, when he emerged from the warm darkness of the bed? It's perfectly possible. So let's say, my dear, that instead of the Louisettes, I could still console myself with the chambermaid. And, as I had no friends to shout it from the house-tops, I did not complain too much of my lot."

Green Sealing-wax

ROUND about fifteen, I was at the height of a mania for "desk-furniture". In this I was only imitating my father whose mania for it lasted in full force all his life. At the age when every kind of vice gets its claws into adolescence, like the hundred little hooks of a burr sticking into one's hair, a girl of fifteen runs plenty of risks. My glorious freedom exposed me to all of them and I believed it to be unbounded, unaware that Sido's maternal instinct, which disdained any form of spying, worked by flashes of intuition and leapt telepathically to the danger-point.

When I had just turned fifteen, Sido gave me a dazzling proof of her second sight. She guessed that a man above suspicion had designs on my little pointed face, the plaits that whipped against my calves and my well-made body. Having entrusted me to this man's family during the holidays, she received a warning as clear and shattering as the gift of sudden faith and she cursed herself for having sent me away to strangers. Promptly, she put on her little bonnet that tied under the chin, got into the clanking, jolting train—they were beginning to send antique coaches along a brand-new line—and found me in a garden, playing with two other little girls, under the eyes of a taciturn man, leaning on his elbow like the meditative Demon on the ledge of Notre-Dame.

Such a spectacle of peaceful family life could not deceive Sido. She noticed, moreover, that I looked prettier than I did at home. That is how girls blossom in the warmth of a man's desire, whether they are fifteen or thirty. There was no question of scolding me and Sido took me away with her without the irreproachably respectable man's having dared to ask her reason for her arrival or for our departure. In the train, she fell asleep before my eyes, worn out like someone who had won a battle. I remember that lunch-time went by and I complained of being hungry. Instead of flushing, looking at her watch, promising me my favourite delicacies—wholemeal bread, cream cheese and pink onions—all she did was to shrug her shoulders. Little did she care about my hunger-pangs, she had saved the most precious thing of all.

I had done nothing wrong, nor had I abetted this man, except by my torpor. But torpor is a far graver peril for a girl of fifteen than all the usual excited giggling and blushing and clumsy attempts at flirtation. Only a few men can induce that torpor from which girls awake to find themselves lost. That, so to speak, surgical intervention of Sido's cleared up all the confusion inside me and I had one of those relapses into childishness in which adolescence revels when it is simultaneously ashamed of itself and intoxicated by its own ego.

My father, a born writer, left few pages behind him. At the actual moment of writing, he dissipated his desire in material arrangements, setting out all the objects a writer needs and a number of superfluous ones as well. Because of him, I am not proof against this mania myself. As a result of having admired and coveted the perfect equipment of a writer's work-table, I am still exacting about the tools on my desk. Since adolescence does nothing by halves, I stole from my father's work-table, first a little mahogany set-square that smelt like a cigar-box, then a white metal ruler. Not to mention the scolding, I received full in my face the glare of a small, blazing grey eye, the eye of a rival, so fierce that I did not risk it a third time.

I confined myself to prowling, hungrily, with my mind full of evil thoughts, round all these treasures of stationery. A pad of virgin blotting-paper; an ebony ruler; one, two, four, six pencils, sharpened with a penknife and all of different colours; pens with medium nibs and fine nibs, pens with enormously broad nibs, drawing-pens no thicker than a blackbird's quill; sealing-wax, red, green and violet; a hand-blotter, a bottle of liquid glue, not to mention slabs of transparent amber-coloured stuff known as "mouth-glue"; the minute remains of a Spahi's cloak reduced to the dimensions of a pen-wiper with scalloped edges; a big ink-pot flanked by a small ink-pot, both in bronze, and a lacquer bowl filled with a golden powder to dry the wet page; another bowl containing sealing-wafers of all colours (I used to eat the white ones); to right and left of the table, reams of paper, cream-laid, ruled, water-marked, and, of course, that little stamping-machine that bit into the white sheet, and, with one snap of its jaws, adorned it with an embossed name: *J.-J. Colette*. There was also a glass of water for washing paint-brushes, a box of water-colours, an address-book, the bottles of red, black and violet ink, the mahogany set-square, a pocket-case of mathematical instruments, the tobacco-jar, a pipe, the spirit-lamp for melting the sealing-wax.

A property owner tries to extend his domain; my father therefore tried to acclimatise adventitious subjects on his vast table. At one time there appeared on it a machine that could cut through a pile of a hundred sheets, and some frames filled with a white jelly on which you laid a written page face downwards and then, from this looking-glass original, pulled off blurred, sticky, anaemic copies. But my father soon wearied of such gadgets and the huge table returned to its serenity, to its classical style that was never disturbed by inspiration with its disorderly litter of crossed-out pages, cigarette-ends and "roughs" screwed up into paper balls. I have forgotten, heaven forgive me, the paper-knife section, three or four boxwood ones, one of imitation silver, and the last of yellowed ivory, cracked from end to end.

From the age of ten I had never stopped coveting those material goods, invented for the glory and convenience of a mental power, which come under the general heading of "desk-furniture". Children only delight in things they can hide. For a long time I secured possession of one wing, the left one, of the great four-doored double bookcase (it was eventually sold by order of the court). The doors of the upper part were glass-fronted, those of the lower, solid and made of beautiful figured mahogany. When you opened the lower left-hand door at a right angle, the flap touched the side of the chest-of-drawers, and, as the bookcase took up nearly the whole of one panelled wall, I would immure myself in a quadrangular nook formed by the side of the chest-of-drawers, the wall, the left section of the bookcase and its wide-open door. Sitting on a little footstool, I could gaze at the three mahogany shelves in front of me, on which were displayed the objects of my worship, ranging from cream-laid paper to a little cup of the golden powder. "She's a chip off the old block," Sido would say teasingly to my father. It was ironical that, equipped with every conceivable tool for writing, my father rarely committed himself to putting pen to paper, whereas Sido—sitting at any old table, pushing aside an invading cat, a basket of plums, a pile of linen, or else just putting a dictionary on her lap by way of a desk—Sido really did write. A hundred enchanting letters prove that she did. To continue a letter or finish it off, she would tear a page out of her household account book or write on the back of a bill.

She therefore despised our useless altars. But she did not discourage me from lavishing care on my desk and adorning it to amuse myself. She even showed anxiety when I explained that my little house was becoming too small for me . . . "Too small. Yes, much too small," said the grey eyes. "Fifteen . . . Where is Pussy-Darling going, bursting out of her nook like a hermit-crab driven out of its borrowed shell by its own growth? Already, I've snatched her from the clutches of that man. Already, I've had to forbid her to go dancing on the 'Ring' on Low Sunday. Already, she's escaping and I shan't be able to follow her. Already, she wants a long dress and, if I give her one, the blindest will notice that she's a young girl. And if I refuse, everyone will look below the too-short skirt and stare at her woman's legs. Fifteen . . . How can I stop her from being fifteen, then sixteen, then seventeen years old?"

Sometimes, during that period, she would come and lean over the mahogany half-door that isolated me from the world. "What are you doing?" She could see perfectly well what I was doing but she could not understand it. I refused her the answer given her so generously by everything else she observed, the bee, the caterpillar, the hydrangea, the ice-plant. But at least she could see I was there, sheltered from danger. She indulged my mania. The lovely pieces of shiny coloured wrapping-paper were given me to bind my books and I made the gold string into book-markers. I had the first pen-holder sheathed in a glazed turquoise-coloured substance, with a moiré pattern on it, that appeared in Reumont's, the stationers.

One day my mother brought me a little stick of sealing-wax and I recognised the stub of green wax, the prize jewel of my father's desk. No doubt I considered the gift too overwhelming, for I gave no sign of ecstatic joy. I clutched the sealing-wax in my hand, and, as it grew warm, it gave out a slightly oriental fragrance of incense.

"It's very old sealing-wax," Sido told me, "and, as you can see, it's powdered with gold. Your father already had it when we were married; he'd been given it by his mother and his mother assured him that it was a stick of wax that had been used by Napoleon the First. But you've got to remember that my mother-in-law lied every time she opened her mouth, so . . ."

"Is he giving it to me or have you taken it?"

Sido became impatient; she always turned irritable when she thought she was going to be forced to lie and was trying to avoid lying.

"When *will* you stop twisting a lock of hair around the end of your nose?" she cried. "You're doing your best to have a red nose with a blob at the tip like a cherry! That sealing-wax? Let's say your father's lending it to you and leave it at that. Of course, if you don't want . . ."

My wild clutch of possession made Sido laugh again, and she said, with pretended lightness:

"If he wanted it, he'd ask you to give it back, of course!'

But he did not ask me to give it back. For a few months, gold-flecked green sealing-wax perfumed my narrow empire bounded by four mahogany walls, then my pleasure gradually diminished as do all pleasures to which no one disputes our right. Besides, my devotion to stationery temporarily waned in favour of a craze to be glamorous. I asserted my right to wear a "bustle", that is to say, I enlarged my small, round behind with a horsehair cushion which, of course, made my skirts much shorter at the back than in front. In our village, the frenzy of adolescence turned girls between thirteen and fifteen into madwomen who stole horsehair, cotton and wool, stuffed rags in a bag, and tied on the hideous contraption known as a "false bottom" on dark staircases, out of their mothers' sight. I also longed for a thick, frizzy fringe, leather belts so tight I could hardly breathe, high boned collars, violet scent on my handkerchief . . .

From that phase, I relapsed once more into childhood, for a feminine creature has to make several attempts before it finally hatches out. I revelled in being a Plain Jane, with my hair in pigtails and straight wisps straggling over my cheeks. I gladly renounced all my finery in favour of my old school pinafores with their pockets stuffed with nuts and string and chocolate. Paths edged with brambles, clumps of bullrushes, liquorice "shoe-laces", cats—in short, everything I still love to this day—became dear to me again. There are no words to hymn such times in one's life, no clear memories to illuminate them; looking back on them, I can only compare them to the depths of blissful sleep. The smell of haymaking sometimes brings them back to me, perhaps because, suddenly tired, as growing creatures are, I would drop for an hour into a dreamless sleep among the new-mown hay.

It was at this point there occurred the episode known for long afterwards as "the Hervouët will affair". Old Monsieur Hervouët died and no will could be found. The provinces have always been rich in fantastic figures. Somewhere, under old tiled roofs, yellow with lichen, in icy drawing-rooms and dining-rooms dedicated to eternal shade, on waxed floors strewn with death-traps of knitted rugs, in kitchen-garden paths between the hard-headed cabbages and the curly parsley, queer characters are always to be found. A little town or a village prides itself on possessing a mystery. My own village acknowledged placidly, even respectfully, the rights of young Gatreau to rave unmolested. This admirable example of a romantic madman, a wooden cigar between his lips, was always wildly tossing his streaming black curls and staring fixedly at young girls with his long, Arab eyes. A voluntary recluse used to nod good morning through a window-pane and passers would say of her admiringly:

"That makes twenty-two years since Madame Sibile left her room! My mother used to see her there, just as you see her now. And, you know, there's nothing the matter with her. In one way, it's a fine life!"

But Sido used to hurry her quick step and pull me along when we passed level with the aquarium that housed the lady who had not gone out for twenty-two years. Behind her clear glass pane the prisoner would be smiling. She always wore a linen cap; sometimes her little yellow hand held a cup. A sure instinct for what is horrible and prohibited made Sido turn away from that ground-floor window and that bobbing head. But the sadism of childhood made me ask her endless questions:

"How old do you think she is, Madame Sibile? At night does she sleep by the window in her armchair? Do they undress her? Do they wash her? And how does she go to the lavatory?"

Sido would start as if she had been stung.

"Be quiet. I forbid you to think about those things.

Monsieur Hervouët had never passed for one of those eccentrics to whom a market-town extends its slightly derisive protection. For sixty years he had been well-off and ill-dressed, first a "big catch" to marry, then a big catch married. Left a widower, he had remarried. His second wife was a former postmistress, thin and full of fire.

When she struck her breastbone, exclaiming "*That's* where I can feel it burning!" her Spanish eyes seemed to make the person she was talking to responsible for this unquenchable ardour. "I am not easily frightened," my father used to say; "but heaven preserve me from being left alone with Mademoiselle Matheix!"

After his second marriage, Monsieur Hervouët no longer appeared in public. As he never left his home, no one knew exactly when he developed the gastric trouble that was to carry him off. He was a man dressed, in all weathers, in black, including a cap with ear-flaps. Smothered in fleecy white hair and a beard like cotton-wool, he looked like an apple-tree attacked by woolly aphis. High walls and a gateway that was nearly always closed protected his second season of conjugal bliss. In summer a single rose-tree clothed three sides of his one-storeyed house and the thick fringe of wistaria on the crest of the wall provided food for the first bees. But we had never heard anyone say that Monsieur Hervouët was fond of flowers and, if we now and then caught sight of his black figure pacing to and fro under the pendants of the wistaria and the showering roses, he struck us as being neither responsible for nor interested in all this wealth of blossom.

When Mademoiselle Matheix became Madame Hervouët, the ex-postmistress lost none of her resemblance to a black-and-yellow wasp. With her sallow skin, her squeezed-in waist, her fine, inscrutable eyes and her mass of dark hair, touched with white and restrained in a knot on the nape of her neck, she showed no surprise at being promoted to middle-class luxury. She appeared to be fond of gardening. Sido, the impartial, thought it only fair to show some interest in her; she lent her books, and in exchange accepted cuttings and also roots of tree-violets whose flowers were almost black and whose stem grew naked out of the ground like the trunk of a tiny palm-tree. To me, Madame Hervouët-Matheix was an anything but sympathetic figure. I was vaguely scandalised that when making some assertions of irreproachable banality, she did so in a tone of passionate and plaintive supplication.

"What do you expect?" said my mother. "She's an old maid."

"But, Mamma, she's married!"

"Do you really imagine," retorted Sido acidly, "people stop being old maids for a little thing like that?"

One day, my father, returning from the daily "round of the town" by which this man who had lost one leg kept himself fit, said to my mother:

"A piece of news! The Hervouët relatives are attacking the widow."

"*No!*"

"And going all out for her, too! People are saying the grounds of the accusation are extremely serious."

"A new Lafarge case?"

"You're demanding a lot," said my father.

I thrust my sharp little mug between my two parents.

"What's that, the Lafarge case?"

"A horrible business between husband and wife. There's never been a period without one. A famous poisoning case."

"Ah!" I exclaimed excitedly. "What a piece of luck!"

Sido gave me a look that utterly renounced me.

"There you are," she muttered. "That's what they're all like at that age . . . A girl ought never to be fifteen."

"Sido, are you listening to me or not?" broke in my father. "The relatives, put up to it by a niece of Hervouët's, are claiming that Hervouët didn't die intestate and that his wife has destroyed the will."

"In that case," observed Sido, "you could bring an action against all widowers and all widows of intestates."

"No," retorted my father, "men who have children don't need to make a will. The flames of Hervouët's lady can only have scorched Hervouët from the waist up since . . ."

"Colette," my mother said to him severely, indicating me with a look.

"Well," my father went on. "So there she is in a nice pickle. Hervouët's niece says she saw the will, yes, saw it with her very own eyes. She can even describe it. A big envelope, five seals of green wax with gold flecks in it . . ."

"Fancy that!" I said innocently.

". . . and on the front of it, the instructions: 'To be opened after my death in the presence of my solicitor, Monsieur Hourblin or his successor.' "

"And suppose the niece is lying?" I ventured to ask.

"And suppose Hervouët changed his mind and destroyed his will?" suggested Sido. "He was perfectly free to do so, I presume?"

"There you go, the two of you! Already siding with the bull against the bullfighter!" cried my father.

"Exactly," said my mother. "Bullfighters are usually men with fat buttocks and that's enough to put me against them!"

"Let's get back to the point," said my father. "Hervouët's niece has a husband, a decidedly sinister gentleman by name of Pellepuits."

I soon got tired of listening. On the evidence of such words as "The relatives are attacking the widow!" I had hoped for bloodshed and foul play and all I heard was bits of gibberish such as "disposable portion of estate", "holograph will", "charge against X".

All the same my curiosity was reawakened when Monsieur Hervouët's widow paid us a call. Her little mantle of imitation Chantilly lace worn over hock-bottle shoulders, her black mittens from which protruded unusually thick, almost opaque nails, the luxuriance of her black-and-white hair, a big black taffeta pocket suspended from her belt that dangled over the skirt of her mourning, her "houri eyes", as she called them; all these details, that I seemed to be seeing for the first time, took on a new, sinister significance.

Sido received the widow graciously, took her into the garden and offered her a thimbleful of Frontignan and a wedge of home-made cake. The June afternoon buzzed over the garden, russet caterpillars dropped about us from the walnut-tree, not a cloud floated in the sky. My mother's pretty voice and Madame

Hervouët's imploring one exchanged tranquil remarks; as usual, they talked about nothing but salpiglossis, gladiolus and the misdemeanours of servants. Then the visitor rose to go and my mother escorted her. "If you don't mind," said Madame Hervouët, "I'll come over in a day or two and borrow some books; I'm so lonely."

"Would you like to take them now?" suggested Sido.

"No, no, there's no hurry. Besides, I've noted down the titles of some adventure stories. Good-bye for the time being, and thank you."

As she said this, Madame Hervouët, instead of taking the path that led to the house, took the one that circled the lawn and walked twice round the plot of grass.

"Good gracious, whatever am I doing? Do forgive me."

She allowed herself a modest laugh and eventually reached the hall where she groped too high and to the left of the two sides of the folding door for a latch she had twenty times found on the right. My mother opened the front door for her and, out of politeness, stood for a moment at the top of the steps. We watched Madame Hervouët go off, keeping at first very close to the house, then crossing the road very hurriedly, picking up her skirts as if she were fording a river.

My mother shut the door again and saw that I had followed her.

"She is lost," she said.

"Who? Madame Hervouët? Why do you say that? How d'you mean, lost?"

Sido shrugged her shoulders.

"I've no idea. It's just my impression. Keep that to yourself."

I kept silence faithfully. This was all the easier as, continuing my series of metamorphoses like a grub, I had entered a new phase—the "enlightened bibliophile"—and I forgot Madame

Hervouët in a grand turn-out of my stationery shop. A few days later, I was installing Jules Verne between *Les Fleurs Animées* and a relief atlas when Madame Hervouët appeared on the scene without the bell having warned me. For we left the front door open nearly all day so that our dog Domino could go in and out.

"How nice of a big girl like you to tidy up the bookshelves," exclaimed the visitor. "What books are you going to lend me today?"

When Madame Hervouët raised her voice, I clenched my teeth and screwed up my eyes very small.

"Jules Verne," she read, in a plaintive voice. "You can't read him twice. Once you know the secret, it's finished."

"There's Balzac up there, on the big shelves," I said, pointing to them.

"He's very heavy going," said Madame Hervouët.

Balzac, heavy going? Balzac, my cradle, my enchanted forest, my voyage of discovery? Amazed, I looked up at the tall black woman, a head taller than myself. She was toying with a cut rose and staring into space. Her features expressed nothing which could be remotely connected with opinions on literature. She became aware I was gazing at her and pretended to be interested in my writer's equipment.

"It's charming. What a splendid collection!"

Her mouth had grown older in the last week. She remained stooping over my relics, handling this one and that. Then she straightened herself up with a start.

"But isn't your dear mother anywhere about? I'd like to see her."

Only too glad to move, to get away from this "lost" lady, I rushed wildly out into the garden, calling "Mamma!" as if I were shouting "Fire!"

"She took a few books away with her," Sido told me when

we were alone. "But I could positively swear she didn't even glance at their titles."

The rest of the "Hervouët affair" is linked, in my memory, with a vague general commotion, a kind of romantic blur. My clearest recollection of it comes to me through Sido, thanks to the extraordinary "presence" I still have of the sound of her voice. Her stories, her conversations with my father, the intolerant way she had of arguing and refuting, those are the things that riveted a sordid provincial drama in my mind.

One day, shortly after Madame Hervouët's last visit, the entire district was exclaiming "The will's been found!" and describing the big envelope with five seals that the widow had just deposited in Monsieur Hourblin's study. At once uneasy and triumphant, the Pellepuits-Hervouët couple and another lot, the Hervouët-Guillamats, appeared, along with the widow, at the lawyer's office. There, Madame Hervouët, all by herself, faced up to the solid, pitiless group, to what Sido called those "gaping, legacy-hunting sharks". "It seems," my mother said, telling the story "that she smelt of brandy." At this point, my mother's voice is superseded by the hunchback's voice of Julia Vincent, a woman who went out ironing by the day and came to us once a week. For I don't know how many consecutive Fridays, I pressed Julia till I wrung out of her all she knew. The precise sound of that nasal voice, squeezed between the throat, the hump and the hollow, deformed chest, was a delight to me.

"The man as was most afeared was the lawyer. To begin with he's not a tall man, not half so tall as that woman. She, all dressed in black she was, and her veil falling down in front right to her feet. Then the lawyer picked up the envelope, big as that it was" (Julia unfolded one of my father's vast handkerchiefs) "and he passed it just as it was to the nephews so they could recognise the seals."

"But you weren't there, Julia, were you?"

"No, it was Monsieur Hourblin's junior clerk who was watching through the keyhole. One of the nephews said a word or two. Then Madame Hervouët stared at him like a duchess. The lawyer coughed, a-hem, a-hem, he broke the seals and he read it out."

In my recollection, it is sometimes Sido talking, sometimes some scandalmonger eager to gossip about the Hervouët affair. Sometimes it seems too that some illustrator, such as Bertall or Tony Johannot, has actually etched a picture for me of the tall, thin woman who never withdrew her Spanish eyes from the group of heirs-at-law and kept licking her lip to taste the *marc* brandy she had gulped down to give herself courage.

So Monsieur Hourblin read out the will. But, after the first lines, the document began to shake in his hands and he broke off, with an apology, to wipe his glasses. He resumed his reading and went right through to the end. Although the testator declared himself to be "sound in body and mind", the will was nothing but a tissue of absurdities, among others, the acknowledgement of a debt of two million francs contracted to Louise-Léonie-Alberte Matheix, beloved spouse of Clovis-Edme Hervouët.

The reading finished in silence and not one voice was raised from the block of silent heirs.

"It seems," said Sido, "that, after the reading, the silence was such you could hear the wasps buzzing in the vine-arbour outside the window. The Pellepuits and the various Guillamats did nothing but stare at Madame Hervouët, without stirring a finger. Why aren't cupidity and avarice possessed of second sight? It was a female Guillamat, less stupid than the others, who said afterwards that, before anyone had spoken, Madame Hervouët began to make peculiar movements with her neck, like a hen that's swallowed a hairy caterpillar.

The story of the last scene of that meeting spread like wildfire through the streets, through people's homes, through the cafés, through the fair-grounds. Monsieur Hourblin had been the first to speak above the vibrating hum of the wasps.

"On my soul and conscience, I find myself obliged to declare that the handwriting of the will does not correspond . . ."

A loud yelping interrupted him. Before him, before the heirs, there was no longer any Widow Hervouët, but a sombre Fury whirling round and stamping her feet, a kind of black dervish, lacerating herself, muttering and shrieking. To her admissions of forgery, the crazy woman added others, so rich in the names of vegetable poisons, such as buckthorn and hemlock, that the lawyer, in consternation, exclaimed naïvely:

"Stop, my poor good lady, you're telling us far more than anyone has asked you to!"

A lunatic asylum engulfed the madwoman and, if the Hervouët affair persisted in some memories, at least, there was no "Hervouët case" at the assizes.

"Why, Mamma?" I asked.

"Mad people aren't tried. Or else they'd have to have judges who were mad too. That wouldn't be a bad idea, when you come to think of it . . ."

To pursue her train of thought better, she dropped the task with which her hands were busy; graceful hands that she took no care of. Perhaps, that particular day, she was shelling haricot beans. Or else, with her little finger stuck in the air, she was coating my father's crutch with black varnish . . .

"Yes, judges who would be able to assess the element of calculation in madness, who could sift out the hidden grain of lucidity, of deliberate fraud."

The moralist who was raining these unexpected conclusions on a fifteen-year-old head was encased in a blue gardener's apron, far too big for her, that made her look quite plump. Her grey gaze, terribly direct, fixed me now through her spectacles, now over the top of them. But in spite of the apron, the rolled-up sleeves, the sabots and the haricot beans, she never looked humble or common.

"What I do blame Madame Hervouët for," Sido went on, "is her megalomania. *Folie de grandeur* is the source of any number of crimes. Nothing exasperates me more than the imbecile who imagines he's capable of planning and executing a crime without being punished for it. Don't you agree it's Madame Hervouët's stupidity that makes her case so sickening? Poisoning poor old Hervouët with extremely bitter herbal concoctions, right, that wasn't difficult. Inept murderer, stupid victim, it's tit for tat. But to try and imitate a handwriting without having the slightest gift for forgery, to trust to a special, rare kind of sealing wax, what petty ruses, great heavens, what fatuous conceit!"

"But why did she confess?"

"Ah," said Sido reflectively. "That's because a confession is almost inevitable. A confession is like . . . let's see . . . yes . . . it's like a stranger you carry inside you . . ."

"Like a child?"

"No, not a child. With a child, you know the exact date it's going to leave you. Whereas a confession bursts out quite suddenly, just when you weren't expecting it, it tastes its liberty, it stretches its limbs. It shouts, it cuts capers. She accompanied hers with a dance, that poor murderess who thought herself so clever."

It shouts, it cuts capers . . . Just like that, then and there, my own secret burst out into Sido's ear: on the very day of Madame Hervouët's last visit I had noticed the disappearance of the little stick of green sealing-wax powdered with gold.

Armande

"THAT girl? But, good heavens, she adores you! What's more, she's never done anything else for ten whole years. All the time you were on active service, she kept finding excuses for dropping in at the Pharmacy and asking if I'd had a letter."

"Did she?"

"She wouldn't leave the shop until she'd managed to slip in her 'How's your brother?' She used to wait. And while she was waiting, she'd buy aspirin, cough lozenges, tubes of lanoline, toilet water, tincture of iodine."

"So naturally, you saw to it she was kept waiting?"

"Well, after all, why not? When I finally did tell her I'd news of you, off she went. But never till I had. You know what she's like."

"Yes . . . No, to be honest, I *don't* know what she's like."

"What do you expect, my poor pet? You made everything so complicated for yourself, you're wearing yourself out with all these absurd scruples. Armande is a very well-educated girl, we all know that. She takes her position as a comfortably rich orphan a shade too seriously. I grant you it's none too easy a one in a Sub-Prefecture like this. But just because of that, to let her put it over on you to that extent, *you*, Maxime, of all people! Look out, this is the new pavement. At least one can walk without getting one's feet wet now."

The September sky, black and moonless, glittered with stars that twinkled large in the damp air. The invisible river slucked against the single arch of the bridge. Maxime stopped and leant on the parapet.

"The parapet's new too," he said.

"Yes. It was put up by the local tradesmen, with the consent of the Town Council. You know they did tremendously well here out of food and clothing, what with all the troops going through and the exodus."

"Out of food, clothes, footwear, medical supplies and everything else. I also know that people talk about 'the exodus' as they do about 'the agricultural show' and 'the gala horse show and gymkhana'."

"Anyway, they wanted to make a great sacrifice."

Madame Debove heard Maxime laugh under his breath at the word "sacrifice" and she prudently left her sentence unfinished to revert to Armande Fauconnier.

"In any case, she didn't let you down too badly during the war, she wrote to you, didn't she?"

"Postcards."

"She sent you food parcels and a marvellous pullover."

"To hell with her food parcels and her woollies" said Maxime Degouthe violently, "*and* her postcards! I've never begged charity from her, as far as I know?"

"Good gracious, what a savage character you are . . . Don't spoil your last evening here, Maxime! Admit it was a charming party tonight. Armande is a very good hostess. All the Fauconniers have always been good hosts. Armande knows how to efface herself. There was no chance of the conversation getting on to that children's clinic that Armande supports entirely out of her own money."

"Who hasn't organised something in the way of a children's clinic during the war?" growled Maxime.

"Why, heaps of people, I assure you! In the first place, you've got to have the means. *She* really has got the means."

Maxime made no reply. He hated it when his sister talked of Armande's "means".

"The river's low," he said, after a moment or two.

"You've got good eyes!"

"It's not a question of eyes, it's a question of smell. When the water's low, it always smells of musk here. It's the mud, probably."

He suddenly remembered that, last year, he had said the very same words, on the very same spot, to Armande. She had wrinkled her nose in disgust and made an ugly grimace with her mouth. "As if *she* knew what mud was . . . Mud, that pearl-grey clay, so soft to the bare toes, so mysteriously musky, *she* imagines it's the same as excrement. She never misses an occasion of shrinking away from anything that can be tasted or touched or smelt."

Dancing owlet-moths almost obscured the luminous globes at either end of the bridge. Maxime heard his sister yawn.

"Come on, let's go. What on earth are we doing here?"

"I'm asking *you*!" sighed Madame Debove. "Do you hear? Eleven o'clock! Hector's sure to have gone to bed without waiting up for me."

"Let him sleep. There's no need for us to hurry."

"Oh yes there is, old thing! I'm sleepy, I am."

He took his sister's arm under his own, as he used to in the old days when they were students, sharing the same illusions, in that halcyon period when a brother and sister believe, quite genuinely, that they are perfectly content with being a chaste imitation of a pair of lovers. "Then a big, ginger-headed youth comes along and the devoted little sister goes off with him, for the pleasure and the advantages of marrying the Grand Central Pharmacy. After all, she did the right thing."

A passer-by stepped off the pavement to make room for them and bowed to Jeanne.

"Good evening, Merle. Stopped having those pains of yours?"

"It's as if he'd said, Madame Debove. Good evening, Madame Debove."

"He's a customer," explained Jeanne.

"Good Lord, I might have guessed that," said her brother ironically. "When you put on your professional chemist's wife voice."

"What about you when you put on your professional quack's voice? Just listen, am I exaggerating one bit? 'Above all, dear lady, endeavour as far as possible to control your nerves. The improvement is noticeable, I will even go so far as to say remarkable, but, for the time being, we must continue to be very firm about avoiding all forms of meat,' and I preach to you and I instruct you and I drench you with awful warnings."

Maxime laughed whole-heartedly, the imitation of his slightly pontifical manner was so true to life.

"All women are monkeys, they're only interested in our absurdities and our love-affairs and our illnesses. The other one can't be so very different from this one."

He could see her, the other one, as she had looked when he left her just now, standing at the top flight of steps that led up to the Fauconniers' house. The lighted chandelier in the hall behind her gave her a nimbus of blue glass convolvulus flowers and chromium hoops. "Good-bye, Armande." She had answered only with a nod. "You might call her a miser with words! If I had her in my arms, one day, between four walls or in the corner of a wood, I'd make her scream, and for good reason!" But he had never met Armande in the corner of a wood. As to his aggressive instincts, he lost all hope of gratifying them the moment he was in Armande's presence.

Eleven o'clock struck from the hospital, then from a small

low church jostled by new buildings, last of all, in shrill, crystalline strokes from a dark ground-floor room whose window was open. As they crossed the Place d'Armes, Maxime sat down on one of the benches.

"Just for one minute, Jeanne! Let me relax my nerves. It's nice out-of-doors."

Jeanne Debove consented sulkily.

"You ought to have worked them off on Armande, those nerves of yours. But you haven't got the guts!"

He did not protest and she burst into a malicious laugh. He wondered why sexual shyness, which excites dissolute women, arouses the contempt of decent ones.

"She overawes you, that's it. Yes, she overawes you. I simply can't get over it!"

She elaborated her inability to get over it by inundating him with various scoffing remarks, accompanied now by a neighing laugh, now by a spurt of giggles.

"After all, you're not in your very, *very* first youth. You're not a greenhorn. Or a neurotic. Nor, thank heaven, physically deformed."

She enumerated all the things her brother was not and he was glad she omitted to mention the one quite simple thing he was —a man who had been in love for a very long time.

Maxime Degouthe's long-persisting love, though it preserved him from debauchery, turned into mere habit when he was away from Armande for a few months. When he was away from her, a kind of conjugal fidelity allowed him to amuse himself as much as he liked and even to forget her for a spell. So much so that, when he had finished his medical studies, he had been paralysed to find himself faced with a grown-up Armande Fauconnier when the Armande he remembered was a gawky, sharp-shouldered, overgrown adolescent, at once clumsy and noble like a bony filly full of promise.

Every time he saw her again, she completely took possession of him. His feeling for her was violent and suppressed, like a gardener's son's for the "young lady up at the big house". He would have liked to be rather brutal to this beautiful tall girl whom he admired from head to foot, who was just sufficiently dark, just sufficiently white and as smooth as a pear. "But I shouldn't dare. No, I daren't," he fumed to himself, every time he left.

"The back of the seat is all wet," said Madame Debove. "I'm going home. What are your plans for tomorrow? Are you going in to say good-bye to Armande? She's expecting you to, you know."

"She hasn't invited me."

"You mean you daren't go on your own? You may as well admit it, that girl's thoroughly got you down!"

"I do admit it," said Maxime, so mildly that his sister stopped cruelly teasing him.

They walked in silence till they reached the Grand Central Pharmacy.

"You'll lunch with us tomorrow, of course. Hector would have a fit if you didn't have your last meal with him. Your parcel of ampoules will be all ready. No one can say when we'll be able to get those particular serums again. Well, shall I ring up Armande and say you'll be coming over to say good-bye to her? But I needn't say definitely you're not coming?"

She was fumbling endlessly with a bunch of keys. Maxime lent her the aid of his pocket-torch and its beam fell full on Jeanne Debove's mischievous face and its expression of mixed satisfaction and disapproval.

"She wants me to marry Armande. She's thinking of the money, of the fine, rich house, of 'the excellent effect', of my career, as she says. But she'd also like me to marry Armande without being over-enthusiastic about her. Everything's perfectly normal. Everything except myself, because I can't endure the idea that *she*, Armande, could marry me without being in love with me."

He hurried back to his hotel. The town was asleep but the hotel, close by the station, resounded with all the noises that are hostile to sleep and blazed with lights that aggravate human tiredness. Hobnailed boots, shuddering ceiling-lights, uncarpeted floors, the gates of the lift, the whinnyings of hydraulic pressure, the rhythmic clatter of plates flung into a sink in the basement, the intermittent trilling of a bell never stopped outraging the need for silence that had driven Maxime to his bedroom. Unable to stand any more, he added his own contribution to the selfish human concert, dropped his shoes on the wooden floor, carried them out into the corridor and shut his door with a loud slam.

He drenched himself with cold water, dried himself carelessly and got into bed quite naked, after having studied himself in the looking-glass. "Big bones, big muscles and four complete limbs, after all, that's not too bad, in these days. A large nose, large eyes, a cap of hair as thick as a motor-cyclist's head-pad, girls who weren't Mademoiselle Fauconnier have found all that very much to their taste. I don't see Mademoiselle Fauconnier sleeping with this naked, black-haired chap . . ."

On the contrary, he saw her only too well. Irritated by fretful desire, he waited for the hotel to become quiet. When—save for a sound of barking, a garage door, the departure of a motor-car—silence was at last established, a breeze sprang up, swept away the last insults inflicted by man on the night, and came in through the open window like a reward.

"Tomorrow," Maxime vowed to himself. It was a muddled vow that concerned the conquest of Armande quite as much as the return to professional life and the daily, necessary triumph of forced activity over fundamental listlessness.

He reiterated "Tomorrow," flung away his pillow, rolled over on his stomach, and fell asleep with his head between his folded arms in the same attitude as a small intimidated boy of long ago who used to dream of an Armande with long black curls. Later on another Maxime had slept like that, the adolescent who had plucked up courage to invite "those Fauconnier ladies" as they were coming out from High Mass, to have lemon ices at Peyrol's. "Really, Maxime, one doesn't eat lemon ices at quarter-to-twelve in the morning!" Armande had said. In that one word "really" what a number of reproofs she could convey! "Really, Maxime, you needn't *always* stand right in front of the window, you shut out the daylight. Maxime, really! You've gone and returned a ball *again* when it was 'out'."

But, when a particular period was over, there had been no more "reallys" and no more reproaches showered on his head. Still not properly asleep, Maxime Degouthe groped around a memory, around a moment that had restored a little confidence to his twenty-five-year-old self and had marked the end of Armande's gracious condescension. That day, he had arrived with Jeanne at the foot of the steps, just as Armande was opening the silvered wrought-iron door to go out. They had not seen each other for a very long time—"Hullo, fancy seeing you!—Yes, my sister insisted on bringing me with her, perhaps you'd rather I hadn't come.—Now, really, you're joking.—A friend of mine in Paris gave me a lift in his car and dropped me here this morning.—How awfully nice! Are you going to be here for some time?—No, the same friend's picking me up tomorrow after lunch and driving me back—Well, that *is* a short stay." In fact, such trivialities as to make either of them blush had either of them paid any attention to what they were saying. From the height of five or six steps, a wide, startled, offended gaze fell on Maxime. He also caught, at the level of his knees, the brush of a skirt-hem and a handbag which Armande had dropped and which he retrieved.

After a gloomy game of ping-pong, a tea composed entirely of sugary things, a handshake—a strong, swift, but promptly withdrawn hand had clasped his own—he had left Armande once again and, on the way back, Jeanne had given her cynical opinion of the situation: "You know, you could have the fair Armande as easy as pie. And I know what I'm talking about." She added: "You don't know the right way to go about it." But those had been the remarks of a twenty-year-old, the infallibility of one girl judging another girl.

He thought he was only half-sleep and fell into deep, but restless dreams. A nightmare tortured him with the shaming illusion that he was dressing old Queny's incurable foot on the steps leading up to the Fauconniers' house and that Armande was enthroned, impassive, at the top of them. Didn't she owe part of her prestige to those eight broad steps, almost like a series of terraces, that were famous throughout the town? "The Fauconniers' flight of front steps is so impressive. Without these front steps, the Fauconniers' house wouldn't have nearly such a grand air . . ." As if insulted, the sleeper sat up with a start. "Grand air indeed! That cube! That block with its cast-iron balconies and bands of tiles!" He woke up completely and once again the Fauconnier home inspired him with the old awed respect. The Fauconnier heliotropes, the Fauconnier polygonums, the Fauconnier lobelias recovered their status of flowers adorning the altar where he worshipped. So, to send himself to sleep again, Maxime soberly envisaged the duties that awaited him the next day, the day after, and all the rest of his life, in the guise of the faces of old Queny, of the elder Madame Cauvain, of her father Monsieur Enfert, of "young" Mademoiselle Philippon, the one who was only seventy-two . . . For old people do not die off in wartime. He swallowed half his bottle of mineral water at one gulp and fell heavily asleep again, insensible to the mosquitoes coming up from the shrunken river and the noises of the pale dawn.

"My last day of idle luxury." He had his breakfast in bed, feeling slightly ashamed, and ordered a bath, for which he had to wait a considerable time. "My last bath . . . I'm not going to get up till I've had my bath! I'm not leaving without my bath!" As a matter of fact, he preferred a very stiff shower or the chance plunges he had taken, straight into rivers and canals, these last months between April and August.

With some caution he made use of a toilet-water invented by his brother-in-law, the red-haired chemist. "Hector's perfumes, when they don't smell of squashed ants, smell of bad cognac." He chose his bluest shirt and his spotted foulard tie. "I wish I were handsome. And all I am is just so-so. Ah, how I wish I were handsome!" he kept thinking over and over again as he plastered down his brilliantined hair. But it was coarse, intractable, wavy hair, a vigorous bush that preferred standing up to lying down. When Maxime laughed, he wrinkled his nose, crinkled up his yellow-brown eyes and revealed his "lucky teeth", healthy and close-set except for a gap between the two upper front ones. Coatless and buckled into his best belt, he had, at nearly thirty, the free and easy charm and slightly plebeian elegance of many an errand-boy you see darting through the crowd on his cycle, nimble as a bird in a bush. "But, in a jacket, I just look common," Maxime decided, as he straightened the lapels of the reach-me-down jacket. "It's also the fault of the coat." He threw his reflection an angry glance. "Nevertheless, beautiful Armande, more than ten others have been quite satisfied with all that and have even said "Thank you." He sighed, and turned humble again. "But, seeing that it's to no one but Armande I'm appealing when I conjure up my poor little girl-friends, what on earth does it matter whether they thanked me or even asked for more? It's not of them I'm thinking."

He packed his suitcase with the care and dexterity of a man accustomed to use his hands for manipulating living substance, stopping the flow of blood, applying and pinning bandages. The September morning, with its flies and its warm yellow light, came in fresh through the open window; at the end of a narrow street a dancing shimmer showed where the river lay. "I shan't go and say good-bye to Armande," Maxime Degouthe decided. "For one thing, lunch is always late at Jeanne's; for another, I've got my case of medical supplies to fill up at the last moment and, if I'm to have time to get a bite of food before the train goes, it'll be impossible, yes, physically impossible."

At four o'clock, he opened the front gate, marched up the gravel path of the Fauconniers' garden, climbed the flight of steps and rang the bell. A second time, he pressed his finger long and vainly on the bell button, sunk in a rosette of white marble. No one came and the blood rushed up into Maxime's ears. "She's probably gone out. But where are her two lazy sluts of servants and the gardener who looks like a drunk?" He rang again, restraining himself with difficulty from giving the door a kick. At last he heard steps in the garden and saw Armande running towards him. She stopped in front of him, exclaiming "Ah!" and he smiled at seeing her wearing a big blue apron with a bib that completely enveloped her. She swiftly untied the apron and flung it on a rose-bush.

"But it suited you very well," said Maxime.

Armande blushed and he blushed himself, thinking that perhaps he had hurt her feelings. "She would take it the wrong way, naturally. She's impossible, impossible! Pretty, those flecks of white soap in her black hair. I'd never noticed that the skin at the edge of her forehead, just under the hair, is slightly blue."

"I was at the end of the garden, in the wash-house," said Armande. "It's laundry day today, so . . . Léonie and Maria didn't even hear the bell."

"I shan't keep you from your work, I only looked in for a couple of minutes. As I'm leaving tomorrow morning."

He had followed her to the top of the steps, and Maxime waited for her to indicate which of the wicker chairs he should sit in. But she said: "From four to seven the sun just beats down on you here," and she ushered him into the drawing-room where they sat down opposite each other. Maxime seated himself in one of the armchairs tapestried with La Fontaine's fables —his was *The Cat, the Weasel and the little Rabbit*—and stared at the rest of the furniture. The baby-grand piano, the Revolution clock, the plants in pots, he gazed at them all with hostile reverence.

"It's nice in here, isn't it?" said Armande. "I keep the blinds down because it faces south. Jeanne wasn't able to come?"

"Goodness, is she frightened of me?" He was on the point of feeling flattered. But he looked at Armande and saw her sitting stiffly upright on *The Fox and the Stork*, one elbow on the hard arm of the chair, the other on her lap, with her hands clasped together. In the dusk of the lowered blinds, her cheeks and her neck took on the colour of very pale terra-cotta, and she was looking straight at him with the steady gaze of a well-brought-up girl who knows she must not blink or look sidelong, or pretend to be shy so as to show off the length of her lashes. "What the hell am I doing here?" thought Maxime furiously. "This is where I've got to, where we've both got to, after ten, fifteen years of what's called childhood friendship. This girl is made of wood. Or else she's choked with pride.

You won't catch me again in the Fauconnier drawing-room." Nevertheless, he replied to Armande's questions, he talked to her about his "practice" and the "inevitable difficulties" of this post-war period. Nor did he fail to remark:

"But you know better than anyone what these various difficulties are. Look at you, loaded with responsibilities, and all alone in the world!"

Armande's immobility was shattered by an unexpected movement; she unclasped her fingers and clutched the arms of her chair with both hands as if she were afraid of slipping off it.

"Oh, I'm used to it. You know my mother brought me up in a rather special way. At my age, one's no longer a child."

The sentence, begun with assurance, broke off on a childish note that belied the last words. She mastered herself and said, in a different voice:

"Won't you have a glass of port? Or would you prefer orangeade?"

Maxime saw there was a loaded tray within easy reach of her hand and frowned.

"You're expecting guests? Then I'll be off!"

He had stood up; she remained seated and laid her hand on Maxime's arm.

"I never invite anyone on washing-day. I assure you I don't. As you'd told me you were going away again tomorrow, I thought you might possibly . . ."

She broke off, with a little grimace that displeased Maxime. "Ah, no! She's not to ruin that mouth for me! That outline of the lips, so clear-cut, so full; those corners of the mouth that are so . . . so . . . What's the matter with her today? You'd think she'd just buried the devil for good and all!"

He realised he was staring at her with unpardonable severity and forced himself to be gay.

"So you're heavily occupied in domestic chores? What a lovely laundress you make! And all those kids at your clinic, do you manage to keep them in order?"

He was laughing only with his lips. He knew very well that, when he was with Armande, love made him gloomy, jealous, self-conscious, unable to break down an obstacle between the two of them that perhaps did not exist. Armande took a deep breath, squared her shoulders and commanded her whole face to be nothing but the calm regular countenance of a beautiful brunette. But three shadowy dimples, two at the corners of the mouth, one in the chin, appeared when she smiled and quivered at every hint of emotion.

"I've got twenty-eight children over at the clinic, did you know that?"

"Twenty-eight children? Don't you think that's a lot for a young unmarried girl?"

"I'm not frightened of children," said Armande seriously.

"Children. She loves children. She'd be magnificent, pregnant. Tall as she is, she would broaden at the hips without looking squat, like short women who are carrying babies. She'd take up an enormous amount of space in the garden, in bed, in my arms. At last she'd have trusting eyes, the lovely, dark-ringed eyes of a pregnant woman. But for that to happen, Mademoiselle has got to tolerate someone coming close to her, and a little closer than offering her a ball at arm's length on a tennis-racket. She doesn't look as if the idea had ever occurred to her, that girl doesn't! In any case, *I'm* giving up all thought of it!"

He stood up, resolutely.

"This time, Armande, it's serious."

"What is?" she said, very low.

"Why, the fact that it's five o'clock, that I've two or three urgent things to do, a big parcel of medical supplies to get ready. My little village is right out of everything in the way of serums and pills."

"I know," said Armande at once.

"You know?"

"Oh, I just accidentally heard them say so, at your brother-in-law's."

He had leant towards her a little; she drew away with such a fierce movement that she knocked her elbow against a monumental lampstand.

"Have you hurt yourself?" said Maxime coldly.

"No," she said, equally coldly. "Not in the least."

She passed in front of him to open the front door, with its wrought-iron lacework. It resisted her efforts.

"The woodwork's warped. I keep telling Charost to fix it."

"Haven't I always known it stick like that? Don't destroy my childhood memories!"

Pursing her lips tight, she shook the door with a stubborn violence that made its panes rattle. There was a loud crash of glass and metal behind her, and, turning round, she saw Maxime staggering among the splintered cups and chromium hoops of the chandelier that had just fallen from the ceiling. Then his knees went limp and he fell over on his side. Prone on the floor, he made an attempt to raise his hand to his ear, could not finish the gesture, and lay perfectly still. Armande, with her back against the front door she had not had time to open, stared at the man lying at her feet on his bed of broken glass. She said in a strangled, incredulous voice: "No!" The sight of a trickle of blood running down behind Maxime's left ear and stopping for a moment on the collar of the blue shirt, which it soaked, restored Armande's power of speech and movement. She squatted down, straightened herself up swiftly, opened the door that was half-obstructed by the injured body, and screamed shrill summonses out into the garden:

"Maria! Léonie! Maria! Maria!"

The screams reached Maxime in the place where he reposed, unconscious. Along with the screams, he began to hear the buzzing of hives of bees and the clanging of hammers, and he half-opened his eyes. But unconsciousness promptly swallowed him up again and he fell back among the swarms of bees and the hammering to some place where pain, in its turn, tracked him down. "The top of my head hurts. It hurts behind my ear and on my shoulder."

Once again, the loud screams disturbed him: "Léonie! Maria!" He came to, very unwillingly, opened his eyes and received a sunbeam full in his face. The sunbeam appeared to be red; then it was cut off by a double moving shadow. All at once, he realised that Armande's two legs were passing to and fro across the light; he recognised Armande's feet, the white linen shoes trimmed with black leather. The feet were moving about in all directions on the carpet quite close to his head, sometimes open in a V and staggering, sometimes close together, and crushing bits of broken glass. He felt an urge to untie one of the white shoelaces for a joke, but at that very moment, he was shot through with agonising pain, and, without knowing it, he moaned.

"My darling, my darling," said a shaking voice.

"Her darling? What darling?" he asked himself. He raised his cheek, which was lying heavily on fragments of pale blue glass and the butt-ends of electric light bulbs. The blood spread out in a pool and his cheek was sticky with it. At the pathetic sight of the precious red spilt all about him, he woke up completely and understood all. He took advantage of the fact that the two feet had turned their heels to him and were running towards the terrace to feel his aching head and bruised shoulder and to discover that the source of the blood was behind his ear. "Good, a big cut. Nothing broken. I might have had my ear sliced off. It's a good thing to have hair like mine. Lord, how my head does ache!"

"Maria! Léonie!"

The black-and-white shoes returned; two knees sheathed in silk went down on the splintered glass. "She'll cut herself!" He made a slight movement to raise himself, then decided instead to lie low and keep quiet, only turning his head over so as to show Armande where his wound was.

"Oh heavens, he's bleeding," said Armande's voice. "Maria! Léonie!"

There was no reply.

"Oh, the bitches," the same voice said violently.

Sheer astonishment made Maxime give a start.

"Speak to me, Maxime! Maxime, can you hear me? My darling, my darling . . ."

Sabots were heard running in the garden, then climbing the steps.

"Ah, there you are, Charost! Yes, the chandelier fell down. A person could die in this place without anyone's hearing! Where *are* those two wretched girls?"

"In the paddock, Mademoiselle, spreading out the sheets. Ah, the poor unfortunate young man! He had a hundred years of life ahead of him!"

"I'm quite sure he still has! Run round to Doctor Pommier, tell him . . . If he's not in, Doctor Tuloup. If *he's* not in, the chemist, yes, the ginger-haired one, Madame Jeanne's husband. Charost, go and get the towels from my bathroom, the little hand-towel from the cloakroom, you can *see* I can't leave him. And the brown box in the cupboard! Hurry up, will you! Get someone to tell those two idiots to leave their washing, don't go yourself, send someone!"

The sabots clattered away.

"My darling, my darling," said the low, sweet voice.

"It really was me, the darling," Maxime told himself. Two hot hands feverishly massaged one of his, interrogating it. "There, there, my pulse is excellent! Don't get in a state! How beautiful she must be at this moment . . ." He groaned on purpose and slid the thread of a glance at Armande between his eyelids. She was ugly, with huge, terrified eyes and her mouth gaping stupidly. He closed his lids again, enraptured.

The hands pressed a wet towel over his wound, pushed away the hair. "That's not right, my pet, that's not right. Isn't there any iodine in the place then? She'll make me bleed unnecessarily, but what the hell does that matter as long as she keeps busy on me?" The ferruginous smell of iodine rose in his nostrils, he was aware of the wholesome burning pain, and relaxed, content. "Well done! But when it comes to putting on an efficient bandage, my girl, I'm streets ahead of you. That one won't ever hold. You ought to have shaved off a bit of my hair." He heard the girl clucking her tongue against her teeth, "tst, tst", then she became despairing.

"Oh, I'm too stupid! A bloody fool, in fact!"

He very nearly laughed but turned it into a vague, pitiful mumbling.

"Maxime, Maxime!" she implored.

She untied his tie, opened his shirt, and trying to find his heart, brushed the masculine nipple that swelled with pride. For a moment, the two of them were equally and completely motionless. As the hand withdrew, after receiving its reassuring answer from the heart, it slowly went over the same ground on its way back. "Oh, to take that hand that's stroking me in this startled way, to get up, to hug that grand, beautiful girl I love, to turn *her* into a wounded, moaning creature, and then to comfort her, to nurse her in my arms. It's so long I've waited for that. But suppose she defends herself?" He decided to go on with his ruse, stirred feebly, opened his arms and fell back into pretended unconsciousness.

"Ah!" cried Armande, "he's fainted! Why don't those imbeciles come!"

She leapt to her feet and ran off to fetch a fibre cushion that she tried to insert between Maxime's head and the splinters of glass. In doing so, the makeshift bandage came off. Maxime could hear Armande stamping her feet, walking away, and slapping her thighs with a forceful plebeian despair. She returned to him, sat down right in the litter of broken glass and the pool of bloodstained water and half-lay down against the wounded man. With exquisite pleasure he could feel she had lost her head and was crying. He squeezed his eyelids together so as not to look at her. But he could not shut out the smell of black hair and hot skin, the sandalwood smell that healthy brunettes exude. She raised one of his eyelids with her finger and he rolled up his eyeball as if in ecstasy or a swoon. With her sleeve, she wiped his forehead and his mouth; furtively, she opened his lips and bent over him to look at the white teeth with the gap between the front ones. "Another minute of this sort of thing and . . . and I shall devour her!" She bent a little lower, put her mouth against Maxime's, then drew back at once, frightened at the sound of hurried footsteps and breathless voices. But her whole body remained close to him, tamed and alert, and there was still time for her to whisper the hackneyed words girls new to love stammer out before the man has taught them others or they invent more beautiful, more secret ones: "Darling . . . My beloved boy. My very own Maxime."

When the rescue-party arrived, she was still sitting on the ground in her soaked skirt and her torn stockings. Maxime was able to wake up, to complete his deception by a few, incoherent words, to smile in a bewildered way at Armande and to protest at all the fuss going on around him. The Grand

Central Pharmacy had provided its stretcher and its pharmacist who constructed a turban of bandages on Maxime's head. Then the stretcher and its escort set forth like a procession incensed by a choir of voices.

"Open the other half of the door. Mind out, it won't go through. I tell you it will go through if you bear a bit to the right. There . . . just a bare millimetre to spare. You've got eight steps to go down."

At the top of the terrace, Armande remained alone, useless, and as if forgotten. But, at the bottom of the steps, Maxime summoned her with a gesture and a look: "Come . . . I know you now. I've got you. Come, we'll finish that timid little kiss you began. Stay with me. Acknowledge me . . ." She walked down the steps and gave him her hand. Then she adapted her step to that of the stretcher-bearers and walked meekly beside him, all stained and dishevelled, as if she had come straight from the hands of love.

The Sick Child

THE child who was going to die wanted to hoist himself a little higher against his big pillow but he could not manage it. His mother heard his mute appeal and helped him. Once again the child promised to death had his mother's face very close to his own, the face he thought he would never look at again, with its light brown hair drawn back from the temples like an old-fashioned little girl's, the long, rather thin cheeks with hardly a trace of powder, the very wide-open brown eyes, so sure of controlling their anxiety that they often forgot to keep guard over themselves.

"You're rosy tonight, my little boy," she said gaily.

But her brown eyes remained fixed in a steady, frightened look that the little boy knew well.

So as not to have to raise his feeble head, the little boy slid his pupils, with their big sea-green irises, into the corners of his lids and corrected her gravely:

"I'm rosy because of the lampshade."

Madam Mamma looked at her son sorrowfully, inwardly reproaching him for wiping out, with one word, that pink colour she saw on his cheeks. He had shut his eyes again and the appearance of being asleep gave him back the face of a child of ten.

"She thinks I'm asleep." His mother turned away from the white-faced little boy, very gently, as if afraid he might feel the thread of her gaze break off. "He thinks I think he's asleep."

Sometimes they played at deceiving each other like this. "She thinks I'm not in pain," Jean would think, though the pain would be making his lashes flicker on his cheekbones. Nevertheless, Madam Mamma would be thinking, "How well he can imitate a child who's not in pain! Any other mother would be taken in. But not me . . ."

"Do you like this smell of lavender I've sprayed about? Your room smells nice."

The child acquiesced without speaking; the habit and the necessity of preserving his strength had ended in his acquiring a repertoire of very tiny signs, a delicate and complicated mime like the language of animals. He excelled in making a magic and paradoxical use of his senses.

For him, the white muslin curtains gave out a pink sound when the sun struck them about ten in the morning and the scratched pale calf binding of an ancient *Journey on the Banks of the Amazon* smelt, to his mind, of hot pancakes. The desire to drink was expressed by three "claps" of the eyelids. To eat, oh, as to wanting to eat, he didn't think about that. The other needs of the small, limp, defeat d body had their silent and modest telegraph code. But everything that, in the existence of a child under sentence of death, could still be called the capacity for pleasure and amusement retained a passionate interest in human speech. This faculty searched out exact and varied words to be employed by a musical voice, ripened, as it were, by the long illness and hardly shriller than a woman's. Jean had chosen the words employed in draughts, in "solitaire", with its glitter of glass marbles, in "nine-holes", in a dozen other old-fashioned games that made use of ivory and lemon-wood and were played on inlaid boards. Other words, mostly secret, applied to the Swiss patience pack, fifty-two little glazed cards, edged and picked out with gold like drawing-room panelling. The queens wore shepherdess hats, straw ones with a rose under the brim, and the shepherd-knaves carried crooks. On account of the bearded kings with rubicund faces and the small, hard eyes of mountain smallholders, Jean had invented a patience that excluded the four boorish monarchs.

"No," he thought, "my room doesn't really smell nice. It isn't the same lavender. It seems to me that, in the old days, when I was able to walk about . . . But I may have forgotten."

He mounted a cloud of fragrance that was passing within reach of his small, pinched, white nostrils and rode swiftly away. His life of being confined to bed provided him with all the pleasures of illness, including the spice of filial malice of which no child can bear to deprive himself, so he gave no hint of his secret delights.

Astride the scented cloud, he wandered through the air of the room; then he got bored and escaped through the frosted glass fanlight and went along the passage, followed in his flight by a big silver clothes-moth who sneezed in the trail of lavender behind him. To outdistance it, he pressed his knees into the sides of the cloud of fragrance, riding with an ease and vigour that his long, inert, half-paralysed legs refused to display in the presence of human beings. When he escaped from his passive life, he knew how to ride, how to pass through walls; best of all, he knew how to fly. With his body inclined like a diver's plunging down through the waves, his forehead passed with careless ease through an element whose currents and resistances he understood. With his arms outstretched, he had only to slant one or other of his shoulders to change the direction of his flight and, by a jerk of his loins, he could avoid the shock of landing. In any case, he rarely did land. Once he had rashly let himself come down too near the ground, over a meadow where cows were feeding.

So close to the ground that he had seen, right opposite his own face, the beautiful, astonished face of a cream-coloured cow with crescent-shaped horns and eyes that mirrored the flying child like two magnifying glasses, while the dandelion-flowers came up out of the grass to meet him, growing bigger and bigger, like little suns. He had only just had time to catch tight hold of the tall horns with both hands and thrust himself backwards up into the air again; he could still remember the warmth of the smooth horns and their blunted, as it were friendly, points. The barking of a dew-drenched sheepdog who ran up to protect his cow gradually faded away as the flying child soared up again into his familiar sky. Jean remembered very clearly that he had had to exert all the strength of his arm-wings that morning to make his way back through a periwinkle-coloured dawn, glide over a sleeping town, and fall on his enamelled iron bed, the contact of which had hurt him very much indeed. He had felt an agonising pain burning his loins and tearing his thighs with red-hot pincers, a pain so bad that he had not been able to hide two pearly traces of tears from Madam Mamma's sharp-eyed tenderness.

"Has my little boy been crying?"

"In a dream, Madam Mamma, only in a dream . . ."

The cloud of pleasant scent suddenly reached the end of the passage and butted its nose against the door leading to the kitchen.

"Whoa back! Whoa back! What a brute! Ah, these lavender half-breeds, with wild-thyme blood! They'd smash your face for you, if you didn't hold them. Is *that* how you go through a kitchen door?"

He gripped the repentant cloud hard between his knees and guided it into the upper region of the kitchen, into the warmed air that was drying the washing near the ceiling. As he lowered his head to pass between two pieces of linen, Jean deftly broke off an apron-string and slipped it into the cloud's mouth by way of a bit. A mouth is not always a mouth, but a bit is always a bit and it matters little what it bridles.

"Where shall we go? We'll have to get back in time for dinner and it's late already. We must go faster, Lavender, faster . . ."

Having gone through the service door, he decided, for fun, to go down the staircase head first, then righted himself by a few slides on his back. The lavender cloud, frightened by what was being asked of it, jibbed a little. "Oh, you great goof of a mountain filly!" said the child, and this boy, who never laughed at all in his cloistered life, burst out laughing. As he rode wildly down, he grabbed hold, in passing, of the tangled fur of one of the house-dogs, the one they told him was so clever he could go down the steps and out on to the pavement, "do his business all by himself", then return to his parents' house and scratch at the front door. Startled by Jean's hand he yelped and flattened himself against the banisters.

"Coming with us, Riki? I'll take you up behind me!"

With a small, powerful hand he caught up the dog and flung him on to the misty, ballooning rump of the lavender mare, who, spurred by two bare heels, galloped down the last two flights. But there the dog, panic-stricken, jumped down from the eiderdown-pillion and fled upstairs to his basket, howling.

"You don't know what you're missing!" Jean shouted to him. "*I* was frightened too, at first, but now . . . Watch, Riki!"

Rider and mount hurled themselves against the heavy street door. To Jean's amazement, they encountered, not the malleable obstacle of yielding oak and melting ironwork and big bolts that said "Yes, yes" as they slid softly back, but the inflexible barrier of a firmly-chiselled voice that was whispering:

"See, he's fast asleep."

Numbed by the shock, anguished from head to foot, Jean was aware of the cruel harshness of the two words "See he's,

Seehees, Seeheeze." They were sharper than a knife-blade. Beside them lay three severed syllables, "fa-sta-sleep".

"Fa . . . sta . . . sleep," repeated Jean. "That's the end of the ride, here comes Fa . . . sta . . . sleep, curled up in a ball! Good-bye. Good-bye . . ."

He had no leisure to wonder to whom he was saying good-bye. Time was running out horribly fast. He dreaded the landing. The foundered cloud missed its footing with all the four legs it never had; before it dispersed in tiny cold drops, it threw its rider, with a heave of its non-existent hindquarters, into the valley of the japanned bedstead, and once again, Jean groaned at the brutal contact.

"You were sleeping so well," said the voice of Madam Mamma.

A voice, thought her little boy, that was all a tangle of straight lines and curved lines—a curved one, a straight one—a dry line—a wet line. But never would he try to explain that to Madam Mamma.

"You woke up moaning, darling, were you in pain?"

He made a sign that he was not, waving his thin, white, well-groomed forefinger from right to left. Besides, the pain was calming down. Falling on to this rather harsh little bed, after all he was pretty used to it. And what could you expect of a big puffy cloud and its scented bumpkin's manners?

"The next time," thought Jean, "I'll ride the Big Skating-Rink." In the hours when he lay with closed lids and they put a screen between the bright bulb and the lampshade, that was the name of the immmmmmense nickel-plated paper-knife, so big that, instead of two m's, it needed three or often four in its qualifying adjective.

"Madam Mamma, would you bring the Big Skat . . . I mean the big paper-knife, a little further forward under the lampshade? Thanks awfully."

To prepare his next ride at leisure, Jean turned his head on the pillow. They had cut his fair hair very short at the back, to stop it from matting. The top of his head, his temples and his ears were covered with curls of pale, faintly greenish-gold, the gold of a winter moon, that harmonised well with his sea-green eyes and his face white as a petal.

"How exquisite he is!" murmured Madam Mamma's female friends. "He looks quite astonishingly like L'Aiglon." Whereupon Madam Mamma would smile with disdain, knowing well that the Duc de Reichstadt, slightly thick-lipped like his mother the Empress, would have envied the firm, cupid's bow mouth with its fine-drawn corners that was one of Jean's beauties. She would say haughtily: "Possibly there is something . . . yes, in the forehead. But, heaven be praised, *Jean* isn't tubercular!"

When, with a practised hand, she had brought the lamp and big paper-knife closer together, Jean saw what he was waiting to see on the long chromium blade, a pink reflection like snow at dawn, flecked here and there with blue, a glittering landscape that tasted of peppermint. Then he laid his left temple on the firm pillow, listened to the music of water-drops and fountains played by the strands of white horsehair inside the cushion under the pressure of his head, and half-closed his eyes.

"But, my little boy, it's just on your dinner-time . . ." said Madam Mamma hesitantly.

The sick child smiled indulgently at his mother. You have to forgive well people everything. Besides, he was still faintly concussed from his fall. "I've got plenty of time," he thought, and he accentuated his smile, at the risk of seeing Madam Mamma—as she did, faced with certain smiles, too perfect, too full of a serenity that, for her, could only have one meaning—lose countenance and rush out of the room, knocking herself against the door-post.

"If you don't mind, darling, I'll have my dinner very quickly all by myself in the dining-room, while you're having yours on your tray."

"Why, of course, of course," answered the white, graciously condescending small forefinger, crooking itself twice.

"We know, we know," also observed the two lash-bordered eyelids, blinking twice. "We know what an over-sensitive lady Mamma is, and how a pair of tears suddenly come into her eyes, like a pair of precious stones. There are lots of precious stones for ears . . . Eye-rings, Madam Mamma has eye-rings when she thinks about me. Won't she ever get used to me, then? How illogical she is."

As Madam Mamma was bending over him, he raised his unfettered arms and gave her a ritual hug. His mother's neck raised itself proudly under the weight suspended on it, pulling up the child's thin, over-tall body; the slim torso followed by the long legs, inert now yet capable of gripping and controlling the flanks of a shadowy cloud.

For a moment, Madam Mamma contemplated her gracious invalid son, propped up against a hard pillow that sloped like a desk, then she exclaimed:

"I'll be back very soon! Your tray will be here in a minute. Besides, I must go and hurry up Mandora, she's never on time!"

Once again, she went out of the room.

"She goes out, she comes in. Above all, she goes out. She doesn't want to leave me but she keeps going out of my room all the time. She's going off to dry her pair of tears. She's got a hundred reasons for going out of my room; if by any chance she hadn't got one, I could give a thousand. Mandora's never late."

Turning his head with precaution, he watched Mandora come in. Wasn't it right and inevitable that this full-bodied, golden, pot-bellied maid, with her musical, resonant voice and her shining eyes that were like the precious wood of a lute, should answer to the name of Mandora? "If it weren't for me," thought Jean, "she'd still be calling herself Angelina."

Mandora crossed the room and her brown-and-yellow striped skirt, as it brushed against the furniture, gave out rich 'cello notes that only Jean could perceive. She placed the little short-legged table across the bed; on its embroidered linen cloth stood a steaming bowl.

"Here's this dinner of yours."

"What is it?"

"First course, phosphatine: there, you know that. After . . . you'll see for yourself."

The sick child received all over his half-recumbent body the comfort of a wide brown gaze, thirst-quenching and exhilarating. "How good it is, that brown ale of Mandora's eyes! How kind to me she is, too! How kind everyone is to me! If only they could restrain themselves a little . . ." Exhausted under the burden of universal kindness, he shut his eyes and opened them again at the clink of spoons. Medicine spoons, soup spoons, dessert spoons. Jean did not like spoons, with the exception of a queer silver spoon with a long twisted stem, finished off at one end with a little engine-turned disc. "It's a sugar-crusher," Madam Mamma would say. "And the other end of the spoon, Madam Mamma?"—"I'm not quite sure. I think it used to be an absinthe spoon." And, nearly always, at that moment, her gaze would wander to a photograph of Jean's father, the husband she had lost so young, "Your dear Papa, my own Jean", and whom Jean coldly and silently designated by the secret words: "That man hanging up in the drawing-room."

Apart from the absinthe spoon—absinthe, absinthe, absent, apse saint—Jean only liked forks, four-horned demons on which things were impaled, a bit of mutton cutlet, a tiny fish curled up in its fried breadcrumbs, a round slice of apple and its two pip-eyes, a crescent of apricot in its first quarter, frosted with sugar.

"Jean, darling, open your beak."

He obeyed, closing his eyes, and swallowed a medicine that was almost tasteless except for a passing, hypocritical sickliness that disguised something worse. In his secret vocabulary, Jean called this potion "dead man's gully". But nothing would have wrenched such appalling syllables out of him and flung them gasping at the feet of Madam Mamma.

The phosphatised soup followed inevitably; a badly-swept hay-loft, with its chinks stuffed with mildewed flour. But you forgave it all that because of something that floated impalpably over its clear liquid; a flowery breath, the dusty fragrance of the cornflowers Mandora bought in little bunches in the street for Jean, in July.

A little cube of grilled lamb went down quickly. "Run, lamb, run, I'm putting a good face on you, but go right down into my stomach in a ball, I couldn't chew you for anything in the world. Your flesh is still bleating and I don't want to know that you're pink in the middle!"

"It seems to me you're eating very fast tonight, aren't you, Jean?"

The voice of Madam Mamma dropped from the height of the dusk, perhaps from the moulded plaster cornice, perhaps from the big cupboard. By a special gracious concession, Jean granted his mother permission to ascend into the alpine world at the top of the cupboard, the world of the household linen. She reached it by means of the step-ladder, became invisible behind the left-hand door and came down again loaded with great solid slabs of snow, hewn straight out of the heights. This harvest was the limit of her ambition. Jean went further and higher; he thrust up, alone, towards the white peaks, slipping through an odd pair of sheets, reappearing in the well-rounded fold of an even pair. And what giddy slides between the stiff damask table-napkins or on some alp of starched curtains, slippery as glaciers, and edged with Greek key-pattern, what nibbling of stalks of dried lavender, of their scattered flowers, of the fat and creamy orris-roots.

It was from there he would descend again into his bed at dawn, stiff all over with cold, pale, weak and impish: "Jean! Oh, goodness, he must have uncovered himself again in his sleep! Mandora, quick, a hot-water bottle!" Silently, Jean congratulated himself on having got back just in time, as usual. Then he would note, on an invisible page of the notebook hidden in the active, beating nook in his side he called his "heart-pocket", all the vicissitudes of his ascent, the fall of the stars and the orange tintinnabulation of the dawn-touched peaks.

"I'm eating fast, Madam Mamma, because I'm hungry."

For he was an old hand at all kinds of deception and didn't he know that the words "I'm hungry" made Madam Mamma flush with pleasure?

"If that's true, darling, I'm sorry I only gave you stewed apples for your pudding. But I told Mandora to add some zest of lemon-peel and a little stick of vanilla to make it taste nice."

Jean resolutely faced up to the stewed apples, an acid provincial girl aged about fifteen who, like other girls of the same age, had nothing but haughty disdain for the boy of ten. But didn't he feel the same towards her? Wasn't he armed against her? Wasn't he an agile cripple, leaning on the stick of vanilla? "It's always too short, *always*, that little stick," he murmured in his elusive way.

Mandora returned, and her billowing skirt with the broad stripes swelled up with as many ribs as a melon. As she walked she sounded—tzrromm, tzrromm—for Jean alone—the inner strings that were the very soul, the gorgeous music of Mandora.

"Finished your dinner already? If you eat so fast, you'll bring it up again. It's not your usual way."

Madam Mamma on one side, Mandora on the other, were standing close by his bed. "How tall they are! Madam Mamma doesn't take up much room in width in her little claret-coloured dress. But Mandora, over and above her great sounding-box makes herself bigger with two curved handles, standing with her arms akimbo." Jean resolutely defied the stewed apples, spread them all over the plate, pressed them down again in festoons on the gilded rim, and, once again, the question of dinner was settled.

The winter evening had long ago fallen. As he savoured his half-glass of mineral water, the thin, light furtive water that he thought was green because he drank it out of a pale green mug, Jean reckoned he still needed a little courage to conclude his invalid's day. There was still his nightly toilet, the inevitable, scrupulous details that demanded the aid of Madam Mamma and even—tzrromm, tzrromm—the gay, sonorous assistance of Mandora; still the toothbrush, the face-flannels and sponge, the good soap and warm water, the combined precautions for not getting the sheets the least bit wet; still the tender maternal inquiries.

"My little boy, you can't sleep like that, you've got the binding of the big Gustave Doré digging right into your side, and that litter of little books with sharp corners all over your bed. Wouldn't you like me to bring the table nearer?"

"No, thanks, Madam Mamma, I'm quite all right as I am."

When his toilet was finished, Jean struggled against the intoxication of tiredness. But he knew the limit of his strength and did not try to escape from the rites that ushered in the night and the marvels it might capriciously bring forth. His only fear was that Madam Mamma's solicitude might prolong the duration of day longer than he could bear, might ruin a material edifice of books and furniture, a balance of light and shadows that Jean knew and revered. Building that edifice cost him his final efforts and ten o'clock was the extreme limit of his endurance.

"If she stays, if she insists, if she still wants to go on watching over me when the big hand slants to the right of the XII, I'm going to feel myself turning white, whiter, whiter still and my eyes will sink in and I shan't even be able to keep answering the no-thank-you—quite-all-right-Madam-Mamma—good-nights that are absolutely necessary to her and . . . and . . . it'll be awful, she'll sob."

He smiled at his mother and the majesty that illness confers on children it strikes down wakened in the fiery glint of his hair, descended over his eyelids and settled bitterly on his lips. It was the hour when Madam Mamma would have liked to lose herself in contemplation of her mangled and exquisite work.

"Good night, Madam Mamma," said the child, very low.

"Are you tired? Do you want me to leave you?"

He made one more effort, opened wide his eyes, the colour of the sea off Brittany, manifested with his whole face the desire to be fit and bonny, and bravely lowered his high shoulders.

"Do I look like a tired boy? Madam Mamma, I ask you now!"

She replied only with a roguish shake of her head, kissed her son and went away, taking with her her choked-back cries of love, her strangled adjurations, her litanies that implored the disease to go away, to undo the fetters on the long, weak legs and the emaciated but not deformed loins, to set the impoverished blood running freely again through the green network of the veins.

"I've put two oranges on the plate. You don't want me to put out your lamp?"

"I'll put it out myself, Madam Mamma."

"Good heavens, where's my head? We haven't taken your temperature tonight!"

A fog interposed itself between Madam Mamma's garnet dress and her son. That night Jean was burning with fever but taking a thousand precautions to conceal it. A little fire was smouldering in the hollow of his palms, there was a drumming woo-woo-woo in his outer ear and fragments of a hot crown clinging to his temples.

"We'll take it tomorrow without fail, Madam Mamma."

"The bell-push is just under your wrist. You're quite sure you wouldn't rather have the company of a night-light, during the hours you're alone, you know, one of those pretty night . . ."

The last syllable of the word stumbled into a pit of darkness and Jean collapsed with it. "Yet it was only a very tiny pit," he rebuked himself as he fell. "I must have a big bump at the back of my neck. I must look like a Zebu. But I zeed, yes I zaw kvite vell that Madam Mamma didn't zee, no didn't see anything fall. She was much too absorbed in all the things she takes off every night gathered up in her skirt, her little prayers, the reports she's got to give the doctor, the way I hurt her so much by not wanting anyone near me at night. She carries all that away in the lap of her skirt and it spills over and rolls on the carpet, poor Madam Mamma. How can I make her understand that I'm not unhappy? Apparently a boy of my age can's either live in bed or be pale and deprived of his legs or be in pain without being unhappy. Unhappy . . . I *was* unhappy when they still used to wheel me about in a chair. I was drenched with a shower of stares. I used to shrink so as to get a bit less of it. I was the target for a hail of 'How pretty he is!' and 'What a dreadful pity!' Now, the only miseries I have are the visits of my cousin Charlie with his scratched knees and his nailed shoes and that word 'boy-scout' half steel, half indiarubber, he overwhelms me with . . . And that pretty little girl who was born the same day as me, whom they sometimes call my foster-sister and sometimes my fiancée. She's studying dancing. She sees me lying in bed and then she stands on the tips of her toes and says: 'Look, I'm on my points.' But all that's only teasing. There comes a time at night when the teases go to sleep. This is the time when everything's all right."

He put out the lamp and peacefully watched his nocturnal companions, the choir of shapes and colours, rising up around him. He was waiting for the symphony to burst out, for the crowd Madam Mamma called solitude. He drew the pear-shaped bell-push, an invalid's toy of moonlight-coloured enamel, from under his arm and laid it on the bedside table. "Now, light up!" he commanded.

It did not obey at once. The night outside was not so black that you could not make out the end of a leafless branch of a chestnut-tree in the street swaying outside one of the panes and asking for help. Its swollen tip assumed the shape of a feeble rosebud. "Yes, you're trying to soften my heart by telling me you're next season's bud. Yet you know how ruthless I am to everything that talks to me about next year. Stay outside. Disappear. Vanish! As my cousin would say: skedaddle."

His fastidiousness about words reared up to its full height and poured one more dose of withering scorn on that cousin with his scratched, purple knees and his vocabulary plastered with expressions such as "And how!" "I put a spanner in the works", "I'm not having any", and "Golly!" Worst of all, Charlie was always saying "Just think!" and "I do understand!" as if those immensely learned crickets, thought and penetration, would not have fled in terror on all their delicate legs from a boy like that, shod in hobnails and dried mud.

At the mere sight of his cousin Charlie, Jean wiped his

fingers on his handkerchief as if to rid them of some kind of coarse sand. For Madam Mamma and Mandora, interposed between the child and ugliness, between the child and scurrilous words, between the child and the baser sorts of reading, had made it possible for him to know and cherish only two forms of luxury: fastidiousness and pain. Protected and precocious, he had quickly mastered the hieroglyphs of print, dashing as wildly through books as he galloped astride clouds. He could compel the landscapes to rise up before him from the smooth page or assemble round him all the things that, for those likewise privileged, secretly people the air.

He had never used the silver fountain-pen, engraved with his initials, since the day when his rapid, mature writing had startled and, as it were, offended the doctor with the cold hands. "Is that really the handwriting of a young child, Madame?"—"Oh yes, doctor, my son has very definitely-formed handwriting." And Madam Mamma's anxious eyes had asked apologetically: "It's not dangerous, Doctor, is it?"

He also refrained from drawing, fearing all the things the eloquence of a sketch might give away. After having drawn the portrait of Mandora, with all her inner keyboard of resounding notes, the profile of an alabaster clock galloping full speed on its four supporting pillars, the dog Riki in the hands of the barber, with his hair done, like Jean's own, "à l'Aiglon", he had been terrified by the truth to life of his efforts and had wisely torn up his first works.

"Wouldn't you like a sketch-book, my young friend, and some coloured chalks? It's an amusing game and just the thing for a boy of your age." At the suggestion, which he considered outside the province of medicine, Jean had only replied by a look between half-closed lashes, a serious, manly look that summed up the doctor who was giving him advice. "My nice barber wouldn't dream of making such a suggestion!" He could not forgive the doctor for having dared to ask him one day when his mother was out of the room: "And why the devil do you call your mother Madam?" The angry masculine glance and the weak, musical voice had answered with one accord: "I didn't think that was any business of the devil's."

The nice hair-cutter performed his mission very differently and told Jean all about his Sunday life. Every Sunday he went fishing round about Paris. With a dazzling sweep of his scissors, he would demonstrate the gesture that flings the float and the bait far out and Jean would shut his eyes under the chill of the water-drops, splashing out in wheels when the fisherman triumphantly hauled up his loaded line. . . .

"When you're well again, Monsieur Jean, I'll take you with me to the river-bank."

"Yes, yes," agreed Jean, his eyes closed.

"Why do they all want me to be well again? I *am* on the river-bank. What should I do with a chub-as-big-as-my-hand-here and a pickerel-as-long-as-your-paper-knife-there?"

"Nice barber, tell me some more . . ."

And he would listen to the story of the hawk-moths clinging under the arch of a little bridge, impromptu bait that had caught a "waggon-load" of trout with a hazel-twig cut from the hedge and three bits of string knotted together.

To the cool, grating accompaniment of the twittering scissors, the story would begin:

"You go as far as a tiny little creek no-broader-than-my-thigh that widens out as it crosses a meadow. You see two-three willows together and a bit of brushwood: that's the place."

On the very first day Jean had transplanted other things round the two-three willows: the tall spikes of common agrimony extracted from the big botany album and pink-flowered hemp that attracts butterflies and tired children and sends them to sleep. The monstrous pollarded head of the oldest willow, crowned with white convolvulus, pulled faces only for Jean. The leap of a fish burst the glittering skin of the river, then another fish leapt . . . The nice hairdresser, busy with his bait, had heard them and turned round.

"Makin' game o' me, those two! But I'll get 'em."

"No, no," Jean protested. "It was me. I threw two little pebbles into the water."

The tree-frog was singing, the imaginary afternoon was passing.

"Singing invisible on his water-lily raft," mused Jean. "Why tree-frog? Why not lily-frog?"

The shearer of golden fleece, the river and the meadow faded away like a dream, leaving behind on Jean's forehead a sweet, commonplace scent and a wavy crest of fair hair. Jean, waking up, heard a whispering coming from the drawing-room, a long low colloquy between Madam Mamma and the doctor from which one word escaped, crisp and lively, and made a beeline for Jean, the word "crisis". Sometimes it entered ceremoniously, like a lady dressed up to give away prizes, with an *h* behind its ear and a *y* tucked into its bodice: Chrysis, Chrysis Wilby-Sallatry. "Truly? Truly?" said the urgent voice of Madam Mamma. "I said: perhaps . . ." replied the doctor's voice, an unsteady voice that halted on one foot. "A crisis, salutary but severe . . . Chrysis Salutari Sevea, a young creole from tropical America, lissom in her flounced white cotton dress."

The child's subtle ear also gathered the name of another person which no doubt it was expedient to keep secret. A name he couldn't quite catch, something like Polly O'Miley or Olly O'Miall and he finally decided it must refer to some little girl, also stricken with painful immobility and possessed of two long useless legs, whom they never mentioned in front of him in case he should be jealous.

Complying with the order it had received, the tip of the chestnut branch and its message of coming spring had foundered in the sea of night. Although Jean had a second time requested it to do so, the pear-shaped bell-push had not yet lit up. Its dim opal flame was not shining on the bedside table that bore the mineral water, the orange-juice, the big nickel paper-knife with the alpine dawn in its hidden depths, the myopic watch with its domed glass and the thermometer . . . Not one book lay on the table, waiting for Jean to choose it. Printed texts, whatever their size and shape, slept inside and ready open in the same bed as the invalid child. At the foot of the bed, a great tile of binding sometimes weighed heavily on his almost lifeless legs without his making any complaint.

He groped about him with his still-active arms and fished up some paper-bound books, tattered and warm. An ancient volume thrust out its friendly horn from under the pillow. The paper-backs, heaped in a cushion, took their place against one of the little boy's thin hips and the soft childish cheek pressed against the light calf binding that was a century old. Under his armpit, Jean verified the presence of a tough favourite comrade, a volume as hard and squat as a paving-stone, a grumpy, robust fellow who found the bed too soft and usually went off to finish his night on the floor on the white goatskin rug.

Angular pasteboard shapes and the sockets and sinuses and cavities of a fragile anatomy interlocked in the friendliest way. The temporary bruising made the chronic pain easier to bear patiently. Certain wayward little tortures, inflicted between the ear and the shoulder by the horned light brown calf, displaced and relieved the torments endured by that region and by the wretched little back with its wings of prominent shoulder-blades.

"Whatever have you got there?" Madam Mamma would

say. "It looks as if you'd had a blow. Really, I simply can't understand . . ." In perfect good faith, the bruised child would think for a moment, then inwardly reply to himself: "There . . . Why, yes, of course. It was that tree I couldn't avoid. It was that little roof I leant on to watch the sheep going back into the fold. It was that big rake that fell on the back of my neck when I was drinking at the fountain. Still, what luck Madam Mamma didn't see the little nick at the corner of my eye, the mark of that swallow's beak I knocked up against in the air. I hadn't time to avoid it, it was as hard as a scythe. True, a sky is so small . . ."

The confused murmur of his nights began to rise, expected, but not familiar. It varied according to his dreams, his degree of weakness, his temperature and the fantasies of a day that Madam Mamma supposed depressingly like all the other days. This new night bore no resemblance whatever to yesterday's night. The darkness was rich in innumerable blacks. "The black is all purple tonight. I've got such a pain in . . . in what? In my forehead. No, whatever am I saying? It's always my back . . . But no, it's a weight, two weights that are hung on my hips, two weights shaped like pine-cones like the ones on the kitchen clock. *You* there, for the last time, will you light up?"

To intimate his order to the enamel bell-push, he leant his temple hard against the pale leather binding and shuddered to find it so cold. "If it's frozen, it means I'm burning." No light flowed from the enamel pear. "What's the matter with it? And what's the matter with me? Only this afternoon, the front-door wouldn't let me go through it." He stretched out his hand into the inhabited night air and found the shadowy pear without groping for it. Capriciously changing its usual source, the light appeared on the fat, short-sighted face of the spherical watch. "What are you sticking your nose in for?" muttered

Jean. "Mind your own business and be satisfied with knowing how to tell the time."

The mortified watch put out its light and Jean heaved a sigh of gratified power. But all he could get out of his rigid sides was a groan. All at once, a wind he recognised among all others, the wind that snaps the pine-trees, dishevels the larches and flattens and raises the sand-dunes, began to roar. It filled his ears and the images, forbidden to the more ordinary dream that does not pierce the curtain of closed eyelids, rose up and longed to run free, to take advantage of the limitless room. Some of them, queerly horizontal, checkered the vertical crowd who had reared straight up on end. "Scottish visions," thought Jean.

His bed trembled slightly, shaken by the vibrating ascent of High Fever. He felt three or four years fall away from him and fear, to which he was almost a stranger, clutched at him. He very nearly called out: "To the rescue, Madam Mamma! They're carrying off your little boy!"

Neither in his rides, nor in the rich kingdom of the very strangest sounds—humpbacked sounds carrying reverberating ampoules on their heads, on their cockchafer backs, pointed sounds with muzzles like mongooses—nowhere had Jean ever seen such a swarm suddenly appear. His hearing tasted it like a mouth; his eye laboriously spelt it out, fascinated. "Help, Madam Mamma! Help me! You *know* I can't walk! I can only fly, swim, roll from cloud to cloud . . ." At the same moment, something indescribable and forgotten stirred in his body, infinitely far away, right at the very end of his useless legs, a confused, scattered crowd of crazy ants. "To the rescue, Madam Mamma!"

But another person, whose decisions depended neither on impotence nor on motherly kindness, made a haughty sign that imposed silence. A magical constraint kept Madam Mamma on the other side of the wall, in the place where she waited, modest and anxious, to become as great as her little son.

So he did not scream. In any case, the unknown beings, the fabulous strangers, were already beginning to abduct him by force. Rising up on all sides, they poured burning heat and icy cold on him, racked him with melodious torture, swathed him in colour like a bandage, swung him in a hammock of palpitations. With his face already turned to flee, motionless, to his mother, he suddenly changed his mind and launched himself in full flight, letting his own impetus carry him where it would, through meteors and mists and lightnings that softly opened to let him through, closed behind him, opened again . . . And, just as he was on the very verge of being perfectly content, ungrateful and gay, exulting in his solitude as an only child, his privileges as an orphan and an invalid, he was aware that a sad little crystalline crash separated him from a bliss whose beautiful, soft, airy name he had yet to learn; death. A little, light melancholy crash, coming perhaps from some planet deserted for ever . . . The clear and sorrowful sound, clinging to the child who was going to die, held on so staunchly that the dazzling escape tried in vain to shake it off and outdistance it.

Perhaps his journey lasted a long time. But having lost all sense of duration, he could only judge of its variety. Often he thought he was following a guide, an indistinct guide who had lost his way too. Then he would groan at not being able to take on the pilot's responsibility and he would hear his own groan of humbled pride, or of such weariness that he abandoned his voyage, left the wake of a spindle-shaped squall, and took refuge, dead-beat, in a corner.

There he was pounced on by the anguish of living in a country where there were no corners, no square, solid shapes; where there was only a dark current of icy air, a night in whose depths he was no longer anything but a small boy, lost and in tears. Then he would rear himself upright on a great many, suddenly-multiplied legs, promoted to the rank of stilts, that a searing pain was slicing off in rattling bundles, like faggots. Then everything would go dark and only the blind wind told him how fast he was travelling. Passing from a familiar continent to an unfamiliar sea he caught a few words in a language he was surprised to find he understood:

"The sound of the glass mug breaking woke me up."

"Madam can see he's smacking his lips, doesn't Madam think he wants something to drink?"

He would have liked to know the name of that voice. "Madam . . . Madam . . . What Madam?" But already the speed at which he was going had swallowed up the words and the memory of them.

One pale night, thanks to a stop that jarred through his temples, he again gathered a few human syllables and would have liked to repeat them. The sudden stop had brought him painfully face to face with a harsh, solid object interposed between two noble and inhabited worlds. An object with no destination, finely striped, bristling with very tiny hairs and mysteriously associated—he discovered this afterwards—with horrible "my-young-friends". "It's a . . . I know . . . a . . . sleeve . . ." Promptly he opened his wings and flung himself head first into reassuring chaos.

Another time, he saw a hand. Armed with slender fingers, with slightly chapped skin and white-spotted nails, it was pushing back a marvellous zebra-striped mass that was rushing up from the depths of the horizon. Jean began to laugh: "Poor little hand, the mass will make one mouthful of it, just imagine, a mass that's all striped in black and yellow and has such an intelligent expression!" The feeble little hand struggled with all its outspread fingers and the parallel stripes began to broaden and bend and diverge like soft bars. A great gap opened between them and swallowed up the frail hand and Jean found himself regretting it. This regret was delaying his journey and, with an effort, he launched himself off again. But he carried the regret with him, just as once, very, very long ago, he had carried the tenacious tinkle of a broken mug. After that, through whatever whirlpools and troughs he swirled and dipped, drowsy and rather pleasantly giddy, his journey was disturbed by echoes, by sounds of tears, by an anxious attempt at something that resembled a thought, by an importunate feeling of pity.

A harsh barking suddenly rent the great spaces, and Jean murmured: "Riki . . ." In the distance, he heard a kind of sob that kept repeating: "Riki! Madam, he said Riki!" Another stammering reiterated: "He said Riki! He said Riki."

A little hard, quivering force whose double grip he could feel under his armpits, seemed to want to hoist him up to the top of a peak. It was bruising him and he grumbled. If he had been able to transmit his instructions to the little force and its sharp corners, he would have taught it that this was no way to treat a famous traveller who only uses immaterial vehicles, unshod steeds, sledges that trace seven-coloured tracks on the rainbow. That he only allowed himself to be molested by those . . . those elements whose power only the night can unleash and control. That, for example, the bird's belly that had just laid itself against the whole length of his cheek had no right at all. And, moreover, it was not a bird's belly because it was not feathered, but only edged with a strand of long hair. "That," he thought, "would be a cheek, if there were any other cheek in the universe except mine. I want to speak, I want to send away this . . . this sham cheek. I forbid anyone to touch me, I forbid . . ."

To acquire the strength to speak, he breathed the air in through his nostrils. With the air, there entered in the marvel, the magic of memory, the smell of certain hair, certain skin he had forgotten on the other side of the world and that started up a wild rush of recollections. He coughed, fighting against the rise of something that tightened his throat, staunched a thirst lurking in the parched corners of his lips, salted his overflowing eyelids and mercifully. veiled from him his return to the hard landing-bed. Over an endless stretch, a voice said, re-echoing to infinity: "He's crying, dear God, he's crying . . ." The voice foundered in a kind of storm from which there arose disjointed syllables, sobs, calls to someone present, but concealed. "Come quick, quick!"

"What a noise, what a noise," thought the child reproachfully. But more and more, he kept pressing his cheek unconsciously against the soft, smooth surface bordered by someone's hair, and drinking up a bitter dew on it that welled out, drop by drop. He turned away his head and, as he did so, encountered a narrow valley, a nest moulded exactly to his measure. He had just time to name it to himself "Madam Mamma's shoulder" before he lost consciousness or else fell asleep on it.

He came to himself to hear his own voice, light and faintly mocking, saying: "Wherever have you come from, Madam Mamma?"

There was no answer but the deliciousness of a quarter of orange, slipped between his lips, made him conscious of the return, of the presence of the person he was searching for. He knew that she was bending over him in that submissive attitude that flexed her waist and tired her back. Soon exhausted, he fell silent. But already a thousand questions were worrying him and he conquered his weakness to satisfy the most urgent one: "Did you change my pyjamas while I was asleep, Madam Mamma? When I lay down, last night, I had blue ones and these are pink."

"Madam, it's past believing! He remembers he had blue pyjamas, the first night when . . ."

He did not listen to the rest of the sentence that a big, warm voice had just whispered and abandoned himself to the hands that were taking off his wet garments. Hands as deft as the waves between which he rocked, weightless and aimless . . .

"He's soaked. Wrap him up in the big dressing-gown, Mandora, without putting his arms through the sleeves."

"The heating's full on, Madam, don't be afraid. And I've just put him in a new hot-water bottle. Gracious me, he's positively drenched."

"If they knew where I've come from . . . Anyone would expect to be drenched," thought Jean. "I wish to goodness I could scratch my legs or that someone would take those ants off."

"Madam Mamma."

He received the muteness, the vigilant stillness that were Madam Mamma's answer when she was strained and on the alert.

"Would you please . . . scratch my calves a little because these ants . . ."

From the depths of silence, someone whispered, with a strange respectfulness:

"He can feel ants . . . He said ants . . ."

Swathed in the dressing-gown that was too big for him, he tried to shrug his shoulders. Why, yes, he had said ants. What was there astonishing about his having said Riki and ants? A reverie carried him away, relieved, to the margin between waking and sleeping; the rustle of some stuff brought him back again. Between his lashes, he recognised the hateful sleeve, the blue stripes, the little hairs of wool, and his resentment restored his strength. He refused to see any more of it but a voice came and opened his closed lids, a voice that said: "Well, my-young-friend . . ."

"I abolish him, I abolish him!" shrieked Jean inside himself. "Him, his sleeve, his my-young-friend, his little eyes, I curse them, I abolish them!" Beside himself with irritation, he was panting.

"Well, well. What's the matter? You're very restless. There . . . there . . ."

A hand laid itself on Jean's head. Powerless to revolt, he hoped to strike the aggressor down with one thunderbolt from his eye. But all he could see, sitting on the bedside chair reserved for Madam Mamma, was a worthy, rather fat, rather bald man, whose eyes, as they met his own, filled with tears.

"Little one, little one. Is it true you've got ants in your legs? Is it true? That's splendid, my word, that's really splendid. Could you manage to drink half a glass of lemonade? Wouldn't you like to suck a spoonful of lemon water-ice? A mouthful of milk and water?"

Jean's hand yielded itself up to some thick, very soft fingers and a warm palm. He murmured a vague acquiescence, not quite sure himself whether he was apologising or whether he wanted the lemon ice, the drink, the "watered" milk. His eyes, paled to a tired grey between the great black rings and the dark eyebrows, gazed amicably into two small eyes of a cheerful blue that were moist and blinking and tender.

The rest of the new era was nothing but a series of muddled moments; a medley of different kinds of sleep, now short, now long, now hermetically sealed, interspersed with sudden sharp awakenings and vague tremors. The worthy doctor indulged in an orgy of great satisfied coughs, ahem, ahem, and exclamations of "Dear lady, this is capital! We're safe now!" All this din was so cheerful that Jean, if he had not been sunk in apathy, would have asked himself what happy event had occurred in the house.

The hours passed inexplicably, signposted by fruits in jelly and milk flavoured with vanilla. A boiled egg raised its little lid and revealed its buttercup yolk. The window, left ajar, let in a breath of spring, heady as wine.

The nice barber was not yet permitted to return. Jean's hair hung down over his forehead and neck like a little girl's and Madam Mamma risked tying it back with a pink ribbon which Jean tore off with the gesture of an insulted boy.

Behind the pane, the chestnut branch's rose-like buds were swelling day by day and all up and down Jean's legs there ran ants armed with little nipping jaws. "This time, I've caught one, Madam Mamma!" But all he was pinching was his own transparent skin and the ant had fled inside a tree of veins the colour of spring grass. On the eighth day of the new era, a great scarf of sunlight lying across his bed moved him more than he could bear and he decided that this very night the daily fever would bring him what he had been vainly awaiting for a whole week. Everything that profound weariness and sleep hewn out of a solid block of black repose had robbed him of would be restored: his faceless companions, his rides, the accessible skies, his security of an angel in full flight.

"Madam Mamma, I'd like my books, please."

"My darling, the doctor said that . . ."

"It's not to read them, Madam Mamma, it's so that they'll get used to me again."

She said nothing and, with some apprehension, brought back the tattered volumes, the big badly-bound paving-stone, the light calf soft as a human skin, a *Pomology* with coloured plates of chubby fruits, the Guérin mottled with flat-faced lions and duck-billed platypuses with beetles big as islands flying over them.

When night came, having eaten his fill—food was now something magical and interesting that he ate with the avidity of children who have come back to life—he pretended to be overcome with sleep and murmured his good nights, and a vague, mischievous song he had recently improvised. Having secretly watched the departure of Madam Mamma and Mandora, he took command of his raft of in-folio and atlas and set sail. A young moon, behind the chestnut branch, showed that the buds, thanks to the warmer weather, were about to open in leafy fingers.

He sat up without assistance in bed, towing his still-heavy legs that were overrun with ants. In the depths of the window, in the celestial waters of night swam the curved moon and the dim reflection of a long-haired child, to whom he beckoned. He raised one arm, and the other child obediently copied his summoning gesture. Slightly intoxicated with the power to work marvels, he called up his boon companions of the cruel but privileged hours; the visible sounds; the tangible images; the breathable seas; the nourishing, navigable air; the wings that mocked feet; the laughing suns.

In particular, he called up a certain spirited little boy who chuckled with inward laughter as he left the earth, who took advantage of Madam Mamma and, lord of her sorrows and joys, kept her prisoner of a hundred loving lies.

Then he waited, but nothing came. Nothing came that night or the following ones, nothing ever again. The landscape of pink snow had vanished from the nickel paper-knife and never again would Jean fly, in a periwinkle dawn, between the sharp horns and the beautiful bulging eyes of cattle azure with dew. Never again would brown-and-yellow Mandora reverberate with all the strings—tzromm, tzromm—humming beneath her vast, generous skirt. Was it possible that the damask alp, piled high in the big cupboard, would henceforth refuse to allow a child who was nearly well to perform the feats a small cripple had achieved on the slopes of imaginary glaciers?

A time comes when one is forced to concentrate on living. A time comes when one has to renounce dying in full flight. With a wave of his hand, Jean said farewell to his angel-haired reflection. The other returned his greeting from the depths of an earthly night shorn of all marvels, the only night allowed to children whom death lets go and who fall asleep, assenting, cured and disappointed.

The Photographer's Missus

WHEN the woman they called "the photographer's Missus" decided to put an end to her days, she set about realising her project with much sincerity and painstaking care. But, having no experience whatever of poisons, thank heaven, she failed. At which the inhabitants of the entire building rejoiced, and so did I, though I did not live in the neighbourhood.

Madame Armand—of the Armand Studio, Art Photography and Enlargements—lived on the same landing as a pearl-stringer and it was rare for me not to meet the amiable "photographer's Missus" when I went up to visit Mademoiselle Devoidy. For, in those far-off days, I had, like everyone else, a pearl necklace. As all women wanted to wear them, there were pearls to suit all women and all purses. What bridegroom would have dared to omit a "string" from his wedding-presents to his bride? The craze started at baptism, with the christening-gift of a row of pearls no bigger than grains of rice. No fashion, since, has ever been so tyrannical. From a thousand francs upwards, you could buy a "real" necklace. Mine had cost five thousand francs, that is to say, it did not attract attention. But its living lustre and its gay orient were a proof of its excellent health and mine. When I sold it, during the great war, it was certainly not for an idle whim.

I used not to wait to have its silk thread renewed till it was really necessary. Having it restrung was an excuse for me to visit Mademoiselle Devoidy who came from my part of the country, a few villages away. From being a saleswoman in a branch of *The Store of a Thousand Necklaces* where everything was sham, she had gone on to being a stringer of real pearls. This unmarried woman of about forty had kept, as I had, the accent of our native parts, and delighted me furthermore by a restrained sense of humour which, from the heights of a punctilious honesty, made fun of a great many people and things.

When I went up to see her, I used to exchange greetings with the photographer's Missus who was often standing outside her wide-open door, opposite Mademoiselle Devoidy's closed one. The photographer's furniture trespassed on to the landing, beginning with a "pedestal" dating back to the infancy of the craft, a camera-stand of carved, beautifully-grained walnut, itself a tripod. Its bulk and its solid immobility made me think of those massive wooden wine-press screws that used to appear, at about the same period, in "artistic" flats, supporting some graceful statuette. A Gothic chair kept it company and served as an accessory in photographs of First Communicants. The little wicker kennel and its stuffed Pomeranian, the pair of shrimping-nets dear to children in sailor suits, completed the store of accessories banished from the studio.

An incurable smell of painted canvas dominated this top landing. Yet the painting of a reversible canvas background, in monochrome grey on grey, certainly did not date from yesterday. One side of it represented a balustrade on the verge of an English park; the other, a small sea, bounded in the distance by a hazy port, whose horizon dipped slightly to the right. As the front door was frequently left open, it was against this stormy background and this slanting sea that I used to see the photographer's Missus encamped. From her air of vague expectancy I presumed that she had come out there to breathe the coolness of the top landing or to watch for some customer coming up the stairs. I found out later that I was wrong. I would go into her opposite neighbour's and Mademoiselle Devoidy would offer me one of her dry, pleasant hands; infallible hands, incapable of hurrying or trembling, that never dropped a pearl or a reel or a needle, that gummed the point of a strand of silk by passing it, with one sure twist of the fingers, through a half-moon of virgin wax, then aimed the stiffened thread at the eye of a needle finer than any sewing-needle.

What I saw most clearly of Mademoiselle Devoidy was her bust, caught in the circle of light from her lamp, her coral necklace on her starched white collar, her discreetly mocking smile. As to her freckled, rather flat face, it merely served as a frame and a foil for her piercing brown, gold-spangled eyes that needed neither spectacles nor magnifying-glass and could count the tiny "seed-pearls" used for making those skeins and twists that are known as "bayadères" and are as dull as white bead trimming.

Mademoiselle Devoidy, living in cramped quarters, worked in the front room and slept in the back one, next door to the kitchen. A double door, at the entrance, made a minute hall. When a visitor knocked or rang, Mademoiselle Devoidy would call out, without getting up:

"Come in! The key turns to the left!"

Did I feel the beginnings of a friendship with this fellow-native of my own province? I most certainly liked her professionable table, covered with green baize, with a raised edge like a billiard-table, and scored with parallel troughs along which her fingers ranged and graded the pearls with the help of delicate tweezers, worthy to touch the most precious matter: pearls and the wings of dead butterflies.

I also had a friendly feeling for the details and peculiarities of a craft that demanded two years' apprenticeship, a special manual dexterity and a slightly contemptuous attitude towards jewels. The mania for pearls, which lasted a long time, allowed the expert stringer to work in her own home and to do as much as she chose. When Mademoiselle Devoidy told me, suppressing a yawn: "So and so brought me *masses* last night, I had to compose till two o'clock in the morning," my imagination swelled these "masses" to fairy-tale size and elevated the verb "compose" to the rank of creative labour.

In the afternoon, and on dark mornings in winter, an electric bulb, set in a metal convolvulus, was switched on above the table. Its strong light swept away all the shadows on the work-bench on which Mademoiselle Devoidy allowed nothing to stand; no little vase with a rose in it, no pin-tray or ornament in which a stray pearl might hide. Even the scissors seemed to make themselves perfectly flat. Apart from this precaution, which kept the table in a permanent state of pearl-decked nudity, I never saw Mademoiselle Devoidy show the faintest sign of wariness. Chokers and necklace lay dismembered on the table like stakes not worth picking up.

"You're not in a great hurry? I'll clear a little place for you. Amuse yourself with what's lying about while I re-thread you. So it refuses to get any fatter, this string? You'll have to put it in the hen-coop. Ah! you'll never know your way about."

All the time Mademoiselle Devoidy was teasing, her smile was busy reminding me of our common origin, a village ringed with woods, the autumn rain dripping on the piles of apples on the edge of the fields, waiting to be taken to the cider-press. . . . Meanwhile, I did, indeed, amuse myself with what was lying about on the table. Sometimes there were huge American necklaces, ostentatious and impersonal; Cécile Sorel's pearls mingled with Polaire's choker, thirty-seven famous pearls. There were jewellers' necklaces, milky and brand-new, not yet warmed into life by long contact with women's skin. Here and there, a diamond, mounted in a clasp, emitted rainbow sparks.

A dog-collar, a fourteen-row choker, stiffened with vertical bars of brilliants, spoke of wrinkled dewlaps, an old woman's sinewy neck, perhaps of scrofula. . . .

Has that curious craft changed? Does it still fling heaps of treasures, defenceless fortunes into the laps of poor and incorruptible women?

When the day was drawing to a close, Madame Armand sometimes came and sat at the green baize table. Out of discretion, she refrained from handling the necklaces over which her bird-like gaze wandered with glittering indifference.

"Well, so your day's work's over, Madame Armand?" Mademoiselle Devoidy would say.

"Oh, me . . . mine doesn't have to be fitted into the day like my husband's. My dinner to warm up, the studio to tidy, little things here and there . . . it's easily done."

Rigid when she was standing, Madame Armand was no less rigid seated. Her bust, tightly encased in a red-and-black tartan bodice with braided frogs, visible between the stiff half-open flaps of a jacket, made me think of a little cupboard. She had something of the fascination of a wooden ship's figurehead. At the same time she suggested the well-mannered efficiency of a good cashier and various other sterling virtues.

"And Monsieur Armand, what nice thing's he up to at this moment?"

"He's still working. He's still on his last Saturday's wedding. You see he has to do everything in a little business like ours. That wedding-procession on Saturday is giving him a lot of trouble, but it means quite a good profit. The couple in one picture, a group of the bridesmaids, the whole procession in four different poses, goodness knows what all. I can't help him as much as I'd like to."

The photographer's Missus turned to me as if to apologise. As soon as she spoke, all the various stiff and starchy phenomena of the close-fitting bodice, the jacket, the imitation gardenia pinned in her buttonhole melted in the warmth of a pleasant voice with hardly any modulations in it, a voice made to recount local gossip at great length.

"My husband gets tired, because he's starting this exophthalmic goitre, I call it his exo for short. The year's been too bad for us to take on an assistant cameraman. The tiresome thing is, I haven't got a steady hand, I break things. A pot of glue here, a developing tank there, and bang, there goes a frame on the floor. You can see a mile off what a loss that means at the end of a day."

She stretched out a hand towards me that was, indeed, shaking.

"Nerves," she said. "So I stick to my own little domain, I do all the housework. In one way it seems to be good for my nerves, but . . ."

She frequently paused on a "but", after which came a sigh, and when I asked Mademoiselle Devoidy whether this "but" and this sigh hid some melancholy story, my fellow-countrywoman retorted:

"What an idea! She's a woman who tight-laces to give herself a slim waist so she has to fight every minute to get her breath."

Madame Armand, who had regular features, remained faithful to the high military collar and the tight, curled fringe because she had been told she looked like Queen Alexandra, only saucier. Saucier, I cannot honestly say. Darker, definitely. Heads of blue-black hair accompanied by white skin and a straight little nose abound in Paris and are usually of pure Parisian origin with no trace of Mediterranean blood. Madame Armand had as many lashes as a Spanish woman and a bird's eyes, I mean black eyes rich with a lustre that never varied. The neighbourhood paid her a laconic and adequate tribute by murmuring, as she passed, the words "Handsome brunette." On this point, Mademoiselle Devoidy's opinion allowed itself one reservation:

"Handsome brunette's the word . . . Especially ten years ago."

"Have you known Madame Armand ten years?"

"No, because she and little old Big-Eyes only moved into this place three years ago. I've been in the house much longer than they have. But I can very well imagine Madame Armand ten years ago. You can see she's a woman who's devouring herself."

"Devouring herself? That's a strong expression. You're not exaggerating?"

An offended look, the colour of spangled iron-ore, passed under the lamp and met my eyes in the shadow.

"Anyone may be mistaken. Madame Armand may be mistaken too. Just fancy, she's got it into her head that she leads a sedentary life. So every evening, either before dinner or after, she goes out on foot to take the air."

"It's a good healthy habit, don't you think?"

Mademoiselle Devoidy, as she pinched her lips, made the little colourless hairs of moustache at the corners of her mouth converge—just as diving seals do when they close their nostrils to the water.

"You know what I think of healthy habits. Now that the photographer's Missus has got a bee in her bonnet that she has breathless fits if she doesn't go out, the next thing will be she'll be found on the stairs one day, dead of suffocation.

"You very seldom go out, Mademoiselle Devoidy?"

"Never, you might say."

"And you don't feel any the worse for it?"

"You can see for yourself. But I don't stop other people from doing what they fancy."

She darted her malicious gaze, directed at an invisible Madame Armand, towards the closed door. And I thought of the tart, ill-natured remarks the women herding the cattle in my native countryside exchange over the hedges as they slap the blood-swollen clegs under the heifers' sensitive bellies.

Mademoiselle Devoidy bent her head over the threading of some very tiny pearls; at the edge of her forehead, between the cheek and the ear, the chestnut hair ended in vigorous down, silver, like her little moustache. All the features of this Parisian recluse spoke to me of downy willows, ripe hazel-nuts, the sandy bottom of springs, and silky husks. She aimed the point of her needle, pinched between the thumb and forefinger that rested on the table, at the almost invisible holes in the small, insipidly white pearls that she spitted in fives, then slipped on to the silk thread.

A familiar fist banged at the door.

"That'll be Tigri-Cohen. I recognise his knock. The key's in the door, Monsieur Tigri!"

The ill-favoured face of Tigri-Cohen entered the little arena of light. His ugliness was now gay and ironical, now sad and imploring, like that of certain over-intelligent monkeys who have equal reason to cherish the gifts of man and to shiver with fear at them. I have always thought that Tigri-Cohen took tremendous pains to appear crafty, reckless and unscrupulous. He adopted, perhaps out of guilelessness, the style and manner of a moneylender who charged exorbitant rates. As I knew him, he was always ready to part with twenty francs or even a "big flimsy", so much so that he died poor, in the arms of his unsuspected honesty.

I had known him in the wings and dressing-rooms of music-halls where Tigri-Cohen spent most of his evenings. The little variety actresses used to climb on his shoulders like tame parakeets and leave wet-white all over this black man. They knew his pockets were full of small jewels, flawed pearls and gems just good enough to make into hatpins. He excited his little friends' admiration by showing them badly coloured stones with beautiful names, peridots, chalcedonies, chrysoprases and pretentious zircons. Hail-fellow-well-met with all the girls, Tigri-Cohen would sell a few of his glittering pebbles between ten p.m. and midnight. But to the rich stars, he presented himself mainly in the role of buyer.

His taste for beautiful pearls always seemed to me more sensual than commercial. I shall never forget the state of excitement I saw him in one day when, going into his shop, I found him alone with a small, unremarkable, expressionless little man who drew out of his shabby waistcoat a sky-blue silk handkerchief and, out of the handkerchief, a single pearl.

"So you've still got it?" asked Tigri.

"Yes," said the little man. "Not for long, though."

It was an unpierced pearl, round, big as a fine cherry, and, like a cherry, it seemed not to receive the cold light shed from the even-number side of the Rue Lafayette but to emit a steady, veiled radiance from within. Tigri contemplated it without saying a word and the little chap kept silence.

"It's . . . it's . . ." began Tigri-Cohen.

He searched in vain for words to praise it, then shrugged his shoulders.

"Can I have it a moment?" I asked.

I held it in the hollow of my palm, this marvellous, warm virgin, with its mystery of tremulous colours, its indefinable pink that picked up a snowy blue then exchanged it for a fleeting mauve.

Before giving back the glorious pearl, Tigri sighed. Then the little man extinguished the soft rays in the blue handkerchief, thrust the whole, carelessly, into a pocket and went away.

"It's . . . repeated Tigri . . . "It's the colour of love."

"To whom does it belong?"

"To whom? To whom? Think *I* know? To black chaps in India! To an oyster-bed company! To savages, to people with no faith and no feelings, to . . ."

"How much is it worth?"

He gave me a look of contempt.

"How much? A pearl like that, in the dawn of its life, that's still going about in its little blue satin chemise at the bottom of a broker's pocket? How much? Like a kilo of plums, eh? 'That'll be three francs, Madame. Here you are, Madame. Thank you, Madame.' Ah! to hear anyone ask *that* . . ."

Every muscle of his ugly, passionate mime's face was working, that face that was always overloaded with too much expression, too much laughter, too much sadness. That evening, in Devoidy's room, I remember he was dripping with rain and seemed not to notice it. He was exploring his pockets with a mechanical gesture, pockets that were secret hoards of necklaces of coloured stones, cabochon rings, little bags in which diamonds slept in tissue-paper. He flung some ropes of pearls on the green baize.

"There, Devoidy, my love, do me that for tomorrow. And that one. Don't you think it's hideous? If you pulled out the pigeon's feather stuffed in the middle of that nut, you could thread it on a cable. Anyway, change the stuffing."

From force of habit, he bent over my necklace, with one eye screwed up.

"The fourth one from the middle, I'll buy that. No? Just as you like. Good-bye, my pets. Tonight I'm going to the dress-rehearsal of the Folies-Bergère."

"Should be a fine evening for business," said Mademoiselle Devoidy politely.

"That shows you don't know a thing about it. Tonight my

good ladies will be thinking of nothing but their parts, their costumes, the audience's reaction and going off into faints behind a flat. See you soon, pets."

Other visitors, especially female ones, passed through the boltless door into the narrow circle of harsh light. I stared at them with the avid curiosity I have always felt for people I run no risk of seeing again. Richly-dressed women thrust out hands filled with precious white grain into the glare of the lamp. Or else, with a proud, languid gesture acquired from constantly wearing pearls, they undid the clasps of their necklaces.

Among others, my memory retains the picture of a woman all silvered with chinchilla. She came in very agitated and she was such a sturdy daughter of the people under all her luxury that she was a joy to the eye. She plumped herself down rudely on the straw-seated stool and commanded:

"Don't unstring the whole row. Just get me out that one, on the side, near the middle, yes, that beauty there."

Mademoiselle Devoidy, who did not like despots, calmly and unhurriedly cut the two silk knots and pushed the free pearl towards her client. The beautiful woman grabbed it and studied it from very close to. Under the lamp, I could have counted her long, fluttering eyelashes that were stuck together with mascara. She held out the pearl to the stringer:

"You, what's *your* idea about this here pearl?"

"I know nothing about pearls," said Mademoiselle Devoidy impassively.

"Sure you're not joking?"

The beautiful woman pointed to the table, with evident irony. Then her face changed; she seized a little lump of cast-iron under which Mademoiselle Devoidy kept a set of ready-threaded needles and brought it down hard on the pearl, which crushed into tiny fragments. I exclaimed "Oh!" in spite of myself. Mademoiselle Devoidy permitted herself no other movement than to clutch an unfinished string and some scattered pearls close against her with her sure hands.

The customer contemplated her work without saying a word. Finally, she burst into vehement tears. She kept noisily sobbing: "The swine, the swine," and, at the same time, carefully collecting the black from her lashes on a corner of her handkerchief. Then she stuffed her necklace, amputated of one pearl, into her handbag, asked for "a little bit of tissue paper", stowed every single fragment of the sham pearl into it, and stood up. Before she left the room, she made a point of affirming loudly, "That's not the last of this business, not by a long chalk." Then she carried away into the outside air the unpleasant whiff of a brand-new, very fashionable scent: synthetic lily-of-the-valley.

"Is that the first time you've seen a thing like that happen, Mademoiselle Devoidy?"

Mademoiselle Devoidy was scrupulously tidying up her work-bench with her careful hands, unshaking as usual.

"No, the second," she said. "With this difference, that the first time, the pearl resisted. It was real. So was the rest of the necklace."

"And what did the lady say?"

"It wasn't a lady, it was a gentleman. He said: 'Ah! the bitch!'"

"Why?"

"The necklace was his wife's. She'd made her husband believe it cost fifteen francs. Yes. Oh! you know, when it comes to pearls, it's very seldom there isn't some shady story behind them."

She touched her little coral necklace with two fingers. I was amazed to catch this slightly sneering sceptic making a gesture to avert ill-luck, and to see the cloud of superstition pass over her stubborn brow.

"So you wouldn't care to wear pearls?"

She raised one shoulder slantwise, torn between her commercial prudence and the desire not to lie.

"I don't know. One doesn't know one's own self. Down there, at Coulanges, there was a chap who couldn't have been more of an anarchist, he frightened everyone out of their wits. And then he inherited a little house with a garden and a round dovecote and a pigsty. If you were to see the anarchist now! There's quite a change."

Almost at once, she recovered her restrained laugh, her pleasantly rebellious expression and her way of approving without being sycophantic and criticising without being rude.

One night when I had lingered late with her, she caught me yawning, and I apologised by saying:

"I've got one of those hungers. I don't take tea and I had hardly any lunch, there was red meat—I can't eat underdone meat."

"Neither can I," said my fellow-countrywoman. "In our part of the world, as you well know, they say raw meat is for cats and the English. But if you can be patient for five minutes, a mille-feuilles will be wafted here to you, without my leaving my chair. What do you bet?"

"A pound of chocolate creams."

"Pig who backs out of it!" said Mademoiselle Devoidy, holding out her dry palm quite flat to me. I slapped it and said "Done!"

"Mademoiselle Devoidy, how is it that your flat never smells of fried whiting or onions or stew? Have you got a secret?"

She indicated "Yes" by fluttering her eyelids.

"Can I know?"

An accustomed hand knocked three times on the front door.

"There you are, here it comes, your mille-feuilles. And my secret's revealed. Come in, Madame Armand, come in!"

Nevertheless, she fastened my little middle-class necklace at the back of my neck. Loaded with a basket, Madame Armand did not at once offer me her chronically-trembling fingers and she spoke very hurriedly:

"Mind now, mind now, don't jostle me, I've got something breakable. Today's chef's special is *bœuf à la bourguignonne* and I brought you a lovely bit of lettuce. As to mille-feuilles, nothing doing! It's iced Genoese cakes."

Mademoiselle Devoidy made a comic grimace at me and attempted to unburden her obliging neighbour. But the latter exclaimed: "I'll carry it all into the kitchen for you!" and ran towards the dark room at the back. Quickly as she had crossed the lighted zone, I had caught sight of her face and so had Mademoiselle Devoidy.

"I must fly, I must fly, I've got some milk on the gas-ring," Madame Armand cried out, in tomboyish tones.

She crossed the front room again at a run and pulled the door to behind her. Mademoiselle Devoidy went out into the kitchen and came back with two Genoese cakes, with pink icing, on a plate adorned with a flaming bomb and the inscription "Fire Brigade Alarm".

"As sure as eggs is eggs," she said, with a thoughtful air, "the photographer's Missus has been crying. And she hasn't any milk on her gas-ring."

"Domestic scene?"

She shook her head.

"Poor little old Big-Eyes! He's not capable of it. Neither is she for that matter. I say, you've got through that cake quickly. Would you like the other one? She's rather put me off my food, Monsieur Armand's good lady, with that face all gone to pieces."

"Everything will be all right tomorrow," I said absent-mindedly.

In exchange for that flat remark, I received a brief, trenchant glance.

"Oh, of *course* it will, won't it? And, anyway, if it isn't all right, *you* don't care a fig."

"What's all this? You think I ought to be more passionately concerned over the Armand family's troubles?"

"The Armand family isn't asking you for anything. And neither am I. It would most certainly be the first time anyone had heard *me* asking anyone for anything . . ."

Mademoiselle Devoidy had lowered her voice in the effort to control her irritation. We were, I imagine, utterly ridiculous. It was this cloud of anger, rising suddenly between two hot-blooded women, that fixed the details of an absurd, unexpected scene in my memory. I had the good sense to put an end to it at once by laying my hand on her shoulder:

"Now, now. Don't let's make ourselves out blacker than we are! You know quite well that if I can be any use to this good lady. . . . Are you frightened about her?"

Mademoiselle Devoidy flushed under her freckles and covered the top of her face with one hand, with a simple and romantic gesture:

"Now, you're being too nice. Don't be too nice to me. When anyone's too nice to me, I don't know what I'm doing, I boil over like a soup."

She uncovered her beautiful moist spangled eyes and pushed the straw-seated stool towards me.

"One minute, you've surely got a minute? That's rain you can hear; wait till the rain's over."

She sat down opposite me in her working place and vigorously rubbed her eyes with the back of her forefinger.

"Get this well into your head first—Madame Armand isn't a tittle-tattle or a woman who goes in for confidences. But she lives very near, right on my doorstep. This place is just a little twopenny-ha'penny block of flats, the old-fashioned kind. Two rooms on the right, two rooms on the left, little businesses that can be done in one room at home. People who live so very near you, it isn't so much that you hear them, anyway they don't make any noise, but I'm conscious of them. Especially of the fact that Madame Armand spends so much time out on the landing. In places like this, if anything's not going right, the neighbours are very soon aware of it, at least I am."

She lowered her voice and compressed her lips; her little moustache-hairs glistened. She pricked her green table with the point of a needle as if she were cabalistically counting her words.

"When the photographer's Missus goes out shopping for herself or for me, you can always see the concierge or the flower-seller under the archway or the woman in the little *bistrot*, coming out, one or other of them, to see where she's going. Where is she going? Why, she's going to the dairy or to buy hot rolls or to the hairdresser, just like anyone else! So then the Nosy Parkers take their noses inside again, anything but pleased, as if they'd been promised something and not given it. And the next time, they start all over again. But when it's me who goes out or Madame Gâteroy downstairs or her daughter, people don't stop and stare after us as if they expected something extraordinary was going to happen."

"Madame Armand has a . . . a rather individual appearance," I risked suggesting. "Perhaps she does somewhat overdo the tartan, too."

Mademoiselle Devoidy shook her head and seemed to despair of making herself understood. It was getting late; from top to bottom of the building, doors were slamming one by one, on every floor chairs were being drawn up round a table and a soup-tureen; I took my leave. The door of the photographic studio, unwontedly shut, turned the camera-pedestal and the crossed shrimping-nets under the gas-jet into an important piece of decoration. On the ground-floor, the concierge raised her curtain to watch me going: I had never stayed so late.

The warm night was foggy round the gas-lamps and the unusual hour gave me that small, yet somehow rewarding pang I used to experience in the old days when I came away from stage performances that had begun when the sun was at its zenith and finished when it was dark.

Do those transient figures who featured in long-past periods of my life, deserve to live again in a handful of pages as I here compel them to? They were important enough for me to keep them secret, at least during the time I was involved with them. For example, my husband, at home, did not know of the existence of Mademoiselle Devoidy or of my familiarity with Tigri-Cohen. The same was true of Monsieur Armand's "Missus" and of a certain sewing-woman, expert at repairing worn quilts and making multi-coloured silk rags into patchwork pram-covers. Did I like her for her needlwork that disdained both fashion and the sewing-machine or was it for her second profession? At six o'clock in the afternoon, she abandoned her hexagonal pieces of silk and went off to the Gaîté-Lyrique where she sang a part in *Les Mousquetaires au Couvent*.

For a long time, in the inner compartment of my handbag, between the leather and the lining, I kept a fifty-centime "synthetic" pearl I had once lost in Tigri-Cohen's shop. He had found it and, before returning it to me, he had amused himself by studding my initials on it in little diamonds. But, at home, I never mentioned either the charming mascot or Tigri himself, for the husband I was married to then had formed such a rigid, foursquare idea of the jeweller, such a conventional notion of a "dealer" that I could neither have pleaded the cause of the latter nor rectified the error of the former.

Was I genuinely attached to the little needlewoman? Did I feel real affection for the misunderstood Tigri-Cohen? I do not know. The instinct to deceive has not played a very large part in my different lives. It was essential to me, as it is to many women, to escape from the opinions of certain people, which I knew to be subject to error and apt to be proclaimed dogmatically in a tone of feigned indulgence. Treatment of this sort drives us women to avoid the simple truth, as if it were a dull, monotonous tune, to take pleasure in half-lies, half-suppressions, half-escapes from reality.

When the opportunity came, I made my way once more to the narrow-fronted house over whose brow the open blue pane of the photographic studio window slanted like a visor.

As soon as I entered the hall of the block of flats, a cleaners' delivery-man in a black apron, and a woman carrying bread in a long wicker *cistera* barred my way. The first, without being asked, obligingly informed me: "It's nothing, just a chimney on fire." At the same moment, a "runner" from a fashion house came dashing down the stairs, banging her yellow box against all the banisters, and yapping:

"She's as white as a sheet! She hasn't an hour to live!"

Her scream magically attracted a dozen passers-by who crowded round her, pressing her close on all sides. Desire to escape, slight nausea and idle curiosity struggled within me, but in the end they gave way to a strange resignation. I knew perfectly well—already out of breath before I had begun to run—I knew perfectly well that I should not stop until I reached the top landing. Which of them was it? The photographer's Missus or Mademoiselle Devoidy? Mentally, I ruled out the latter as if no peril could ever endanger her mocking wisdom or the sureness of those hands, soft as silky wood-shavings, or scatter the milky constellations of precious, tiny moons she pursued on the green baize table and impaled with such deadly aim.

All the while I was breathlessly climbing the storeys, I was fighting to reassure myself. An accident? Why shouldn't it have happened to the knitting-women on the fourth floor or the bookbinding couple? The steamy November afternoon preserved the full strength of the smells of cabbage and gas and of the hot, excited human beings who were showing me the way.

The unexpected sound of sobbing is demoralising. Easy as it is to imitate, that retching, hiccuping noise remains crudely impressive. While I was being secretly crushed to death between the banisters and a telegraph-boy who had pushed up too fast, we heard convulsive male sobs and the commentators on the staircase fell silent, avidly. The noise lasted only a moment, it was extinguished behind a door that someone up there had slammed again. Without having ever heard the man whom Mademoiselle Devoidy nicknamed little old Big-Eyes weep, I knew, beyond a shadow of a doubt, that it was he who was sobbing.

At last I reached the top floor, crammed with strangers between its two closed doors. One of them opened again and I heard the biting voice of Mademoiselle Devoidy.

"Ladies and gentlemen, where are you going like that? It doesn't make sense. If you want to have your photographs taken, it's too late. Why no, don't worry, there hasn't been any accident. A lady has sprained her ankle, they've put a crêpe bandage on it and that's the beginning and end of the story."

A murmur of disappointment and a little laughter ran through the crowd flocking up the stairs. But it struck me that, in the harsh light, Mademoiselle Devoidy looked extremely ill. She proffered a few more words designed to discourage the invaders and went back into her flat.

"Coo, if that's all . . ." said the telegraph-boy.

To make up his lost time, he jostled a cellarman in a green

baize apron and a few dim women and disappeared by leaps and bounds, and, at last, I was able to sit down on the Gothic chair reserved for First Communicants. As soon as I was alone, Mademoiselle Devoidy reappeared.

"Come in, I saw you all right. I couldn't make signs to you in front of everyone. Do you mind? I wouldn't be sorry to sit down for a moment."

As if there was no refuge except in her regular, everyday haunt, she collapsed into the chair she worked in.

"Ah, that's better!"

She smiled at me with a happy look.

"She's brought it all up, so we needn't worry any more."

"All what?"

"What she'd taken. Some stuff to kill herself. Some disgusting filth or other."

"But why did she do it?"

"There you go, asking why! You always have to have three dozen reasons, don't you? She'd left a letter for little old Big-Eyes."

"A letter? Whatever did she confess?"

By degrees Mademoiselle Devoidy was recovering her composure, and her easy, mocking way of treating me.

"You've got to know everything, haven't you? As to confessing, she confessed all. She confessed: 'My darling Geo, don't scold me. Forgive me for leaving you. In death, as in life, I remain your faithful Georgina.' By the side of that, there was another scrap of paper that said: 'Everything is paid except the washerwoman who had no change on Wednesday.' It happened about quarter-past two, twenty-past two . . ."

She broke off and stood up.

"Wait, there's some coffee left."

"If it's for me, don't bother."

"I want some myself," she said.

The panacea of the people appeared with the sacred vessels of its cult, its blue-marbled enamel jug, its two cups adorned with a red-and-gold key-pattern and its twisted glass sugar-bowl. The smell of chicory faithfully escorted it, eloquent of ritual anxieties, of deathbed vigils and difficult labours and whispered palavers, of a drug within reach of all.

"Well, as I was saying," Mademoiselle Devoidy went on, "about two or a quarter past, someone knocked at my door. It was my little old Big-Eyes, looking ever so embarrassed and saying: 'You haven't happened to see my wife going down-stairs?'—'No,' I says, 'but she might have gone down without my seeing her.' 'Yes,' he says to me. 'I ought to have been out myself by now, but, just as I was on the point of leaving, I broke a bottle of hyposulphite. You can see the state my hands are in.'—'That was bad luck,' I says to him. 'Yes,' he says to me, 'I need a duster, the dusters are in our bedroom, in the cupboard behind the bed.'—'If that's all,' I says, 'I'll go and get you one, don't touch anything.' 'It isn't all,' he says to me, 'What's worrying me is that the bedroom's locked and it never is locked.' I stared at him, I don't know what came into my head, but I got up, nearly pushing him over, and off I went and knocked at their bedroom door. He kept saying: 'Why, what-ever's the matter with you? Whatever's the matter with you?' I answered him tit-for-tat: 'Well, what about you? You haven't taken a look at yourself.' He stayed standing there with his hands spread out, all covered with hyposulphite. I come back in here, I snatch up the hatchet I chop up my firewood with. I swear to you the hinges and the lock bust right off at the same blow. They're no better than matchwood, these doors."

She drank a few mouthfuls of tepid coffee.

"I'll get a safety-chain put on mine," she went on. "Now that I've seen what a fragile thing a door is."

I was waiting for her to continue her story, but she was

toying absently with the little metal shovel that gathered up the seed pearls on the cloth and seemed to have nothing more to say.

"And then, Mademoiselle Devoidy?"

"Then what?"

"She . . . Madame Armand . . . Was she in the room?"

"Of course she was. On her bed. Actually in her bed. Wearing silk stockings and smart shoes, black satin ones, embroidered with a little jet motif. That was what struck me all of a heap, those shoes and those stockings. It struck me so much, that, while I was filling a hot-water bottle, I said to her husband, 'Whatever was she up to, going to bed in her shoes and stockings?' He was sobbing, as he explained to me: 'It's because of her corns and her crooked third toe. She didn't want anyone to see her bare feet, not even me. She used to go to bed in little socks, she's so dainty in all her ways.' "

Mademoiselle Devoidy yawned, stretched, and began to laugh:

"Ah! You've got to admit a man's a proper muff in circumstances like that. *Him!* The only thing *he* could think of doing was crying and keeping on saying: 'My darling . . . My darling . . .' Lucky I acted quickly," she added proudly. "Excuse details, it makes me feel queasy. Oh, she's saved all right! But Doctor Camescasse, who lives at number eleven, won't let her have anything but a little milk and soda-water till further orders. Madame Armand swallowed enough poison to kill a regiment, apparently that's what saved her. Little old Big-Eyes is on sentry duty at her bedside. But I'm just going to run in and have a look at her. Shall we be seeing you again soon? Bring her a little bunch of violets, it'll be more cheerful than if you'd had to take one to her in the Montparnasse cemetery."

I was already on the pavement when, too late, a question crossed my mind; why had Madame Armand wanted to die?

At the same moment, I realised that Mademoiselle Devoidy had omitted to tell me.

During the following days, I thought of the photographer's Missus and her abortive suicide; this naturally led me on to thinking about death and, unnaturally for me, about my own. Suppose I were to die in a tram? Suppose I were to die while having dinner in a restaurant? Appalling possibilities, but so highly unlikely that I soon abandoned them. We women seldom die outside our own homes; as soon as pain puts a handful of blazing straw under our bellies, we behave like frightened horses and find enough strength to run for shelter. After three days, I lost the taste for choosing the pleasantest mode of departing. All the same, country funerals are charming, especially in June, because of the flowers. But roses so soon become overblown in hot weather. . . . I had reached this point when a note from Madame Armand—admirable spelling and a ravishing curly handwriting like lacework—reminded me of my "kind promise" and invited me to "tea".

On the top landing, I ran into an elderly married couple who were leaving the photographer's studio, arm in arm, all got up in braided jacket, four-in-hand tie and stiff black silk. Little old Big-Eyes was showing them out and I scanned his heavy eyelids for traces of his passionate tears. He greeted me with a joyful nod that implied mutual understanding.

"The ladies are in the bedroom. Madame Armand is still suffering from slight general fatigue, she thought you would be kind enough to excuse her receiving you so informally."

He guided me through the studio, had a courteous word for my bunch of violets—"the Parma ones look so distinguished" —and left me on the threshold of the unknown room.

On this narrow planet, we have only the choice between two unknown worlds. One of them tempts us—ah! what a dream, to live in that!—the other stifles us at the first breath. In the matter of furnishing, I find a certain absence of ugliness far worse than ugliness. Without containing any monstrosity, the total effect of the room where Madame Armand was enjoying her convalescence made me lower my eyes and I should not take the smallest pleasure in describing it.

She was resting, with her feet up, on the made-up bed, the same bed she had untucked to die in. Her eagerness to welcome me would have made her rise, had not Mademoiselle Devoidy restrained her, with the firm hand of a guardian angel. November was mild only out of doors. Madame Armand was keeping herself warm under a little red-and-black coverlet, crocheted in what is called Tunisian stitch. I am not fond of Tunisian stitch. But Madame Armand looked well, her cheeks were less parched and her eyes more brilliant than ever. The vivacity of her movements displaced the coverlet, and revealed two slim feet shod in black satin, embroidered—just as Mademoiselle Devoidy had described them to me—with a motif in jet beads.

"Madame Armand, a little less restlessness, please," gravely ordered the guardian angel.

"But I'm not ill!" protested Madame Armand. "I'm coddling myself, that's all. My little Exo's paying a woman to come in and do the housework for me in the morning, Mademoiselle Devoidy's made us a lemon sponge-cake and you bring me some magnificent violets! A life of idle luxury! You will taste some of my raspberry and gooseberry jelly with the sponge-cake, won't you? It's the last of last year's pots, and, without boasting . . . This year I made a mess of them, and the plums in brandy too. It's a year when I've made a mess of everything."

She smiled, as if making some subtle allusion. The unvarying glitter of her black eyes still reminded me of some bird or other; but now the bird was tranquil and refreshed. At what dark spring had it slaked its thirst?

"In that affair, however many were killed and wounded, nobody's dead," concluded Mademoiselle Devoidy.

I greeted the sentence that came straight out of our native province with a knowing wink and I swallowed, one on top of the other, a cup of very black tea and a glass of sweet wine that tasted of liquorice: what must be, must be. I felt ill at ease. One does not so quickly acquire the knack of conjuring up, in the straightforward light of afternoon, such a very recent suicide. True, it had been transformed into a purging but it had been planned to prevent any return. I tried to adapt myself to the tone of the other two by saying playfully:

"Who would believe that charming woman we see before us is the very same one who was so unreasonable the other day?"

The charming woman finished her wedge of lemon sponge before miming a little confusion and answering, doubtfully and coquettishly:

"So unreasonable . . . so unreasonable . . . there's a lot could be said about that."

Mademoiselle Devoidy cut her off short. She seemed to me to have acquired a military authority from her first act of life-saving.

"Now, now! You're not going to start all over again, are you?"

"Start again? Oh! Never!"

I applauded the spontaneity of that cry. Madame Armand raised her right hand for an oath.

"I swear it! The only thing I absolutely deny is what Doctor Camescasse said to me: 'In fact, you swallowed a poison during an attack of neurasthenia?' That infuriated me. For two pins I'd have answered him back: 'If you're so certain, there's no point in asking me a hundred questions. *I* know perfectly well in my own mind that I didn't commit suicide out of neurasthenia!' "

"Tst, tst," rebuked Mademoiselle Devoidy. "How long is it since I've seen for myself you were in a bad way? Madame Colette here can certify that I've mentioned it to her. As to neurasthenia, of course it was neurasthenia; there's nothing to be ashamed of in that."

The crochet coverlet was flung aside, the cup and saucer narrowly escaped following suit.

"No, it wasn't! I think I might be allowed to have my own little opinion on the subject! I'm the person concerned, aren't I?"

"I do take your opinion into account, Madame Armand. But it can't be compared with the opinion of a man of science like Doctor Camescasse!"

They were exchanging their retorts over my head, so tensely that I slightly ducked my chin. It was the first time I had heard a would-be suicide arguing her case in my presence as if standing up for her lawful rights. Like so many saviours, heavenly or earthly, the angel tended to overdo her part. Her spangled eye lit up with a spark that was anything but angelic, while the colour of the rescued one kindled under her too-white powder.

I have never turned up my nose at a heated argument between cronies. A lively taste for street scenes keeps me hovering on the outskirts of quarrels vented in the open air which I find good occasions for enriching my vocabulary. I hoped, as I sat at Madame Armand's bedside, that the dialogue between the two women would blaze up with that virulence that characterises feminine misunderstandings. But incomprehensible death, that teaches the living nothing; the memory of a nauseous poison; the rigorous devotion that tended its victim with a rod of iron; all this was too present, too massive, too oppressive to be replaced by a healthy slanging-match. What was I doing, in this home timidly ruled by little old Big-Eyes? What would remain to me of his "Missus", whom death had failed to ravish, beyond a stale, insipid mystery? As to Mademoiselle Devoidy, that perfect example of the dry, incorruptible spinster, I realised that I could no longer fancy she was anything of an enigma and that the attraction of the void cannot last for ever.

Sorrow, fear, physical pain, excessive heat and excessive cold, I can still guarantee to stand up to all these with decent courage. But I abdicate in the face of boredom which turns me into a wretched and, if needs be, ferocious creature. Its approach, its capricious presence that affects the muscles of the jaw, dances in the pit of the stomach, sings a monotonous refrain that one's feet beat time to; I do not merely dread these manifestations, I fly from them. What was wrong in my eyes about these two women, who from being gratitude and devotion incarnate, were now putting up barriers between them, was that they did not proceed to adopt the classic attitudes. There was no accompaniment of scurrilous laughter, of insults as blinding as pepper, of fists dug well into the ribs. They did not even awaken minute old grievances, kept alive and kicking by long stewing over and brooding on. Nevertheless, I did hear dangerous exchanges and words such as "neurotic . . . ingratitude . . . meddlesome Matty . . . poking your nose in . . ." I think it was on this last insult that Mademoiselle Devoidy rose to her feet, flung us a curt, bitter, ceremonious "good-bye" and left the room.

Somewhat belatedly, I displayed suitable agitation.

"Well, really! But it's not serious. What childishness! Who'd have expected . . ."

Madame Armand merely gave a faint shrug that seemed to say "Forget it!" As the daylight was going fast, she stretched out her arm and switched on the bedside lamp which wore a crinoline of salmon-pink silk. At once the depressing character of the room changed and I did not hide my pleasure, for the lamp-shade, elaborately ruched and pretentious as it was, filtered an enchanting rosy light, like the lining of a sea-shell. Madame Armand smiled.

"I think we're both of us pleased," she said.

She saw I was about to mention the disagreeable incident again and stopped me.

"Forget it, Madame, these little tiffs—the less one thinks about them the better. Either they sort themselves out of their own accord, or else they don't, and that's even better. Have another drop of wine. Yes, yes, do have some more, it's pure unadulterated stuff."

She leapt from her couch, deftly pulling down her dress. In those days, women did not let themselves slide off a sofa or out of a car revealing a wide margin of bare thigh as they do nowadays with such cold and barbarous indifference.

"You're not overtaxing your strength, Madame Armand?"

She was walking to and fro on her jet-and-satin-shod feet, those feet that had been modest even in death. She poured out the pseudo-port, pulled an awning over the ceiling skylight, displaying a briskness that was not without grace, as if she had grown lighter. A likeable woman, in fact, whose thirty-six years had left few traces. A woman who had wanted to die.

She switched on a second pink lamp. The room, extraordinary by its very ordinariness, exuded the false cheerfulness of well-kept hotel bedrooms.

My hostess came and picked up the chair abandoned by Mademoiselle Devoidy and planted it firmly beside me.

"No, Madame, I won't allow people to believe that I killed myself out of neurasthenia."

"But," I said, "I've never thought . . . Nothing gave me any reason to believe . . ."

I was surprised to hear Madame Armand refer to her failed

attempt as an accomplished fact. Her eyes were frankly presented to me, wide open and looking straight into mine, but their extreme brightness and blackness revealed hardly anything. Her small, smooth, sensible forehead, under the curled fringe, really did look as if it had never harboured the regrettable disorder called neurasthenia between the two fine eyebrows. Before she sat down, she straightened the violets in the vase with her unsure hands; I saw their stalks tremble between her fingers. "Nerves, you know." Hands that were too clumsy even to measure out an effective dose of poison.

"Madame," she said, "I must tell you first of all that I have always had a very trivial life."

Such a prelude threatened me with a long recital. Nevertheless, I stayed where I was.

It is easy to relate what is of no importance. My memory has not failed to register the idle words and the mild absurdities of these two opposite neighbours and I have tried to reproduce them faithfully. But, beginning with the words: "I have always had a very trivial life . . ." I feel absolved from the tiresome meticulousness imposed on a writer, such as carefully noting the over-many reiterations of "in one way" and "what poor creatures we are" that rose like bubbles to the surface of Madame Armand's story. Though they helped her to tell it, it is for me to remove them. It is my duty as a writer to abridge our conversation and also to suppress my own unimportant contribution to it.

"A very trivial life. I married such a good man. A man as perfect and hard-working and devoted as all that really oughtn't to exist. Now could you imagine anything unexpected happening to a man as perfect as that? And we didn't have a child. To tell you the honest truth, I don't think I minded much.

"Once, a young man in the neighbourhood . . . Oh, no, it's not what you're expecting. A young man who had the cheek to accost me on the staircase, because it was dark there. Handsome, I have to admit he was handsome. Naturally, he promised me the moon and the stars. He told me: 'I'm not going to take you under false pretences. With me, you'll see life in the raw. You can reckon I'm quite as likely to make you die of misery as of joy. Things will go my way, not yours.' And so on, and so on. One day he said to me: 'Let me have a look at your little wrist.' I wouldn't give it to him, he grabbed hold of it and twisted it. For more than ten days I couldn't use my hand and it was my little Exo who did it up for me. At night, after he'd put a clean crêpe bandage on my wrist—I'd told him I'd had a fall—he would stare for a long time at that bandaged wrist. I was ashamed. I felt like a dog who's come home with a collar no one's ever seen it wearing and they say to it: 'But where on earth did you get a collar like that?' That shows the least evil-minded people can be sharp in their way.

"With this young man, it was all over before it began. Do you know what I couldn't abide? It was this gentleman I'd never spoken three words to daring to call me '*tu*'. He just sprang up before my feet as if he'd risen out of the earth. Well, he vanished back into it again.

"Since then? Why, nothing. Nothing worth mentioning. There's nothing to surprise you in that. Plenty of women, and not the ugliest ones either, would be in my state if they didn't lend a helping hand. You mustn't believe men throw themselves on women like cannibals. Certainly not, Madame. It's women who spread that idea about. Men are much too anxious not to have their peace upset. But lots of women can't stand a man behaving decently. I know what I'm talking about."

"Personally, I'm not the kind that thinks much about men. It's not my temperament. In one way, it might have been better for me if I had thought of them. Instead of that, whatever do you think came into my head one morning when I was cutting up some breast of veal? I said to myself: 'I did breast of veal with green peas only last Saturday, all very nice, but one mustn't overdo it, a week goes by so fast. It's eleven already, my husband's got a christening group coming to pose at half-past one, I must get my washing-up done before the clients arrive, my husband doesn't like to hear me through the wall rattling crockery or poking the stove when clients are in the studio . . . And after that I must go out, there's that cleaner who still hasn't finished taking the shine off my husband's black suit, I'll have to have a sharp word with her. If I get back to do my ironing before dark, I'll be lucky; never mind, I'll damp my net window-curtains down again and I'll iron them tomorrow, sooner than scorch them today. After that, I've nothing to do but the dinner to get ready and two or three odds and ends to see to and it'll be finished.'

"And instead of adding, as I often did: 'Finished . . . And none too soon' I went on: 'Finished? How d'you mean, finished? Is that all? Is that the whole of my day, today, yesterday, tomorrow?' That night, when I was in bed, I was still going over and over all my idiotic thoughts. The next day, I felt better and I had to make some jam and pickle some gherkins, so you can imagine I sent Mademoiselle Devoidy out to do the shopping, it was well and truly her turn, so as to give all my time to hulling my strawberries and rubbing my gherkins in salt. I was deep in my work, when suddenly it came over me again: 'The events of my life, so today's jam-making day? Be careful about the copper preserving pan, it's got a rounded bottom, if it tips over on the hole of the cooking-range, what a catastrophe! And I haven't got enough glass jam-jars, I'll have to borrow the two jars Madame Gâteroy uses for her potted goose if she can spare them. And when I've finished my jam, what will come along in the way of a sensational event?' At last you can see the picture.

"It wasn't five o'clock by the time my jam was done. Done and very badly done. The worst failure I'd ever had, all the sugar burnt to caramel. Luckily, the strawberries cost next to nothing. And there, off I went again: 'Tomorrow, let's see, tomorrow . . . Tomorrow we've got that lady who comes to mount the proofs on fibre-board.' Fibre-board was a novelty imitation felt that made a lovely background for sports photos. But it needed a special knack and special kind of glue. So once a week this lady used to come and I used to keep her to lunch, it made a change for me. We didn't lose by it, she made good use of her time and it was better for her than running round to the little eating-house. I added something special in the way of a sweet, or something good from the pork-butcher's.

"But this day I'm telling you about, I felt that everything was all one and the same to me, or rather that nothing satisfied me. And the following days . . . I pass them over in silence.

"What did you say? Oh! no. Oh! you're quite wrong, I didn't despise my occupations, on the contrary. I've never put my mind to them so much. Nothing went amiss. Except that I found the time long and at the same time I kept looking about for something I could do to fill it up. Reading? Yes. You're certainly right. Reading makes a good distraction. But I've got such a twisted character that everything I tried to read seemed to me . . . a little thin, sort of poor. Always this mania for something big. When I'd done my housework and finished the day's jobs, I used to go out and take a few breaths on the landing—as if I'd been able to see further from there. But landing or no landing, I'd had enough and more than enough.

"Pardon? Ah! you've put your finger right on the trouble. Enough of what, precisely? Such a happy woman, as Madame Gâteroy used to say when she talked about me. Such a happy woman, why exactly, that's what I would have been if, here and there, in my trivial little life, I'd had something great.

What do I call great? But I've no idea, Madame, because I've never had it! If I'd had it even once, I guarantee I'd have realised straight away, without a shadow of doubt, that it *was* great!"

She rose from her chair, sat down on the bed, rested her elbows on her knees and propped up, her chin. Like that, she was facing me direct. With a wrinkle incised between her eyebrows and one eye nervously screwed up, she did not appear uglier to me, on the contrary.

"What queer things presentiments are, Madame! Not mine, I'm talking of my husband's. Just about that time, he said to me point-blank: 'If you like, in July we'll go off for a month to Yport, as we did two years ago, that'll do you good.' Yport? Yes, it's not bad, mainly a family holiday place, but quite a lot of Paris celebrities go there. Fancy, when we were there before, we saw Guirand de Scevola, that painter who's become so famous, every single day. He was painting the sea in anger, from nature, with the legs of his easel in the foam of the waves. It was a real sight. Everyone used to stare at him. Naturally, I said to my little Exo: 'You're choosing a nice time to go and squander what little money we have at the seaside!'—'When it is a question of you,' he answered, 'nothing else counts.' That day and many days after, I absolutely swore to myself never to do anything to hurt a man like that. Anyway, it wasn't going to Yport that would have brought something great into my life. Unless saving a child who was drowning . . . But I can't swim.

"Little by little, I admit I made myself very unhappy. In the end, what did I go and imagine? I went and imagined that this thing life couldn't do for me, I'd find it in death. I told myself that when death is approaching, not too fast, not too violently, you must have sublime moments, that your thoughts would be lofty, that you'd leave behind everything that's petty, everything that cramps you, nights of bad sleep, bodily miseries. Ah!

what a wonderful compensation I invented for myself! I pinned all my hopes on those last moments you see.

"Oh! But yes indeed, Madame, I did think of my husband! For days and days, for nights and nights. And about his unhappiness. Do me the honour of believing that I weighed it all up and envisaged this, that and the other before setting out on the road. But once I had set out, I was already far on my way."

Madame Armand looked down at her hands, which she had clasped, and gave an unexpected smile.

"Madame, people very seldom die because they've lost someone. I believe they die more often because they haven't had someone. But you think that, by killing myself, I was cruelly deserting my husband? Well, if the worst came to the worst, my beloved Geo could always have followed me, if it had been too much for him to bear . . . Give me credit for this, before I set out on my way, I worked everything out to the smallest detail. It may seem nothing, but I had all sorts of complications. One thinks it's ever so simple, just to lie down on one's bed, swallow some horrible thing or other, and good-bye! Just to procure this drug, goodness knows what trouble I had and what fibs I had to tell! I had to make up my mind on the spur of the moment one day when I got the chance . . . there'd been an accident to the red light in the dark-room which meant my husband had to go out immediately after lunch. For two pins I'd have chucked the whole thing. But I recovered my nerve, I was sustained by my idea, by the thought of this . . . this kind of . . ."

I risked suggesting a word which Madame Armand pounced on eagerly:

"Yes, Madame, apotheosis! That's exactly it, apotheosis! That particular day I was uneasy, I kept wondering what other hitch might still occur. Well, the morning slipped by as easy as slipping a letter in the post-box. Instead of lunch, I took some herb-tea. The embroidered sheets on the bed, all the housework properly done, the letter to my husband sealed up, my husband in a hurry to go out. I called him back to give him his lightweight overcoat and I thought he'd gone when really he was still there, he'd broken the bottle of hyposulphite, you remember?

"I think I'm alone at last, I lock the door, and I get myself settled. Yes, here, but inside the bed, the embroidered pillows behind my back, everything all fresh and clean. Right! I'd hardly lain down when I remembered the washerwoman. I get up, I scribble a word on a slip of paper and I lie down again. First of all, I swallowed a pill to stop stomach spasms, and I waited ten minutes, as I'd been told to do. And then I swallowed the drug, all at one go. And believe me"—Madame Armand twisted her mouth a little—"it was anything but delicious.

"And then? And then I wait. No, not for death, but for what I'd promised myself before it. It was as if I were on a quay, waiting to embark. No, no, I wasn't in pain but I could feel myself getting old. The last straw was that my feet—I'd got my shoes on—were getting hot at the bottom of the bed and hurt like fury wherever I'd got a bad place. Even worse than that, I imagine I hear the door-bell ring! I think: 'It's happened on purpose, I'll never get through.' I sit up and try and remember if someone's made an appointment for a sitting. I listen hard. But I think it was the buzzings in my ears beginning. I lie down again and I say a little prayer, though I'm not particularly religious: 'My God, in your infinite goodness, take pity on an unhappy and guilty soul . . .' Impossible to remember the rest, on my word. But that might have been enough, mightn't it?

"And I went on waiting. I was waiting for my reward, my great arrival of beautiful thoughts, a great pair of wings to carry me away, to sweep me right away from being myself any more. My head was going round and round, I thought I saw great circles all round me. For a second it was like when you dream you're falling from the top of a tower, but that was all. Nothing else, would you believe it, but all my everyday thoughts and fidgets, including that very day's? For example, I kept worrying like anything that my little Exo would only have cold meat and salad and warmed-up soup when he came in that night. At the same time, I thought: 'Even that will be too much, he'll be so upset over my death, it'll put him off his food. Everyone in the house will be so kind to him. My God, take pity on an unhappy and guilty soul . . .' I'd never have believed that, when I was dying, it would be my feet that I suffered from most.

"The buzzings and the circles went on going round and round me, but I still kept on waiting. I waited lying down, as good as gold." She slid towards the middle of the bed, resumed the attitude and the stillness of her postponed death and closed her eyes so that I could see nothing of them but the feathery, black line of the lashes.

"I didn't lose my head, I listened to all the noises on, I went over everything that I had forgotten, everything I had left in a muddle on the other side, I meant the side I was leaving. I reproached myself for those evening walks I used to take without bothering whether my husband might be bored all alone, when his day's work was over. Trifles, petty little things, uninteresting thoughts that floated on the top of the buzzings and the circles. I remember vaguely that I wanted to put my hands over my face and cry and that I couldn't, it was as if I hadn't any arms. I said to myself: 'This is the end. How sad it is that I haven't had what I wanted in life even in my death.'

"Yes, I think that's all, Madame. A terrible icy cold came and cut off the thread of my thoughts and yet I'm not sure, even of that. What I am sure of is that never, never again will I commit suicide. I know now that suicide can't be the slightest use to me, I'm staying here. But, without wanting to offend Mademoiselle Devoidy, you can see for yourself that I'm in my right mind and that a neurotic woman and myself are two utterly different things."

With a jerk, Madame Armand sat up. Her story had left her with a feverish flush that animated her pale skin. Our conversation ended in "Good-bye, see you soon!" as if we were on a station platform, and after exclamations about the "shocking lateness" we parted for a very long time. She held the door of the flat open behind me, so that the light in the studio should illuminate the landing for me. I left the photographer's Missus in her doorway, slender and solitary, but not wavering. I am sure she did not stumble a second time. Whenever I think of her, I always see her shored up by those scruples she modestly called fidgets and sustained by the sheer force of humble, everyday feminine greatness; that unrecognised greatness she had misnamed "a very trivial life".